PRAISE FOR THE WORLD OF THE THRALL

"Unveiling a new paranormal series, the brilliant team of Adams and Clamp crafts an exceedingly intriguing heroine trying to survive a dangerous and complex world. Told in first person, the resilient Kate's struggles and choices are both vivid and terrifying. This is an unbeatably good paranormal!" —*Romantic Times BOOKreviews*
(4½ stars, Top Pick)

"Adams and Clamp are adept at incorporating riveting twists into this fully imagined world, and they don't stint on the romance." —*Booklist* (starred review)

"*Touch of Evil* receives *The Road to Romance* Reviewers' Choice Award for the great writing of the author duo C. T. Adams and Cathy Clamp. This book has it all and more. Readers don't want to miss this perfect example of fantastically vivid paranormal fiction." —*The Road to Romance*

**Tor Paranormal Romance Books by
Cathy Clamp and C. T. Adams**

*Forthcoming

TOUCH OF MADNESS

C. T. ADAMS &
CATHY CLAMP

TOR®

tor paranormal romance

A TOM DOHERTY ASSOCIATES BOOK
NEW YORK

This is a work of fiction. All the characters, organizations, and events portrayed in this book are either products of the author's imagination or are used fictitiously.

TOUCH OF MADNESS

Copyright © 2007 by C. T. Adams and Cathy Clamp

All rights reserved.

A Tor Book
Published by Tom Doherty Associates, LLC
175 Fifth Avenue
New York, NY 10010

www.tor-forge.com

Tor® is a registered trademark of Tom Doherty Associates, LLC.

ISBN 978-0-7653-6512-5

First Edition: June 2007
Second Edition: January 2010

Printed in the United States of America

0 9 8 7 6 5 4 3 2 1

DEDICATION AND
ACKNOWLEDGMENTS

As with all of our books we would like to dedicate this work first to James Adams and Don Clamp, along with the rest of our family and friends who have offered patience, kindness, and unswerving support throughout the years.

Any book is a group effort, and we want to take the time to specifically thank our wonderful agents, Merrilee Heifetz and Claire Reilly-Shapiro, who have helped us so much and so often. Thanks to our terrific editor, Anna Genoese, at Tor and all of the other wonderful staff members who have worked so hard on our behalf.

Finally, thanks to our readers for spending their hard-earned money and their time to share in our worlds.

TOUCH OF MADNESS

1

*S*omething was lurking behind the clean white paint and tasteful carpet of the hospital hallway where I walked. It raised the hairs on my neck and tingled right at the edge of my psychic senses. My mind screamed *vampires,* even though I couldn't see them. But that was to be expected. After all, despite my better judgment, the Thrall were the reason I was here.

"Hey, Reilly! Kate!"

I started at the sudden noise hard enough to nearly stumble, and realized just how tightly strung I was today. Denver Detective John Brooks was walking toward me, looking natty, but uncomfortable. While I hadn't expected to see him here, when I thought about it I realized I shouldn't be surprised. After all, he's Not Prey, just like me.

He smiled, but underneath was the same tension I was feeling. I knew he couldn't sense the Thrall parasites that had nearly killed us both a few months before, he was too head blind for that. But that didn't mean he was any happier to be here than I was.

"I was hoping I'd know at least one other Not Prey here today. How you doing?"

"Better than last time you saw me." I raised my arm over my head and wiggled my fingers. "See, I've got use of the shoulder again. Definitely an improvement. How about you?"

"Well, I'm still employed and haven't been demoted—which is saying something after the fallout of Queen Monica's death." He raised up the corner of one snow-white cuff, with a real gold cufflink attached, reminding me he looked good today, better than me. Despite being a large man, made of muscle, not fat, he's one of those almost impossibly well-groomed people. Today his suit was a dark charcoal that wasn't quite black. His shirt nearly gleamed under the fluorescents, and his perfectly knotted tie was red with charcoal stripes that matched the suit. He's shorter than I am, but is almost as broad as he is tall. It made me wonder if somewhere in the background there was a Mrs. Brooks who took care of getting his suits specially tailored and his shirts starched. I'd never asked. There hadn't really been the opportunity when we'd first met, and it hadn't come up since.

I could see three pale, shiny lines against his ebony skin that disappeared up under the cloth. "Your fingernails left a nice set of scars down one arm, though. I can't *tell* you how much I've enjoyed the ribbing about that down at the station." He snorted and it made me laugh. First time today, which is why I like the man.

"Well, it's not my fault you only had one set of handcuffs to hold me down while that *thing* tried to turn me into the freaking new vampire queen." I paused for a moment and fought off a shudder. Maybe a subject change, even though it wouldn't be much of one. "So, how did they drag you into this?"

Brooks's eyes darkened. He gave me a look of utter disgust. "Office politics. The Chief of Police called me personally. He went on and on about how we need to do everything we possibly can to reassure the public under the circumstances."

"Under what circumstances?"

"We had a hundred and fifty corpses, Kate, including political bigwigs. The whole mess was on the national news, complete with photos. All the people who'd tried to pretend vamps don't exist came face to face with the ugly truth. Now they expect *us* to do something about it." He gave a derisive snort. "How about you?"

"Familial blackmail," I answered dryly.

He laughed loudly enough to draw the attention of several of the nurses who stood down the hall leaning against the raised counter, their brightly colored cotton scrubs still immaculate. One or two of them waved, still cheerful and energetic. It was early, the beginning of a new shift. I could tell. Everybody was too clean, too happy. That shiny good humor usually wears off about the first time they wheel a gunshot wound or accident victim through the doors.

"My brother Joe—you remember him, don't you?" When Brooks nodded, I continued. "Well, he works here at St. Elizabeth's, and he's been getting a lot of pressure from higher up in the food chain. They pushed him to convince me to participate in this stupid research study. Naturally, I told him where to go and how to get there, so he finally had to resort to emotional blackmail to get me walking down this hallway." I paused. "The last thing I ever wanted to do again in this lifetime was deal with those damned parasites."

Brooks nodded and his whole body took on a serious-as-death stance. "It almost *was* the last thing you did. But we don't have any choice—not really. As two of only a dozen or so humans acknowledged as Not Prey we get a certain level of hard-earned respect, but there's a price."

"I'll admit that it's useful that the Thrall have to treat me as an equal, that they can't lie to me and have to negotiate. But if I could have that without the psychic side effects of having been bitten it would be *so* much better." Shaking my head, I turned and we started toward the elevator, side by side. We garnered more than a few nervous glances as we did. I'm six foot one, a redhead, and was clad in thick black leather with plenty of snaps and zippers. I was keeping a brisk pace with an obviously annoyed black man who is built like a brick wall, and has that undefined quality that screams *cop*.

"It's more than that, Reilly. When you're Not Prey there are *rules*. The queens may have set them, but all the Thrall have to follow them or risk getting killed by their own or cut off from the hive. It gives you a handle on the situation—a little bit of control."

"Yeah, yeah. I know. You'd think being bitten but avoiding infestation would be enough, wouldn't you? My natural psychic abilities have given me a near-permanent connection to the hive. Only three things seem to help shut them out."

"Yeah?" he asked as he pushed the button to call the elevator. "What works?"

The bottom of my braid had gotten caught in one of the sleeve zippers again, so I yanked it free. "The first, heavy metal or hard rock music played *loud*."

"Better you than me. I can't stand rock. I'm a jazz and blues sort of guy."

I laughed, because I could actually imagine Brooks hanging out in a smoky Harlem speakeasy in the '20s. "The second is shielding—something I'm just beginning to learn. The third, and most effective by far, is to stay in the presence of a lycanthrope."

His eyebrows rose slightly and he fought not to smile. "I'll bet I know your preferred choice of werewolf, too. How is Mr. Bishop lately?"

I did smile, because he was right. The werewolf I met when Queen Monica targeted me as her replacement, and who had risked his neck to save me from losing my mind to the hive, was pretty much my steady date now. So far, we're pretty happy. "Tom's doing well. He kept his job, too, and is hoping to get into smokejumping school. The jury's still out on that."

Brooks checked the heavy gold watch on his wrist and frowned. "That elevator had better get moving. We're going to be late."

The bell rang and the doors opened with a soft *whoosh*. We rode up in silence. A moment later the doors reopened and we stepped into the brightly lit hall with a faint antiseptic smell. I felt . . . something, a much stronger something than downstairs. I stopped, laying my hand on Brooks's arm.

"Do you feel that?"

"Feel what?" His eyes narrowed. He looked from one end of the hall to the other, his expression cautious.

I shook my head. There was something stirring. The hair on the back of my neck stood on end and I felt my skin begin to crawl under the heavy leather of my biker jacket.

"I'm not sure," I admitted. "You don't feel anything?" I knew I shouldn't expect him to, but the sensation was so *strong*.

"Nah." He snorted instead of laughing. "But I never do."

"Lucky bastard." I meant it. My latent psychic abilities were what had drawn the Thrall to me in the first place. They'd tried twice now to make me the local queen. If I'd been as head blind as Brooks they might have left me the hell alone.

"Oh, I don't know. It might be handy having an early warning system."

It was my turn to snort. "That advantage is *so* outweighed by the problems it isn't even funny."

"Let's get this over with." He loosened my grip on his suit coat and started down the corridor, turning left and following the little black and white sign glued on the wall at eye level. I followed a few steps behind. I tried to convince myself there was no reason to be nervous. Even I didn't believe me. Brooks sure as hell didn't. I could tell from the tension in his shoulders and the way his eyes darted suspiciously around the hall, missing nothing.

Dr. Miles MacDougal was waiting in the corridor outside the conference room. He's a small, slender man standing five foot six or so with a huge, bushy moustache that unkind souls would say is meant to compensate for the thinning dark hair that barely covers his head. He kept checking his watch, then looking down the hall impatiently.

When he saw the two of us approaching his homely face broke into a satisfied smile.

"Kate! John! You came!" He sounded both delighted and relieved. I could tell he'd had his doubts about whether Joe could deliver me as promised . . . money or no. Actually, I'd lied a little to Brooks. The truth was, money had swayed me—especially since the money from selling my motorcycle was nearly gone.

He turned, pulling open the door and holding it open for us.

"Samantha, they've arrived."

A stunningly beautiful woman stepped forward. She had dark hair and wide blue eyes set in a heart-shaped face. The body beneath her white lab coat was slender, but perfectly proportioned. She turned, giving Dr. MacDougal a dimpled smile that would've melted a heart of stone. His reaction was typical. There was a good three-second pause before Miles collected himself enough to make introductions.

"Kate, John, this is Dr. Samantha Greeley. Dr. Greeley is in charge of the study—"

"I thought—" I started to interrupt, but he talked over me, as if he'd actually expected the interruption.

"She's managed to gather together Not Prey from all over the world to participate." He gestured to the oblong conference table. Eight of the seats were taken by a remarkable variety of people, all of whom were eyeing Brooks and me with interest as they munched on their bagels or sipped the drinks they'd selected from a refreshment table tucked discreetly into the corner of the room. Next to it was a young black man half-hidden behind a tripod and video equipment.

"Ms. Reilly, Mr. Brooks, it's a pleasure. I've heard so much about you both." She gestured for us to take a seat as she began making introductions around the table. "Mr. Yakimoto is visiting us from Japan." I gave a brief nod to a tall, elderly Japanese man with thick rimless spectacles and a crisply pressed navy pin-striped suit and received a similar nod in return.

Greeley continued down the table, introducing a teenaged girl wearing an oversized letter jacket of green wool and white leather as Antonia Webster, who was here with her mother, Julia. Next were Digby Wallace, a redheaded Aussie with a broad freckled face, and a 350-pound, bleached-blonde biker chick named Rikki Jacobs.

She sat silently, staring into space, her eyes vaguely unfocused. I recognized the gang logo on the sleeveless vest she wore over her black Harley-Davidson tee-shirt. There were elaborate "sleeve" tattoos on each of her arms, beautiful work if you appreciated such things. She turned slowly at the sound of my name. The look she gave me was . . . unsettling. I didn't have time to dwell on it, though. Samantha Greeley had moved on to introduce Mrs. Emily Patterson, a prim little schoolmarm of a woman in a pretty floral print dress with a white lace collar. I wondered what might have caused her to earn the Not Prey title. She didn't seem capable of much more than attending a quilting bee.

Last, but not least, was Henri Tané, a small, withered black man with liquid brown eyes and a stiff new suit. Something in the shape of his face made me think of Jamaica or one of the other tropical islands.

Haiti. A voice leapt into my head, thick accent and all. *It is a true pleasure to meet you, Kate Reilly. I have heard much about you, though perhaps from unusual sources.* He smiled, showing slightly crooked white teeth.

Following good meeting etiquette, Brooks pulled his seat forward and turned toward the screen. I, on the other hand, was much too unsettled to do anything of the sort. I'm paranoid by both profession and nature. It's served me well over the years. I took my chair and pulled it away from the table until I sat with my back to the corner with a clear view of the door. While his eyes were focused steadily on Dr. Greeley, Henri continued speaking to me mind-to-mind while I poured a glass of water from the sweating pitcher on the large black tray in the center of the table.

You felt it as well? I do not know what it is she plays at—but it is a dangerous game. We shall be cautious, you and I.

I couldn't help but glance at him. I'm just not accustomed to talking without looking at the person. *I'm always cautious.*

Which is why you are here—and why they *fear you.*

I somehow doubted the Thrall *feared* me—or much of anything else. Although things had certainly changed in the past few months. The Thrall had always been a fact of life, existing mostly in the shadows, in the larger cities. The nests and herds had generally been kept small and secret enough that most people had considered them to be yet another "urban legend." The previous queen of Denver had changed all that. She'd increased the size of both the nest and the herd, and had chosen prominent, highly placed people. The plan had worked to a point. Under her "rule" herd members lived longer, healthier lives. The nest, too, had prospered. But she'd made two major mistakes. Ignoring her own mortality, she left off breeding her replacement queen until almost too late. As her host body weakened so had her hold on her nest, so that a few of the strongest and most desperate had gone against the orders of the queens and attacked me directly.

Her second mistake was to choose me as the replacement host. It had been touch and go, but with the help of my friends and family I'd managed to kill the eggs and hatchlings—causing the death of the Denver nest and most of its herd. I gave an involuntary shiver and pulled my jacket tight around me to fight a chill that had nothing to do with the breeze blowing down from the air-conditioning duct.

Did you notice, all of us here are from the Western nations? Do you know why? Henri's voice in my mind was pleasant, almost amused.

I hadn't noticed until he mentioned it. I shook my head no, ever so slightly, while fighting to keep my eyes on Dr. Greeley at the front of the room.

When you destroyed the nest the pictures were shown all over the world. In those countries less sensitive to human rights issues anyone even suspected of being host or herd was hunted down, executed.

I snorted lightly and took a sip of water to cover it. *Bet quite a few political dissidents were accidentally eliminated in the process.*

No doubt. But the queens, they are afraid now. They were few, now fewer. They fear extinction.

Aw damn. Wouldn't that just break my heart?

I saw Henri's shoulders shake with silent laughter. Brooks might not be psychic enough to have heard the conversation, but he's observant as hell. He noticed the old man's mirth and gave me a warning look just as Dr. Greeley turned to glare at me.

I didn't wilt. Then again, I never do. I went to Catholic schools for twelve years. Far as I've been able to determine nobody, and I do mean *nobody,* can give you a worse glare than a pissed-off nun.

"Now that everyone is *here,*" she said the word to have double meaning, "I'll begin the presentation."

I gave her my brightest smile. It wasn't sincere, but it was sweet enough to rot the teeth out of her head. It didn't take a psychic gift to know I had thrown her off her game. "Mason, get the lights . . . and hurry it up."

I turned to see the young black man step from behind the tripod long enough to turn off three of the four rows of

overhead lights. She hadn't introduced him, and the conde-
scension in her voice when issuing the order had been
enough to raise my hackles. Mason didn't appear offended:
his entire being seemed focused on his work. Brooks's
eyes, however, had narrowed significantly, and I could see
the tension spread in his massive shoulders.

Dr. Greeley hit a button on her laptop and a PowerPoint
slide appeared on the screen on the far wall. It depicted the
life cycle of a Thrall in sterile, clinical detail. She began
speaking to us, using a voice polished from frequent public
speaking. "The *Heterotroph hippocratia* are a highly developed species with a unique culture and highly evolved hive
society. Until very recently, the exceptionally short life span
of the host/heterotroph symbiont—" she prompted the next
slide to appear, as she continued unabated—"created a fun-
damental conflict between the two primary intelligent
species of our planet."

I saw her glance discreetly around the room to see if
she'd lost us yet. While none of the audience appeared particularly riveted, nobody's attention seemed to be wandering . . . except for Rikki. But she was no more unfocused
than she'd been when I'd walked in, so I was betting it
wasn't the lecture.

"Recently, however, a particularly intelligent *heterotroph*
queen discovered a means of significantly extending the
life span of a symbiont. By working with this queen we
were able to obtain a number of eggs, which were cryogenically preserved until funding could be obtained for the full
project."

There was no hiding the admiration in her voice. I sat
dumbstruck. The queen she was referring to was the late
Queen Monica, and a nastier piece of work you've never seen.

"Until *heterotrophs* merge with their human hosts and
enter the symbiont stage, they are only able to communicate telepathically. Since telepathy is a very rare gift among
the human population, early communication has never pre-

viously been attempted." She hit the button and a slide showing a new hatchling appeared. I gave an involuntary shudder. Only a few months ago I'd had one of those slimy little maggots trying to climb into my mouth to take over my mind and my body. The mental wound was too new, too raw, for me not to react.

Dr. Greeley was droning on. "Until recently, becoming a host meant a severely shortened life span, along with the loss of free will. The goal of this study is to cut off the original bond to the heterotroph collective and create a conduit of communication between the heterotroph eggs and psychically gifted humans so that both species can work together to find a way to live a full cooperative life span with joint awareness and control of the shared body." She turned, looking at each of us in turn, her smile bright and shiny as a newly minted coin, while a weight, heavy as lead, began to form in my stomach.

"We hope that by working together we can come up with solutions to so many of the issues that try our peoples, where telepathy could play a significant and helpful role. The possibilities are nearly endless, but some examples would be the ability to communicate with coma patients, the possibility of reviving Eden zombies, and so very much more."

I understood now why Joe had been so insistent—and how Miles had "hooked" him on the idea. My baby brother Bryan is a former Eden zombie. The only good thing that had come from my confrontation with Monica was that he'd had what the doctors were referring to as a "partial recovery." Now instead of being a total zombie, he had the mind of a four-year-old child. Since not one single Eden zombie had ever recovered even that much of their ability, physicians from around the world were flying in to study my brother to see if there was any way to duplicate the effect.

Drug abuse, in general, was up in all the developed countries. But Eden was the worst. Not only was it the most addicting—but one single misstep in the preparation would result in anyone who used the "bad" drugs becoming empty shells with no mind or will of their own. Hope for a cure was no doubt the lure Greeley had used to obtain her funding.

While my mind had been wandering Greeley kept talking. I missed some of it, and would have missed more if I hadn't heard Henri gasp inside my mind.

"You *what?*" Brooks's voice was a controlled roar and I fought my way back to reality to figure out what was happening.

Greeley gave him a steely glare. "We have incubated one hundred of the eggs provided by Queen Monica—"

I stared at her, horrified. "Where?" I kept my voice controlled, despite the panic that was tightening my chest. I asked, though I was very much afraid I knew the answer. Suddenly the buzz that had been in the back of my mind from the time I'd entered the hospital had a logical explanation.

"The eggs are being maintained in a safe, sterile—"

"WHERE?"

She placed hands on her hips, which caused the wireless remote in her hand to flip to the next slide—and a picture of what must be an incubation chamber appeared twice real-life size. "Really, Ms. Reilly! There's no need to shout!"

It took every ounce of my self-control not to rise from my seat, grab her by the lapels, and *shake* the information out of her. Instead, I gripped the edge of the conference table, my nails digging little half-moon shapes into the blond wood.

"Oh my God." I heard a whisper from the far side of the table. The teenager in the letter jacket was staring at the screen. She'd paled until her skin was the color of bleached paper. "Mom, we need to go NOW." She turned to face her mother, white showing all around the irises of her eyes. "She has them *here!*"

Mrs. Webster didn't need to be told twice. She rose to her feet abruptly enough to send her chair clattering backward onto the floor. "Dr. Greeley, you'll receive our check returning your money within the week."

"Antonia, Mrs. Webster, there's no need—" Dr. Greeley's protests were nearly inaudible over the sound of chairs scraping back from the table as most of the meeting participants prepared to leave.

"Ladies and gentlemen . . . if you'll just—"

It was no good, and she knew it. I could see it in the thinning of her lips, the angry set to her shoulders as she watched her hopes dwindle as the others walked out. Frankly, I didn't give a damn about her feelings. I was much more worried about what was in the incubator. I knew how powerful the mind control of a hatchling was. I'd had one in my mind once, and to this day didn't remember everything that happened that night. All it would take was one susceptible human walking by and opening the lid for all hell to break loose. I shuddered at the thought.

Only Henri, Brooks, the videographer, and I remained.

"Well, aren't you going?" Her acid-tinged words were directed at me. "This is *your* fault after all. They were fine until you started a wholly unnecessary panic."

"Hardly," Brooks corrected. "If it's anyone's fault it's yours for getting us here under false pretenses."

"No one was lied to."

Henri and Brooks snorted in unison at her feeble protest. By their own rules they couldn't/wouldn't lie to the Not Prey, but the Thrall were champions of misdirection and omission. I was used to it. That wasn't the problem to my mind. But it occurred to me, and probably to the others as well, how much her logic was like that of the Thrall collective. Just to be safe, I opened my senses, searching for any parasite inside the good doctor. There was none, but I couldn't guarantee that she wasn't herd—one of their meals and, thereby, under the control of a queen.

Henri gave a curt nod to me, and said, "You two do as you will, *I* will go find Dr. MacDougal. It was at his request that I am here, and I want an explanation and assurances that the situation is not as bad as we believe it to be." Eyes blazing with a dark anger, he strode out of the room.

I wasn't leaving until I was satisfied about the safety of the public. The critical issue was that there were one hundred parasite eggs close to hatching in a public building. It was a recipe for disaster.

I stood slowly. It was taking every ounce of my self-control not to throttle the stupid little bitch. I forced myself to speak softly, enunciating each word with exquisite care. "Where . . . is . . . the . . . incubator?"

Her eyes shifted from me to Brooks. You could almost see the gears shifting behind those beautiful baby blues.

"Fine. Give me five minutes to get things set up in the other room, then you can come see for yourself the protocols that have been instituted to protect both the eggs and the public."

"Five minutes," Brooks agreed, but his voice was heavy with controlled anger. "But know this. If the three of us don't agree that your 'protocols' are adequate to protect the public, you *will* be shut down."

Greeley's voice was cold. "I'm not intimidated by your threats, Detective Brooks."

"That wasn't a threat, Dr. Greeley. It's a promise."

She didn't have a reply for that, so she turned to Mason. "Bring the video equipment," she snapped, then left, her heels beating an angry tattoo on the linoleum. He hurried after her, awkwardly juggling his camera and tripod.

I hate waiting. I'm not good at it. As the second hand crawled around the face of the wall clock I found myself twitching in my seat. My stomach was in knots, and I desperately wished that I had stayed home, or gone for an early morning run with Tom. I'd rather be anywhere than here, in this hospital right now.

I lurched to my feet as a male shriek rent the air. Brooks beat me out the door and into the hall, his gun drawn. The sound was cut off abruptly, with a wet gurgle that I recognized from past experience. Apparently Brooks did, too, because his face paled and set into stony lines. He gestured for me to follow behind him. I had a knife drawn, and didn't remember pulling it.

I looked down the hall, wondering where the reinforcements were. People *had* to have heard that scream. But there were no running footsteps, no Code Blue pages on the intercom, just an eerie silence so complete that I could hear every rasping breath, hear my own pulse pounding in my ears. Keeping his back against the wall, Brooks turned the knob and flung open the door.

It was a scene from one of the lower levels of hell. Samantha Greeley knelt on the floor next to Mason, the videographer. He lay on the ground, his throat torn out. Blood pumped from the severed arteries in his neck, spraying against the wall as a living blanket of squirming, writhing maggots swarmed up the clear plastic walls of the opened incubation tank and up Greeley's arms. She reared back at the sound of the door slamming against the wall. The front of her clothing was so soaked with blood it clung wet and impossibly red against the milk white of her blood-splattered skin.

She hissed, lips pulling back to expose brand-new, bloodied fangs.

"Shit!" Brooks swore.

I couldn't hear him, even though I saw his lips move. The collective mind of the hatchlings crashed into mine like a sledgehammer blow between my eyes. Instead of the many voices of the hive it was one voice—one being with a hundred bodies.

I AM FREE.

2

The district courthouse in Denver is an elegant old building. The front has huge columns that flank a main entrance that faces the state capitol across Civic Center Park. It was winter, so the view from the top of the steps wasn't as impressive as it would be once the spring flowers were planted. But it was still worth seeing. Once you come inside the building the marble, polished dark wood, and ornately decorated ceilings with gold-foiled relief are meant to impress, even awe.

Unfortunately, the old girl is beginning to show her age, and while they are working hard on the restoration project, it's hard to ignore the scaffolding and plastic sheeting that drapes sections of the second floor where the trial was being held.

I was being sued—along with everybody else involved in Samantha Greeley's project. Well, everyone except Samantha herself. She is missing. Since the Supreme Court had recently ruled that anyone under the control of a Thrall is not considered *in their right mind,* she probably wouldn't be found culpable even if the cops could find her.

So the plaintiffs, being the family of the late videographer, Mason Watts, had decided not to wait to find her. And in a freak of scheduling that had more to do with the notoriety of the case than justice, we were on the docket and in front of the judge a mere three months after the incident. Not long after this ended I was scheduled to appear in criminal court on charges of destruction of hospital property.

I was seriously hoping that I wasn't going to get paint or something on my suit. It was brand-new, and expensive as hell. I probably wouldn't have bought it if Tom hadn't talked me into it. I'm not much of a clotheshorse, and the coral designer suit had a jacket cut to emphasize my athletic build, with a skirt short enough to make me worry every time I crossed my legs. I had bought pumps and a bag and had them dyed a shade of peach that exactly matched the silk blouse I wore. The outfit had cost more than the rest of my entire wardrobe combined. Thank God for gift certificates and the after-Christmas sales. Still, the look on Tom's face every time he saw me in it was worth the price. I'd also left my long red-gold hair down, loose except for a pair of small gold combs that pulled the front sections away from my face. None of it was practical for fighting, but I really didn't expect a pitched battle in the halls of justice.

I glanced over at the man holding my hand. Tom Bishop is gorgeous. We're talking calendar model, stop in the middle of the street and gawk at him gorgeous. He has hair that shade of dark brown that isn't quite black, and even though he keeps it fairly short it falls in soft curls that I can't resist running my fingers through. His eyes are the warm brown of good milk chocolate and shine with intelligence and good humor. I still can't quite believe my good luck to have hooked up with him.

He'd shown up on my doorstep this morning, dressed in the gray pin-striped suit he'd had on the first day I met him and told me he'd taken the week off to be with me during the trial. I hadn't asked him to. He'd just done it. He's like that—kind, thoughtful, supportive.

"Penny for your thoughts," he whispered into my left ear after we were seated behind the table in the courtroom. The acoustics are such that sound carries clearly, not only from the witness stand, but frequently from the audience as well. The judge had made it very clear that he wasn't going to put up with any interruptions from the spectators, and that included snide remarks.

At the moment, though, we were just sitting waiting as the plaintiff's attorney and his assistant set up equipment for everyone to watch the videotape that had just been put into evidence.

"I'm wishing I was back home in bed," I whispered back.

Tom gave me his most lascivious grin, flashing bright teeth and deep dimples. I blushed. I hadn't exactly meant that the way he'd taken it. Not that I minded, but the relationship was still new enough that I kept waiting for something to go wrong. I have always had a *very* bad history with relationships. I mean, my first serious boyfriend left me *to become a priest.* The second one cheated on me with a woman I had thought was my best friend and tried to help turn me into a queen vampire. To say I have trust issues is like calling the Grand Canyon a pothole.

The lights in the courtroom dimmed, and the screen in the front left corner that had been angled to maximize the viewing of the jury, judge, and spectators lit up. Silence settled heavily over the audience, until the only audible sound was of people breathing.

The attorney's voice carried clearly through the courtroom. "Ladies and gentlemen, the video you are about to see contains graphic violence. Anyone in the courtroom and not of the jury who has a delicate constitution should consider leaving now."

Nobody rose to leave. If anything there was a collective gasp of excitement and the room took on the same kind of energy you find just before the showing of a much-anticipated horror movie.

The attorney began speaking again, listing the people who would be appearing on screen. My name was among the first: defendant, Mary Kathleen Reilly. When he finished there was silence except for the shifting of people in their seats and the running of the equipment.

Dr. Samantha Greeley appeared on the video screen. She wore the same white lab coat over traditional business clothes. The beautiful face I remembered had been transformed by rage, her blue eyes blazed with fury.

"They're idiots. Superstitious idiots, all of them." She let out her breath in a long, irritated sigh. Squaring her shoulders, she turned to the camera. "Come along, Mason. You might as well get a good look at what it is that has them so terrified. It's feeding time anyway."

"Hang on, let me get the camera onto the tripod."

The picture jiggled slightly, then settled.

People shifted in their seats in the dim courtroom. When the image steadied, we had a good view of the laboratory. Microscopes and test tubes adorned a black counter that ran the length of the far wall. Underneath were cabinets. But dominating the room, in the center of the screen, was a huge glass incubation case. Tubes ran to and from a pair of pumps to the case, one pumping clear fluid, the other a red fluid I knew was blood.

I heard the click of latches, saw her lift the top of the plastic case an inch or two. "Help me with the lid," Greeley ordered.

"Is that a good idea?" A handsome young black man joined Greeley onscreen. He kept his distance. His body language screamed reluctance and suspicion.

"Don't tell me you're afraid, too!" Greeley sounded utterly exasperated.

"Of course not." Her words had pricked his vanity, which was probably exactly what she'd intended. He took a pair of steps toward her, but stopped short of the case. Her hand snaked out in a lightning fast move to grab his arm and jerk him toward her.

He jumped backward, his eyes wide, but she had his arm in a vise-like grip.

"What in the hell!" He struggled, managing to pull loose. Stumbling over a stool, he tried to feel his way to the door of the lab without ever taking his eyes from her.

She lunged for him, but he dived out of reach. She hissed then, and it was not a human sound.

When he shrieked, I closed my eyes, covering my face with my hands, unable to watch any further. I knew how the story ended. She'd caught him, and ripped his throat out. A dozen or more of the hatchlings had escaped and fed, and then crawled into the doctor's willing mouth while we watched, frozen and horrified for the brief moment it took. All hundred would have gotten loose if it hadn't been for Brooks. We'd burst in together, but it was Brooks who had risked everything to close the incubator. I'd been too busy fighting the good doctor—fighting, and losing. Because of me, she'd escaped down the hospital hall, leaving the door to the lab unlocked.

I heard Brooks stomping on the hatchlings that had escaped before he stooped to check on me.

"I'm fine!" My voice from the video was choked with pain. "GO, catch her!"

There was the slamming of a door, and the thud of footfalls retreating in the distance.

In the courtroom Tom put his arm around me, holding me close. "It's all right." He murmured the words in my ear. "You did your best."

It wasn't all right. The boy in the video was dead. But so were most of the hatchlings. I straightened up, opened my eyes and forced myself to watch the screen where I saw myself using the counter to haul my body up from the floor. I dragged myself across the room, my left leg useless from the kick she'd used to dislocate my knee. Wearing heels today had probably been a bad idea, since it might give the jury the impression I was faking just how much pain I was in every day.

I watched myself grab a lab stool and throw it through the glass window of MacDougal's adjoining private office. There was the sound of me rummaging through various drawers. When I came back on screen I was carrying a large bottle of single malt scotch. Without hesitation I limped over to the case, disconnected the blood bag, and poured the amber liquid from the bottle to make its way through the pumping system. It was obvious when it did, because the hatchlings began to writhe and shrivel. Onscreen I dropped the empty bottle to slam both palms against my ears before I collapsed to the floor with an agonized scream.

Somewhere in the courtroom a woman, probably Mason's mother, was quietly weeping. A gagging sound came from the jury box. I leaned into Tom's body, and took slow deep breaths while counting to a hundred.

The sound of movement drew my attention back to the picture. I looked up at the screen in time to watch Henri Tané and Miles MacDougal stride into the room. Kneeling beside the fallen boy, Miles tried to find a pulse in a throat that was mostly ravaged meat. He closed his eyes, muttering what looked like a quick prayer, before grabbing the phone and calling in a Code Blue.

The judge called for a break. It wasn't quite time for lunch, but several of the jurors were looking more than a little bit sick. I doubted that anybody was hungry. I certainly wouldn't be able to eat. My head was pounding and I was nauseous from the rage of a thousand Thrall that had watched the event through my eyes—another side effect of being connected.

Once upon a time my life had been relatively normal and my thoughts had been my own. Now I was reviled in the press and facing a wrongful death suit, even though I hadn't been responsible for Mason's death. And suing me, or taking money from my insurance company, wasn't going to bring the Watts' son back to them.

I'd let my insurance company talk to them, but the lawyer for the Watts family had wanted more money than the insurance company had been willing to pay. So, I was here in civil court, defending myself. I'd be *back* in front of a judge again in a few weeks facing criminal charges of destruction of property and vandalism because of my actions in the lab. Oh fucking goody.

I stood and gathered up my coat and purse from the seat beside me, then followed Tom behind the retreating backs of people filing from the courtroom. I hadn't seen Brooks here. That surprised me a little. As one of the other defendants, I would've expected him to be present. I considered asking my attorney about it, but changed my mind. He was in the middle of an animated debate with opposing counsel.

"Kate . . . Kate, wait." I recognized the voice calling behind me as my hand touched the brass guard plate of the courtroom door. Miles MacDougal hadn't spoken a civil word to me since that morning in the lab. Joe said Miles blamed me for what happened, which didn't make sense to my mind. But emotions frequently *don't* make sense, and Miles had lost the woman he loved that morning. Samantha Greeley wasn't dead, but she wasn't Samantha any more either, and God alone knew where she was. Even the collective didn't seem to have knowledge of her. Or, if they did, they were hiding it from me.

I made sure to keep my expression completely neutral as I turned to face him. I liked Miles. His anger had hurt me more than I'd care to admit. I'd tried to hide my pain by acting pissed. It hadn't fooled Tom or my brother. They were both being very gentle with me at the moment because I still wasn't completely over it. But I wanted to be. I wanted things to be right so that I could have my friend back.

Miles approached carefully. He looked older than he had a few weeks ago. There was gray in the bushy moustache, and in the thinning hair. But more than that, the shoulders beneath the navy suit slumped, and there were dark circles under his eyes that spoke of sleepless nights.

"I'll meet you outside." Tom gave me a quick peck on the cheek and ducked out the doors that led to the hallway. He was giving us privacy, and I appreciated it. A lot of the guys I know wouldn't have been able to suppress their protective instincts. My brother Joe, for example, would've hovered, glowering. Fortunately for me he was out of town at a conference.

"Miles." I kept my voice steady and neutral.

Miles MacDougal straightened his shoulders and took a deep breath to gather his courage. His gaze locked with mine with no flinching. "I owe you an apology." His eyes were red with suppressed tears, but his voice was strong. "I needed someone to blame. It was easier than blaming myself. This wasn't your fault."

"No," I agreed.

"It was mine."

"No. You're wrong." I spoke firmly. "It wasn't. It was her mistake. She underestimated them. Most people do. They don't look threatening. They're small, not physically imposing, so people let their guards down."

He shook his head, sadly. "Thank you for saying that. But you're wrong. I . . . I had misgivings about the project from the beginning, but Samantha was so enthusiastic. She wanted it so *very* badly. I let her talk me into it—helped her get funding and volunteers. She wouldn't have been able to get hospital approval without my backing the project."

I wanted to comfort him, but I didn't know what to say. He'd made a horrible, tragic mistake. He obviously had been in love with the woman, hell, still was. People in love do stupid things all the time. His mistake had just had tragic consequences.

"I'm sorry." It wasn't enough, and I knew it the moment the words passed my lips. But nothing I said was really going to matter. Miles blamed himself. It didn't matter if anyone else blamed him, or what they might say. This was his very own, personal hell.

Miles gave me a weak smile, and held out his hand. Instead of shaking it, I pulled him into a hug. It was awkward. I'm not really the "huggy" kind and I didn't think he was either. But he needed comfort and it was the best I could do for him.

"You'd better get out of here. Tom's waiting." He pulled back slowly. I let him go.

"Are you going to be okay?" I caught his gaze and kept it.

He didn't dignify the question with a response, just gave me a sad smile and a gentle shove toward the door. I went, both because he wanted me to and because I was too awkward and chicken to know how to deal with such raw emotions.

Tom was waiting in the hall just outside the door. Putting his hands on my waist, he looked me straight in the eyes. The kindness in his gaze warmed me to my toes, made me wonder, yet again, what I'd done to deserve this man. "How'd it go?"

I gave a small shrug. "He blames himself."

"No surprise there." Tom pulled me into his arms. I didn't fight it. It felt so good to rest my head on his shoulder, feel his heart beating and listen to the soft, quiet hum that blocked out the angry voices in my head. I took a deep breath, inhaling the masculine scent of skin and soap. We were still standing like that when the police officers rounded the corner and said my name.

"Excuse me, are you Mary Kathleen Reilly?"

I stepped out of Tom's embrace reluctantly, taking a small step back. Tom took my hand in his and gave it a gentle squeeze.

"That would be me."

There were two of them, both a few years older than me, probably thirty-five to my twenty-eight. Both wore suits that fit well enough and looked as though they got a fair amount of use. Not shabby, but not new either. The one on the left stood about five feet ten. He wore a tan suit with a brown belt and loafers. The color suited his sandy blond hair and hazel eyes. The man on the right was Italian-American. It showed in his olive coloring, his features, and somehow, in his attitude. I would be hard pressed to say how I could tell, but it was unmistakable, at least to me. And while they weren't uniforms, and weren't flashing their badges, it was just as obvious they were cops.

"Could we have a word with you?" The blond gestured toward a wooden bench a short distance down the hallway.

"May I ask what's going on?" Tom's voice was even, but I could feel the tension singing through his arm and the hand that held mine. Something about them was bothering him. Normally, I've learned to trust his supernatural instincts, but I let go of his hand instead, turning to rest it lightly on his chest. The gesture was meant to reassure him. I wasn't sure it would work, but I knew that any more strain and he wouldn't be able to hold onto his beast. The last thing he, I, or anyone else wanted was for him to change form in the middle of a crowded courthouse. Unlike most of the werewolves, he retained his personality, but that didn't make changing unexpectedly a good thing. Nobody else in this hallway would know he was still himself. There could be a panic. With the rampant prejudice and fear that lycanthropes faced it wasn't inconceivable that one of the officers might draw a weapon. There were far too many negative possibilities for me to be willing to risk it. I might not be armed with weapons, but I was still pretty good in a fight if it came to it. But my psychic senses told me neither of the men were Thrall hosts.

"We just want to ask Ms. Reilly a few questions." The blond smiled as he said it, raising one hand in a placating gesture. But there was a tension in his body language that I didn't like.

"Fine. No problem," I agreed. I started walking toward the bench they'd indicated earlier. Tom came with me. Apparently his willingness to let me handle things myself only went so far. For the life of me I couldn't decide whether that was a good thing or a bad thing. But I didn't have time to think too much about it. As soon as my butt hit the wood the Italian introduced himself and his partner and started in on the questions.

"I'm Detective Frank Martinelli. This," he gestured toward the blond, "is my partner, Detective Al Cook."

Neither one held out a hand for me to shake, so I nodded my acknowledgment.

Cook took the lead then. "Ms. Reilly, can you tell us where you were last night at around 10:00 P.M.?

Tom was still standing. He looked from Martinelli to Cook, then back at me. "I think I'll go get your lawyer."

"I really don't think that's necessary, sir." Cook forced himself to smile when he said it. He was being the very picture of the polite police detective in dealing with Tom, but I got the impression he wasn't happy about it.

"I do." Tom gave me a look that said as clearly as words that I should shut up and wait for the attorney. It was probably good advice. That didn't mean I was going to take it.

I watched him hurry toward the courtroom. He'd barely stepped through the door when I turned my attention back to the detectives and answered the question.

"Last night at ten I was watching a DVD with Father Michael O'Rourke and my brother Bryan in the rectory at Our Lady of Perpetual Hope parish."

Cook's expression changed. He looked almost like he'd swallowed a bug. Martinelli let out a bark of laughter. He stifled it with difficulty in response to a glare from his partner, hiding it behind a cough.

"Right." Cook pulled a small spiral notebook and pen

from his trouser pocket. It reminded me forcibly of all the police procedurals I'd watched on television. I wondered just exactly what crime had been committed. I didn't, however, ask. I hadn't done anything wrong. I really *had* been at the rectory. But I already had one pending criminal case and as the saying goes, anything I said can, and would, be used against me. I wasn't looking to get myself into any more trouble.

"And Father O'Rourke can verify this?"

"Of course. Let me get you his number." I took a minute to rummage in my bag to pull out my cell phone, by which time Tom and the attorney were walking out of the courtroom and hurrying toward us.

"Officers." The attorney's voice was smooth, cultured. It matched his appearance perfectly. He wore a suit in dove gray with a faint charcoal pinstripe. It was almost the exact same shade and cut as Tom's, but I'd have bet most of a paycheck that it cost at least twice as much. It had been cut to perfection and had that indefinable *something* that made me think it had been hand tailored. If I was right, that suit had cost him more than my last, lamented vehicle. He had been selected by the insurance company to represent me, and while I probably wouldn't have chosen him if it were up to me, I had no complaints thus far. "May I ask what this is about?"

"Ms. Reilly has been charged with vandalism of a laboratory and destruction of specimens at St. Elizabeth's hospital. Last night, someone broke into that same laboratory and stole similar specimens. We thought that was quite a coincidence, and decided we'd like to have a chat with her." Cook was pissed and it showed. Either that or he was putting on an act. Most cops don't rise to detective, and the ones who do don't make it by losing their tempers just because someone brings in a lawyer.

"First." The lawyer held up his index finger as he spoke. "She has been charged. She has *not* been convicted." He held up a second finger. "Second, as you no doubt know, my client has been declared *persona non grata* at St. Elizabeth's Hospital. Security has been ordered to escort her off the premises on sight. Since, as you can see, she has a very distinctive appearance, I doubt she could have made it through the doorway, let alone to the laboratory."

"The perp didn't come in the front door," Cook answered.

I heard him, but I wasn't really listening. My mind was spinning. Someone had broken into the lab and *stolen similar specimens*. Shit. Specimens . . . he meant eggs. There had been more Thrall eggs somewhere in that lab, and somebody had stolen them. Oh, this was *so* bad.

3

I sat squirming in the uncomfortable wooden seat most of the afternoon. I couldn't keep my mind on the trial. I was too distracted from the questioning by Cook and Martinelli. Fortunately, they didn't call me up to the stand to testify. I'm fairly certain I wouldn't have sounded coherent. My mind just kept going over the same two questions again and again: *who the hell would steal Thrall eggs and why?*

The obvious answer was the Thrall. They were sentient, thought of eggs as their unborn children, and were facing a crisis. Tané hadn't been wrong in his assessment that morning in the conference room. Thrall hives had been decimated throughout the world. They had to be worrying about extinction. While I wasn't thrilled by the notion that they had recovered some of Monica's eggs, at least that explanation made sense. But the moment I'd learned of the missing eggs I had dropped my shields and actually tried to hear what was going on in the hive. Instead of the usual angry buzz of the queens and hive there was utter silence. They were blocking me out. While a part of me really did appreciate their absence, the more sensible part knew that it couldn't be good.

The witness stood and left the stand. I hadn't heard any of the testimony, but my attorney had one of those smug little smiles he wore when he felt we'd scored major points.

The judge glanced at the clock. He leaned forward to speak into the microphone in front of him. "We'll adjourn for the day. Court will resume tomorrow morning *promptly* at eight."

He gave a brisk nod of his head, and the bailiff called out. "All rise."

We rose. As soon as the judge exited the room through a door behind the bench people began gathering up their belongings and leaving the courtroom. Tom and I joined the general flow headed toward the door. When we reached the hall people herded toward the exits, flowing steadily around the construction debris.

Tom was helping me into my coat when a voice called out his name, the sound echoing off the stone floors and cream-colored walls.

He turned abruptly, automatically putting himself between me and any possible danger. I turned to see Jake and Rob, a pair of teenage boys who were members of his pack, approaching at a fast walk from the direction of the stairwell. I knew both boys.

I'd met Rob in July. At the time he'd been painfully thin, with straight blond hair and a penchant for chains and leather. I realized looking at him now that he'd grown. Regular meals had put meat on his bones. Daily workouts had given him bulk and definition. More than that, there was a confidence in his bearing that hadn't been there before. He still wore all black, but instead of the biker jacket I'd seen before, today it was an expensive full-length trench coat. He was living with his girlfriend in one of the apartments in my building for free, and an uncharitable part of me wondered how he could afford the coat and not afford rent. I clamped my mouth shut, because while I think Rob needs to develop more of a sense of responsibility, my saying so wasn't going to help today's situation.

I'd also met Jake during the crisis with the Thrall. He hadn't liked me much then, and he didn't like me now. He was still whipcord thin, with noticeably long arms and legs that ended in oversize hands and feet—both common traits of lycanthropes that Tom didn't share. Anger flashed in the dark eyes that weren't quite hidden beneath a fringe of dark hair.

"I was afraid we'd miss you," Rob admitted. "Traffic was a bitch."

Neither boy greeted me. I wasn't surprised. Rob and I get along well, but he's not big on good manners. Jake is of the opinion that even being civil might give me the mistaken impression that he approves of Tom being with me. In fact, none of the wolves are in favor of our relationship.

Werewolves are a matriarchal society, but the females are sterile. In order to maintain a healthy pack size, they use human surrogates to carry the pack's children, which are then raised by the group. Rob's current girlfriend, Dusty Quinn, is one of the surrogates. She's the reason I got involved with the Thrall last time, because she was Monica's runner-up for the queen crown and my former fiancé, Dylan Shea, was her uncle. He begged me to save her life and, sucker that I am for innocent teenagers, I agreed.

Unfortunately, while she and Rob had been going at it like little bunnies from the strange sounds I've been hearing through my apartment wall for the last few months, she still wasn't preggers. Neither was their second hope for kids, Jake's girlfriend Ruby. Mary Connolly, the wolf pack leader, was getting nervous. She'd already warned me that only the strongest males can breed, and Tom's one of those males. Jake not only supports the pack leader's position that Tom is supposed to remain unattached until both Dusty and Ruby are pregnant, but he's been actively trying to turn some of the other pack members against me.

"We've got a pack meeting in a half hour." Rob brushed a section of hair back from his face. His voice was tense, nervous. He kept shifting from foot to foot, his narrow face pinched with worry. Without even intending it, my mind brushed his, even though it shouldn't be possible. He was afraid. I saw bits of conversations he'd had recently. The pack meeting had been called to discuss whether he and Jake would be given another month, or if both surrogates would need to choose another male from the pack for breeding. There was a good chance it would be Tom. Rob didn't want to lose Dusty, and he was more than a little afraid of how I would react if the pack forced Tom and me to separate.

"Haven't you people ever heard of artificial insemination—or free will?" The words popped out of my mouth. I hadn't meant to say them, hadn't even realized I was thinking them.

Tom's eyes bugged out. Rob stepped back a pace, looking shocked. Jake gave a harsh bark of laughter that had very little humor in it. "That's not how it works." He gave me a long look. "The male who breeds has to be there to *raise* the cubs as well."

"So? They live right downstairs. From what I was told the whole pack raises the children. Does it really matter whether the biological parents are actually sleeping together?"

"That's not how it's *done*." Jake's voice dropped into a lower register. He stepped forward, shoulders hunched aggressively. Both Tom and Rob stepped between us, and I heard a low, menacing growl come from between my sweetie's lips. "Besides," he glared at Tom, his eyes narrowed to mere slits. "You were *ordered* not to get too close to her." He nodded in my direction. "She *shouldn't* know this much about our business. *She isn't one of us.*"

Rob stepped forward, placing a restraining hand on Jake's arm that earned him a baleful glare from the dark-haired wolf and a growl that raised the hairs on the nape of my neck.

"She knows what our Acca has chosen to tell her. No more," Rob assured him.

"How would you know what he whispers in her ear in bed at night?"

Rob snorted in derision at the same moment I did. "Somehow I don't think pack politics interests her as pillow talk."

He was right about that.

Jake pressed on. "But you don't *know*. None of us *know* anything other than that his loyalties are in question. I'm not the only one who feels this way, either, and you know it!"

My mouth went dry. My heart was pounding with a fear that had nothing to do with physical danger. I'd really hoped Jake was the only one working against me. If he was telling the truth, and he believed he was, then the situation might be worse for Tom than I'd imagined. When we'd first started seeing each other I'd had no idea that being with me was going to cause him this kind of trouble. But even if I'd known I wasn't sure I'd have done anything different. I was pretty sure I was in love with Tom. I sure as hell didn't want to lose him before I knew for certain. But if some of his pack mates had their way, I just might.

"We aren't going to discuss this here." Tom's voice was deceptively smooth, but I could sense the anger beneath the calm words. "And we don't have time to waste if we're going to make it to the meeting on time." He turned to me then. "I'll call when I get back."

"Do that."

I didn't make any move to kiss him goodbye in front of Jake. Tom gave me a sad little smile to let me know he appreciated the thought, but pulled me close. "I think they already know I kiss you, Katie," he said teasingly. With that he moved his mouth over mine.

It wasn't a gentle kiss. He took my mouth, muscles in his mouth and jaw working with almost bruising force until I opened my lips and let him in, his tongue tangling with mine. I moved my hands to his chest, sliding underneath the jacket. I felt his heart pounding through the thin fabric of his shirt. I forgot where we were; forgot Jake and Rob were watching us. My whole body ached with the need to touch and be touched by this man. When he pulled away, I let out a small involuntary sound of regret. I would've staggered if his arm hadn't been there to steady me.

He smiled. It was obvious he was pleased that I still reacted to him this way nearly every time we kissed.

Jake growled, and the sound made the hairs all over my body stand on end. Both Rob and Tom put themselves between Jake and me once more.

"We'd better go." Tom didn't look at me when he spoke. His eyes were all for Jake. It wasn't a friendly look. "I'll see you after the meeting."

"See you then."

I watched them go, my body seemingly frozen in place. I'd known I cared about Tom, almost from the beginning. I hadn't realized until that moment just how *much* I cared. They say you don't know what you've got 'til it's gone. I just hoped I wasn't about to find out.

I don't know how long I stood there. Long enough, at least, for the hallways to clear and the clerks to lock up their offices for the night. The building was nearly empty by the time I started making my way slowly to the elevators in the main hallway. The light shining through the tall windows had taken on the blue and pinkish tint of sunset.

I was so lost in thought that I didn't even notice the two men who stood in a shadowed corner beneath the state and federal flags that flank the entrance to the city council chambers until they stepped forward, into the light.

"Good afternoon Ms. Reilly, I don't believe we've had the chance to meet. I'm P. Douglas Richards."

I tensed immediately. He was right, we hadn't met. But I'd heard of him. Doug Richards was the new queen of the Denver hive. They'd brought him in from New York City. He was short, probably five feet five, but he had a runner's build: strong and wiry. His face was all sharp angles, with a prominent brow and heavy silver eyebrows over a beakish nose. He wore a heavy wool coat unbuttoned over a suit of expensively tailored silk in a shade of charcoal that exactly matched the color of his eyes and looked great with his salt and pepper hair.

Standing next to him was a man who needed no introduction—at least not to anybody who'd ever looked at the sports page of the newspaper: Lewis Carlton, former bad boy of the NBA. He stood a solid seven feet two, had a shaved head, and wide expanses of his coffee-colored skin had been tattooed. More to the point, he was built like a brick wall. He wasn't wearing a coat, or even a warm-up jacket. He stood in the halls of justice in a white tank top and white warm-up pants with navy piping. Every inch of him was rock solid muscle. He looked me slowly up and down, his gaze assessing. It was positively scary, and I wished to hell I was wearing my leathers and had found a way to get through the metal detectors with my weapons. And I was still wearing heels, damn it!

"I see you recognize Lewis."

"Mr. Carlton, Mr. Richards." I greeted them politely. After all, if they'd intended to attack me, they could've done it. I'd been ripe for an ambush. "To what do I owe this . . . *honor?*"

Lewis Carlton smiled, deliberately flashing an impressive set of fangs that hadn't been there back when he was playing power forward. *Shit.*

"We have a business proposition for you." Richards said *we* with that special emphasis that told me he was referring to the hive rather than himself and Lewis.

"And if I don't want to do business?"

He smiled pleasantly, showing his own fangs. "Then Carlton here is going to challenge you to a little game of one-on-one—without a basketball. Right here. Right now." He used Lewis's last name. Then again, after all the years of hearing him referred to that way on television play-by-play it's how I thought of him, too.

Well isn't this just ducky. I opened my senses and knew, without them saying a word, what they wanted. The hive hadn't stolen the eggs. They wanted me to find out who had them so that they could get them back.

"You'd be better off hiring a detective." Why pretend I wasn't connected? They knew better. The statement wasn't a lie, either. Lying cost me my status. But more to the point, I believed it. If the Thrall hadn't been the ones to steal the eggs, and they truly wanted them back, they should hire somebody who would know what in the hell they were doing.

"No." Douglas's voice was firm. He didn't elaborate why and blocked me out when I popped in to find out.

I sighed and shook my head. "I don't have the proper connections, experience, *anything,* to do this sort of thing. The last time was a fluke. I'm just a simple bonded air courier."

"Perhaps you don't have the proper connections," Doug agreed, with a slight nod that reminded me a lot of my attorney. "But you have access to those who do. And through you *we* can observe and participate."

Oh fucking goody.

A smile twitched at the corner of Carlton's mouth and his dark eyes sparkled for an instant. I wondered if he'd heard the thought. He might have. Like it or not, my psychic abilities had grown even stronger after my last encounter with the Thrall. I find myself hearing things I didn't mean to, and responding as though they'd reached air. The confrontation with the wolves a few minutes ago was just another in a long line of incidents over the past few months.

Before he'd left town, Henri Tané had started working with me, teaching me how to control my gifts, which are quickly becoming a curse. Even since returning to Haiti, he's kept in touch, contacting me mentally once a week to see how I'm progressing. Our last conversation had been almost three weeks ago. It had ended with me smashing an alarm clock into the wall in frustration—a bad habit, but cheaper than drinking. He had accused me of blocking my own abilities because I'm not willing to accept them. I probably wouldn't have been nearly as angry if there hadn't been at least a bit of truth to the charge.

A few days ago I received a package via FedEx. It was from Henri and contained several books dealing with psychic phenomena and a letter warning me that if I didn't control the gifts, they would control me. He suggested that when I was ready and capable I contact *him*.

Richards's voice brought me back to the present. He spoke to me with the condescending attitude I see a lot of bosses use with underlings they consider beneath them. I gritted my teeth and held my tongue, but it certainly wasn't easy.

"Unfortunately, there is a deadline involved, Ms. Reilly. Without implantation or cryogenic preservation, the eggs will only be viable for a week to ten days. You are to find and return them to us before they perish." He took a deep breath and continued. "We will, of course, pay your customary fee for your time."

He took the two steps between where he stood and a glass display case of trinkets from various trips around the world made by the mayors of Denver throughout history. He set his briefcase on top of the glass and opened it, pulling out a bulky 11×13 padded envelope that had my name emblazoned on it in black block letters. He handed it to me, along with his business card. The front of the card had the printed information for his downtown law office. On the back, in that same neat block print, was a cell phone number.

"Keep in touch. Don't make Carlton track you down." He reached over, closing the case. He nodded to Carlton and the two of them strode across the hall to the staircase. Carlton stopped at the top of the stairs. He turned, giving me one last assessing look before following Doug down the stairs and out of sight.

As I listened to their retreating footfalls I wondered just what in the hell I was getting into.

I left the building through the main doors on the second floor. It meant I had to go down a long set of stone steps in my high heels, but it put me on the same side of the building as Civic Center Park and the last stop of the mall shuttle. I'd save a lot of time if, rather than waiting for a cab, I just walked the couple blocks from the courthouse to the station and took the shuttle.

Normally I would have just taken a short cut through the park, but my encounter with the Thrall queen and his oversize flunky had made me realize just how vulnerable I was in my current outfit, and it was nearly full dark. So I took a slightly longer route, crossing Colfax, walking quickly and with attitude across the various cross streets until I reached the bus stop.

I waited beneath metal and plastic awnings that looked vaguely like umbrellas and turned up my blazer collar against the icy breeze that whipped through the skyscrapers. The white fluorescent lights reflected oddly off the black and gray stone that formed the building. I heard the rumbling of a bus motor, and watched one of the crosstown express buses make its way up the ramp from the underground garage.

If I'd arrived a few minutes earlier I might have caught the outgoing shuttle. I could see it moving down the street, only a block or so away. But I'd missed it. So I either had to wait a few minutes for the next one, or walk the distance in uncomfortable shoes. I decided to wait.

I wanted to be home. Home, for me, was a converted

brick warehouse in Lo-Do, the opposite end of downtown
from where I was currently standing. I'd bought the property back in the days when the neighborhood was bad and
property was cheap. It had been structurally sound, but in
sorry shape. Still, it was all I had been able to afford with
the savings I had accumulated from my career as a professional volleyball player, and my portion of the inheritance
from the death of my parents. It was taking a lot of work to
convert it into lofts. But it was work I loved, and was good
at. It really bothered me that because of my injuries, and
lack of funds, it was taking me so long to finish.

Even with the renovations half-done the building had
been appraised at more than four times what I'd paid for it.
I'd been lucky rather than smart. The once derelict area of
lower downtown had become über trendy. Now expensive
restaurants, fern bars, and lofts compete for space, butting
up against the seedy old remnants of the past.

The last traces of daylight smoothed into a deep sheet of
black as the late stragglers who'd worked overtime in their
corporate offices wandered up to join me in my wait. Eventually our patience was rewarded. The shuttle made its way
back around. It rang its bell, the doors opening to disgorge
one or two passengers before the rest of us climbed in.

I grabbed a seat in the back, my purse and the envelope
in my lap. I stared blankly out the window as the bell rang
and the bus jerked into motion.

It was a slow ride from one end of the route to the other.
We passed all the landmarks, The Pavilions, the clock
tower, the Cheesecake Factory, several local microbrew-
eries, and a couple of art galleries. Every so often the bell
would chime, and the bus would come to a stop, picking up
or disgorging passengers. I watched as a mountie rode his
patient horse down the opposite side of the mall, keeping an
eye on the street kids who hung out in doorways or leaned
against the kiosks that had closed and locked up for the day.

I sat on the uncomfortable bus seat, thinking about Tom

and his meeting with the pack; about Carlton Lewis and the package in my lap; about the unknown someone who managed to break into the hospital to steal the eggs of an insane vampire; and even about the court case. Not one thing on my mind was comfortable or pleasant. I almost wished that way back when, I'd made my way into the corporate maze like so many of the people I knew. Almost. I still valued my freedom too much. Besides, I was a smart ass. With my mouth I wouldn't have made it long.

The bus pulled to a halt. I'd reached my stop. As the bell rang and the doors whooshed open I rose to my feet. I stepped down onto the pavement and started the short walk to my building.

I entered through the parking gate, rather than through the front door. The front lobby is beautiful, with an art deco feel to it. That elevator serves all the apartments. But during the remodel I'd left the old freight elevator in place. It's big, noisy, and opens directly into the garage, and into my apartment. It's my own private entrance, and private was what I needed right now. I was in no mood to meet up with any of the tenants. God knows how I'd react if one of them had a complaint.

I'd locked off the freight elevator this morning when I left, so I had to use the key to get it running. As I pulled the gates closed and hit the button for my floor I closed my eyes and told myself to concentrate on the positive.

It wasn't as easy as it should have been. Yes, I'd gotten out of the situation with Richards without getting hurt, but I don't like being threatened. I particularly didn't like being *successfully* threatened. I rode up to the apartment in the freight elevator, telling myself I'd been sensible—there had been no way I could have survived a fight with Lewis Carlton unarmed. It didn't make me any happier.

A lawsuit, possible additional criminal charges, the frigging Thrall. Could my day get any worse? Of course it could, I told myself sourly. I just hoped it wouldn't.

The elevator shuddered to a stop. I opened the doors, used my key to lock it off, and stepped into my apartment.

"Home sweet home." I flicked on the light switch and saw my massive white cat, Blank, run headlong across the living room and up the stairs that led to the bedroom. Grinning at his antics, I kicked the shoes off my feet, watching as they dropped over the edge of the steps leading down to the conversation pit. I felt the tension in my shoulders start to ease as I tossed the envelope on the kitchen island and slid out of my coat.

When I'd hung it neatly in the closet, I padded over to the windows.

I'd left the vertical blinds fully open this morning, so I had an unobstructed view. The sky was a deep, vivid blue flecked with tiny pinpricks of pure white starlight. As I watched, the lights lining the street below flickered on. The glare of the light pollution made all but the brightest stars disappear. Ah well.

I took a deep breath, the scent of green plants and loamy soil filling my nostrils. The windows I stood at take up one entire wall of my apartment, and I had taken advantage of the natural sunlight to plant my own personal jungle. The plants thrive, thanks in no small part to timed misters that I had put in so that I'd never forget to water them. I travel a lot, delivering other people's valuables, and I got tired of coming home to dead plants.

I'd designed the entire apartment to be my own personal refuge, a place I could go to escape . . . everything.

It takes up what were once the entire third and fourth floors of the old warehouse. The east wall has the front door, the freight elevator, and the back wall of the kitchen. The west wall is a bank of floor-to-ceiling windows. I left the north wall bare red brick, the only decoration a six foot framed coat of arms with the Reilly family history.

There is only one interior wall on the lower floor, where a set of wide steps curve up to the bedroom loft. The wall is painted pale peach. One section is adorned with all my important photographs, another third is taken up by the entertainment center. The downstairs bathroom and walk-in closet are cleverly concealed behind the wall.

Looking around I saw little reminders of Tom almost everywhere, bits and pieces of things that have migrated from his apartment downstairs up to mine. I've never been one for reading the news, but the newspaper sat folded on the coffee table next to an empty coffee cup. Every morning, he goes on his run, gets a paper and reads it over coffee. We used to run together, until the dislocated knee. It's healed, but I have to be very careful of it. I can run, but not too far, and I have to make sure it's well wrapped.

Tom's laptop sat open on top of my desk next to a huge stack of mail. A bowl of fresh fruit sat in the center of the kitchen island, a canister of sugar on the counter. We weren't living together, but even before Dusty and Rob moved into the apartment next to his, he'd spent as much time up here as in his place downstairs.

I didn't want to lose that, and it pissed me off that the pack might force the issue. I had thought I understood and accepted what being a part of a pack meant to the wolves. Apparently I'd been wrong. The thought of them telling Tom, and by extension me, how I was going to live my life got my back up. But losing my temper would only make things worse.

Think about something else. Of course that was like telling myself *not* to think of pink elephants. Still, determined not to brood, I took my mother's advice from my childhood. When in doubt, eat. She would never have understood the whole eating disorder thing. People actually deliberately starving themselves? You've got to be kidding! For her, food was how you showed comfort. Period. I was my mother's daughter. Since I was in dire need of comfort and hadn't eaten since an early breakfast, food seemed like a good idea.

I went to the freezer and looked over what was left of my

last big cooking session. There wasn't much. I'd been home a lot more than I was used to lately, recovering from the injuries inflicted in my last run-in with the vampires. There were only four of my homemade pasties left. Pasties are one of my favorite things in the world, meat pies with vegetables and gravy. I always use my mother's recipe except for one small change. No turnips. I *hate* turnips.

In the next day or so I'd need to take time to cook up a freezer full of single-portion meals to get me through. Otherwise, I was liable to get too busy and not bother to eat. I cringed. I wasn't completely broke, but damned near. I'd been living off of my short-term disability payments. The insurance pays out at half of what I usually make. Unfortunately, I don't eat half as much, and the mortgage company hasn't cut my payment in half either—while I bought the place for cash, I'd had to refinance to make a lot of the repairs. Money was tight enough that I'd had to use the check from the insurance company paying for my stolen truck to pay the power bill. The big check I'd gotten for doing a process service had kept the roof over my head and groceries on the table. But it, too, was almost gone. I'd been as conservative as I knew how to be. Even Christmas this year had been "intimate" (read: grim) with "small tokens of my affection." But despite my best efforts, I was losing ground, and fast.

I took two of the pasties out of the freezer and unwrapped them. I set them in a dish and slid it in the microwave to heat. While they defrosted, I poured myself a nice glass of wine, fed the cat, and headed over to the counter to check the answering machine and retrieve my messages.

My answering machine is a black plastic monstrosity that takes up the better part of one end of the counter. I realize it's hopelessly old-fashioned. I don't care. My brother Joe keeps nagging me to get voice-mail, but I *like* the machine. It works fine for me. I'm used to it. And, though I'd never admit it to him, I'm contrary enough that, the more he pushes me, the more I dig in my heels.

At the moment the light was blinking, and the screen showed three new messages. Unfortunately, I was pretty sure none of them were from clients needing deliveries. While I was anxious to get back to work, the doctor had been dragging his feet. He'd only *just* cleared me—right before the blasted trial started. Now I can't leave town until the trial is over, judge's orders. Then there were the hearings on the criminal charges, which might lose me my bonded and concealed carry permits. I knew there were things I could do to drum up business. But they had to wait for now. I'd just have to budget carefully and tighten the old belt a little bit more.

At least the Thrall are going to pay. The thought soured me even further. It was small consolation. Still, while they will twist the truth into corkscrews they do not flat out lie to the Not Prey and they'd promised to pay. Of course they hadn't named a price. For all I knew, I could be doing this for the price of a cup of coffee.

I hit the button to rewind and play the answering machine tape as I sipped the wine from my glass.

The machine beeped, and I heard my own greeting play back. "You have reached Kate Reilly, bonded air courier. I'm not available to take your call at the moment. Please leave your message after the tone." Another beep, followed by my older brother's voice. "Kate, it's Joe. Give me a call on my cell to let me know how it went, okay?"

Beep.

"Kate, it's Mike. I just got a call from the police checking to make sure you were here last night at ten. Is something wrong? Give me a call."

Father Mike sounded concerned, and for good reason. Yes, something was wrong. No, I wasn't going to call him: at least not until after I had a good meal in me and took a look at whatever was in the padded envelope Doug had given me.

Beep.

"Ms. Reilly, this is Dr. Edgar Simms. I took over from Matt Quinn as chairman of the hospital board at St. Elizabeth's. I would appreciate it if you would call my office to-morrow to set up an appointment over lunch. It has to do with a research study involving Eden victims. We are continuing on with the study, despite the . . . circumstances. We would still like to have your participation."

Yeah, right. That's what you said last time, and look where it got me. Thanks, but no thanks!

He continued after a brief pause. "I can understand why you would have some reservations, but if you would be willing to at least discuss the matter, I am sure we can re-solve the previous misunderstandings."

Misunderstandings—like the threat of losing my home and business, and those pesky little criminal charges the hospital asked the district attorney to investigate?

"My number is 555-1748. I'll look forward to your call. Perhaps a timely call from our office to the district attorney could help with your decision?"

The machine shut off, leaving me debating whether or not I was going to call him back. I'm not a big fan of legal fees, and if there was even a slim chance they could talk the DA out of prosecuting—

I took another sip of wine and decided to think about it over dinner.

A glance at the microwave showed me that I still had a few more minutes to wait for the pasties. With a sigh, I called the hotel to talk to Joe. He didn't answer his line. Considering the time, he'd probably gone out to dinner. I left him a quick voice-mail saying everything was fine and hung up the phone. Filial duty accomplished, I retrieved the envelope I'd gotten from Doug the vampire and tore it open.

Inside there was a DVD, several neatly typed sheets of paper, and a check. I tilted the envelope and they fell onto the couch beside me. The check was made out to me from the Law Offices of Richards, Harlan, Morris, and Dow, P.C. The amount was exactly what I had always charged Morris Goldstein for runs to Tel Aviv.

I set my wine glass onto a coaster on the coffee table. Before I did anything else I was going to hang up this suit. Otherwise, no matter how careful I tried to be I was almost guaranteed to get something on it. I climbed upstairs and changed, making sure to hang it carefully so that it wouldn't wrinkle, and put the shoes, purse, and jewelry where they belonged. That done, I pulled on an oversize tee-shirt and sweats. I padded barefoot down the stairs, picked up the disk, and slid it into the DVD player. I was as ready as I'd ever be to see what they'd sent. Unfortunately, I couldn't find the remote. After checking all the various surfaces, then crawling around to reach under the couch and chairs, I finally found it jammed down between the couch cushions.

I climbed onto the couch and settled in with a sigh. As soon as I was comfortable, Blank wandered over and jumped in my lap. He purred a greeting, rubbing his entire body against me, decorating my clothing with long, white cat hairs. I scratched him under the chin, and the volume of his purr intensified until he sounded like a miniature motorboat.

Despite all of my problems, I found myself smiling. I had *missed* this cat. No matter how bad I felt, he could always make me smile. Dylan had taken him from me years ago when he left me and I'd gotten him back after Dylan died—finally a hero, despite everything. I'd named him Blank when he was a kitten, a small bundle of white fur with huge paws and pale eyes. He'd looked unfinished, like a blank canvas. He'd grown into the paws, and developed an attitude. Both of which were just fine with me.

I hit the play button. The image on the screen was a digital copy of a surveillance video. At the bottom of the screen there was an indicator giving the date and time. The black and white image was grainy, and showed one of the unmarked back entrances of a building. I realized after a few seconds it was the hospital's back entrance. I'd walked out that very door on occasion when going out to dinner with Joe.

A hunched figure in a dark hooded sweatshirt and jeans lurched up a pair of steps. There was something wrong with the way the figure moved, but I couldn't quite pinpoint what it was. As I watched a gloved hand reached out and punched the series of numbers onto the keypad that unlocked the door. He/she entered the building at 10:02 P.M. At precisely 10:36 the figure emerged carrying a large leather doctor's bag.

The screen went black and I sat back into the cushions, thinking about what I was supposed to be seeing. I pressed the button to turn off the DVD player and wound up staring at the pretty night anchor from Channel 4 News. She was standing in front of the courthouse summarizing what had happened in the trial. The wrongful death case was big news.

In the background I could dimly see demonstrators carrying signs. They were from a new group called "Share the Planet." They'd formed somewhere on the Western Slope shortly after my confrontation with Monica left the entire nest dead. The group's purpose was a push for vampire rights. Their position was that the vampires were a fully sentient species and should receive the same rights and treatment as human beings. It was a lovely sentiment, but given the fact that the only way the species could live was as a parasite, I was pretty sure it wasn't going to play in Peoria. Still, I'd gotten more than my fair share of boos as I passed by them on the way to court. Every one of them had recognized me and several of them had started a chant of "murderer."

I cringed at the memory and used the remote to turn off the television. Despite what people may think, I do *not* like being the center of attention, and certainly not *that* kind of attention. Whatever the news stations had to say about today, I didn't want to hear it. Instead, I shifted the cat from my lap and began reading the pages that had been given me.

There were a three-page double-spaced list of the names of hospital employees who were known to have the access code to that door; a much shorter list of people who had access to the code to the laboratory; and the names of the nurses on duty on that floor the night of the theft. All of it very useful information, assuming I knew what I was doing.

What I really wanted to do was to talk to Brooks. He'd at least have suggestions about how to proceed. If I was really lucky, he'd jump at the chance to help clear his own name; effectively giving me access to the considerable resources of the Denver Police Department. Of course, that assumed he would talk to me. It was entirely possible his lawyer had advised him to keep his distance. I was fairly sure the politicos in the police department had. My name was poison in political circles right now. And while I was pretty sure Brooks wouldn't care, I didn't want to get him in trouble.

Decisions, decisions.

My internal debate raged back and forth for several minutes. In the end I decided it wouldn't hurt to call. After all, he could always say no. It wasn't until after I'd reached the decision that I realized I didn't know his telephone number. We were friends of a sort, but I'd never had occasion to call him. Our relationship had been forged in a crisis. We really hadn't ever had the chance to learn the everyday details of each other's lives. Not knowing what else to do, I called the police station with a street address closest to the Shamrock Motel and asked for him by name. I was told he was off duty, but they offered to transfer me to his voicemail.

"Sure." I waited, trying to think of what to say as the officer in charge of receptionist duties transferred my call. His smooth near-bass voice came over the wire. "You have reached Detective John Brooks. If this is an emergency, please hang up and dial 911. Otherwise, please leave a message after the tone."

"Hey Brooks, it's Kate Reilly. I've run into a situation and I could really use some help if you're available. Either way, give me a call when you can. The number is 555-2155."

I set the phone back in its cradle and went into the kitchen. The pasties were ready to eat. I sat on a stool at the kitchen counter, munching absently on meat-filled goodness and tried to figure out what my first move should be. When I caught myself dozing off mid-bite I decided to hell with it. It had been a rough day. Plans and decisions would have to wait until I'd gotten a little rest. So I went upstairs, pulled on a nightgown, set the alarm, and went to bed.

I dreamed. I knew it was a dream, because I was floating above a foreign landscape. The parking lot could have been anywhere, but the plants that lined it seemed . . . odd. In the distance I heard laughter and the distinctive sound of billiard balls being struck. There were loud music and voices raised to be heard over the din.

I heard a door open, and saw a man exit the building, keys in hand. He was small and wiry, with curling red hair and a no-nonsense attitude that showed in his body language. He walked briskly across the lot to a battered and ancient pickup truck that might have been blue in a previous lifetime. Now plastic had been taped over the driver's side window, and dust and caked mud coated the paint job until it was impossible to be sure of the color.

A hooded figure moved stealthily between two nearby parked cars. The man turned, his expression wary. "Who's there?"

The voice was familiar. In the dream I struggled to shout a warning, struggled to come in closer for a clearer look. It was hopeless.

The man stared into the darkness, slowly turning to scan the parking lot. Every muscle was tense, alert. For long, silent moments he stood poised and still, keys in his left hand, his right hand resting on the hilt of the knife on his belt.

Nothing.

Eventually, he turned back to the vehicle, sliding the key into the lock.

The attacker pounced, but the man was ready. He fought hard and dirty, using his knife with the skill that

comes from regular practice. But his opponent was ru-
inously quick—too quick for a mere human. Nor did it
have merely human strength.

It darted in close. Grabbing his knife arm in both
hands, the attacker jerked the arm sharply down at the
same time that it raised its knee.

Bones snapped audibly, and the man screamed in pain
and rage. He head-butted his attacker, pounding with his
uninjured fist. It was no use. The creature grabbed the
knife where it had fallen. In a smooth motion, almost too
fast to see, it gutted the man with his own weapon.

Blood and worse poured from the wound as the at-
tacker relentlessly sought for his victim's heart. The
man threw his head back to scream and the attacker's
fangs struck home.

I woke screaming, my heart racing. The alarm was blaring. In those first startled seconds, I fumbled around for it in the dark and wound up knocking it to the floor. It broke. Swearing, I threw back the covers and climbed out of bed, carefully avoiding the broken plastic. I went and got the broom and dustpan from the linen closet and swept up the mess. It occurred to me that this was the first time I've ever broken a clock accidentally. Amazing.

I dumped the bits of plastic in the trash but saved the battery to use in the replacement clock I pulled from the shelf.

I was awake, but I wanted coffee. It was, after all, only 5:30 A.M.

I wandered downstairs and started the coffeemaker. I automatically pulled out the creamer and sugar, before I realized Tom wasn't here.

I stood frozen, the refrigerator door wide open, the cat twining around my legs. He hadn't come back last night. *Shit.* A million what-ifs chased through my mind before I saw the note he'd taped to the freezer.

Kate:
Paul caught the chicken pox from one of his kids. I have
to cover the last day of his shift at the station. I'm
sorry! I really wanted to be at the trial for you! Call me
on my cell and let me know how it goes.
   See you soon.

                                                    Tom

I let out my breath in a relieved sigh. He was all right. The
note didn't say anything about the pack meeting though. I
had no idea whether that was a good or bad thing.

I fervently wished Dusty would just get pregnant. She
wanted the baby, after all. With at least one of the surrogates expecting a lot of the pressure on Tom would let up.
Oh, the pack still wouldn't be *thrilled* that he was with me.
They'd *prefer* he hooked up with some sweet little werewolf, or a fertile human woman who could bear more children for the pack. I'm not fertile. In fact, like Mary and the
others, I'm sterile—a heartbreaking effect of all the Thrall
yolk running in my veins. But they might at least tolerate
the idea. I wasn't sure I wanted to live *without* Tom.

Would he choose me over the pack? I didn't know. Werewolves are people, but the wolf traits are part of them, too.
They crave pack, family. I didn't want being with me to cost
Tom something that was integral to who he was. But I
wasn't willing to give him up either. I couldn't change my
genetics. There has never been a werewolf in the Reilly
family tree. Not one. Nor could I make myself fertile, no
matter how much I might have wanted to.

I sighed. *Think about something else, Reilly. You'll just*
depress yourself worrying about things that you have no
control over. Tom hasn't *had to choose. He may* never *have*
to choose. He hasn't left you. He's just working.

It wasn't the first time he'd gotten called in to work unexpectedly. He was single, and had a flexible schedule.

When things went wrong at work he was one of the first to get called to cover for an absent coworker. Still, the little, suspicious corner of my mind wondered at how *convenient* it was that it came up right when the pack was trying to get him to keep his distance from me.

I shook my head. I was being unfair. I'd let a simple nightmare get under my skin. I shuddered. It had seemed so *real*. I'd felt the breeze against my skin, smelled the metallic scent of the spilled blood.

I shivered with cold that had nothing to do with the ambient temperature. I needed to clear my head. Exercise would be good. But I didn't want to go for my run until after I did my meditation.

I went to the closet and retrieved the kit I'd set up for myself. It consists of a large box, a gray floor mat, white pillar candle, incense and burner, and matches. I carried the box to my usual spot, underneath the plants, with a clear view of the scene outside my windows.

It took only a minute or two to roll out the mat, turn the box over to use as a table, and set up and light the incense and candles. I sat Indian style on the mat, my forearms resting on my knees, palms up, and began deliberately relaxing each muscle in turn.

The sweet spicy scent of sandalwood filled the room. I let my mind float, relaxing the barriers that I normally fought so hard to keep in place. Slowly, the muscles in my back and shoulders began to unclench. I took deep, slow breaths, watching the flickering blue and yellow of the candle flame. I felt light-headed, suffused with warmth and power. I was ready. It was time. I closed my eyes and sent my mind outward, thinking of Henri Tané, his voice, his face as it was the last time I saw him.

A crowd of people stood in a cemetery, all wearing white. The priest stood in front of the casket, speaking

in a language I couldn't understand. It wasn't French.
Perhaps Creole. They were the two national languages.
   A beautiful young black woman wept, her arms
wrapped around a small boy with Henri's features. She
looked up, and for a moment it was as though she saw
me. Her eyes burned with pain and rage.
   A feminine voice filled my mind, the English heavily
accented. "Find the thing that murdered my man. Find
it and kill it."

I was back in my body so suddenly it startled me. I was
shaking, cold. Tears streamed down my face. The candle
had blown out, the incense was ashes. My mind reeled, as
though from a blow. I knew, *knew* that Henri was dead,
murdered. I hadn't known him long, but he had been my
friend. He alone of the people I knew actually understood
what being Not Prey meant. He'd been the one who brought
me relief by teaching me how to shield and block out the
hive most of the time. Thanks to Henri I have another way
to be alone in my mind. The queens would have to launch a
full attack to break through my shields now.

I stood shakily and made my way to the bathroom. Using
toilet paper to blow my nose, I tried to think who to contact
to find out what had happened. I didn't know. From what
I'd read there'd been unrest in Haiti for years. According to
the news I'd read, UN peacekeeping forces had clashed
with local gangs and the unrest made everything more
complicated.

I could talk to Miles when I saw him at the courthouse,
see if I could get him to retrieve contact information for me
from the hospital files. He might refuse, but it was worth a
try. Because, while a part of me absolutely believed in my
vision, another part held out hope: maybe what I'd seen was
simply the product of an overactive imagination. Or maybe
it was a premonition that could be avoided if I gave Henri

warning. I was new at this. I didn't control it very well yet. Other things I'd seen had been from the past, or the future. Not everything I saw was in real time no matter how urgent it felt.

I told myself all those things and more. I didn't believe any of it. With a heavy heart I tossed the tissue in the trash and went back in the living room to put away the meditation gear. Normally I put nearly a full hour into the exercises. Today I'd barely done fifteen minutes. But I couldn't bring myself to try again. Not right now. So I repacked the box, loaded it into the closet, and went upstairs.

I wrapped my knee and then pulled on a sports bra, followed by a navy sweat suit with white stripes down the jacket sleeves that matched the stripes on the outside of the pants. Thick socks and comfortable running shoes completed the outfit except for the accessories. I clipped one of my favorite knives onto the waistband of my pants, tucked my iPod into the pocket of my jacket, and strapped on the man's sports watch I wear when I run. A quick glance at the watch let me know I could run for a half hour, but that was all. I tucked my house keys in my jacket pocket and rode the freight elevator down to street level. I exited the parking garage through the gate. It was chilly, but not really cold. Still, I did a couple of quick stretches to limber up, touching my fingertips to the tops of my Nikes and stretching until the bones in my spine popped and the handle of the knife I'd clipped into the waistband of my pants dug painfully into my waist. I rolled my body upward, clasping my hands together and reaching toward the sky, then bent from one side to the other.

It felt good, really good, to be moving my upper body without pain. My shoulder had finally healed, as had my elbow. Oh, I'd be doing physical therapy for months yet to get full strength back, but I had mobility, and function, so I wasn't complaining. The stitches on my forearm were gone, replaced by a really interesting pattern of scars. I shivered at the memory of sharp fangs digging into the vein, and the throbbing pain of twelve, individual eggs absorbing the blood from my body.

I closed my eyes, saying a quick prayer of thanks for my survival and the survival of my loved ones and another prayer for Henri. Then I slipped my iPod on, cranked up the tunes, and started off at a slow jog, my feet moving in time with the music coming through the headphones. Yeah, I'd promised to wait until spring, but what Joe didn't know, wouldn't hurt me.

I'd run less than half a block when I started to sweat through the fabric of the sports bra. The calendar might say January, but the weather didn't believe it.

Rather than take my usual route on the trail that runs next to Cherry Creek, along Speer Boulevard I ran down Fifteenth Street past the underpass, until I came to the park and trails that had been put in between an entire development of high-end apartments and condominiums. The prices advertised on the billboard outside the building that housed the management offices took my breath away. They'd taken the price I originally paid for my building, and added a one on the front—*per unit!* I couldn't believe anyone would pay that much, but they obviously were. The sign in front read "Only four units left."

Amazing. If I ever *did* decide to go condo with the building, it was good to know that the sky was the limit as far as pricing. But despite my current financial woes, I just wasn't ready to parcel out my building. For one thing it was *my* building, and I liked it that way. Still—

I felt, then saw, movement out of the corner of my eye. I turned my head to see a huge shape emerging from the doorway of one of the condos. It was Carlton. He'd covered his head with a Rockies baseball cap, and wore dark sunglasses, but there was no mistaking him.

Not for the first time I wished that vampires really were the evil undead of legends. If that were the case, he would be bursting into flame right about now, and fear wouldn't be trying to claw its way out of my stomach like a trapped animal. Instead, as I watched he adjusted the drawstring at the waist of his pale blue satin warm-up suit and started heading my way at an easy lope.

I am Not Prey. Prey run. I will not *run.* But oh God I wanted to.

He came up next to me, his long legs making it easy for him to keep pace. "Morning, Buffy. How's tricks?"

"Buffy?" I didn't break stride, just kept moving at a steady pace, my feet thudding in a steady rhythm against the pavement. "I'm *Kate*."

He grinned, flashing white teeth and fangs. A lot of new vamps try to be subtle about what they've become. Carlton wasn't the subtle type.

"What, you don't like the nickname? I mean, hell, aren't you just the heap big vampire slayer? You're the one to beat, baby. I've done my homework. The rest of the Not Prey—they've taken maybe one minor vamp to earn their status. You've taken down two entire hives. I mean . . . *damn, girl.* You have those old broads shittin' a brick every time you so much as say boo."

Somehow I doubted that. I glanced over at him. "You don't look too intimidated."

His grin widened, but something in the set of his face made it look fake. "Like I said, I like a challenge. It's why I accepted their offer to come out to Denver."

"And why you jog in broad daylight."

He laughed, a deep joyous sound, and flashed those oh-so-sharp teeth again. "It stings like a bad sunburn, and it's hard on the eyes. But I don't mind a little pain."

Why doesn't that surprise me?

I decided to ask Carlton the question that had been tugging at the back of my mind ever since Richards handed me the packet last night. He might choose not to answer, but it couldn't hurt. Who knew, maybe I'd actually find out something.

"Why can't the queens track the eggs mentally? They had an awareness. I could feel it when I was in the hospital."

"Those were the incubated eggs. They had either hatched or were close to hatching. The ones that have been stolen were cryogenically preserved. They've never been connected to the hive, so the queens can't find them."

"They've tried?"

"Oh, hell yeah." He shook his head. "Do you really think they'd deal with *you* if they didn't have to? Get real, Reilly. They hate your ass. To them you're a fucking mass murderer."

"Funny, I feel the same way about them."

We continued running in silence for several minutes, stride for stride. He could easily have outdistanced me if he'd wanted to, but seemed content to just keep pace, his breathing perfectly easy, expression calm.

"Do they know anything about Henri Tané?"

I could barely see his eyes behind the dark glasses, but I felt his consciousness shift. He didn't break stride, but he did slow the pace a little. I matched my stride to his.

After a long moment he said. "He's dead. And before you ask, nobody connected to the hive did it. The queens didn't want to risk it. They considered him almost as much of a pain in the ass as you."

"Only almost?"

"Baby, *nobody* is more of a pain than you are." His voice was hard.

I looked over at him, deliberately keeping my expression neutral. "Am I supposed to be flattered?"

"Don't be."

We reached a fork in the sidewalk. I stayed on the main track. He turned off. In less than a minute he was gone.

4

I made it back to the apartment with plenty of time to shower and change. I didn't dawdle. I didn't want to be late.

The 16th Street Mall has a set of shuttle buses that run from one end of downtown to the other, stopping every couple of blocks. They're busy most of the day and night, but during peak times, when all the good little commuters are making their way to the high-rise office buildings, they run extra buses. Even so, people pack in like sardines.

I had climbed on at the Union Station stop. It's the start of the line, so I'd been able to snag a seat. It was more comfortable than swaying on my feet with somebody's brief-case jabbing into my back, but only barely. If I hadn't been due to testify this morning I'd have walked. But I didn't want to take the stand in front of an entire courtroom full of people, including reporters, soaked in sweat and stinking to high heaven.

Winter in Denver, you had to love it. Frigid one minute, hot the next. The old saw about "You don't like the

weather? Wait a few minutes. It'll change" is actually true
here. Since Tom hadn't been on hand to choose an outfit,
I'd gone for a more comfortable and practical look today.
My jacket and slacks were light-weight wool in a deep, for-
est green that brought out the color of my eyes and made
my hair look even more red than usual. I'd pulled all of that
hair back into a tight French braid that hung down to the
middle of my back. I left the jacket open to show off a soft
cotton tee in a flattering shade of cream with a floral and
leaf pattern embroidered around the scooped neck. Practical shoes with no heel in basic brown matched the bag I
carried. It might not be a *great* outfit for fighting, but it
would be a damned sight better than what I'd had on yesterday. Not that I was likely to have to fight any Thrall today.
No, apparently for the moment I was on their side. Made
me nauseous just thinking about it.

I checked my watch as the shuttle bell rang. The doors
were sliding closed, we were one block from Civic Center
Station; only a couple blocks from the courthouse. I'd
make good time by cutting through the park that takes up
nearly the entire block between the Denver courthouse and
the state capitol building. It has trees, gorgeous flowerbeds
in the summer, fountains, Greek columns forming an open
theater area and, at this time of day, more than a few homeless still huddled against the warm air exhaust grates in
sleeping bags.

I crossed Colfax with the light and began hurrying along
the sidewalk, the heat from the concrete sidewalks seeping
through the thin soles of my shoes.

I had only gone about half-way across the park when I
stopped cold. There had been about a dozen demonstrators
yesterday. Today there had to be over a hundred, waving
signs, chanting. It was a mess. There were police there to control the crowds, and vans from all of the local news affiliates.

"Shit."

The clock in the bell tower struck the quarter hour. Judging from the crowds by the front door, there was no way I was going to make it through security and up to the courtroom before eight going that way. Turning on my heel, I took one of the sidewalks that angled to the corner of the park. There was a visible line at the back entrance to the courthouse, too, but at least there wouldn't be reporters and chanting demonstrators.

I moved as quickly as I could, my purse slapping against the side of my leg, shoes clicking on the concrete.

I reached the edge of the park across the street from the courthouse in less than two minutes. I'd missed the light, and was getting ready to jaywalk when someone spotted me.

"It's *her!*" someone in the crowd shouted.

The demonstrators surged forward, knocking over the wooden barriers. I couldn't tell if the police were holding the demonstrators or vice versa. There were screams of "Murderer!" and "Bitch!"

Two teenage boys managed to break from the pack. They did an end-run around cops and the rest of the crowd, each running full out toward me. They ignored the squeal of traffic on Court Street, their eyes intent.

I dropped my purse. Kicking it out of my way, I braced myself as well as I could for attackers approaching from opposite sides.

The first boy, to my left, reached into the side pocket of his baggy jeans and pulled out what looked like a red water balloon. Time seemed to slow. As if from a distance I heard a booming voice shout "Put down the weapon!" I turned and saw the second boy pull a blue balloon out from his jacket. As the first boy cocked back his arm to throw, a dark-uniformed figure launched himself into a flying tackle, bringing the boy to the pavement with a bruising impact, the balloon smashing against the ground inches away from them.

I spun, toward the second attacker, even as the smell of rotting meat hit me like a slap to the face. He'd let go of his balloon. I had all the time in the world to see it sailing toward me, and no time at all to avoid it. It hit me in the center of my chest and exploded, soaking me with red paint mixed with what smelled suspiciously like fly attractant.

Police officers had cuffed both boys and were hauling them toward the squad cars. A third cop crossed the street to check on me, leaving his buddies to deal with the wildly cheering crowd of demonstrators.

"Ma'am, are you all right?"

"I'm fine." I reached down to grab my purse. I wasn't hurt, but I was humiliated. My clothes were ruined, and I stank like road kill left in the mid-July sun for a couple of days. I was scheduled to be in the courtroom in less than five minutes to testify. Oh, and all of the local news cameras were aimed in my direction.

"Do you want to press charges for assault?"

I thought about it and decided that, while a part of me really *did* want to, I also didn't have time to deal with it right now. I turned to the cop. "I'm scheduled to testify in Courtroom Four in a few minutes."

"I'll walk you through the line, but you'll have to wait and go through security. If you decide to press charges, stop by the station." He gave me an address over on Cherokee, only a couple blocks from the courthouse, escorted me past the line to the back door, through security, and to the bathroom door. He promised to go into the courtroom and let my attorney know what had happened, and that I would be there in just a few minutes.

I hated being late. It would probably piss off the judge. But I had to at least try and clean up.

I was scrubbing my face with a coarse paper towel and the cheap pink soap they keep in the dispensers when a woman opened the restroom door. Her nose twitched, she gagged, and retreated rapidly back into the hallway.

The jacket had been one of my favorites. But it was completely soaked and totally unsalvageable. I shoved it through the hinged lid into the trash can. The pants were ruined, too, but I couldn't exactly take them off until I had something else to wear. The tee-shirt had only been splattered. I'd go ahead and wear it, but the odds were good that the stuff would stain, despite my efforts to blot at the spots.

There was a brisk knock on the outer bathroom door. "Ms. Reilly, they're ready for you in the courtroom." I recognized the voice of my attorney's legal assistant.

"All right." I turned off the sink, dried my hands, and retrieved my purse.

The assistant was waiting for me outside the door. He manfully managed not to gag, but he couldn't keep from sneezing. He escorted me past the scaffolding, down the hall. When we reached the courtroom, he held open the heavy wood door for me. Steeling myself, I passed through.

Back rigid, I walked straight up the center aisle. There were gasps. More than a few people made choking noises. I couldn't blame them. The stench was really, seriously disgusting, and this was the improved model. Short of utter desperation I didn't believe anybody would set foot in the women's restroom on this floor until the janitors had emptied the trash.

In a loud voice my attorney announced, "I call Mary Kathleen Reilly to the stand."

The bailiff held open the little gate to the front of the courtroom and I walked over to the witness stand. I put my left hand on the bible, my right in the air and swore to tell the whole truth. And I did, so help me God.

I glanced at the judge and fought not to blush as he winced from the smell. "No need to explain, Ms. Reilly. The bailiff informed me of the altercation outside. Normally, I'd reschedule your testimony and allow you to go change, but this courtroom is needed in a few days, so we need to finish this trial up."

I nodded and the questioning began. When my attorney was done with our planned questions, I was cross-examined by the attorney for the other side. I'd been warned he'd bait me—try to get me to yell or argue, and he did. He tried valiantly to make me lose my temper so that I would say something he could use against me. I could feel the heat of blood rushing to my face, but I held onto my temper. I was polite. I was civil. I wasn't even sarcastic. If Tom had been here, he'd have been damned proud. Of course if Tom had been with me outside, there was a good chance we'd have had a pair of mauled teenagers. Was that a good or bad thing?

"I'm sorry, could you repeat the question?" I said the words sweetly. I didn't really think that he'd asked a question. It had sounded more like a sarcastic comment. But I was being good.

He gave me a truly nasty look, but announced, "No more questions, Your Honor."

"Attorney Jones, do you wish to reexamine the witness?"

"I do."

My attorney stood up and walked calmly over to stand in front of me. He didn't sneeze, but his nose wrinkled, and his eyes looked a little more moist than was normal. I watched him take a few steps back, until he was standing next to the air conditioner vent. It was a smart move. The vent was angled in a way that would blow the scent away from him.

The judge, meanwhile, had pulled an old-fashioned handkerchief from a pocket beneath his robes and was holding it over his nose and mouth. It wasn't exactly subtle, but maybe it helped.

I felt sorry for the poor court reporter. She needed both her hands to run the transcription machine. She was just going to have to suffer until I was done with my testimony.

"Ms. Reilly, would you say that you are an expert with regard to the *Heterotroph hippocratia*, or Thrall as they're more commonly called?" Jones asked.

"I wouldn't say that."

"You wouldn't? But aren't you Not Prey?"

"Yes. I am. But that doesn't make me an expert. It just makes me a survivor."

One or two people in the room chuckled. I hadn't meant it as a joke. It was the simple truth. If there was such a thing as a Thrall expert, it was somebody like Miles MacDougal. Not me.

"So, again, being Not Prey doesn't mean you've studied the Thrall, or have any special knowledge of them that you could be expected to pass on to others? It simply means that you have fought off a vampire attack and survived. Is that correct?"

"Yes." I spoke clearly into the microphone, making sure everyone in the room could hear.

"I have no more questions, Your Honor."

The judge discreetly slipped his handkerchief back beneath his robes. "Ms. Reilly, you may step down. And I want to thank you on behalf of this court for your appearance today in spite of the . . . adverse circumstances."

"Thank you, Your Honor." I stood up and stepped down from the witness box. The bailiff held open the little gate for me to leave. I walked out of the courtroom with as much dignity as I could muster. Then I called a cab to one of the smaller side exits of the building and went home to clean up.

5

I had a starring spot on the local news on every station at both 5:00 and 6:00 P.M. There were pictures of me with my clothes plastered to my body, with red paint splatters decorating a face set in lines of fury. The voice-over rehashed the death of Monica and the Denver hive back in July, and discussed the manifesto of Share the Planet. If it had been my place, I would've turned off the television. Unfortunately, we were at the rectory, so it wasn't my call.

The rectory at Our Lady of Perpetual Hope is a two-story, brick building that shares a basement with the church proper. The building is old, with steam heat and hardwood floors, fireplaces, built-in bookshelves, and lots and lots of real wood paneling. The ceilings are high, which makes it hard to keep the place heated in winter. Today, however, it was a dim, cool, haven. Mike—Father Michael O'Rourke to the parishioners—and I were sitting in the library. He was in his favorite battered recliner. I kept shifting in my seat, trying to find a comfortable position on the horsehair sofa, but no matter what I did, the coarse little hairs kept poking at me through my clothes, making me *itch*.

"They used red paint and *fly attractant?*" I could hear the suppressed laughter in Mike's voice. If I'd been injured, he would've been furious. But I hadn't been. As it was, he was trying very hard not to laugh.

I glared at him. He didn't even flinch. Then again, it's hard to be intimidating when you've grown up with someone. Mike has been a part of my life since we were kids. When my parents moved us away from Denver I'd been heartbroken. After their death, my brothers and I came back. By then Mike was a tall, devastatingly handsome blond rake whose passion for girls was only surpassed by his love of hockey. I'd fallen for him hard, had dreamed of us spending the rest of our lives together. God, and Mike, had other plans. I still love him, just not in the same way. And I really do believe that things worked out for the best. He's a terrific priest. And we're far too much alike to have made a life together. We'd have been ready to kill each other in no time.

"And you had to go up on the stand and testify like that?" He chortled. There was no other word for it. He *chortled*.

"It isn't funny, Mike! I had to throw out the clothes, even the tee-shirt. And I spent over an hour trying to scrub the paint and smell from my hair and skin. Even now I'm not sure I got it all." I had on fresh blue jeans and a pale yellow sleeveless shell. My still-damp hair was pulled back into a braid. The brown purse had been ruined, so I'd tucked my wallet into my back pants pocket. I knew I looked okay, but I still felt as though I stunk.

"No, of course not." He fought his amusement manfully, but his voice cracked just a little. "I'm sorry." His face was pink from the effort it was taking to control himself, his blue eyes dark and sparkling.

I glared at him some more. Eventually he began to look a

little repentant. He even started to apologize. "I'm sorry. Really. It's just—"

I took a deep breath and let it out slowly, telling myself as I did that Mike is my parish priest and one of my best friends. He was not deliberately trying to piss me off, although if he had been, he'd be succeeding admirably. I normally have a pretty good sense of humor, but I wasn't seeing anything funny about this morning.

I decided to change the subject so that I could speak without saying something bitchy. "So, you called me last night and wanted to talk?"

"Right." The amusement left his face in a rush. The serious expression made him look older. "Kate, what in the hell is going on? The police—"

I interrupted him before he could get any further. "Somebody broke into a lab at St. Elizabeth's and stole the vampire eggs they had in storage. The police were looking at me as a suspect."

"Kate—" He spoke carefully, as though a part of him might not want to know the answer to the question he was about to ask.

"Michael O'Rourke! I am *not* a thief. And I'm insulted as hell that you'd think I might do something like that!"

He blushed, until even the scalp beneath his thinning blond hair was bright red. "I'm sorry, Katie." He spoke softly, his expression contrite. "It's just . . . I know how much you hate them. And with good reason."

I wasn't mollified. "Which makes it all the harder to have to work for them."

"*Excuse me?*" He actually fell back into the chair from shock.

"You heard me." I started explaining. I talked fast. First, I wanted to get this over with. Second, any minute now one of Mike's assistants would be bringing Bryan and the other zombies back from dinner. I wanted to keep this conversation as private as possible. The other zombies were empty shells. They'd never know or care what anyone said. But my younger brother, Bryan, had gotten enough of his individual awareness back that he'd be likely to ask questions. Worse, he was likely to repeat the whole thing to Joe. He'd do it in all innocence, but I didn't want to deal with my older brother's reaction.

Mike started swearing. Since he became a priest he watches his language. He's very careful not to say anything that would shock people. But back in high school, when we were dating and he was playing hockey, he'd been able to turn the air blue when circumstances warranted it. Apparently he considered this to be a suitable occasion to trot out his old vocabulary.

"It's not like I have a good choice, Mike. I can't fight Carlton. The man could palm my *head* and crush it. He's bigger, stronger, has better reach." I was ticking off the items on my fingers.

"I know, I know," Mike agreed. He was drumming his fingers on the arms of the recliner in an uneven rhythm. "But that doesn't mean I have to like it."

"Well, if it makes you feel any better, neither do I."

"It doesn't." Mike ran his hands through his hair, leaving it standing up in odd directions. It was a gesture of frustration he used often around me. "God, Katie, the messes you get into! What are you going to do? You're not a detective. Do you even have any idea where to start looking?"

"I'm going to try to get Brooks to help me," I assured him.

Mike gave an approving nod. He'd met Brooks, liked and respected him. "Good idea."

"I hope he'll help. But even if he doesn't, I have a couple of ideas." That was a lie, but only a little one. Mike had enough on his plate. I didn't need him spending extra energy worrying about me.

He stood up and made his way across the room to the huge old desk that had come with the place. Opening the bottom left drawer he pulled out a bottle of whiskey and a pair of short glasses of heavy, cut crystal. He poured a generous portion from the bottle into each glass and walked over to where I sat so that he could hand me one of them.

"I hate to make things worse for you. God knows you have enough on your plate right now."

"What?" My voice was hard, suspicious. It drew his gaze to me, and he gave me a look that was both pained and embarrassed.

"What?" I repeated.

He took a long pull of alcohol. It made me nervous. Whatever he was going to tell me had to be bad. I don't drink much, and neither does he. The fact that he thought that we both might need fortification for what he was about to say scared me more than I was willing to show him.

"We have a problem." Mike had his back to me when he spoke, but he turned. Sitting on the edge of the desk, he took another long pull from his drink. I could see him gathering his thoughts, trying to come up with the right words.

"Just say it."

"Fine." He drained his glass, setting the empty tumbler onto the desk blotter. "Bryan has the curiosity and self-control of a four-year-old child."

I nodded.

"But he has the physical needs and body of an adult male."

I choked on my liquor, spewing alcohol onto the worn Oriental rug. My eyes were burning, and filled with tears. Partly from the alcohol, but partly from the logic jump that had followed his words.

Mike grabbed the tissue dispenser from off the desk and held it out to me. I grabbed a couple to wipe my face. He dropped to his knees and used a few more to clean the mess from the floor. He didn't speak again until he stood up and took the used tissues over to the trash.

"Oh shit."

"Twice, with two different nurses, I have caught him in . . . compromising situations. He wasn't *forcing* anyone, but—" Mike was struggling, and I was simply too shocked to say anything useful.

"I've been trying to find a male nurse to help take care of him, or even a male volunteer, but I haven't had any luck. I'm going to keep trying, but if no solution presents itself by the end of the week you'll need to start looking for another placement for Bryan."

"Michael!"

"I'm sorry, Kate. I've prayed long and hard about this. I don't know what else to do! Bryan needs more and different care than I can give him as short handed as I am—and I'm not willing to shirk my duties to my other charges just to take care of him. I hate this! You and Joe are like family to me. But I have to do what's right for *everyone*."

"Right." I choked the word out around the bitterness that tightened my throat. I stood, and Mike stood. Stepping forward he started to set a hand on my arm, to stop me, but I shook my head and stepped sharply away.

"I'd better go." I set the unfinished drink onto the coffee table. I wouldn't look at him. I was too angry, too hurt. If I looked at him I'd do something—say something I shouldn't. The hardest part was that a part of me *wanted* to say it. He'd hurt me, and a part of me wanted to hurt him back.

"Kate—" He started to say something, but I spoke over the top of him.

"I'd better get started, making those *other arrangements*." He flinched from the bitterness in those words.

I walked out the front door before he could respond. I very carefully didn't slam the door behind me.

Normally when I'm this upset, I go *into* the church. But if I went there, Mike would follow. He'd want to explain, talk things out. I didn't want to talk to him, and I sure as hell didn't need any more of an explanation than he'd already given me.

Having Bryan come even partially back had been such a miracle. Every other one of them was an empty shell. The bodies worked, but no one was "home." They could follow the most basic commands, if they were supervised. Unsupervised, they didn't have enough sense to eat, or stay out of traffic. Mike had made it his mission to care for them, because they were completely incapable of caring for themselves. I'd always admired his dedication. I'd appreciated everything he'd done for my baby brother. It had never occurred to me that there might come a time when he wouldn't be able to continue.

I walked the two blocks to Colfax. It was after dark and not a good neighborhood, but nobody bothered me. I was almost sorry. A part of me really wanted to hit something. As it was, I sat down on the bench at the bus stop, fighting back tears. It wasn't Mike's fault. If he said he couldn't handle Bryan, then he couldn't. But dear God, what was I going to do?

My cell phone rang. I thought about not answering it. I really wasn't in a mood to talk with anyone. All I wanted to do was ride the bus home, get some food, and have a good, long cry. I pulled the phone out of my pocket, intending to just turn it off. The number on the screen was Tom's. I hit the button to take the call.

"Hello." My voice was thick and rough with unshed tears.

Tom's voice came on the line. "Katie? Honey, are you okay? You sound terrible! I saw the news—"

I felt some of the tension leave my shoulders at the sound of his voice. I didn't want to say too much. Other people were starting to join me at the bus stop. But oh, it felt good to hear from him.

"I've had a rough day."

"Come home." He spoke gently, as though he were talking me down from some high ledge. Maybe he was. "Just come home. We'll have dinner. We'll talk. You can tell me all about it."

I let out a slow, shaking breath that was almost a sob. "It's going to be a while. I'm clear out by the church."

"That's all right. It'll give me time to pick up some wine. Just come home."

Home and Tom sounded exactly perfect right now, which should really scare me—but didn't. It was exactly what I wanted and needed. "Okay."

The bus pulled up, and the various passengers started climbing on. I stood up and moved into line. "I gotta go. The bus is here."

"All right. I'll see you when you get here. I . . . I *love* you, Katie."

I stopped, in shock, my finger hovering over the cut-off button. He'd only said that to me once before—when Amanda Shea, Dylan's former wife, had tried to kill me. Of course, she was insane, and had done something . . . *strange* to herself with Thrall eggs that had turned her into something not quite human, yet not a vampire either. But I've convinced myself over the past few months that he'd said it sincerely, despite being completely freaked out by her walking away from a three-story fall onto concrete, and me bleeding on the floor.

"Um . . . you, too." I closed the phone with shaking fingers and slid it into my left pocket, then started digging in my right pocket for change. Luckily, I had enough. Originally Mike was going to drive me home, so I hadn't thought I'd need it. But the drivers don't carry change, and I wasn't about to pay five dollars for a bus ride.

I dropped the change through the slot and stumbled to the back of the bus. I'd have to call Mike, either tonight when I got home or tomorrow to let him know that it wasn't really him I was angry with. Although, frankly, he's a smart man and knows me well. He'd probably already figured it out. Still, I owed him an apology. Damn it.

I slid into an open seat and stared out the window at the passing streetlights. My emotional turmoil was affecting my shielding. The buzz of the hive was growing stronger in the back of my head. Most of the vamps in this hemisphere were up and moving, ready to go on the prowl in search of a meal. I concentrated on controlling my breathing in preparation for reinforcing my shields.

Before I could finish, though, the queens' consciousness slammed into me. They were angry, impatient with me, and more than a little bit worried. They wanted the eggs back *now,* and they weren't happy that I wasn't devoting my entire attention to the assignment. I felt a headache beginning to build behind my left eye, and knew that they were causing it.

Fuck you. If you don't like the way I do things, find someone else to do your dirty work. I'm in the middle of a court case and I have a life to take care of. I'll do what I said, but on my *terms and on* my *schedule.*

The pressure behind my eyeball let up, and the buzz of the hive stopped for a full three count. When they spoke, the words were chosen with care. Even in my head, it was a sing-song collection of voices—all saying the same thing, in the same rhythm, but with various tones and accents.

When your brother was taken, what would you have done to get him back safely? If you had hired someone, and they didn't give their best . . .

I fought not to growl, or telegraph my mental conversation to anyone on the bus. *But you didn't just* hire *me. You threatened me. Under the circumstances, are you surprised that I'm not exactly chomping at the bit? I don't like being bullied. I never have. If I'd had a chance in hell of surviving I would've taken the challenge then and there.*

Another long silence. I felt a single entity pull itself separate from the hive.

I believe we owe you an apology, Not Prey, whether or not you would be willing to accept it. But we did not, and I do not, believe that you would have assisted us otherwise. Were we wrong?

I didn't even have to think about that one. I knew the answer. *No.*

I felt her wry amusement, completely separate from the anger of the hive. I hadn't known that any of the queens could pull away from the hive to think or act as an individual. I'd thought Monica an aberration.

Monica was insane. In that, at least, she was an aberration. But the most powerful of the queens can, if they wish, pull themselves from the hive. But I digress.

Not Prey, we need you to find and retrieve our young, and time is of the essence. I will consult with the others as to what payment we could make for this service that you would accept as adequate.

She was gone. My head was suddenly echoingly silent; my thoughts my own. I stared out the bus windows, trying to make heads or tails of the fact that the Thrall queens actually seemed to be acting . . . reasonable. That was just *so* wrong.

6

The mouth-watering scents of garlic bread and Italian food wafted to me as the freight elevator rose toward my apartment. My stomach was growling audibly before the car had come to a stop. The gates opened to reveal an apartment lit by dozens of white candles.

I looked around, taking it all in as Tom stepped forward.

My eyes widened, and my breath caught in my throat. He looked utterly amazing. He wore perfectly tailored black dress slacks, and a black collarless shirt in raw silk. The matte black of the fabric was the perfect frame for the warm tanned skin of his throat and chest.

He smiled at my reaction, flashing deep dimples, the skin at the corners of his chocolate brown eyes crinkling a little.

"Glad you like it." He took both my hands in his and pulled me into the apartment until we were next to the kitchen island. Letting go of my left hand, he reached over and plucked a wine glass from the counter and handed it over to me.

"Wow." I took a sip. It wasn't the cheap stuff I occasionally buy. This stuff actually tasted good. "I feel seriously under-dressed."

"You always look beautiful, Katie." Tom reached up to cup my face in his hand before laying a gentle kiss on my lips. Soft, warm, it tasted just a little of red wine.

I shivered, as my body reacted to his touch, my pulse racing at the thought of what I wanted to do with him.

"Dinner first," he teased, pulling back a step and letting go of my hand. "Don't want to waste perfectly good take-out."

I laughed. Tom doesn't cook. He considers it a failing of his. I don't. If I need something cooked, I can do it myself. When I don't, there's always take-out, and the man does know *all* the best take-out joints in Denver.

His grin warmed me to my toes. "Good to see you can still laugh. I was worried about you." It felt good to hear him say that; to know that he really *had* worried, that there was someone in my life who cared enough to want to share not only the good times, but the tough ones as well.

I nodded. "Rough day."

"Tell me over dinner," he suggested. "Then *after* dinner I'll see what I can do to make you forget all about it." He winked, and I laughed again.

The timer on the oven dinged, and Tom walked over to turn it off. He started gathering dishes and silverware from the various cupboards as I watched.

"So, which do you want first, the bad news, the *really* bad news, or the completely horrible, unbelievably rotten news?" I forced myself to keep the tone light. He was trying so very hard to cheer me up. Hell, I *wanted* him to cheer me up. *Then* I wanted wild, passionate sex, and to curl up against him and sleep in blessed silence for the night.

"Gee, honey," he teased, "you make them all sound wonderful. *You* pick." He picked up a wine glass that matched mine and raised it in a mock toast.

I gave a snort of laughter. I started with the problems with Bryan, because they were the ones that hurt the most. It didn't take long to tell, but before I'd finished my throat was tight and there were tears in my eyes again, damn it. My hand was shaking enough that I was afraid I would spill what was left of the wine, so I set the glass onto the smooth, tile surface of the counter.

Tom set his glass beside mine and pulled me into a hug. "It'll be all right. We'll think of something." He buried his face in my hair—and sneezed. I gave a shaky laugh and pulled back a couple of steps. "I take it I didn't get all the rotten meat scent out."

"Not quite," he admitted. "Somehow I don't see eau de chemical as your signature cologne. But it doesn't smell a thing like rotten meat to a werewolf nose." He grabbed an oven mitt from a hook on the wall and walked over to the oven.

"Thank God for that." I took another drink. The wine and the company began working their magic, helping me back away from the despair that was threatening to overwhelm me every time I thought about Bryan. Some hard decisions needed to be made, but not right this minute.

"I can't believe the demonstrators did that! Are you going to press assault charges?" Tom pulled the pan from the oven and set it on top of the stove, then reached in to retrieve a foil-wrapped loaf of bread. That, he placed on the counter. Closing the oven door with his hip he started rummaging in the utensil drawer for a spatula and bread knife.

"I decided against it. They *want* publicity. If I prosecute, there'll be another trial, and another chance for them to raise hell."

"Makes sense, I suppose. But I hate to see them getting away with it."

"Oh, they won't get away with it; at least not completely. I'm betting they'll be facing charges of disturbing the peace and disobeying a police officer at least, and maybe inciting a riot on top of that."

"Good!" The word and his expression were fierce. He

unwrapped the garlic bread and began slicing it with vigor. He slid a couple of pieces on each plate before serving the lasagna. "Can you get the glasses and silverware? I figured we'd eat in the living room."

"Good plan."

It wasn't until we were halfway into the living room that I realized I hadn't seen Blank since I'd been home. Since candles and the cat hadn't proven to be the best mix a couple of weeks ago, I had to ask. "Where's the cat?"

"In the upstairs bathroom, stoned out of his mind on catnip."

It made me smile. "You really *did* think of everything."

"We aim to please, ma'am." He winked at me.

I sighed. It was so nice to just relax and let someone else cut the bread and serve the lasagna. All I had to do was numbly fill my empty stomach. I told him about Henri's death, and the dream where I'd watched another man get killed.

He'd closed his eyes because, even though he hadn't met Henri, he'd heard me talk about him so often of late, it felt like losing a distant family member . . . a favorite uncle or grandfather. "I'm so sorry, Katie. I know how much he'd come to mean to you."

"I saw his wife in my mind . . . or thought I did. She asked me to hunt down his killer."

"I'm sorry, Kate. I was drifting. What did you say?"

"His wife, or someone, asked me to track down his killer. But with everything else going on—"

"Sweetie, you've already got such a full plate, I can't imagine how you'd have *time* to find out anything about his death in . . . where did he live? Haiti?"

I nodded and proceeded to stuff a hunk of bread in my mouth so I wouldn't say anything else stupid.

We finished the meal mostly in silence, even though I wanted to ask about the pack meeting. But the fact that he hadn't volunteered anything wasn't a good sign.

Finally, when we'd eaten all we could manage, he led me gently, as one by one he blew out each of the candles in the kitchen, then the living room. Slowly he put out each light up the stairs until the only light remaining came from a pillar candle that rested on the wall of my loft bedroom. Its soft glow cast flickering shadows over the bedroom. I turned to face him, enjoying the play of light and shadow over the perfect planes of his face. There was an intensity to his gaze—not just lust, although it was certainly there. But it was so much more.

Seeing that expression on his face made my knees weak. All the playfulness was just . . . gone, washed away in a wave of emotion and need.

He kissed me then, slowly and gently. The feel of his lips on mine, the warmth of his hands sliding beneath my top, took my breath away.

I gasped, my mouth opening wider as his tongue danced with mine. He unfastened my bra and pulled it and my tee-shirt from my body, throwing them onto the floor. I stood naked from the waist up, my body aching with the need for his touch. His stare devoured my body, his eyes dark and hungry. He dropped to his knees on the floor in front of me. Hooking his right hand through my belt, he pulled me close, until his breath burned hot against the skin of my chest. His mouth closed over my left breast, tongue and teeth teasing the nipple as his left hand worked the same magic on my right. I cried out, my body arching, my head thrown back in reaction to a pleasure that walked the fine edge of pain.

Even as his mouth teased and pulled, his hands were busy, unbuckling my belt, unzipping my jeans.

He pulled my pants and underwear down in a single rough gesture that made me stagger. I put my hands on his shoulders to steady myself, or I would've fallen. My knees didn't seem capable of holding me, not when he was trailing hot kisses down the front of my body, ever closer to where I wanted, needed, his touch.

He rose to his feet in a single, fluid movement, and I wanted to scream with frustration. Before I could make a sound, his mouth was on mine. He took one of my thighs in each hand, lifting me from the floor, raising me to the height of his waist before running my body slowly along his until I felt every long inch of him even through the thick cloth of his trousers.

I whimpered into his mouth, my body writhing with the need to have him inside me.

He carried me easily the few steps to the bed and lay me gently on my back. Once again he went to his knees, this time moving my legs over his shoulders. Slowly, gently, he kissed and licked his way from my knees upward, as I squirmed and bucked, my hands clutching at the comforter.

By the time his mouth had reached me, I was already on the edge of an orgasm. The first lick sent waves of pleasure through me. Then he began working in earnest, licking and sucking in a fierce rhythm until I screamed his name, my body spasming again and again.

Breathless and weak on the bed, my eyes closed, I continued to shudder in reaction to the intensity of the orgasm. I heard the sound of a zipper, the soft plop of clothing falling to the floor, but I was too drained to even open my eyes.

The bed shifted, and I felt a warm hand sliding along my thigh as he lay on the bed beside me. "Wake up, sleeping beauty. I'm not nearly finished with you yet." There was a huskiness in his voice that belied the playful words. He kissed me. A gentle brush of lips. I opened my eyes to stare into his from inches away.

I let my eyes move down the length of his body. I knew he could see the naked need in my face. I didn't care. I traced my index finger down the finely muscled expanse of his chest, over those washboard abs, until my hand reached its goal. It was my turn to tease him. With a feather light touch I traced my finger around the wide, swollen head, then ever so slowly the length of his shaft, down between his balls. His eyes closed and he let out a low groan. With one deft movement he rolled on top of me, his hips pressing against mine, while his arms held him propped up above me.

"Are you ready?"

I nodded, the movement of his body on mine sending new thrills through my stomach. "Oh yes."

He smiled at me and then lowered his face next to mine to nuzzle my neck. His hands slowly traced the curve of my waist as he whispered, "Tell me what you want, Kate. Soft or hard . . . slow or fast."

I honestly didn't care and was quickly losing rational thought. But then he pressed down against me again with force; urgently, and my body decided for me. The spasm inside me nearly hurt—and it felt good. I gasped out the word. "*Hard*. And . . . fast."

His lips on my neck pulled back into a smile and then my eyes flew open wide when his mouth opened and his teeth bit down into my shoulder. I couldn't move, couldn't breath as his fingers dug into my legs, pulling them wider open with a force that surprised me.

He was inside me before I could take a second breath and my muscles contracted around him hard enough to make him hiss and chuckle lustfully.

He pulled out, nearly completely, and then slammed into me again. A cry escaped me and white lights erupted in my vision. I dug fingernails into his back as a second orgasm swept through me. Time slowed to crystalline intensity as he took me like I wanted him to. Rising to his elbows, his mouth moved from nipple to nipple—biting, licking, sucking—while he ground himself into me over and over. The slapping sounds of flesh on flesh and the musky scent of him made me even hotter; I needed more of him. I wrapped my arms and legs around him, pushing when he pulled and rising up to meet every thrust. Before I realized what I was doing, I'd bitten into his neck and was raking nails down his back while he rode me hard and fast. The noises I was making in the back of my throat weren't quite words. They were guttural, animalistic and, apparently, he liked them.

"God, what you do to me, woman!" he growled and then threw his head back with a fierce cry. He swelled, pushing even deeper inside and liquid heat flowed into me, so hot I could actually feel each burst. But even then, he wasn't done. He kept pumping just as hard, groaning with each thrust—fully enjoying what must be an incredible climax. It was almost a full minute later before he collapsed on top of me, panting, sweating, and utterly spent.

I woke to the sound of Blank scratching at the bathroom door. Tom was snoring heavily. A glance at the alarm clock on the nightstand showed that it was 2:30 in the morning. I slid from beneath his arm, moving carefully so as not to wake him, and padded naked over to open the door.

The cat scooted out, warm fur brushing against my ankles as he rushed over to the litter box.

I was wide awake. If I climbed back in bed I'd just wind up disturbing Tom's sleep, too. It would be an inconsiderate thing to do. Besides, the quiet time in the middle of the night is often when I do my very best thinking.

I tiptoed over to the dresser, sliding the drawer open as quietly as I could. I grabbed at random. I just needed something to keep me warm while I was downstairs. I didn't need to be a fashion plate. Clothes in hand, I ducked into the bathroom, closed the door, and started to dress. The sweatshirt was one of the oldest and most beat-up I own. Black, with a small gold tiger on the chest: the Our Lady of Perpetual Hope High School mascot. I'd earned it by lettering in gymnastics and volleyball. The sweatpants were gray, and splattered with Navajo White paint from the building renovations. Finally, I slid my feet into a pair of thick white tube socks, turned off the bathroom light, and headed downstairs in the dark.

I'd had an idea, up in the bathroom. It might be nothing. Then again, it was at least worth another look.

I poured myself a glass of milk, grabbed a couple of chocolate chip cookies from the cookie jar on the counter, and wandered into the living room. While my head was not silent, the buzz of the Thrall hive was low enough that I could ignore it. I grabbed the remote for the DVD from the coffee table and hit the play button. As I watched, the familiar grainy picture came on screen. As the figure lurched up the steps I saw . . . something. I hit pause, and reversed. When I hit play, I noticed it again, but it was too quick. *One more try.* I used the remote to move the action forward one frame at a time. When the figure's foot touched the first step I pressed pause and hit the jackpot.

I could see the edge of a gold image and lettering on the front of the sweatshirt. I used the remote again to hit zoom, until the image was four times as large, as big as I could make it.

"What's that?"

I jumped, letting out a little squawk of surprise. I hadn't heard Tom come downstairs. My heart thundered in my ears from the shock. "You startled me."

"I can tell." He was wearing a pair of striped boxers and nothing else. I was distracted. He wasn't. He nodded at the screen. "What are you watching?"

"A surveillance video," I answered. "Take a look at her chest, can you read the logo?" I tried to keep my voice light. I didn't want this to start a fight, but it just might. Vampires and werewolves are the bitterest of enemies. I hadn't *deliberately* concealed the fact that I was working for the Thrall from Tom, but I sure as hell wasn't looking forward to breaking the news. I really didn't know how he'd take it.

"It's got the word 'Our' and the edge of what looks like a paw. I'd say it was like the one you're wearing, but your tiger is crouching. Yours doesn't have a single paw sticking up."

Shit. He was right. I hadn't noticed it before. Was it something subconscious that caused me to wake up and come look at the video again?

Tom walked over to the couch and pulled the padded envelope from where I'd lodged it between the cushion and the frame. His nostrils flared.

"Kate," he spoke softly, his voice tightly controlled, "why does this envelope smell like vampires?"

"You know how last night I said I had three pieces of rotten news?"

"Yes."

"This is the third one." I watched as he set the envelope onto the coffee table, oh so carefully. "It's kind of a long story," I said awkwardly.

"I'm in no hurry." He didn't look at me as he said it, just stood with his back to me, those amazing shoulders tight with the beginnings of anger.

Shit. Shit. Shit! I hate this. I really, truly, hate this.

I told him.

He turned very slowly. His face was slack with shock.

"You—" he spoke slowly, enunciating each word separately and with great care, "are . . . working . . . for . . . the . . . vampires."

"Tom—"

He held up his hand to stop me from speaking. "I know. You said it yourself. It's not like you had a lot of choice."

He was still angry. I could feel it beating off of him like waves of dry heat. I watched him standing there, clenching and unclenching his fists. I recognized what he was doing. I'd seen him do it before when he was fighting to control his beast.

"But you're still pissed."

"Not at you. At them. If I'd been there—"

"If you'd been there they still would've confronted me, or else waited until another time when I was alone. But they wouldn't let it go. You can't protect me from this, and I don't *expect* you to. It's my problem, not yours."

"Not *my* problem." The bitterness in his voice cut like broken glass. "No, of *course not*. You're the *Terminator*." He used the nickname from my volleyball years as though it were a curse. "You don't *need* anybody. I'm just the eye candy that warms your bed at night."

"Tom! That's not fair. And it's not true!"

"Isn't it? Are you sure . . . really *positive* about that?" He glared at me. His anger was scalding hot, but his eyes had gone dark and cold. "I've been with you for months, and all I've ever asked is that you let me in; share your life with me. But something this important, this *dangerous* comes up, and you deliberately leave me out—hell, would you even have *told* me if I hadn't walked down here?"

"Tom—" I stepped forward, reached for him, but he waved me away with an angry gesture.

"I'm out of here. You decide you need me as something more than a boy toy, give me a call."

7

I spent a miserable rest of the night not sleeping. My life sucked right now, and I didn't have any answers. I didn't want to go to court. I wanted to curl up under the covers and give the world the finger. Unfortunately, I didn't think I would be given that option.

At 7:00 A.M. I called attorney Jones on his cell phone to see if I really did need to go to the hearing. He told me they were having closing arguments today. Then the jury would deliberate, and it would be over. He said he'd check with the judge and call me back, but until I heard otherwise I should assume they wanted me to stay away from the courthouse.

I didn't do the happy dance, but I was relieved. I so wanted the trial to be over. All week I'd been paying attention, trying to see the situation from the jury's perspective. I honestly had no idea who was winning. If it had been up to me I would've held the hospital liable, but cut the rest of us loose. We'd see if the jury agreed with me in a day or two.

I flipped on all the lights in the living room. Normally, there's enough sunlight coming through the windows that I don't need to, but today the weather was as stormy as my mood. Thick black clouds, heavy with rain, had rolled into the city from over the mountains.

A crack of lightning striking nearby was followed by the deep rumble of thunder. Rain slashed at the windows, as if the lightning had hit some switch that released the full fury of the storm.

My stomach was in knots as I waited for the attorney's return call. Part of it was the trial. Most of it was the fight with Tom. *Had* I been shutting him out again? I didn't think so. He wasn't the only one working at this relationship. I've spent most of my life since my folks died trying to take care of everything myself, not trusting *anybody*. I'm more open with Tom than I ever was with Dylan. Hell, I'm closer to him than I was with Michael. That was saying something, since Mike and I were together when I was a kid in school, before life taught me even more hard lessons in self-reliance.

Frankly, I'd been far more worried about Bryan than myself. The situation at the parish was on a short time line, and I couldn't think of a single, decent solution to it. Second, I hadn't wanted to ruin the mood. Tom had gone to so much trouble . . . and, damn it, I'd needed the break he was offering me. In case . . . well, in case he did just what he ended up doing. The pack has made me so damned paranoid I'm afraid if I say anything . . . let him in any further to my whacked-out life, he'll walk. Damn it!

I ached to tell him that. But would he listen? Would he accept the explanation? I hoped so, but maybe not. Tom is one of the most reasonable human beings I've ever met, but he isn't perfect. He has his sore spots. I'd just run foul of one of the big ones. There were no guarantees. All I could do was try.

Sighing, I went upstairs to get dressed. Since I probably wasn't needed at court, I chose clothing that suited my mood. Black jeans, new enough to still be stiff with sizing, worn over a black tee-shirt printed with silver roses crossed under a skull.

The power flickered and went out while I was brushing my teeth. Swearing, I rummaged in the bathroom drawer for the matches I put there the last time Tom and I had a romantic bubble bath together.

The memory didn't improve my mood. I closed my eyes, fighting the sting of tears. When I had myself back under control, I lit the candle still sitting on the wall from last night and brought it back into the bathroom to finish getting ready. Blank had dived under the bed at the first crack of thunder. I had learned his nature well-enough over the past few months to know he wouldn't resurface until after the storm was long past.

The printing on my shirt shone eerily, reflecting the dim light as I braided black and silver ribbons into my hair. Usually candlelight softens features, which is why it's considered romantic. But the face reflected in the mirror now was stark, the light casting dark shadows that threw the bone structure of my face into sharp relief. I was still debating whether to put on makeup when I heard the heavy pounding of a fist on my front door.

"I'm coming," I yelled down. Grabbing the candle in my left hand I hurried downstairs. I sent a tendril of thought outward and realized that it was Mary Connolly. I *so* didn't want to talk to her, since she's the one person with final say over both the dyad, the breeding part of the group, and the pack, the hunting portion. Tom's a member of both.

Ultimately, she would decide whether or not Tom was *allowed* to stay with me long term, and she'd already said no. Have I mentioned how much I hate that? Still, we knew each other in high school, and if I *had* to pick someone to be in charge, she'd be it. Mary is tough as old boot leather, but she is fair.

I opened the door to find her looking totally drenched and thoroughly disgusted. Her short dark hair was dripping in her golden-brown eyes, and water ran in rivulets onto the carpet, off the black trench coat that made her look almost too small. Her jeans were soaked up to the knees, and I heard a definite squishing noise when she walked through the open doorway.

"Let me get you a towel and some dry clothes. We can hang your coat up in the bathroom and toss your clothes in the dryer downstairs when the power comes back on," I suggested.

"Thanks." She looked at me oddly, as though she hadn't expected me to be nice. Then again, maybe she hadn't. As Not Prey, we were technically equals in the predatory food chain, and she did stand between me and a happily ever after with Tom. Always assuming, of course, that he still wanted one.

I lit a couple of last night's candles and took her coat and left her stripping out of her wet things on the tile floor of the kitchen. It only took a moment to hang up the coat in the bathroom and retrieve both a towel and a set of sweatpants for her to wear.

"What brings you here in this weather?" I asked as I set the pants on the counter next to her.

"We need to talk."

Uh-oh. "Oh?" I tried to keep my tone neutral—and failed miserably.

Mary laughed. "Subtle, Reilly, very subtle." She toweled her hair vigorously for a minute, then hand-combed it in place.

I gave her a wry grin in acknowledgment. Subtle has never been my best thing. Hers either, if it came to that.

She handed me the damp towel, which I hung over the back of one of the kitchen stools to dry.

"Look," said Mary, the laughter fading from her eyes, leaving her expression serious and a little bit vulnerable. "I like you. I respect you. So I'm not going to bullshit you or beat around the bush." She emptied the pockets of her jeans, placing the contents onto the kitchen island. I didn't watch her undress, but heard the sucking sound of her peeling the wet denim from her legs.

I nodded, even though I wasn't sure she could see it with my back to her. I just didn't trust myself to speak. My heart was suddenly in my throat, and I felt like I was choking on it.

"Dusty wants to be with Rob. Fair enough. But it's been months, and no baby." She sighed. "Then, last night, I find out that Rob's been out of a job all this time, and that they've been living here without paying rent."

"Mary," I turned around, started to speak, but she held up a hand to stop me.

"Look, the fact is, if he can't support a family, we can't let him have one. It's that simple." She shook her head. "But then he pipes up and says that if he gets a job, even if he doesn't get her pregnant, what about artificial insemination? Says that someone else could father the child, but let them stay together. He said that it shouldn't matter since we raise the baby as a pack anyway." She gave me a long look. "He didn't come up with that one by himself. God love him, he's not that bright."

"No." I smiled at little. "He's not."

She stared at me for a long moment. I could almost see the thoughts moving behind her eyes. "So it was your idea."

She took my silence as an admission of guilt. Heaving a huge sigh, she asked the inevitable question. "Just how serious is it between you and Tom?"

I threw my hands in the air. "Hell, I don't know. I think I love him. More than I've ever loved anyone."

"Including Dylan?"

"Including *Michael*."

Her eyebrows rose so high they disappeared beneath her still-damp bangs, and her mouth formed a small "o" of surprise. Michael had been my first love, my first *real* love, and she knew it. Mary had been a freshman when I was a sophomore. We'd played softball together. She knew better than most the special place Mike would always have in my heart.

The silence seemed to stretch on for an eternity. When she finally spoke she sounded tired. "You sure as hell don't make things any easier on me, Reilly."

"It's not deliberate." I turned away from her, so that she wouldn't see my expression. "But it may be moot anyway."

I could feel her eyes boring into the back of my skull. When she spoke, her voice was surprisingly gentle. "Let me guess, you had a fight?"

I nodded, I didn't completely trust myself to speak, damn it.

"Do you want to talk about it?"

I shook my head no. It would've been nice to talk to someone about it. But while I like Mary, she had the whole pack to think of. Besides, this was private business between Tom and me.

"Fair enough," she agreed. "So let me change the subject. I brought you a check for the rent on Dusty and Rob's apartment."

I didn't have to pretend to be shocked. "You don't have to do that."

She gave me a stern look. "Kate, it was nice of you to let them stay here without paying, but Dusty's our surrogate and our responsibility. We pay our bills." She grinned, and it softened her features. I'd never noticed before that she was pretty. But she was, with her shining hair and her dark eyes sparkling in the candlelight. "Besides, I know you can use the money. You haven't been able to take a courier job since you got injured."

She held out a check, face up. I blinked at the amount. "Mary, that's—"

"Nine months' rent, plus a damage deposit based on what you charge Tom. Take it."

I looked at the check. She wasn't wrong. I needed the money badly. I hadn't been in great financial shape *before* I got laid up.

She set the check onto the counter. "Look, I have to think of the good of the pack. Do you really think you'd be all right with Tom having a child with another woman?"

I turned away, walking across the room to stand by the windows. I looked out at the rain-soaked scenery rather than try to meet the intensity of her gaze. "I can't have children, Mary. The only chance I'll ever have of being a parent is either adoption or as a stepmother." There wasn't a lot of emotion in the words. I'd lived with the knowledge for a long time that I wouldn't be bearing children. Usually it didn't bother me. After all, my lifestyle hasn't exactly been conducive to motherhood. I wouldn't want my child to end up orphaned. I knew too damned well what that was like. And while Monica might be dead and gone, she wasn't my only enemy. Not by a long shot.

"I hadn't realized you even wanted kids." Mary's voice was surprisingly gentle.

I shrugged. "It's not something that comes up in casual conversation. But yeah, I do." I could see her reflection in the glass of the windows, the image distorted by the rivulets of water running down the outside of the pane.

"No, it's not." She sighed again. "I need to think about this and talk it over with my people."

I nodded my assent. "I'll have Rob or Tom get your pants back to you." She retrieved her coat from the bathroom and left without another word.

8

The power came on around 10:00 A.M. and the rain slowed to a drizzle. I hopped in the shower and started cleaning up. Normally, I prefer a bath, but I was getting a late start on the day. Of course, as soon as I got the shampoo in my hair the phone started ringing. Rather than run naked through the house with soap in my eyes, I let the machine take the calls. I did hurry the process up a bit, and when I was out and dry I pulled on my robe and rushed downstairs and played back the messages.

The first call was from the attorney. Closing arguments went well, the jury was in deliberation. He'd be in touch. My stomach tightened into a painful knot. Closing my eyes, I said a quick prayer as the next message cued up in the machine.

"Kate, it's Mike. You're a genius! He's perfect! And he said he might know someone else to cover the second shift! I should've known you'd come up with the answer. Sorry I was such an ass yesterday. Call when you get the chance."

Hunh? I had no clue what Mike was talking about. *Who*

was perfect? It certainly sounded as though he'd found someone to work with Bryan, but I sure as hell hadn't sent anyone. My heart was thundering in my ears as I picked up the phone and dialed. I hadn't forgotten that Bryan had been kidnapped once already because of me. He was an absolute innocent, and the perfect hostage. Mike still blamed himself for the carelessness that made Bryan's capture possible, but if he believed I'd sent someone. . . . With trembling fingers I punched in the number to the church.

A familiar voice answered the line on the second ring. "Our Lady of Perpetual Hope, Rob speaking."

"Rob?"

"Katie! I got the job! Tom talked to me about it at breakfast this morning and I came right over." Excitement bubbled in his voice. "I really needed the break! Thank you *so* much! I swear I'll do a good job, too. I know how much your brother means to you."

He was babbling. Not that it mattered. I couldn't have spoken anyway. I was just too relieved. Rob might be young, and a little immature in some ways, but I trusted him, and as a wolf, he was certainly strong enough. He'd guard Bryan and take care of him. Between him and Mike, my baby brother would get the best possible care and protection. Thank *God* . . . and Tom.

"Kate? You okay?"

"I'm fine." I said the words with a smile. I meant it. If the trial went badly and I lost, the insurance would pay. I could deal with performing the investigation for the Thrall. But the thing with Bryan; that had me terrified. Tom had known it, and despite our fight, he'd found a solution. "Tell Mike I apologize for being an ass yesterday."

He snorted lightly and let thick, teasing sarcasm play through his voice. "*You*, an *ass*? No, surely not."

"Rob—" I wasn't really angry, but I put a warning in my voice.

He let out a joyful bark of laughter. "Gotta go. Catch you later, Reilly."

"Later," I agreed.

I hit the button to end the call, then pressed again for a line out. I forced myself to hit the number for Tom's cell phone quickly, before I chickened out and hung up the phone. I owed him a thank you, *and* an apology. I'm pretty good at gratitude—*apologies*, though, not so much. But I'd do it. First, I owed it to him. More important, he was a terrific guy, and I didn't want to lose him for any reason.

"Hi." His voice sounded tentative; cautious.

"Hi." I was suddenly tongue-tied. There were so many things I wanted, needed to say, and I couldn't quite come up with the words.

"Kate . . . I—"

"Tom." We each spoke the other's name simultaneously, then laughed.

"Awkward, isn't it?" he admitted.

"I'm so sorry!" I sighed. "I didn't mean to cut you out. I planned to tell you. But then I met with Mike, and you'd fixed dinner, and I got distracted."

Tom heaved a long sigh. "I know. I realized that when I took the time to think it over. But Kate, you have a cell phone. Why the hell didn't you just *call* me?"

"You were going to the . . . well, the *pack meeting*. Can you imagine a worse possible time to call and bring this up? Well, and it's just really not a good idea to bring it up on the phone at all."

He thought about that for a long moment. "You're right. And it probably wouldn't be a good idea for the pack to overhear you telling me that you're going to be working for the vamps either." He spoke slowly, as though he was choosing each word with extreme care. "Look, we need to talk. Why don't you meet me for lunch at Guiseppe's. I'll set the reservation for 11:30 so we can beat some of the lunch crowd."

Guiseppe's was a very nice, very expensive, Italian restaurant on the 16th Street Mall. It caters to the very wealthy business types and is a "must" for celebrities passing through the Mile High City. Normally, neither Tom nor I go to restaurants in that price range. Yes, the food is wonderful, but I just can't justify the extravagance, even with the check from Mary. I could hear a small choke in my voice when I responded. "Guiseppe's?"

"Yes, and *I'm* paying—no arguments. I want to make up with you for not giving you the chance to explain."

"You could make up with me at the Spaghetti Factory for a lot less." I was only half-joking.

"I know." I could hear the smile in his voice. "But they aren't open for lunch and I want to see you dressed up. You won't do that if I don't pick somewhere nice."

He knows me well. I consider dressing up a nuisance and wearing panty hose to be one short step above torture. Tom's solution to that, of course, was to suggest garters and thigh highs. His birthday is coming up soon. I plan to surprise him by doing just that. But not today. I didn't have the time or money to go shopping for lingerie before lunch.

"Fine, Guiseppe's it is," I agreed. "And Tom—" I took a deep breath. I knew it should be easy for me to tell him, but it never is.

"Yes?"

Hesitating would make me sound uncertain, so I just blurted it out. "I love you."

He paused, and his voice softened. "I love you, too."

I was smiling when I hung up the phone. He loved me. He forgave me. My stomach fluttered with happy butterflies.

Tom wanted me dressed up and at Guiseppe's by 11:30. I've never been one to buy a lot of dressy clothes. I have business clothes. I have casual clothes. I just didn't *do* dressy often enough to need a wardrobe for it. He'd have to live with something he'd already seen on me.

I flipped through the various hangers in my closet looking for something suitable. I finally realized there *was* an
outfit he hadn't seen me in. I'd bought it for Joe's graduation from medical school. I'd only worn it that one time a
few years ago, but fortunately I'd chosen a classic look that
hadn't gone out of style. The dress was sleeveless linen,
with a low scoop neckline, in a small floral print on a
daffodil-yellow background. The collarless jacket was a
matching solid yellow. The color looked good on me, the
tailoring was feminine enough that Tom would like it, and
comfortable enough that I'd be able to move in it. Somewhere in the back or bottom of the closet there were even
matching shoes and a purse.

Of course it was a spring outfit, not exactly perfect for a
winter lunch, but I told myself I refuse to be dictated to by
fashion norms. Besides, it was clean.

I was dressed, pressed, and wearing makeup and jewelry
by the time the cab arrived at the front door. It was a bit of
an extravagance to take a cab just those few blocks, but I'd
gone to a lot of trouble with my appearance. And damn it, if
Tom could spring for lunch at Guiseppe's, then I could
spring for a short cab ride—hopefully, the cab driver
wouldn't mind a handful of change for his tip.

At exactly 11:28 the cabbie dropped me off at the side
street that intersected Sixteenth Street nearest the restaurant
entrance. Tom came running over as I was pulling my wallet out of my purse. He paid the driver before I could, giving him a hefty tip. As the cab drove off he looked me up
and down, letting out a whistle of appreciation. "I like the
outfit. I haven't seen that one before."

He planted a kiss in my hair before I could speak, and I
found myself inhaling deep to catch the clean scent of him.
It wasn't cologne, it was just *Tom,* and my heart tightened
in my chest.

"I save it for special occasions."

"Ah. And this is a special occasion?"

Any date with Tom was a special occasion, but I'd feel like an idiot saying so. So I blushed and stammered, which made him chuckle low in his throat.

"You look pretty spiffy yourself." I wasn't the only one who thought so either. More than one woman walking along the mall was staring at him. He was worth a stare, too, no doubt about it. The tan dress pants he wore had been perfectly tailored to show off the best backside God had ever put on a human male. His shirt fit just as well, showing off a broad, muscled back and narrow waist. His belt and shoes were shined to a high gloss and were almost exactly the same shade of brown as his hair. He was absolutely gorgeous and completely unaffected by it.

"You know, there are lots of people in this world who think kissing in the rain is romantic." He gave me a sly look. "Wanna try it?"

I laughed, but he kissed me anyway. It was warm, sweet, and yes, very, very romantic.

"We'd better get inside." Putting his hand around my waist we walked to the front of the restaurant. He held open the door for me, and in we went.

The first thing that struck me was the smell of freshly baking bread. It made my mouth water. I wasn't the only one. Behind me, I could hear Tom's stomach rumbling as the maitre d' led us to an intimate, linen-draped table at the far side of the restaurant. Already it was beginning to get crowded as men and women in business suits settled down to power lunches. A large group was already at the long table in the corner, laughing and teasing a man who was retiring. Black balloons with snarky sayings danced in the breeze from the heater vents.

At least a dozen servers in starched white shirts and crisp black pants were moving swiftly through the dimly lit room to a counterpoint of clinking glass and muted voices.

The maitre d' managed to scoot my chair in beneath me

as I sat without either of us looking too awkward. At his signal, a young man came over with a pitcher of ice water and our server appeared with menus and a bread basket and introduced himself.

There were no prices on my menu. To me, this is never a good sign. I frowned, and Tom caught the look. "It's all right, Katie. I can afford it. Really. Remember I told you the rent you charge was saving me a bunch of money every month. Well, today you're getting some of it back."

I made little grumbling noises and he laughed. "You worry too much."

I didn't have a ready answer to that, and I was spared the necessity of coming up with one by the appearance of a stranger at our table.

He was tall, thin, with close-cropped silver hair that was a shade or two lighter than the gray of his suit. The white shirt he wore had enough starch to stand up without him in it. His perfectly knotted raw silk tie was exactly the same shade of pale blue as his eyes. He held out a manicured hand to me and introduced himself in a voice that would have screamed self-confidence if screaming just weren't so tacky.

"Ms. Reilly, you don't know me, but I'm Edgar Simms. I've left some messages on your machine. I'm sorry to interrupt, but when I saw you here, I couldn't pass up the opportunity." He smiled, and it was both subtly smug and predatory.

I shook his hand. After all, he was my brother Joe's ultimate boss. It wouldn't hurt to be nice. At least that's what I told myself. "Doctor Simms, this is Tom Bishop, he's a firefighter here in Denver."

"Mr. Bishop, it is a pleasure." Simms shook Tom's hand and smiled, but immediately turned his attention back to me. Tom was watching him with wary eyes, and I didn't blame him. I really wished I hadn't left my weapons at home. I probably could have managed to fit one arm sheath under the jacket if I'd tried.

"Ms. Reilly, I know your reputation. You do not know mine." He smiled to take the sting out of the words. It wasn't sincere, but it was definitely pretty. His dentist had done a fine job on an expensive set of caps.

"Which is?" Tom kept his face completely bland, but there was an energy, a tension in the way he held himself, that was a warning.

"I am not used to being refused."

Why doesn't that surprise me? I bit my tongue so I didn't say it out loud, but Tom blinked, as though he'd heard the thought. Maybe he had.

"And what is Kate refusing you?" The warning wasn't hidden this time. It was there in the almost growling quality Tom's voice had taken on.

Dr. Simms didn't flinch. He did, however, raise an eyebrow in surprise. Still, he answered the question. "Bryan Reilly is the first Eden zombie ever to make even a partial recovery. Doctors from all over the world have been clamoring for the opportunity to work with him. But I've read the police report filed by Detective Brooks. I believe that Bryan's recovery is *directly* tied to her psychic abilities. Studying one without the other would be pointless."

"I participated in one of your studies once." I kept my voice polite, but it took more effort than I would've liked to admit. "It didn't work out well."

Dr. Simms gave a polite, manufactured chuckle, but his eyes hardened to chips of blue ice. "Quite the understatement."

I shrugged.

"Kate—"

"Ms. Reilly, if you please." I hadn't told him he could call me Kate, and I realized, when he said it, that it bugged me. I'd only just met the man, and already I didn't like him. He struck me as being a well-bred, well-heeled bully. I don't like bullies.

"Of course . . . *Ms. Reilly*. I can understand your reluctance. But I am in a position to do you a service. You currently have criminal charges regarding destruction of hospital property worth thousands of dollars."

I sighed. Who'd have known the damned incubator would be so expensive? By pouring alcohol into the system I had damaged it irreparably. I couldn't honestly say I was sorry. I wasn't. But I really did hate the fact that I was probably going to have to pay for it. I might even have to go to jail. Although I was pretty sure that most jurors would be on my side in this one, particularly if they got to see the video.

"I can see to it that those charges are dropped if you would be willing to cooperate."

"I doubt that. Only the DA can make that determination. It's not your choice to make."

We stared at each other, neither of us blinking until I felt the weight of Tom's hand on mine.

"Dr. Simms." Tom spoke softly, but there was a weight behind the words. Simms turned to meet Tom's gaze. Whatever he saw there made his back stiffen, and his jaw thrust stubbornly forward. Still, the words Tom spoke were completely polite and utterly mild. "Ms. Reilly and I came here for a quiet . . . *private* luncheon. If you don't mind, we really would like to get back to it."

"Of course." Simms gave Tom the kind of nod you would give an opponent in a fencing match. "But I would like to leave you with this thought, Ms. Reilly. I have more than just business motives for pursuing this. My daughter Melinda is an Eden zombie. I would, *will,* do anything to bring her back." He turned to Tom, his voice hard. "I'll leave the two of you to your *private* luncheon."

He stalked off, his back rigid beneath the elegant suit.

"Well, he certainly knows how to ruin a mood, doesn't he?" Tom observed.

"Yes indeed," I agreed.

"And did you see whose table he sat down at?"

I turned, following Tom's gaze, and began swearing

softly under my breath. Dr. Simms was just pulling up a chair to join P. Douglas Richards and Lewis Carlton. Even if Tom hadn't recognized Richards, *nobody* can miss Carlton in a crowd.

The waiter arrived. Tom ordered lobster. I chose rare steak. Neither was a particularly "Italian" dish, but we'd had lasagna the night before. At first I had my back to Carlton and company, but I just couldn't stand it. So, as subtly as I could manage, I shifted seats, moving one over, so that I was both closer to Tom and had a better than peripheral view of their table. Tom noticed, but didn't comment.

We didn't talk much during the salad course. We were both too distracted and tense. Fortunately, they were getting ready to leave before our main course arrived. When Carlton stood to leave, he looked full at me . . . and winked before deliberately stretching up his arms to put on his winter jacket. He must not be trying to impress today or he wouldn't bother with the jacket. Tom got a relatively close look at the sheer *size* of him as his hand flattened briefly on the overhead ceiling beam, and understanding dawned.

"*Damn,* but that's a big man."

I nodded, even though his eyes were still locked on the former NBA star. "A big *host*."

"Shit. Unarmed he would've killed you. Hell, even if you were *armed* he probably would."

"But I'd hurt him first. Maybe snap off one of those pearly white teeth." I sipped my water, knowing it was true. I'd learned back during my last adventure with the Thrall that breaking off one or both feeding tubes, which drop down behind the human's eye teeth after the parasite attaches to the spinal cord, can stun the parasite. It can even cause enough shock to kill it.

Tom's expression softened. He turned, his eyes meeting mine. There was pride in that look, and a little possessiveness. "You bet your ass."

The waiter came with our food and poured the wine. I

took a sip from my glass. It was excellent. Until I started dating Tom I'd never been much for wine, or any other alcohol. But he liked wine with meals, and was enjoying introducing me to new vintages. As time went by I found I was enjoying the taste of it. I'd never be a connoisseur, not by a long shot. But I was starting to get a handle on what kinds of wine went best with different sorts of food.

The waiter bowed his way away from the table, leaving us to our meal.

The steak was excellent. I was grateful. So often, because of health issues, they overcook the meat. From the first bite I could tell it was *perfect,* tender, juicy, just the way I like it. I savored the taste in my mouth, and followed it with a sip from my wine glass. It was almost enough to drive away the tension of having run into Dr. Simms and the others. Almost.

"The problem," I spoke softly, so that only Tom would hear, "is that I can't keep backing down, or they'll rule me. Now that they have someone I'm intimidated by, they'll use him every time they want something. I won't live like that."

Tom's fork stopped halfway to his mouth. "So what are you going to do?"

I shrugged. "I haven't got a clue. Any suggestions would be welcome."

"Let me think on it for a bit."

We shared a slice of double chocolate fudge cake with ice cream for dessert. Tom's not nearly as big a chocolate fan as I am, but he'd been willing to indulge me. We didn't linger after the meal. Both of us had other things we needed to do.

We parted with another kiss in front of the door to the restaurant and a promise of dinner at home tonight. Tom had a meeting to attend down at the station. I needed to go to the bank and deposit the money from the Thrall and the check Mary had given me. After that I would take a trip down to Our Lady of Perpetual Hope and deliver my apology to Mike in person, and maybe talk to him a little about things. He gives great advice, even if I don't always follow it.

9

The rain had slowed until it was little more than heavy mist. I walked to the bank, staying mostly under the cover of store awnings, hurrying across the streets with the lights, always careful not to break my neck, or twist my knee again. Wet pavement and high heels are a recipe for disaster as far as I'm concerned. I know there are women who do just fine. I'm not one of them.

The nearest branch of my bank was on the first floor of one of the office towers. I'd come to this same building many times for work purposes as well. One of my best former clients, a jewelry designer and gem buyer, had an office on the tenth floor. A part of me still missed Morris Goldstein, despite the fact he'd gone host and had tried to capture me for Monica.

But more than that, I missed all the other people involved with my Tel Aviv runs. From Gerry Friedman, the old Jewish cutter who was a flirt, to Marta, the receptionist here in Denver. I'd lost a lot of people the day I fought Monica—more than just those who'd died, and there was no bringing them back. It reminded me forcibly that I needed to get back to work—the sooner the better. The longer I was out of the game, the more likely my customers would be permanently snapped up by the competition. I'd worked too hard to build my client base to have to start again from scratch. And . . . I missed my old life. A lot.

"Can I help you?" The bank teller brought my attention back to the present. While I'd been daydreaming, the line had moved forward until it was now my turn.

"Yes, thank you." I smiled and went to the open space at the counter, sliding the deposit slip across the desk to her. "I want to make a deposit."

"And how would you like your cash back?"

"Small bills, please."

She counted out my cash, putting it into a bank envelope with the deposit ticket before handing it back to me.

"Is there a phone where I can call a cab?"

"You can use the one at reception if you want, but there are always cabs waiting at the hotel across the street."

Of course there were. That made perfect sense. I felt stupid for not having thought of it myself. "Thank you. I'll catch one there."

By the time the cab dropped me off at the church, the rain had stopped altogether. Bright sunlight speared through the clouds and a breathtaking rainbow arched through the sky. I closed my eyes, making a wish the way my mother had taught me.

Rob and Bryan were outside, playing catch, heedless of the muddy grass. In that moment, my brother looked absolutely normal, the sunlight catching the red and gold of his hair until it shone. He was laughing, his handsome features open and happy. My heart lurched in my chest and I remembered for an instant how it used to be before the drugs took him. I wanted that back, so badly I ached from the wanting. But the chances of it were worse than slim. Not impossible. I believe in miracles. But we'd already had one miracle. No other Eden zombie had ever recovered even this much. I should be grateful, and was . . . but still, I couldn't help but wish for more.

"Hey, Kate!" Rob called out with a wave.

Bryan turned around to see and missed catching the ball completely. It bounced past him to stop at my feet.

I squatted down to pick it up for him. When I rose, I looked up, and for the first time saw what he was wearing.

It was a black hooded sweatshirt from back when he'd played baseball in high school. It had the imprint that read "Our Lady of Perpetual Hope." It had a tiger. But it was not the same logo as when I'd been in school. This tiger had a paw sticking up.

Sometimes it is better to be lucky than good. I had a flash of insight and just suddenly knew who else would have a shirt like this; who would steal Monica's eggs if she could. My stomach lurched, and my lunch moved restlessly at the thought.

Amanda.

I remembered the last time I'd seen her. It had been in my apartment, after Monica had died, taking the hive with her.

Amanda slid her fingers into the metal guides of the massive veterinary needle and held out her other arm, where I could see a string of puncture wounds in a trailing line below her elbow. "I thought so, too, but there's another way. It wasn't easy to figure out how, but I've got the technique down. Once you're a queen, you'll be alone. All alone, like Monica was. Will you go insane? Or will you turn all your friends? What will you do to survive, Kate? Monica told me that not everything goes away. You'll remember them. You'll know what you've done, but you won't be able to stop yourself."

My heart was beating like a triphammer. She was insane. What the hell had she done to herself?

"Kate, are you all right?" Mike's words jerked me back to the present like a lifeline. He and Rob had joined us. I hadn't seen them move. I think Armageddon could've started in the couple of minutes when I had that brainstorm and I wouldn't have noticed it.

"When did they change the mascot logo of the school? The crouching one?" I asked Mike as I pointed to the symbol on Bryan's chest.

"The year after you graduated. Why?"

Amanda was in Mary's class, a year behind me. She was a cheerleader, a gymnast, and played varsity softball. She would've bought a letter jacket and the school warm-ups, just like the rest of us.

"Ka-tie?" Bryan's voice was a deep baritone, but the tone was somehow childlike. It wasn't the voice itself, but the phrasing he used, the little break between the first and second syllables of my name.

"I'm right here, Bryan. I'm just thinking."

Rob let out a low growl. "You're thinking at *them,* aren't you?"

"No. Just thinking." I tried to keep my voice neutral when I said it. Rob's a friend, but he's a werewolf, one of Tom's pack mates. I really couldn't expect him to be reasonable about the Thrall, despite championing me with the pack. I didn't think Rob knew about my working for the Thrall, but I hadn't told Mike it was a secret. Stupid of me; I should have. Because working with the Thrall was bound to piss off *all* the wolves, and that was a complication I really didn't need in my life right now.

"Kate?" Mike's concern was obvious in the way he said my name. "Are you in trouble?"

"I'm always in trouble, Mike." I tried to make it a joke, but it fell flat. "It's my basic nature."

"Then why don't the two of us take this inside?" He gestured in the direction of the front steps of the church.

"Sounds like a plan to me," I agreed. I turned, tossing the

ball underhand. Rob caught it easily. I gave him a little salute and started up the steps with Mike behind me.

In my peripheral vision I saw Bryan start to follow, but Rob stopped him with a gentle hand on his arm. "Come on, Bryan," Rob offered, "let's play some more catch. We can talk to Ka-tie later." I thought it was nice how he said my name the same way as Bryan.

"Okay," Bryan agreed readily, his head nodding before he started to skip back across the grass. Until he was out of sight, every few steps Bryan would turn around and wave. It made me laugh and I waved back. Mike joined me. But his face sobered a moment later.

"How bad is it?" He pushed on the brass plate to open the door to the church.

As I stepped into the foyer I gave an involuntary shudder. I rubbed my arms from a chill that stemmed not from cold, but from a particularly intense memory. It had happened here.

I'd laid on that marble floor, let Brooks handcuff me to the baptismal font. I'd stared at the painted ceiling, where hidden in the clouds were the images of angels and saints, while my arm was sliced open and one by one the eggs Monica had implanted there were pulled from my vein to burn and sizzle in a silver bowl of alcohol.

I felt a wave of rage from the Thrall hive. Instinctively I slammed shut the door in my mind. Blessed silence. I said a heartfelt prayer for the soul of Henri Tané. If it hadn't been for him I'd still be trapped living my life to an increasingly loud soundtrack. It really was because of him that I was now able to live alone in my own head most of the time.

I turned to Mike. "Before I forget, I'd like to arrange a mass to be said in someone's honor."

"Whose?"

"His name was Henri Tané."

Mike pulled his keys from the pocket of his trousers and unlocked the door to his parish office. It was a small space, crowded with vestments, a battered old desk, and the various other tools of his trade. "Wasn't he the guy you were working with from Haiti?"

"Yes."

Mike led me into his office. He sat down and pulled out a desk drawer. He took out a journal calendar and pen and set them onto the desk in front of him.

I sat across from him and watched, trying to hide my amusement. Just recently he'd started getting absent-minded. I'd tried to tease him, but he was too sensitive about it. He'd gotten seriously angry the one time I had. It didn't make sense to me, but I wasn't stupid enough to make the same mistake more than once.

"When did he die?" Mike flipped pages in the journal until he found the one he wanted, then used the pen to scribble notes across the page.

"A few days ago . . . I think."

"Was this what you wanted to talk about?"

I sighed. He just had to burst my balloon. "Not really. It's just sort of an aside. One of the questions I had got solved outside."

I glanced around the room, buying time to organize my thoughts. The place was cluttered with the stuff of his work. All of it was familiar to me, giving me a strong sense of belonging, from the spare candles and prayer books to the long-handled crucifix that Rob had used to bar the church doors against the vampires. Everything was familiar. Even the silver fruit bowl was back on his desk. I reached out to run a finger along the rim of the cool metal. This, too, had been used that night. It was the same one that had held the alcohol they'd used to kill the eggs and the hatchling.

The phone rang. Mike excused himself to take the call. I wasn't sorry, it gave me an excuse to wander the church to "give him privacy."

There were so many memories here in this church. Most of them were good. I'd had my first communion here, with

Father John presiding. My confirmation was here, too. I'd even planned to marry Dylan here, before I'd found out he'd betrayed me, both with Amanda and Monica.

I loved this place, but there was a sadness to it today. It felt, somehow, as though the life of the building were drawing to a close. It didn't make sense, really, but I felt it nonetheless. There were tears in my eyes as I stared up at what was still the most beautiful stained-glass window I'd ever seen. The *Pietà,* the afternoon sun streaming through it until the colors were almost too much for the eye to bear.

I had hoped that, if things worked out, Tom and I could wed here. Somehow, though, I knew that wasn't going to happen. Not here . . . not ever, and I couldn't figure out why. But it made my heart wrench in my chest.

"Penny for your thoughts?" Mike spoke softly from the doorway that led from the lobby to the main church.

"They're going to close the parish, aren't they?" I didn't take my eyes off of the window.

He stared at me for a long, silent moment. "Sometimes you really do scare me, Kate. I just got the call, but you already knew."

"When?"

"I have until the end of the quarter. Then they'll close our doors and I'll be reassigned."

"I'm sorry." This time I did look at Mike, let him see the tears in my eyes.

"Do you know what the monsignor told me?" Mike acted as though I should know, but I didn't. I shook my head, watching as he walked into the church proper and lowered himself onto one of the polished wood pews. "To everything there is a season."

"It's been coming for a while, hasn't it?" I knew it had, just as I'd known the church was closing. There was no real parish here now, only a soup kitchen, and the home for the zombies. The church and school buildings were old, in need of repairs, with no income to support it. It had only been a matter of time. And the time was almost up.

"I managed to talk them into running a mobile soup kitchen, bringing food and supplies down to the poor in a van from one of the suburban churches. I'm still working with them about the zombies."

"They'll be all right," I told him.

His eyes looked like his heart was breaking at the thought. "You don't know that."

I smiled then. "Have a little faith."

He laughed then, and there was a trace of bitterness in it. "That's rich, you preaching to *me* about faith."

"Apparently you need it."

He snorted—a bit of his old hockey self. "Smartass."

"Always." I sat next to him on the pew. "So, where is your next parish going to be? Or did they tell you?"

He gave me a meaningful look. I caught the anger, and frustration, but there was something positive there, too. A level of excitement, liberally mixed with guilt. *As if they've offered him something he's always wanted, but with strings attached. He wants it, but he doesn't trust it.*

"I'm not getting a parish." He spoke with a soft intensity. "In fact, if I could be *sure* my charges would be safe, I'd say this was the most amazing thing that could happen in my life."

"So what is it?"

He took a shaky breath. His eyes locked with mine, as though he were looking to me for reassurance. "I've been invited to go to Rome."

"Rome . . . as in Italy, where the Pope lives Rome?" I know my eyes were a little wide.

He nodded mutely, his eyes searching my face.

"Holy shit!"

"I suppose that's there, too." His nervous laugh was a little shrill, but I didn't blame him. This was *huge*. I was so proud and happy for him I felt as though I might burst from it. I threw my arms around him.

"That's *wonderful*! What do they want you to do?"

"The church has an International Commission on Youth. They've got a committee going, studying the problems of drug abuse in general, and Eden in particular, along with the resulting Zombie problem. They want me on the committee."

"Um . . . *wow!*"

He grinned, and it was his old grin. "Yeah. Wow. If I could only be sure—" He turned his head in the direction of the building that he'd converted from nuns' housing to a home for the zombies and the grin faded. I didn't need any psychic ability to follow his thoughts.

"They'll be fine. *We'll* be fine. You'll see." I slugged him playfully on the arm. "God really *does* know what he's doing, you know."

"Oh shut up!" He gave me a gentle shove in return. We wrestled like kids for a couple of minutes, like we used to in grade school, before we started thinking of each other as more than just friends. But eventually, breathless and laughing, we settled back down into behaving like the adults we were supposed to be.

"You said the end of the quarter? That's not very long."

"Only a few weeks. I'll have to push hard to wrap things up here, get a passport. That sort of thing." He ran a hand through his hair at the mere thought of everything he needed to accomplish in the short time he'd been given.

"Let me know if there is anything I can do to help."

"As a matter of fact—" His voice took on the wheedling tone I knew so well.

I sighed, knowing that I would be here for hours working my ass off. Still, if I hadn't meant it, I shouldn't have made the offer. "Fine, what do you want?"

"Lots and lots of things. You'll be working for hours. And just so you don't ruin that nice outfit I'll dig you up another of the old sets of warm-ups. We've got a bunch of them downstairs."

"That reminds me." I glanced over at the file cabinets tucked up against the wall. There were only two of them. I might be out of luck. Still, there was no harm in asking. "Do you have the old school records? I'd really like to know if Amanda had one of the warm-up sets with the new logo."

"The records are in the basement." He grinned at me, his blue eyes sparkling. The same basement, coincidentally, that I need to start cleaning out."

"Oh goody."

I followed him into the basement. I hadn't been down there in a while. Either my memory was off, or it had gotten even more cluttered than I remembered. Cleaning it out was going to be a serious pain.

"We had to move the school records in here," Mike explained, gesturing toward six stacks of boxes, each stack containing five neatly labeled cartons. They took up the entire center portion of the basement, not quite blocking the door to the storage room or the staircase leading up to the rectory. I noticed that one or two of the cartons had water stains on them and stank of mildew. "The school roof started leaking."

I wrinkled my nose and fought off a sneeze. "Ick."

He nodded his agreement before he disappeared into the storage room, reappearing with plastic-encased clothing in his arms. "These should fit you." He passed them to me.

"They're brand-new!"

"Yeah. Apparently the coach ordered a bunch for all the teams, thinking the school would be open the next year. When the archbishop decided to close our doors, the church got stuck with them. They've been locked in storage ever since. I just found them a couple of days ago." I could see the frustration in his face. "If I'd *known* I would have distributed them to the homeless. They always need warm clothes in winter."

I heaved an inward sigh of relief. If he had, then there would be no way to know who would have had a set from way back when. This way, I might have a chance. Because while I was pretty sure I knew who the culprit was, hard evidence would be useful in convincing the police *and* the Thrall.

The boxes were clearly labeled and well organized, so it only took me a few minutes to find the right records. Amanda had ordered five sets of sweats, three with hooded shirts, two without, along with five of the matching tee-shirts. Her mother had paid by personal check. Mike told me I could keep the file, if I carried the rest of the box out to the dumpster. Apparently the only records he was going to deliver to the diocese were the old academic records. Everything else had to go.

I changed clothes in the restroom upstairs, and spent several hours working on inventory and cleaning out the basement. Mike wouldn't let me lift anything heavy. He was worried I'd rip up my shoulder. So he had Rob and Bryan help by loading boxes onto a dolly and wheeling them either to the dumpster, or out to the van. Mike went back upstairs to deal with his other parish duties. He wanted to accomplish as much as he could while the zombies in his care were at the free clinic getting their monthly check-ups because he could never manage to get everything done otherwise. I finally got around to apologizing to him for having been an ass the previous night, an apology he accepted with only the minimal amount of ribbing. At four o'clock we piled into his car and Mike drove Rob and me home. Rob seemed happy and excited about his job, and I didn't feel like bringing him down with the news that he wouldn't have it for long. I didn't even want to think about what that would mean to *my* life.

I kicked off my shoes and dropped the lunch outfit into the laundry the minute I made it through the front door. It was good to be back. I felt a lingering sadness about the church, but there was nothing I could do. Besides, I really was proud of Mike. He was being transferred to Rome. That was just so *cool*. He'd been working so hard, for so long. It felt good to see him succeed.

I was sweaty and stinky from dealing with dusty old boxes of records and the amazing volume of mostly useless stuff that had accumulated in the church basement. I needed to clean up. A shower would get me clean, but it wouldn't do anything to head off the sore muscles I'd earned from good old-fashioned hard work. Besides, I like long, hot bubble baths. Yeah, it's girly. So sue me.

I ran water into the tub, digging under the bathroom sink for the aromatherapy mixture. In no time the room filled with fragrant steam as sparkling white bubbles foamed up from the water. I eagerly stripped off the soiled sweat suit, kicking it into the corner near the hamper. I turned off the taps and climbed into the tub, sliding my body under the suds with a sigh of utter contentment.

I dropped my shields, and immediately felt the buzz of the hive in the back of my mind.

I think I may know who stole the eggs. She's a human who was tied to Monica and the Denver hive. Would it be possible for you to track her and see?

The sing-song trilling replied immediately. *With effort we can track nearly any human. Only the strongest of you can block us out. Who is this woman?*

Her name is Amanda Shea. She was married to Dylan Shea, who was one of your hosts.

There was a pause that lasted long enough to surprise me. *We remember her, Not Prey. We will check.*

Fair enough. I cut the connection and resumed my bubble bath with a thrill of absolute delight. When the bubbles were gone I scrubbed myself clean and climbed out to dry off. Even though it was early, it had been a rough day. I wanted to be at my best when Tom came home, so I decided to take a nap.

We all make mistakes.

10

I dreamed of Amanda. We were in the high school gym and she was screaming at me about something or other. A crowd of kids were gathered around, sniggering. I might be older, but she was popular, the first freshman to make it onto the varsity cheerleading squad. She wore the uniform, the black sweater stretched tight across her ample chest, the short pleated skirt showing off a pair of muscular legs. Every time she moved you could see a flash of the gold fabric inside the pleats of the skirt. Her face was distorted with rage, and she kept screaming that I was a fucking murderer who deserved to die along with all the other Not Prey.

The kids in the background started laughing, and as I looked from one to another I noticed that every one of them had fangs. Amanda moved, drawing my eyes to her, but she'd changed. Instead of the angry cheerleader, I saw the deranged woman who'd attacked me in my apartment. Her eyes were wild, with no hint of sanity. She held the same old-fashioned needle she'd used to try to infest me. The same scars marred her arm. "We'll make you pay, Katie.

Pay for everything you've done to us." A kid with Dylan's face stepped forward, he pulled up his sleeve, extending his arm. She plunged the needle into his flesh, and he screamed. As I watched, the egg hatched beneath the skin. I could *see* the movement of the hatchling through his veins.

I struggled, tried to force myself to wake, but the dream was too powerful. All I succeeded in doing was to shift the image.

I floated above a scene from suburbia. Below me was a split-level house of white wood and tan brick with an attached garage. A basketball hoop had been mounted above the garage door. The whole scene was illuminated by a pair of bright halogen security lights mounted on the front eaves. The yard was as perfectly groomed as any golf course, not a weed in sight, every blade of grass of an exact height. I could make out individual leaves moving in the chest-high hedge that lined the concrete driveway.

My eyes zoomed in, focusing on the movement.

There was a figure crouched behind the hedge, hidden by a veil of leaves. It waited with patient malice.

A car rounded the far corner, slowing to pull into the driveway. It was an older model Ford Mustang, candy-apple red, with a gleaming white leather interior. The girl driving it was high school age. She was very pretty, and very familiar, though I couldn't place where I'd seen her before.

The girl pulled the car to a stop in the driveway. I saw her reach across to retrieve her purse from the floorboards.

The bushes shifted, the figure moving carefully up to the small gap between the hedge and the corner of the garage. The car door opened, causing the interior light to come on. When the girl turned to close the car door with a brisk slam, a figure in a hooded sweatshirt leaped forward and struck.

There was no fight. The first blow, a brick to the back of the girl's skull, dropped her to her knees. I watched, helpless, as a gloved hand used the girl's hair as a handle and pulled her head back to expose her vulnerable neck.

Fangs struck home, and the vampire fed.

Try as I might I could not see the creature's face. Its body was hidden, so I couldn't even tell if it was male or female. When it had finished feeding, it pulled a knife hidden somewhere on its person, and with one smooth movement, slit the girl's throat.

"Kate, are you all right?" Tom's hands shook me awake. "You smell terrified."

I gasped for air, my hands automatically going to my own throat. He pulled me close, and I let him hold me until my breathing steadied and my pulse slowed to its normal rate. *It was just a dream. Just a nightmare. You've had nightmares before. They don't mean anything.*

It hadn't felt like a nightmare. It had felt real. I could still smell the sweat and blood, hear the night sounds in the distance. I shuddered again.

"Do you want to talk about it?"

I shook my head and forced myself to speak. "No." I pulled back, and he let me. "Just a bad dream. I'm being an idiot."

"You are never an idiot." He gave me a smile, but the wattage was lower than usual. There were lines of exhaustion around his eyes, and I caught a faint whiff of smoke.

"What time is it?"

"3:00 A.M."

"And you're just getting in? What happened?"

Tom lowered himself onto the edge of the bed. He was moving slowly, as if it were an effort to do even the smallest things. "I was at the station for the safety meeting when a call came. All available units, so I got snagged to help out. A small commuter jet crashed into the shopping center where Stapleton Airport used to be."

"Oh shit."

He closed his eyes, and there was such pain in his expression that I cupped my hands around his face. "It was bad." He whispered the words.

"I can guess. You look exhausted."

He barely had enough strength to nod. People think that werewolves are super-strong, and they are—but spending even supernatural energy comes with a price. "I am. I spent most of the night in wolf form, searching for survivors. We got a lot of people out. Even the ones who died during the impact. It's . . . hard when there's nothing left for people to bury."

I knew he was remembering his own family, who all died in a blaze when he was a teenager. He got out his sister, who died at the hospital, but they never found his parents. I smoothed down his wet, still smoke-scented hair gently. "Then take off your clothes and lay down. Get some sleep."

"I think I'll do that." He was slurring his words a little, as though it almost took too much energy to speak. I'd seen him like this once before, after another bad fire, when he'd worked himself to the point of collapse trying to find and save victims trapped inside the burning building. It was part of what made him such a valuable member of the fire department—his ability to become a search and rescue animal that didn't burn and could breathe smoke without suffocating.

He managed to get his shoes off before he fell over and began snoring. I managed to tug and roll him until he was fully on the bed. That done, I slid naked onto the bed beside him. I fell asleep with my body curled around his and didn't dream this time.

I woke before Tom did. Bright sunlight was flooding the apartment. I slid carefully out of bed so as not to disturb his sleep. He'd taken a week of vacation, but thus far it hadn't been at all restful. Still, he wouldn't have it any other way. He's a firefighter now because of his family. He hadn't been able to save them, though he'd tried. So he saves other people, other families. I can understand that.

I pulled my running clothes from the dresser and carried them into the bathroom. It had felt so good yesterday that I decided to try it again. Probably pushing myself, but hey— whatever works.

I brushed my teeth and hair, then wrapped my knee. That done, I pulled on my mint green shorts with a matching jacket over a white sports bra and plain old cotton underwear. I dug around in the clean laundry basket until I found a pair of matching tube socks to wear under my favorite running shoes. I finished dressing and was ready to face the morning in just under fifteen minutes. Still, before I went out the front door I made sure to tie on my fanny pack and clip on a knife. I probably wouldn't need to be armed for a quick run to the newsstand for the morning paper and cinnamon rolls, but I prefer safe to sorry.

I got the coffeemaker started on the way out the door, and was off and running while Tom snoozed away upstairs.

I love Denver. I love the sights, the smells. Most of all, I love the weather. You never know what you're going to get from one hour to the next. Seasons exist, but because of the altitude, the mountains, and just the nature of things you would have random warm days midwinter. Conversely, you could get a sudden snow or frigid temperatures in late spring. You just never know. Today was gorgeous. The sky was clear. Bright sunlight peeked between the skyscrapers, slowly taking the worst of the chill from the concrete caverns. Seventeenth Street was already humming with traffic. I'd chosen Seventeenth to avoid the foot traffic that clogs the mall during the early commuter influx.

I caught a good rhythm and was breathing easy when I turned onto Broadway. My goal was Lenny's Newsstand on the corner of Colfax. He calls it a newsstand, but it's a good-sized store crammed with not only newspapers and magazines from around the world, but a fair number of books, magnifying glasses, reading lamps, and miscellany. It has that musty smell that comes whenever you gather together enough books and old newspapers and is run by Leonard Levine, named for the grandfather who founded the place. It gets a lot of traffic from the political types who work just down the street at the state capitol.

The bell to the shop door rang as I pushed open the door and stepped inside. Several patrons were inside, most of them middle-aged to elderly men, dressed in elegant suits in traditionally muted colors, carrying expensive briefcases. It wasn't until I was nearly to the counter that I recognized the man paying Lenny for his *Wall Street Journal*.

P. Douglas Richards turned to face me. His welcoming smile didn't show even a hint of fangs and didn't reach his eyes.

"Good morning, Not Prey." It wasn't his voice that came through his lips, or at least not *only* his voice. No, there was that odd, sing-song choral tone to it that meant I was speaking to the entire Queen collective.

I stood stock still, trying to act casual despite the fact that every human in the store had frozen in place, their eyes glazed and blank.

"We would speak with you."

It looked to me as though they *were* speaking to me, but I bit back the smartassed comment.

"You are correct. Amanda Shea is in possession of our young. But we cannot *find* her. We have tried. There is something wrong with her."

Their collective anger stabbed at me like a knife, and I felt the pain building behind my left eyeball. But my shields held. They weren't in my mind. Yippee!

"It is much like your new talent for blocking us out."

I considered that for a moment. It wasn't easy. Their power and rage beat at me like a club, and the throbbing pain made my skull feel like it was going to explode.

The last time I'd seen Amanda had been when she attacked me in my apartment. We fought. I won. She'd fallen out the window to the pavement below *and it hadn't killed her*.

"You've thought of something." The voice belonged to P. Douglas alone.

"What would happen if a human tried to infest herself and couldn't?"

He paled and stepped back, his expression horrified. "Tried *how?*"

I dropped my shield, opening the door to my mind, letting him see the memory of a wild-eyed Amanda, wielding the syringe like a weapon as she showed me her arm, told me how she planned to infest me, make me queen.

"That . . . that's an abomination."

I couldn't argue, and didn't try.

Not Prey. You cannot lie to us. Is this true? Did she do this thing?

She did.

There was a long silence, as if the world itself held its breath.

She is insane and dangerous. Not just to our young, but to you humans as well. Every egg that hatched inside her body released its yolk, making her stronger, faster, and increasing her psychic power exponentially. She will be able to heal nearly any injury. If she has done this thing, she is a monster, a monster of great and terrible power. Without the control of a hatchling tied to the hive—

I shuddered in reaction to their horror, their fear.

Do you know where this woman is?

No. I didn't have a clue.

Can you find out?

I'm not a detective. You'd be better off—

They cut me off mid-thought. *Not Prey, we offer you a deal. Find this woman for us and, should you survive, we will show you a way to bring your brother and many others like him fully back to themselves.*

My jaw dropped. It must have for the sudden amount of cool air and exhaust fumes that assaulted my tongue. You know what they say about deals that sound too good to be true. They are. But maybe I'd misunderstood. *Find her*. Just *find her and you'll do this?*

Their words left me feeling sudden chills up my spine. *Find her and* survive.

But then I thought about Bryan, the way he used to be; thought about Michael, and his fear about what would happen to the zombies in his care when they closed the church. I even thought about Dr. Simms, and the daughter he was so desperate to save. I said the only thing I could say under the circumstances.

I'll find her.

11

A gleaming black Lamborghini Diablo with tinted windows was parked at the curb in front of my building by the time I finished the run home. The driver's side window rolled down. From what little I could see, Carlton looked particularly spiffy this morning. He was wearing a black dress shirt artfully unbuttoned to show an expanse of muscular chest, over black dress pants. I couldn't see, but was willing to bet the watch on his wrist was a Rolex, and the shoes were hand-sewn Italian leather.

"Mornin', Buffy."

I put on my very best manners. "Good morning, Carlton. This is quite the surprise. I wouldn't have expected to see you here bright and early on a Wednesday morning." I put the emphasis on the word bright. It earned me a smile that flashed his fangs.

"Yeah, well, I've been ordered to keep tabs on you. Seems the ladies think you'll lead us to the eggs, but they don't expect you to survive the process. I'm supposed to be the clean-up crew."

"Good to know they have so much faith in me."

He laughed. "I think I'm beginning to like you, Buffy."

"Take a couple aspirin and lie down. I'm sure you'll get over it."

His chuckle followed me as I went through the front door of the building and hit the elevator button. By the time it had reached the third floor Tom had the apartment door open and was waiting for me. He wore only a pair of red and white striped boxers and a thunderous expression.

"Lewis Carlton is parked downstairs, Katie. What in the hell is going on?"

I shoved the newspaper and bag of cinnamon rolls into his hands as I passed by. He stared at me, openmouthed. I pretended not to notice, going into the kitchen and pouring myself a huge mug of steaming coffee. "It's a long story. We may as well talk about it over breakfast."

Tom turned slowly, his eyes following my every movement. "You're actually going to tell me?"

Sighing, I turned, leaned my back against the kitchen cabinets and gave him the dirty look that comment deserved. "I don't *want* to screw things up with you, Tom. I just don't know any other way to operate. But I'm trying really hard, so give me a break. Yes, I'm going to tell you."

"Am I going to like it?" He pulled the apartment door closed and walked over to the kitchen island. He dropped both the newspaper and pastry bag onto the white tile surface before he pulled up the nearest stool.

"Hell no," I admitted. "Even *I* don't *like* it." I took a long pull of coffee. It had cooled enough during the trip home that it was the perfect temperature. I let the taste rest on my tongue for a few seconds. The scent wafting from the cup was absolute heaven.

"So . . . spill."

I did.

He stood there blinking stupidly long enough that I had time to pour myself another mug of coffee to drink while I waited for the inevitable explosion of recriminations. When I turned back, he was still silent, but his expression was determined. "What's the plan?"

I probably blinked stupidly, just like he had. "Um . . . the short version? We find Amanda, try not to get killed, and save my brother."

He gave a low growl, but not as if he really meant it.

I shrugged. "Seriously, I'd gotten as far as renting a car. After that, I don't have a clue."

"Fine, go online and rent a car from that place that'll deliver. Then come upstairs. We'll figure out the rest of it in the shower."

I raised my brows in mock concern. "Tom, if we share the shower, I won't be thinking about the plan."

The smile he gave me as we headed upstairs was positively wolfish. *Yay.*

He was out of his boxers in one swift movement. With him standing nude in front of me I couldn't think. My heart sped up, beating like thunder within my chest. He was so beautiful. Handsome just didn't do it justice. Every muscle was toned, his golden brown skin perfectly smooth. My hands sought his chest of their own accord. I lay my palms against his skin and felt his nipples tighten in response. The rest of his body responded as well, he grew firm, then hard as his erection grew.

His hands on my waist pulled me close against him so that his mouth could claim mine. His erection pressed against the front of my body. I felt every inch of it, wanted it all inside me. I let out an involuntary whimper that was swallowed up in the heat of Tom's kiss. I deliberately trailed my hand down the length of his torso, my fingers barely skimming along that long expanse of hot smooth skin, until I could cup him in my hand, gently squeezing.

He pulled back from the kiss with a groan, his head thrown back, his body shuddering. His cock jerked in my hand, and I moved my grip so that I could caress the head of it with the pad of my thumb.

"Katie—" Tom took my wrist in his hand, guiding my hand away. "If you don't stop this, I won't be able to last long enough to do you any good." His voice was rough, as though he were having a hard time talking.

"You can't even imagine the good this is doing me." I gave him a knowing smile before moving my head to kiss the center of his chest. Ever so slowly, I kissed and licked my way downward, my tongue teasing his belly button before following the trail of hair that led downward. I knelt on the floor in front of him, using my hands to caress the softness of that most delicate skin before guiding him tenderly into my mouth.

He groaned, and I think if he hadn't moved his hands to my shoulders he might have stumbled, his legs were that unsteady as I used my tongue and mouth to bring him pleasure until he came in a shuddering burst that sent his semen down my throat.

I pulled back slowly, letting the now soft flesh slide from my mouth. I looked up at him, and it pleased me to see the small shudders that ran through his body like aftershocks, his hands tightening on my shoulders in an almost bruising grip.

He opened his eyes, looking down at me, and I saw him lick lips gone dry. "That—" his voice was rough, hoarse from pleasure, "That was . . . *amazing*. You've never gone that far before. *You're* amazing."

"Thank you." I rose to my feet and leaned forward to lay a gentle kiss on his lips.

His laugh was a little shaky. "No, thank *you*."

We stood there for a moment, not moving. I finally spoke. "I still do need a shower."

"Right." He stepped out of the way, so that I could close the shower curtain and start the water running at the perfect temperature. But when I tried to step back, he was behind me. His mouth moved to the base of my neck, the sensitive skin where neck meets shoulder. He bit me gently, and his breath against my throat brought my breath in a gasp. His left arm wrapped around my waist, pulling me tight against him. His flesh against mine was so warm. He held me gently, but though he held it in check I could feel his strength.

"Tom—" I turned my head slightly, intending to say something. I wasn't sure what.

"Shhh." He took my earlobe between his teeth, nibbling at it. He unfastened the fanny pack, stepping back to let it fall to the floor. When it was out of the way his right hand slid beneath the fabric of the shorts, between the soft cotton underwear and my skin. Fingers teasing at my hair, his hand moved between my legs, finding me warm, wet, and ready.

He traced the edges of my opening, flicking, teasing, but not entering me. I whimpered, and my knees wouldn't have held me if it hadn't been for the strong arm around my waist. My body writhed in response to his touch. "Please. Please." The words were a hoarse whisper. But instead of thrusting fingers inside me, he pulled back. With both hands at my waist, he turned me to face him. In one harsh movement he pulled shorts and underwear down my legs. The knife clattered to the floor, forgotten, as I stepped out of the ring of fabric.

He stood. Eyes locking with mine, he pulled the jacket from my shoulders. It fell to the floor next to the discarded shorts. All that was left of my clothes was the sports bra and the bandage on my knee. He made short work of both. When, at last, I was naked he stepped back. His eyes roamed the length of my nude body, the very look a caress.

"You are so beautiful."

I wasn't, or at least I didn't think so. The scars that crisscrossed my body were angry and spoke of terrible things and lives lost. But I wanted to be beautiful, and I loved that he believed it to be true.

He stepped forward, and I got ready for a kiss. But instead, he reached past me to pull back the shower curtain. "Get in."

I climbed in. The shower massage was on, and the water beat at me with a pulsing rhythm that made my sensitized skin tighten. My nipples hardened, and I gave an involuntary shudder.

Tom climbed into the shower behind me.

He used a washcloth to clean the outside of my body very, very thoroughly, and later used his tongue to clean the spots the washcloth wouldn't reach. He brought me to a screaming orgasm that was strong enough to roll my eyes back in my head and make my knees give way. I would've fallen except for the pair of strong hands that pressed my hips against the wall of the shower.

The water got cold before we finally got out. If phenomenal sex was my reward for keeping Tom informed, I was going to spill the beans more often. I just wouldn't be able to help myself.

Tom dried off and dressed in some spare clothes he had lying around the apartment. It took me longer to get ready. I'd shampooed my hair, and combing out the tangles was an extensive project. To entertain me, distract me, and keep me from using language that would curl *his* hair, Tom brought the newspaper up and was sitting on the bed reading to me.

Most of the paper was dedicated to the plane crash. After looking at the pictures, I decided it was best if he didn't give me details about it. He'd seen the destruction firsthand, so instead he was reading to me from an article buried in one of the back sections while I figured out what to wear. It was an in-depth article on Share the Planet. While it had since gone worldwide, the home office was based out of some teenager's garage in a town too small to warrant a dot on most maps.

Tom talked to me from the doorway, well out of reach of the clothes I was flinging out of the hope chest as I searched for the neck brace I wear as protection from the vampires.

"Forney, Colorado, is on the Western Slope of the Rocky Mountains. Once the home of the Forney Miners, the high school was closed in 2005 due to declining enrollment, and the students are now bused to Bear Creek."

The brace had sunk to the bottom of the chest. I ran my hands over the hard, acrylic surface, looking for any cracks or flaws. Made of two rigid pieces hinged together, it was made to go over my shoulders and around my neck and fasten shut with a small padlock. It's heavy. It itches, and every time I hear that lock snick shut I get a little claustrophobic. The key was still in the padlock from the last time I'd worn the brace back in July. I opened the lock and pulled on the guard, pushing aside memories I didn't want to deal with by listening to Tom's lecture.

"Worldwide, Share the Planet has members from all age groups, but it has a particularly large base among those aged fifteen to twenty-one. This is due in no small part to active recruiting by the founder on the World Wide Web and in Internet chat rooms."

I shifted the brace around, trying to get comfortable with the weight of it, then closed the hasp and set the lock. I slid the key into the front pocket of my jeans before reaching into the pile of clothes on the bed to retrieve a navy turtleneck sweater. I was pulling it over my head when there was a knock on the door. I sent a wisp of thought outward.

"It's the rental company delivering the car," I said.

"I'll get it." Tom dropped the newspaper onto the top of the dresser. "You finish getting ready."

I'd selected business clothes for the day. They're not as comfy as jeans, but people really do treat you differently when you are dressed for business than when you dress casually. I wasn't sure who or what I'd be facing today, so it was better to be prepared.

The turtleneck I chose was dark brown. It hid the neck brace nicely, and had an added bonus of looking good with my coloring. I wore it over camel-colored business slacks and finished with a man-cut blazer and a pair of battered brown pumps that had low enough heels to run in. I would've preferred another pair of shoes, but the only other brown pair I owned had been ruined in the paint attack.

I took my wallet out of the fanny pack and tucked it into the blazer pocket. A quick minute to put on lipstick and a little blush, and I was ready to go downstairs. There were forms for me to sign, including the optional, additional insurance, credit card slip, and standard rental agreement. The nice man in the bright green jacket read off the terms in a bored, inflectionless voice as he passed the clipboard to me. When he'd finished his spiel the three of us went downstairs so I could make sure there wasn't any preexisting damage to the car they'd be handing over the keys to.

The dark blue rental sedan was parked at the meter directly in front of Carlton's Lamborghini and suffered badly from the comparison. Still, it seemed to be a nice enough car; clean with a gray leather interior that still smelled new, and not so much as a ding on the painted finish of the doors. I was pleased to find out it was a front wheel drive model as the skies were darkening, and the temperature was dropping like a rock. It was days like this I really missed Edna, my old classic pickup. She could handle any weather and was made of real steel. She'd been stolen from the parking lot at the Shamrock Motel the night Monica Micah had tried to infest me and make me Thrall Queen of Denver. There'd been no sign of her since, and the insurance company had paid up. If I had been able to work I would've bought another vehicle after I had to sell the motorcycle—which was pretty worthless in the winter anyway. Instead, I had to use the money to live on. Even though I knew I'd probably never see Edna again, I kept hoping to find her. I know it's not sensible, but I can't seem to help it.

Unless I missed my guess we'd be getting snow some time this afternoon. I wasn't sure how Carlton's Lamborghini handled in bad weather, but if it had been mine I wouldn't want to risk it. Then again, I probably would never have the courage to drive a car worth more than my building.

I reminded myself that it was not my problem. Ignoring Carlton's look of disdain, I climbed into the driver's seat of the rental. Tom apparently couldn't resist a little bit of teasing. He slid his sunglasses to the tip of his nose. Eyes alight with mischief, he looked over the tops of the lenses at the man lounging against one of the fastest cars ever made and in total deadpan said: "Try to keep up."

Carlton managed not to grin in return. Thrall hosts and werewolves are not supposed to do the buddy thing. "I'll do my best."

We started with the obvious, driving out to Dylan and Amanda's house in the suburbs. It should have been easy to find, but it wasn't. Whoever had been responsible for naming the streets in the suburb had been an idiot. There was an Elm Street, Elm Court, Elm Drive, and Elm Way. It was the same for every other common tree or shrub. I pitied the poor pizza deliverymen trying to drive through a covenanted community like this where each house was a cookie-cutter image of the last and with street names as similar as the floor plans.

We drove around in circles for nearly an hour before we finally pulled in front of the correct address. The house was vacant, with a For Sale sign in the lawn. Pulling the cell phone from my pocket, I dialed the number on the sign and was rewarded when a pleasant female voice answered on the third ring.

I lied, pretending an interest in a house that I wouldn't

buy if it were quite possibly the last residence on the planet. But my fibs at least earned me a kernel of information. Mrs. Shea was not available to answer questions, but the woman holding the power of attorney could. The real estate agent helpfully offered to take down my inquiries and pass them on to Ms. Ryan and get back to me with the answers.

I pretended to think about it, thanked her for her time, and hung up. Sliding the phone into my pocket, I started up the car and pulled away from the curb.

"Where now?" Tom asked.

"Amanda's mother has power of attorney. She's a partner in a law firm downtown. I figured I'd stop by her office and see if she might be able to squeeze us in between appointments. If she's still speaking to me, that is."

"Ah." Tom turned to look through the back window. In the mirror I saw Carlton give a cheery little wave before blowing us a kiss.

"God, that man is annoying," Tom announced, but there was a hint of amusement in his voice.

"Better watch it. You sound like you're beginning to like him."

"He's a *vampire*, Katie." Tom's voice was thick with scorn.

"Yeah. I know." I did know. But in the silence of my own mind I had to admit that there was a little part of me that found Carlton fascinating and amusing. He was irreverent, clever, and scary as hell. It was a titillating combination.

A companionable silence stretched between Tom and me. I was grateful for it. So many people simply can't stand not having some noise, be it music, talking . . . whatever. After years of living to a hard rock soundtrack I was finally able to have moments of blessed quiet.

I concentrated on driving. There was plenty of traffic on I-25, despite the fact that it was a weekday morning. Nowadays there almost always is. The city is growing. The government tries to keep up, but the infrastructure wasn't built to support as many people as we've got and more keep coming. I love the city, but I don't love the traffic.

"Why do you suppose he did it? I mean, he was a professional athlete. He had fame, money, everything! It doesn't make sense!"

"Don't look at me. I'd rather die than have one of those damned things in my head."

"So would I. Not that it would ever be an issue." Tom looked over his shoulder, watching Carlton's car slipping smoothly in and out of traffic. "It doesn't make sense," he repeated the words, speaking more softly this time.

"Well, if you really want to know, ask him." I pulled onto the Speer exit and headed over the bridge to downtown. Our tail kept up with us with ease—right up until it was time to find on-street parking. I was able to get a metered spot on Tremont by waiting for someone to pull out. But it was the only spot available for blocks in either direction. Carlton was either going to have to keep circling the block or pull into a parking garage. Either way, there was a good chance he'd lose us. I didn't mind. I might be starting to like Carlton personally, but his constant presence in the background was getting annoying.

Small, hard pellets of snow began falling as I was sliding coins into the parking meter. I put in enough for the full one hour. If I could get in and out of the office quickly I'd be all right. More likely, I'd get a parking ticket. The City of Denver makes damned good money off folks trying to get business done downtown. The new mayor had fun with it during his campaign and has made a little progress. But the fact is that it costs money to run a city. The traffic fines provide an income stream.

I was thinking about that for the first five floors of the elevator trip. The next twenty-five were spent remembering.

I'd known Victoria Ryan since I'd been in high school. Amanda's mother was very much an older version of Amanda: short, stacked, with dark hair and perfect features.

I remembered her being smart, but not brilliant. She was steady, someone you would rely on in a crisis. She'd been at every gymnastics meet her daughter competed in, every ball game Amanda cheered at or played in. I'd heard she was called "the dragon lady" by her opponents and was a stone cold bitch in the courtroom, but I'd never seen that side of her. Couldn't say I was sorry to miss it.

When I first was starting up my business I did some courier work for her firm, which was how Amanda and I had met back up as adults. She'd been manning the reception desk over the summer. I'd gotten the vague impression Victoria had disapproved of my becoming best friends with her daughter. The courier work had definitely dried up. But nothing had ever been *said*. As commuters exited on the various floors it occurred to me that I wasn't looking forward to this meeting at all. Amanda blamed me for Dylan's death. It was quite likely Victoria would, too.

"Why the hell am I doing this?" I muttered the words under my breath.

Tom leaned into me, his expression sympathetic. Giving me a quick one-armed hug, he whispered. "Because you love your brother and it's the right thing to do."

"Yeah," I agreed, "but you'd better keep reminding me of that, otherwise I'm liable to chicken out."

The elevator stopped and the last of the commuters had stepped off. The next time the doors opened we'd step into the middle of Logan, Ryan, Leary, and Meyers, P.C., one of the premier law firms in Denver, occupying both the thirtieth and thirty-first floors of the building.

"Mary Kathleen Reilly, you have never chickened out of anything in your life," Tom teased. He'd taken off his sunglasses somewhere along the way. It gave me a chance to see his face.

Looking into those chocolate brown eyes, I felt a little of the tension ease out of my shoulders. I smiled. I couldn't help it. Tom was here. It would be all right. The worst thing that could happen would be that the receptionist would call security and I would be escorted from the building. Embarrassing, but far from fatal.

The bell rang and the elevator doors opened. It was time to beard the dragon in her lair.

12

The view from the thirtieth floor of a skyscraper is phenomenal. Tom and I had been escorted by the receptionist into a small conference room. The entire west wall from the waist up was windows, giving a glorious panorama of the Rocky Mountains in the distance. The clouds weren't even this high up—I could see their tops, slumming around the twenty-third floor. The ground seemed *very* far below. The pedestrians scurrying to work weren't much bigger than ants, cars and trucks were the size of the Micro Machines I'd given Bryan for Christmas when he was five. I sat in a very comfortable burgundy leather chair, one of four spaced evenly around a circular conference table of highly polished cherry wood that matched the built-in bookcases and window ledges. The drapes were a geometric pattern in burgundy, teal, and gold in a shade that exactly matched the plush carpet. There was an original painting on the east wall. It was nonobjective: white mostly, on a glossy black background, but with splashes of vibrant teal, red, and lavender in a simple cherry frame.

Tom settled into the chair directly across from me, turning slowly to take in every detail of both the room and the view.

"Nice, very nice," he observed.

"Thank you."

Victoria Ryan stepped into the room carrying a sealed brown envelope. She hadn't changed much in the years since I'd seen her. There was a little more gray in her hair, but it looked good on her. Her body was still trim and toned beneath the red power suit. The blouse she wore was snow white silk, her jewelry heavy and gold. It was all very impressive, understated and businesslike, with one exception. On her lapel she wore a large pin. Jeweled and enameled it was just a fraction away from gaudy. It was in the shape of a traditional Chinese dragon.

I laughed. I couldn't help it. She smiled and said. "Do you realize you are only the second person with enough nerve to laugh at the joke?"

"Who was the other?" Tom asked.

"A U.S. District Court judge."

She dropped the envelope onto the table between Tom and me, but didn't sit down. Instead, she walked over to the windows, her high heels sinking deep and silently into the carpet. She stared outward, but not as though she was actually looking at the view.

"My daughter said you'd be coming here."

"She did?" I didn't bother to hide my surprise. "When?"

"Shortly after Dylan's death." She turned and looked at me, her expression carefully neutral. "I love my daughter."

"I know."

"I wish I was one of those mothers who could rationalize everything, tell myself that anything Amanda does is all right, simply because it's her doing it." Her eyes met mine, and it was a hard look. "I'm not."

There wasn't much I could say to that, so I kept my mouth shut. Tom must have agreed with me, because he seemed to be doing his absolute best to remain invisible.

She sighed and turned back to the window. "We disagreed about her obsession with you and her involvement with the parasites. It put a significant strain on our relationship."

"I'm sorry to hear that."

She turned, giving me a small smile. "I believe you actually mean that."

"I do. As I recall the two of you were very close."

"Yes." She crossed to the table and primly took her seat. "We were." Sadness touched her eyes, and her shoulders drooped a little beneath the padded jacket, but only for a moment. I watched as she very deliberately put the pain aside and took back up the armor of business.

"At any rate, she said you'd be here, and here you are. I was asked to give you this envelope and tell you that she'll be waiting." I reached for the envelope, but she set a manicured hand on top of it, holding it in place. "There's something I feel I need to tell you, but I'm not sure how to word it."

"Just say it." Tom softened the words with a smile. She looked at him, then at me, and I saw recognition of our relationship in that look. It was as though until that moment, I'd been alone in the room as far as she was concerned, but now Tom and I were a couple, or even a team.

"Amanda blames you for Dylan's death, Kate, and for everything else that happened that night. I think . . . I'm afraid it may have unhinged her. I tried to convince her to get help, but all I succeeded in doing was to drive her further away from me. But judging from how she was behaving the last time we spoke, I'd have to say that, where you're concerned, she might well be dangerous."

I thought of Amanda's attack on me at my apartment and gave an involuntary shudder. Amanda was unhinged all right, and more dangerous than her mother even imagined. "I know."

She stared at me for a long moment before giving a small nod of acknowledgment. "Please don't kill her, if she's still sane." She paused and I watched her blink away a moment of wetness. "I have to ask you for that. She *is* my child." She took her hand off the envelope, rose in one fluid movement, and cleared her throat. "Now, if you'll excuse me. I have another appointment. I'll have Rachel come back in a few minutes to show you out." She paused at the door. "Be careful, Katie." She was gone before either of us could answer.

I shifted my gaze from the closing door to the envelope in my hand. My stomach was tight with nerves, and there was a fine trembling in my fingers. I undid the clasp and used a fingernail to slit open the flap. Inside there were a sheet of paper with a handwritten address, a printout of a map, and directions. It was a trap. Sure as God made little green apples, Amanda had laid out a trap for me—months ago, and she'd had all this time to perfect it. The question was, what was I going to do about it?

We walked out of the building to find Carlton double-parked next to the rental car and signing autographs. We had to wade through an actual *crowd* to get to the vehicle. Tom was shaking his head in disbelief. I couldn't blame him. It was just . . . surreal.

I wanted to hate Lewis Carlton. I mean, he's big, he's scary, and he's a vampire. And still something about him appealed to me. Under other circumstances, I'd probably be friends with him. A part of me wanted dealing with the Thrall to be black and white. But the fact was that the parasites infested *people*. Sometimes the host's mind was even strong enough to briefly override the influence of the hive. Morris had done it. Nor was Carlton the first person I'd known to willingly accept a parasite. Dylan had made the same choice. Amanda would've if she could. Hell, she'd even tried. I didn't know what was wrong with her that she couldn't be a host, but I'd seen the results. I couldn't understand why Dylan had agreed to be infested, but I couldn't hate him for it either. In the end, he'd died saving Tom and my brother Joe.

Don't think about it, Reilly. Think about what you're going to do about Amanda.

I had options. First, I could call Brooks, tell him that I had a good idea who took the eggs and where they were. Problem with that was, Amanda was completely insane, and, according to the hive, a big, strong bad-ass who'd wipe the floor with the nice police officers.

Second, she'd issued a direct challenge. If I didn't meet it, the Thrall could use it as an excuse to revoke my Not Prey status. I *like* my status. Admittedly, part of it is ego. But more than that, being Not Prey makes them deal with me as an equal. It's kept them from simply hunting me down and killing me as a threat. Granted, there have been times when it's been a damned nuisance. But more often than not it's been a good thing.

I thought about all of this on the long, silent ride back to the apartment. Only a few blocks, but the drive seemed to take forever.

I turned the car into the drive, stopping at the parking gate to punch in the access code. Carlton pulled to the curb. His window rolled down and I heard him call my name.

"Reilly!"

I leaned out the driver's side window. "What?"

"You going anywhere for the next couple hours? I could stand a bite to eat, and I want to switch vehicles." He nodded toward the bank of ominous clouds rolling in over the mountains. A snowstorm was headed this way, and from the looks of things it was going to be a beaut.

I looked at Tom to get his opinion.

"It's going to take more than a couple hours to work up a plan. I vote we let him go."

I didn't disagree, and a little privacy might be a nice thing.

"Go ahead and go."

"That doesn't answer my question." He smiled to take the sting out of the words.

"I'm not trying to ditch you, Carlton. I honestly don't care if you follow me around. It'll take us at least two hours to come up with a plan of attack—"

"Whoa, whoa, whoa." He opened the door and climbed from the vehicle with amazing speed. "*What* exactly did you find out that you're talking 'bout a 'plan of attack'?"

I blinked stupidly. I'd just assumed that the queens had been in my head and seen what was going on, and that they would pass the information on. Apparently I was wrong. I looked at Tom, who shrugged his shoulders. He was leaving the decision up to me.

"I thought you knew." I reached over and grabbed the envelope from where it was sitting on the seat between Tom and me. "Amanda anticipated my move. She left a message for me at her mother's office." I handed the envelope out the window to Carlton. "She gave me a map showing how to get to her."

"It's a trap." Carlton slid the pages from the envelope and looked them over.

"Ya think?" Tom rolled his eyes and growled.

Carlton's smile evaporated as he replaced the pages and passed the envelope to me through the car window. "I'll be back in two hours. Give me your word you won't take off without me. And I don't mean telling the queens in your head—you tell *me . . . personally*."

I thought about that for a second, searching for his angle and not finding it. "Give me your cell phone number. If we decide to leave early, I'll give you a call."

Carlton pulled his wallet from the back pocket of his slacks and removed a business card. Using a Mont Blanc pen he scrawled a series of numbers on the back of the card.

"You're going to be needing back-up on this one, Reilly."

"I'll be going with her." Tom's voice had a bass rumble to it.

Carlton put both massive hands on the window frame and leaned forward to get a better look inside the car. "Yeah, but you're only *one* wolf." His expression grew grave as he turned to me. "Just how well does this bitch know you?"

"I've known her since high school. We were best friends once."

"Shit. Then she'll be able to anticipate exactly what you're going to do."

I thought about that for a second. Once upon a time that would have been true. But a lot had happened in the past few years. I'd changed. Like it or not I was a harder, colder person than the girl Amanda had known. "I don't think so." I smiled a quick baring of teeth. "But she'll *think* she can."

"She anticipated you going to her mother."

"Hell, that's just logic, Carlton. Anyone who has ever watched a cop show knows you start with the next of kin."

He thought about that for a moment. When he answered, his voice was quiet and firm. "Just don't leave before I get back." He straightened up and stepped away from the car. As I entered the code and drove into the garage I caught a glimpse of him driving off.

Tom shook his head as I pulled the car into its usual space. "A vampire. He's a friggin' vampire. It doesn't make sense."

I didn't comment. I couldn't fathom it either. I couldn't imagine that Lewis Carlton wouldn't be strong enough to fight off an attacking Thrall, even a queen. Which meant he'd gone into being a host willingly. It made no sense. Why accept a parasite *knowing* it would kill you in just a few years? There are people who are just stupid, or crazy, but Carlton demonstrably wasn't. So why?

I hopped out of the car, shutting the door with a brisk slam before hitting the lock button on the keychain. The car beeped, its lights flashing to let me know that the alarm was on.

"I'm going to head up to my apartment," Tom announced. "I'll come up in a few minutes." He circled around the vehicle, taking me into his arms for a sweet, gentle kiss. "Promise you won't leave without me."

"I promise."

He gave me a quick squeeze and another kiss before sprinting over to the staircase. I stood in the near-empty garage for a long moment, listening to the thunder of his feet echoing in the stairwell before I went over to activate the freight elevator.

Alone in the elevator, I scratched irritably at the skin under the neck brace. The rough acrylic was miserably uncomfortable, but it was worth it to have my neck protected in case of a bite. I'd learned from past experience just how much of an advantage it was, because a Thrall that broke off its teeth went into shock, leaving it totally vulnerable.

I had the key in the socket and was locking off the elevator when the phone rang. I wasn't really in any mood to talk to anyone. I had things to think about, plans to make, so I let the machine take it, grabbed the remote from on top of the counter, and flipped on the television with the volume muted. It was almost time for the news. I didn't want to hear about Share the Planet, or the trial, or even the plane crash. I did need to check out the weather report. If it was snowing in the mountains there was a good chance the passes would be closed to traffic. I didn't want to drive all the way up there only to find I couldn't get through.

After the fourth ring I heard my voice saying "I'm not available to take your call, please leave a message after the tone." The machine beeped, and I heard Miles MacDougal's voice on the line.

"Kate, I got a very strange call from Henri Tané's wife. I'm very worried. *Please* call me."

I stopped in my tracks. Guilt washed over me in a tidal wave. How could I have forgotten about Henri? I leapt across the room, grabbing the receiver while Miles was still talking.

"Miles, I'm here. You caught me coming in the door."

"Kate. I'm so glad I was able to reach you!" His relief was obvious, even over the phone. "I got the strangest call from Yvette Tané. She said that Henri had been murdered. She also said she saw you at Henri's funeral, but that's impossible. In Haiti the custom is normally to bury the dead within twenty-four hours of their death. I saw you in court, and there's no way you could've flown down to Port-de-Paix and back."

"No. I didn't." I didn't explain about the psychic connection. It was just too weird. Miles was a scientist. He'd be utterly fascinated and would keep me on the phone for hours talking about it. I didn't *have* hours. I needed to plan.

"Did she say anything about how it happened? Who did it?"

"She didn't say. In fact, she acted as though you already knew. Does this have to do with the Thrall?"

"I don't know. I'd thought so, but I talked to one of them about it and he said that it wasn't them."

"Then who—" He let the sentence trail off.

"I don't know. I assume the Haitian police are looking into it?"

"Yvette didn't seem to have much faith in them."

I didn't answer. There wasn't anything to say. From what I've seen, most people don't have a lot of faith in the police—anywhere in the world. It's a shame, really. Most of the cops I've met are basically good guys doing a tough job. But I live in Denver, not Haiti. With the unstable political situation there, Yvette might have a valid point. Or not. I just didn't know.

"Do you think the Thrall lied to you?"

"Maybe. But I doubt it. They're pretty careful about not breaking the rules. They'll bend them all to hell, but not break them." I drummed my fingers against the tiled surface of the kitchen island, trying to remember word-for-word what Carlton had said. I couldn't do it. I remembered the gist, but somehow that didn't seem good enough.

"Monica broke the rules." Miles spoke softly, each word chosen with obvious care.

"Monica was insane. The queens lost control over her."

Miles didn't answer. The silence stretched between us for long moments before he finally spoke. "Henri was a friend of mine, Kate. His wife is a lovely woman, left to raise her son alone in a country torn by violence. The person who did this needs to be brought to justice."

I didn't disagree. In fact, I figured Miles and I were probably even on the same page as to what constituted justice. The problem was, if the Thrall hadn't been responsible, I didn't have a clue who would have done it.

I paced the floor with the receiver in my hand. I was tired, angry, and sad. It occurred to me that even though Carlton had told me Henri was dead, despite the fact I'd asked Mike for a mass, a part of me had clung to a tiny thread of hope that they were wrong and Henri was alive. Now I knew for a fact he wasn't. I wouldn't get the chance to apologize to him for being a jerk, or laugh at his dry wit and endless supply of Haitian proverbs. He'd been so vibrantly alive, it was hard to imagine him gone.

"Kate?" Apparently the silence had gone on too long for Miles's comfort.

"I'm here."

"I'm sorry. I know that the two of you had become close."

"I'll miss him." My voice was tight with unshed tears of both anger and grief.

A pause, and it sounded like Miles's tears weren't so unshed. "I'll miss him, too."

We ended the conversation shortly after that. There was really nothing more to say, and neither of us was capable of small talk.

I put the phone in its cradle and sank onto the nearest stool. I let my head fall into my hands. I was still sitting there when Tom came through the front door. He came up to me slowly, gently wrapping me in his arms before speaking. "What's wrong?"

I lay my head against his chest, wrapping my arms around his waist and holding him tight. He stood in front of the stool, my knees on either side of him, just holding me. "Henri Tané really is dead. Somebody murdered him."

"I'm sorry. I know you liked him." Tom moved his hand beneath my chin and tilted my head upward. With infinite tenderness his lips met mine, his fingers wiping away my tears. When the kiss ended he pulled back only a little, so that he could look me in the eyes. "There's more, isn't there?"

"I'm not sure." I took a deep breath, trying to gather my thoughts. "You know I've been having nightmares."

"Yes."

"I'm beginning to wonder whether they're just dreams, or if maybe they're something more. And while I didn't recognize them at first, I think . . . I think the victims in the dreams were the Not Prey who participated in the study."

His brow furrowed and he was suddenly very, very serious. "Tell me everything." Tom reached back to pull the second stool out. He took a seat, but covered my hands with his. That touch was an anchor, holding me together.

It took time, but I described the dreams, giving him every detail I could remember. When I finished, I felt drained, exhausted, but strangely lighter. It was almost as if the information had been a weight dragging me down.

"You need to call Miles back. Ask him to pull the contact information on all of the Not Prey from the study files. If what you've been seeing are just dreams, no harm done. But if someone is stalking the Not Prey, they need to be warned."

He reached past me to grab the phone, putting it onto the counter in front of me. Sighing, I picked it up and dialed the number for the hospital. Miles wasn't in his office; maybe he'd been calling from home. If so, I was out of luck. I'd never gotten his home number. So I left a voice-mail explaining the situation and asking him to call me back. I felt like a fool and an idiot. But it was possible that lives were at stake. My embarrassment was irrelevant.

When I hung up the phone, Tom reached over and hugged me close. "I'm proud of you."

"Why?"

"I know how hard it is for you to accept your psychic talent. Since you don't completely believe in it yourself, it was asking a lot for you to make that call."

"Was it that obvious?"

"Only because I know you so well." He smiled, and the expression warmed me to my toes. "Tell you what," he suggested. "Why don't you order us a pizza for dinner while I check out the weather reports?" I nodded my agreement and reached for the phone at the same time he went for the remote. Our hands brushed against each other, and it made me smile.

As I dialed out I watched Tom settle himself comfortably into the recliner. He switched channels and then turned off the mute, but kept the volume low enough that he could hear it without it bothering me.

"Holy crap!"

"What?" I put my hand over the mouthpiece and turned to find him staring at the television screen in absolute awe. Following his gaze, I stared at the picture being transmitted by Channel 5's "MountainView" camera. It showed some of the worst blizzard conditions I'd ever seen. We usually get at least one or two really good storms a year, but this was just . . . amazing.

"There's no way we're driving to the Western Slope in that," Tom observed. "We're going to have to wait until the storm blows over."

"You're right," I admitted. I wasn't even sorry. The confrontation with Amanda was inevitable and dangerous. We needed to plan our attack. I knew it logically, but emotionally I simply wasn't up to it. I was hoping that maybe some food and a good night's sleep curled up next to Tom would help. If it didn't I was going to be so screwed.

The person at the pizza place came onto the line to take our order. She was obviously harried, and told me the delivery time was liable to be over an hour—*if* the storm didn't worsen. I put my hand over the speaker and asked Tom if he minded.

"Perfect. They can even take two hours if they want."

"No problem," I told the woman. She quoted the price and hung up the line. By the time I'd placed the phone back in the cradle Tom was in front of me. He was smiling. I'd come to recognize that look on his face. It was the look he wore when he intended to seduce me.

"However shall we pass the time?" He batted his lashes at me in mock innocence.

I laughed right up until the instant our lips met. His lips were warm and gentle, moving carefully against mine, as though my mouth was precious and fragile. He used both hands to cup my face. His strong fingers held me with a tenderness that took my breath away. He pressed gentle kisses in a line down my jaw line toward my throat, but was stopped by the turtleneck and brace.

"Let's go upstairs and get you into something more comfortable," he whispered.

I was a little surprised: twice in one day? But I nodded my agreement, and he moved his hands. Taking my right hand in his he led the way upstairs.

I would not have thought it was possible to make unlocking the neck brace sexy, but damned if he didn't manage. His teeth nibbled my earlobe, his breath hot against my neck. He shifted positions, pressing his hips against mine, pinning me to the wall next to the bed. I could feel every hard inch of him pressed against me. He spread my legs with one knee as his hand slid into the front pocket of my jeans to retrieve the key.

His mouth locked on mine, and our tongues tangled as the kiss deepened into a fierce claiming of my mouth. I moaned because while his hands were working the catch his hips worked a slow movement that made my body ache with the need for his touch.

My hands struggled to unfasten his belt. Once it was loose I pulled hard at his shirt. I wanted, *needed* the touch of his bare skin. He was so warm, his skin utterly smooth beneath my seeking hands.

The lock clicked loose, and he pulled back enough to lift the brace off my shoulders and toss it aside. I watched it drop unceremoniously onto the bed. When my gaze turned back to him he was smiling. It was a wicked little smile that told me he planned to do all sorts of things with my body and knew that I wouldn't stop him.

He used his hands to cup my breasts, his thumb and fingertips teasing my nipples through the thin silky fabric of my bra. His mouth moved to my throat, nibbling, kissing, licking as I writhed against his hips. Little whimpering noises escaped my mouth. I couldn't help myself. He was driving me wild. I was hot, wet, and aching to be touched.

He pulled back, a little, just enough to let me catch my breath and to give him room to unfasten my jeans.

Sliding his hand between the fabric and my skin, his hand sought my opening. Using his fingers he teased my body, bringing me closer and closer to climax. He pulled away before I could reach orgasm, and I wanted to scream in frustration.

He kissed me hard. Using his hands, he pulled me off balance, pulling me with him onto the floor. His mouth never left mine as he stripped the jeans from my body as I used my hands to caress him. He was so hard, so ready, his cock throbbing as I traced my finger down his shaft and cupped his balls in my hand.

With a low groan he grabbed my thighs, pulling them wide so that I was open and ready. This time it was not tender, not slow. His body pierced mine, again and again. The silken hardness of his shaft slid in and out in an ever faster rhythm.

The first orgasm hit hard and fast, my body bucking against him as my hands dug into his hips, pulling him even deeper inside my body until, with a shout of triumph, he came inside me.

It took almost two hours for the pizza to arrive. I was so happy about it that I gave the deliveryman a twenty-dollar tip.

13

Most of metro Denver was buried under a thick blanket of glistening white snow and it was still coming down. The windows of the apartment were limned with frost. If I hadn't looked at the clock I wouldn't have been able to tell that it was almost dawn. What I could see of the sky was a uniform gray. I was glad I'd called ahead yesterday to change my rental car over to something with four wheel drive. It would be more expensive, but worth every penny.

I stared out the windows at the city below. It was quiet, the snow muffling what few of the city noises remained after nearly everyone had deserted the streets to avoid the snow. Only the distant sound of the snow plows and salt trucks working on Speer, and the ticking of the kitchen clock, could be heard from where I stood.

The only light in the apartment was the light in the stove hood. It gave me just enough illumination to make my way around the apartment, but wasn't bright enough to wake Tom, who was snoring away upstairs.

Blank came up, wending his body around my bare ankles, purring like a miniature motorboat. I scooped him up, settling him against my shoulder. I ran my hands through his thick fur, feeling the purr rumbling against my chest through the fabric of my robe. He butted his head against my chin.

"Demanding little cuss, aren't you?" I whispered, but used my fingernails to scratch his favorite spot. His eyes narrowed, and his body went almost limp with pleasure. I closed my eyes and leaned back against the wall, enjoying a few minutes of peace before the world woke and the day went to hell.

It was the cat that woke her. He jumped on the bed, giving a soft, high-pitched growl unlike anything she'd ever heard from him. She sensed . . . something . . . something not right, not normal. Sitting up in bed she reached over to the nightstand and grabbed her glasses from beside the water glass. Once she'd slid them on and could see what she was doing she slipped quietly from beneath the covers and eased the drawer open.

The knife was large and honed to a razor's edge. People didn't expect her to own such a knife, let alone know how to use it. But her father had insisted she learn. He'd sensed she'd need the knowledge. She'd inherited her ability to sense things from him, just like she'd inherited his blue eyes. She might be a little old lady, but she was no pushover, and whoever was in the house was about to find that out.

She stood, her bare feet sinking into the thick Oriental rug, and sent her mind outward, seeking the source of the disturbance. The cat's growl faded into the background of her awareness.

Her mind slammed against something feral and deadly. This was no random attack. It knew who, and what, she was.

She edged slowly forward, moving with absolute stealth through the familiar room. Her heart was pounding. She could taste the adrenaline on her tongue.

She had reached the center of the bedroom when a shape filled the doorway. She had a flash of recognition. "You!"

"Ouch! Damn it, Blank!" The cat thudded to the floor and dashed upstairs. I gasped in pain, my mind brought forcibly back to my own body. He'd dug in claws as he jumped, drawing blood. I padded across the room to the kitchen sink and washed the puncture wounds with antibacterial soap, drying them off with a paper towel.

Was it a dream, or was it a vision? I needed to be sure. I concentrated, trying to reconnect with the woman in the bedroom. Nothing. Either it had all been my imagination, I was doing it wrong, or the old woman was dead.

Shivering from a cold that had nothing to do with the weather outside, I pulled the robe tighter around my body. Coffee, coffee would warm me up. I puttered around the kitchen getting the first pot of the day brewing and tried very hard not to think of some little old woman fighting for her life against someone she knew.

One of the things I hate most about the psychic stuff is that what I'm seeing doesn't always happen in real time. The attack in that bedroom could be happening now, or last year, or next week. There was no way of knowing. If I didn't distract myself, I was going to go nuts worrying, so I turned the volume down low and started listening to the messages that had accumulated on the answering machine.

Most of it was crap. There were a couple of social calls from Peg my best female friend in the world—who often called from strange, exotic locations because of her job as a flight attendant. Joe called to say he was due back in on Saturday and asking me to *please* call and let him know what the verdict had been. There was the call from Miles, a return call from Brooks giving me his cell phone number, and finally, a call from the lawyer.

The jury had found the hospital 100 percent liable. The rest of us had been found to have zero liability. I wasn't going to owe a thing.

I staggered backward and felt my way onto one of the stools by the breakfast counter. I'd pretended to myself and everyone else that I wasn't worried. I'd lied. A part of me had been terrified that I'd be found responsible for the death of Mason Watts to the tune of several million dollars I didn't have. The whole mess had been consuming my thoughts for months. I felt bad for his parents, guilty I hadn't saved him, and terrified that I'd lose my home and everything else I'd worked so hard to earn. Now it was just, suddenly . . . over. Stress I'd been rationalizing away just vanished, leaving me limp and weak from the lack of adrenaline.

I heard movement on the steps and saw Tom padding downstairs wearing one of my pairs of sweatpants. He looked rumpled and delicious, the dim light casting shadows in the muscular hollows of his body. Normally my body would have reacted to the sight of him like that. I knew I was seriously stunned because it didn't.

"Did I hear that correctly? You were cleared?"

I nodded, still unable to speak.

"WHOOO HOOO!" He let out a celebratory war cry that echoed through the large living room. "YES!" He pumped his fist in victory. He leaped down the last few steps and bounded over to me. Putting one hand on the counter on either side of me he leaned in and kissed me senseless, his mouth opening mine so that our tongues could dance. It was a couple of minutes before he pulled back, by which time I could see from the fit of the sweats that he was a very happy man.

"A good omen to start the day," he observed.

"I'm not sure I believe in omens."

"Party pooper. And you a psychic." He was playing with my braid when he said it, twisting it around his fingers, playing with the loose hairs at the end. "Katie, sweetheart, things are getting better. We can deal with the pack; your legal problems are working out. It's going to be all right. We'll face Amanda together, and then, just imagine. Your brother will be all right again." There was awe and excitement in his voice as if he couldn't quite imagine it himself.

I wanted to believe. I truly did. But I was terrified. I almost didn't dare hope. Because, honestly, in the time since my parents died things have never really been easy, never really been "all right." There have been good times, but they've been leavened with enough disaster to keep me on edge. For years I've spent my life waiting for the other boot to drop. Even though I wanted to, I didn't know how to stop, how to change my entire way of relating to the world. I just don't have that much trust left in me any more. And there was still the niggling knowledge that Tom never had told me what happened at the pack meeting, despite the repeated nudging into the topic.

Tom sensed it, or else he just knows me well enough to guess. "It's okay to be scared." He put his hands on my waist and pulled me close. I buried my head against the warm skin of his chest, my hands resting on his shoulders.

"Good, 'cause I'm terrified." I took a deep breath, not daring to look up into those gentle, knowing, eyes. "I—"

Tom put a finger under my chin, tilting my face up so that I was forced to look at him. "Shhh. We're going to take it one step at a time: plan our attack, defeat the bad guy, and live happily ever after."

"You sound so sure."

"Trust me."

14

There are some arguments you are not going to win. The trick is to accept it, and move on. I would love to say I'm good at that. I'm not. But at some point I realized that unless I wanted to spend the next forty years or so arguing in the basement of my building, I was going to have to give in. Because Rob and Dusty weren't about to back down, and Tom agreed with them.

They'd been waiting by the rental car when Tom and I exited the freight elevator. Dusty looked small and vulnerable in a lavender down jacket, zipped up to her chin—her hair hidden by a matching pull-on cap that was decorated with white and silver snowflakes. Her black jeans were tucked into an ugly set of glossy royal purple snow boots that were lined with thick crimson fake fur. Her hands were covered by the lavender and white mittens that had come with the hat. Despite the warm clothes, her face seemed pinched with the cold, or maybe with worry. Normally she tries to act aggressively tough. Today she didn't bother.

Rob was in his black leather trench coat. He wore boots,

but more as a fashion statement than in reaction to the weather. They were heavy and black, and came up to his knees, fastening with complicated-looking steel buckles. There was probably some trick to fastening them that I wasn't going to figure out at just a casual glance.

"What are you doing here?"

"Dusty sensed that something was up. She said we needed to be here," Rob explained.

I wasn't sure how to answer that. Dusty's psychic talent was what had made her Monica's second choice for a replacement queen. But she'd never said or done anything to show off her talent before now, so I'd pretty much forgotten all about it.

I turned to Tom. "If I take the two of them with me, Amanda won't have to kill me, Mary will do it for her."

Dusty flinched a little, but didn't say anything to deny it. It was Rob who argued, "You need us, Kate. I don't know what you're going up against, but you need reinforcements. Dusty saw it. If you don't take us along willingly, we'll just follow you in Dusty's car, so you might as well stop arguing."

The little shit meant every word. At least he wasn't smug. If anything, he seemed a little nervous, as though he was afraid I might try to kick his ass.

"I think we should bring them," Tom said. "Rob knows how to fight, and Dusty can drive us to the hospital, in case anybody gets hurt." By "anybody" he meant me. Werewolves aren't issued driver's licenses because the condition is triggered by adrenaline. If we got in a fight, Rob and Tom were almost guaranteed to be in wolf form.

He had a point. I didn't *like* it, but there was a good chance I'd be hurt. Hell, Carlton and the queens thought I'd be killed. Having Dusty as a back-up driver could make the difference between life and death for me, Tom, or Rob. It made perfect sense, but that didn't make me like it any better. "Fine." I didn't sound gracious, but none of them expected it. "Just as long as Dusty agrees to stay in the car, no matter what."

"Agreed." Tom and Rob said it in unison. Dusty didn't respond. She was already climbing into the back seat of the sedan. I noticed, but didn't say anything. She wasn't stupid. I knew she understood why we might need her as a driver. I was hoping it was incentive enough to keep her in the car and out of trouble.

Our first stop was the car rental lot. I'd called ahead to arrange an exchange. Since we were going up to the mountains I wanted a four wheel drive vehicle. We might not need it, but I wanted to be prepared.

It was a good thing I'd called ahead. We got the last SUV on the lot, a red Jeep Grand Cherokee. It was roomy, with a luxurious leather interior, and heating and cooling *zones*. We'd be driving into the trap in comfort and style.

According to the map and directions in the envelope, the drive to meet with Amanda would take approximately three hours and four minutes. The destination was halfway between the towns of Grizzly and Bear Creek. Most of the trip would be spent on I-70. Tom and I had spent a fair amount of time this morning looking for another route, but there just wasn't one. There simply aren't that many roads through the mountains. The terrain is too rough. The road is an intruder, a thin ribbon of pavement carved onto the edge of steep cliffs of tan stone. At any time the mountain may hurl a boulder downward, smashing its way through everything in its path. The signs say "Watch for Falling Rock," but the boulders themselves, wedged deep into the pavement of the road's shoulder, are a better warning. Nor is it the only danger, there are hairpin turns. The runaway truck ramps bear witness to how easy it is for the driver of a semi or heavy truck to lose control of a vehicle in the mountains. The first ramp we passed already had a tanker buried in snow and sand. The truck had been going fast enough that momentum had carried it more than halfway up the steep incline before the loose sand beneath the tires slowed it to a stop.

Still, dangerous as it is, there are the morons who insist

on driving twenty to thirty miles over the speed limit, and the others whose vehicles chug along in the slow lane, barely able to make the climb at all.

I wasn't thrilled that we were driving into a trap with my enemy knowing exactly how we were coming in, but I just didn't see any way around it. Amanda *didn't* know I was bringing reinforcements. I didn't know if she knew about Tom or not, but Rob and Dusty coming along was not something she would anticipate, and Carlton was trailing along behind in his Hummer.

Of course, I wouldn't want to bet on the vampire actually doing anything to help. The hive would probably be more than happy to see me dead, and he'd already referred to himself as the "cleanup crew."

We'd left early enough to arrive in full daylight, on a clear, bright day. Whether sunlight bothered Amanda in her current state I didn't know, but I'd take any possible advantage. Besides, in daylight I, at least, would be able to see what the hell I was doing.

It was a long, tense drive. I could hear Rob and Dusty whispering in the back seat from time to time, but other than that, we traveled in silence. Tom alternately stared out the window at the passing scenery, or into the rearview mirror at Carlton.

Traffic was heavy. It hadn't occurred to me that it would be, but it should've. The Rocky Mountains have some of the best skiing in the world, and from Denver you have to take I-70 most of the way up to get to the resorts.

Things were at a dead standstill going into the Eisenhower Tunnel. I waited impatiently, my eyes straying to the left to watch the colorful chair lifts of Loveland Ski Resort making their way up the snow-covered mountain.

"I have an idea." Rob's voice interrupted my musings. He spoke softly, as if he wasn't sure how I'd react. It made me wonder just how much of a bitch I'd been recently. I didn't like thinking that way, but it was probably the truth. I was gearing up for a battle, and it probably showed.

Tom turned, looking over the top of the front seat. I met Rob's eyes in the rearview mirror. "What?"

"Amanda knew you when. She's going to expect you to come riding in like the Lone Ranger. So why don't we show her just that?"

I thought about that. It actually wasn't such a bad suggestion.

"Go on." Tom's voice was likewise thoughtful.

Rob, his eyes on Tom, cleared his throat and continued with more confidence. "There's only one road out to this place, but if you and I go in wolf form, we don't have to use the highway. We can go cross-country and have the element of surprise. Hell, the adrenaline in this car is thick enough to walk on. It's all we can do to hold in the beasts. So we don't. We use our wolves."

"I thought you couldn't think clearly in animal form?" I phrased the question carefully. I didn't want to insult him, but Tom's ability to keep his human mind when he shifted was, from what everyone told me, a very rare talent. Call me selfish, but I didn't want my back-up to run off on the trail of some elk. It was perverse of me. I'd argued against Rob and Dusty coming along, and now I didn't want him to go. "And what about Dusty?"

She spoke softly, but there was pride in her voice. "Rob's been practicing with Tom. He's getting really good at controlling his wolf and keeping his identity." She continued. "I'll hide on the floor of the back seat. If things go bad, I can drive to the rescue."

"Not if, when," I said.

"You don't know that." Her eyes flashed when she said it, as though she was insulted that I thought the wolves couldn't take Amanda.

Tom looked at me for a long moment. I think he saw something in the way I held myself, or maybe scented something coming off my body. "Yeah, she does."

I didn't *know*, not exactly. There was nothing specific

about the premonition. But I had a feeling, the kind of feeling that generally means there's going to be trouble. "Dusty, I know Amanda is your aunt, but I'm not really certain you understand just what she's become. Hell, even I'm not sure what she's become."

Rob nodded and touched Dusty's arm. "I didn't let you see the sidewalk until after I cleaned it up, honey. But there's no way she should have survived that fall."

"I know that!" she protested. "But it's a really good idea!" Her voice sounded huffy, like she felt insulted on behalf of the wolves.

"Which is why we're going to do it." I smiled and tried to put some enthusiasm into the words. Out of the corner of my eye I noticed the cars ahead of me moving a few feet forward. I put the Jeep in gear and followed them.

Dusty settled back against her seat. She was smiling, still tense, but better. Looking at her in the rearview mirror, it hit me again just how *young* she was. She'd opened her ski jacket in the warmth. Underneath was a tight black top with a plunging neckline made all the more impressive by lavender lacings that pulled together the front until her breasts were prominent enough to put your eyes out. She'd matched her belt to the ties in her blouse. I watched her strip off the mittens and hat until I could see her hair. It was styled in dark purple dreadlocks. Her makeup was perfectly applied until she was the absolute picture of goth beauty. She'd had some hard times, but her brush with death and her new role in the wolf pack hadn't changed her basic nature. She was still a kid inside, a kid who very much wanted the grown-ups to take her seriously.

Rob was nearly the same age chronologically, but experience had toughened him. There was a shadow in his eyes that never quite went away. Back in July when Tom had been kidnapped and I was infested by the Thrall queen, it had been Rob who offered to rip off the infested arm if that's what it took to save me. If push came to shove, he'd do whatever it took. He caught my eyes in the mirror and gave me a nod of acknowledgment. It was almost as if he could read my mind. Hell, maybe he could. Or maybe I'm not all that subtle. Nah, couldn't be.

It only *seemed* to take forever to get through the tunnel. Once we were on the other side, traffic loosened up a little. After a quick drive through at a fast food restaurant in Frisco we were back on our way.

Some time during the traffic jam, or maybe during the stop for food, we lost Carlton. I wasn't sure what I thought of that. Of course I was pretty sure that, like the proverbial bad penny, he'd turn back up.

Eating seemed to improve everybody's mood. We joked a little, argued about music, politics, and recent movies. Rob and Dusty were big fans of the horror genre: *Friday the 13th, The Ring, Dawn of the Dead, Nightmare on Elm Street*. My life is way too much of a horror movie for me to enjoy watching them on the screen. I'm not a big fan of epic dramas either. Give me a good car chase and then blow something up. I love the smartassed banter in a good action flick—it's pure dumb fun. If the reviewers say something is moving, or intelligent, I'll stay home and read a good book. I'm plebian to the core and make no apologies for it.

Tom was arguing the relative merits of the various slasher movie villains when we passed the exit for Grizzly. I slowed, pulling off at the next wide spot in the road.

Silence descended instantly. There was only the crunch of gravel, and the sharp intake of breath. "This is it." The words sounded harsh, even to my own ears.

"Right." Rob leaned over and kissed Dusty. Then he started stripping. I glanced away, trying to give him a little privacy, and caught Tom's eye.

My heart lurched painfully in my chest. This *was* it. We were headed into a situation where one of us might not make it out. I wished he weren't here, and at the same time wouldn't have wished him anywhere else.

"I hate this." He breathed the words so softly I could barely hear them.

"Me too."

"I love you, Katie, and I want you safe."

I agreed with him wholeheartedly. I wanted us all safe. There were so many things I wanted to say, and no time or privacy to say them. So I unfastened my seatbelt and leaned across the seat, using a kiss to show him all the things I couldn't find the words for.

It was everything a kiss should be, warm, deep, passionate. Tears filled my eyes and threatened to spill when he pulled back, and I buried my face against his neck and fought for self-control. I was moving awkwardly from the neck brace hidden beneath my clothing, but I didn't care. For just this one moment I needed to be like this, curled against the man I . . . *loved*. Yes, really truly loved. There was no denying it now, and here was yet another opportunity to lose him forever. He ran his hands over my braid and I took a shaking breath.

Rob let out a soft cough. I pulled reluctantly away.

"Sorry," he apologized. "But we lost hours in that traffic jam. We're running out of daylight."

"No. You're right." Tom picked the envelope up off of the seat and pulled out the papers to take one last look at the directions. He dropped the pages onto the seat and started pulling off his clothes. "We need to get moving."

I stared out the driver's side window of the Jeep. For probably the first time I really didn't *want* to see Tom undressed. I heard the passenger door open a second before I felt the shiver of power down my spine that told me they were shifting. I heard the back door open, then slam shut just before there was a thud of paws impacting against the door. I turned to see the two of them bounding away.

"Tom!" He paused on top a half-buried boulder, turning his head toward me. I shouted, "I love you!" He wagged his tail vigorously and gave a sharp bark. Then he jumped from his perch and was gone.

I took a ragged breath and reached over to close the car door. Dusty was staring at me, her eyes a little too wide.

"What?" I hadn't meant to sound so angry.

"It's not important." She swallowed audibly, then tore her eyes away from me. She unfastened her seatbelt and turned to lie down across the back seat. "I'm going to pull Rob's coat over me to hide."

"Good."

I refastened my seat belt, checked the mirror, and strapped myself in. *Okay, Just Do It.* After checking for traffic I pulled back onto I-70.

The turnoff for the private road I was supposed to take was four miles away. It was narrow, rutted, and so well hidden that I nearly missed it. I hit the brakes hard enough to send Dusty rolling off the seat. She let out a grunt of displeasure that turned into vigorous swearing as the Jeep jerked and jolted over the rutted gravel surface of what could only loosely be termed a "road." The snow was knee deep in spots shaded by the thick cover of pine boughs. Where the sun shone through, the snow had melted, forming a slimy mud that threatened to swallow the tires. I fought to maintain control of the vehicle, clenching my jaw shut to keep from accidentally biting my tongue.

I forced the Jeep around a sharp turn. Up ahead, there was a wide clear area and the burnt-out husk of what had once been a cabin.

As I pulled to a stop Amanda rose from her seat on the stone steps leading up the ruin. As if her movement were a signal, five ATV's swarmed in from various points around the clearing. Each vehicle carried two teenagers. None of them looked old enough to be out of high school. They pulled to a stop, forming a loose circle around Amanda, the cabin, and the Jeep. Like Amanda they all wore black hooded sweatshirts. Each shirt had the logo of Share the Planet emblazoned on the chest.

The odds sucked: even if Tom and Rob did arrive in time,

we were outnumbered. I checked my knives, said a quick prayer, and climbed from the vehicle, leaving the keys in the ignition.

"Hello, Katie." Amanda took two steps forward and I noticed that her left leg was dragging. Her voice sounded different . . . odd, and the left side of her face didn't move in time with the right, as though she'd had a stroke, or something had broken and not healed properly.

"Amanda."

"You came alone."

I decided to bluff. It couldn't hurt and it might buy me time. "Your message wasn't specific, but I got the impression you were issuing a personal challenge. You don't want witnesses for that sort of thing." Not the truth, but not an outright lie either. She wasn't a queen, wasn't Not Prey. But she wasn't a human anymore either. It was revealed in the power that practically shimmered around her. It smashed against my shields, like a tide against a levee, as she looked for a vulnerability.

The shields held, and she snarled a curse. All around me people hissed. It was not a human sound. I looked around and I caught a glimpse of sharp fangs in each face. My throat tightened with fear as I realized exactly what she'd done with the eggs.

Apparently I didn't hide it well enough, because she laughed, a wild, hysterical burst of sound, harsh as nails on a blackboard. Her power surged, and I ground my teeth, rather than cry out from the pain.

"You killed my husband," Amanda accused. "You killed my queen, and my people." Her hands tightened into fists, her face contorting into an ugly mask of rage. "You murdered ninety-nine innocent babies!" She roared the last. If her goal was to work the others into a frenzied mob it was working. They were shouting and waving their fists as they poured off of the machines. "You don't *deserve* a 'challenge.' You don't deserve to live." She smiled a satisfied little smirk without warmth or humor. "Thank you for being so honest and . . . predictable by coming alone. Because now you're going to die."

The vampires surged forward.

15

The engine of the Jeep roared to life. The machine surged forward, slamming into a crowd of vampires on my left at the same moment Tom and Rob leaped out from the cover of the trees, diving into the group on my right. There were screams of pain, and blood everywhere. My world narrowed to the two vampires who had escaped being mowed down by Dusty. One was tall, the other short, but they both had the build of football players and acted as though they were used to working together. The good news, they didn't know how to fight. I train, I practice, and I'd been in more than one situation where my skills were all that stood between me and an untimely death. I was holding them off without too much trouble, landing the occasional good blow and parrying their attacks.

I heard a wolf's howl of pain, and instinctively started to turn. The tall one thought it was an opening and lunged forward. I ducked under his roundhouse swing and was able to drive my elbow into his kidney that dropped him to his knees. I was turning, ready to use the knife to finish him when shorty stepped up, swinging a length of tree limb at my head.

I turned, and ducked my head, taking the blow across my shoulders. There was enough power behind the blow to break the wood, but the neck shield did me proud. It absorbed most of the force. The edge of the fiberglass dug into my skin, cutting me, but my spine wasn't shattered, and I could still fight.

I gave a hard side kick to the outside of shorty's left knee. He gave a hideous, high-pitched squeal as the joint gave way and he fell to the ground.

I felt, rather than saw, movement behind me. I dove out of the way, and rolled so that I could regain my feet.

Amanda had come for me, and she was swinging a bat. Blood vessels had burst in her eyes until there was no white left. I didn't know how she could see, but each swing of the bat was well aimed, and strong enough to make the wood whistle through the air. Her speed was breathtaking—nearly that of Monica at her peak. I couldn't attack. It took everything I had just to avoid her blows.

The ground was uneven. I staggered and fell, slamming first my body, then head with jarring impact against the rocks. I saw stars, bright shots of light in my vision, and for a few seconds I was incapable of movement. Time froze. I had an eternity to watch her raise the bat over her head with both hands; to see the look of fierce triumphant joy on her face. Then I heard the crack of a gunshot. Amanda's body jerked back as a spot of bright crimson bloomed in the center of her chest. The back of her torso exploded outward in a shower of blood and bone. She staggered. The weight of the bat pulled her until she fell backward, where she lay utterly still.

I rolled and turned to see who was shooting. Lewis Carlton stood limned in glorious oranges and purples made by the setting sun through clouds, his arms propped on the roof of his dark green Hummer. There was no expression on his face as he lifted the barrel of the 9mm Beretta, and started to scan the battlefield, looking for another target. If he felt anything, I couldn't see it.

The fighting stopped. Amanda's followers stared in stunned silence from her body to the man holding the gun. Their faces were empty, their bodies as still as any zombie I'd ever seen. It was as though, without her will, they had none of their own.

Tom's voice called me. I dragged myself to my feet and staggered over to him as fast as I could. He was naked, human, his body battered from more wounds than I could count. Blood coated his chest. He knelt among the dead and wounded Thrall, but he paid them no mind. His eyes were all for Dusty. She sat tailor-style on the rocky ground, keening; Rob's broken and blood-drenched body in her arms.

Someone had torn a ragged wound in his throat. He was alive, blood was still pouring from the wound, but his skin was the greenish gray of near death. But every time Tom tried to come close enough to do first aid, she turned on him, fighting, and he was too wounded to beat her off *and* tend to Rob.

I grabbed her hands. She fought me, but I held on. "Dusty," I dropped my shields and *pushed* at her with my mind as I called her name. "He's *not dead*. We may be able to save him if you just *let* us. Tom's a fireman. He knows first aid."

We can help you save the wolf, Not Prey, but first you must agree to help us save our children.

Dusty's eyes widened. She could hear them. I was surprised, even though I shouldn't have been.

You hate the wolves. Why would you save one?

We do not have enough power to both heal our young and bind them to Lewis. With your help we can. We can bring them to themselves and *make them part of the hive.*

I looked from Rob's ravaged body to Dusty's tear-stained face. She wasn't begging with words, but the plea was in her eyes, in the cant of her body.

Agreed. What do I need to do?

No words would adequately describe what they wanted, so they didn't tell me. They showed me. I closed my eyes and felt the essence of my power slip out of my skin. I could see my body as though from above, could see *everything*. It felt wonderful, right.

Come. The consciousness of the hive led me inside Rob's body. I was sending power into each individual hurt. I wouldn't heal him. His body would heal itself. My purpose was to provide the power, the energy to speed the process. I let go, and felt each injury sucking at my energy like a leech sucks blood. In my mind I watched as new flesh was born, sealing the horrible wounds, as new blood cells formed to replace those spilled onto the ground.

Enough. He will live. They pulled me away, and his body fought to hold on. The more I struggled, the more tightly he clung. I felt a wave of panic and *yanked* with all of my strength.

I came to myself, gasping for enough air to scream. I was in Tom's arms. I clung to him, shivering and terrified.

Rob coughed. Rolling off of Dusty's lap he rose to his hands and knees. I turned, burying my face in Tom's shoulder, but I could hear him throwing up. When he could speak, he whispered the words "I'm sorry" over and over again.

Lewis Carlton walked over to join us. He'd retrieved Rob and Tom's clothes from the Jeep, and dropped them onto the ground next to us.

"Do you know what we're going to do?" I asked him.

"Yeah."

"Are you okay with it?"

He shrugged. "Don't have a lot of choice. They're just a bunch of stupid kids, Reilly. I won't just let 'em die." He gave me a wry grin. "So I guess I get to be king."

"Queen, Carlton. You get to be a queen."

His eyebrows raised and his massive arms crossed over his chest with a finality that nearly made me laugh. "Not in this lifetime."

If I hadn't let my butt sink onto my feet I would have been swaying on my knees. The day hadn't been an easy one, and the thing with Rob had drained me badly. But I'd made a deal, and looking at Dusty and Rob holding each other I wouldn't even bitch about holding up my end.

What do I need to do?

There was a long pause. I felt their impatience, their anger. I'd drained myself too much on the wolf. I might not be strong enough to be of use to them and that frustrated them beyond belief.

"Dusty." I spoke softly. "I think I may need your help with this."

She nodded. Laying a kiss on Rob's lips she moved away from him. She scooted over until she was directly in front of me, and took my hands.

I, and they, felt her warmth, her strength. She had ability to burn. It was untrained and untapped, but it was there. She left it bare and unprotected, ready for me to use. *Do it.*

The queens' consciousness settled around me like a mist, and then *I* was the mist. It was similar to what I'd done healing Rob, but it was different, too. One by one my awareness went into each of the hosts, seeking the Thrall inside. When my mind brushed against each symbiont, I could feel the *wrongness* of it. It should have been vibrant, glowing with life and power. Instead, each one was closed off, alone, and very nearly dead. The creatures had been born without the connection they needed. Amanda had been psychic enough to contact them, but she wasn't a queen. She couldn't give the creatures what they needed. When she fell, they weren't tied enough to go with her. They weren't dead, but each symbiont was alone and in shock. I felt the queens focus their will. They sent a current of power pulsing into each creature, trying to jump-start its awareness. One by one they came shuddering into awareness. I felt a wave of crushing *need*, a sorrow and loneliness deep enough to swallow your sanity.

We are here, little ones. We are here.

I felt Carlton's presence moving to the front of my mind, so closely joined to that of his symbiont there was no separation between the two. In that instant I knew that he had chosen his fate, and knew why. Nor could I fault him for it. In the background I sensed thousands of individual personalities. Some were evil, some not. More than a few hated and feared me with a frightening intensity. They would see me dead if they could.

Carlton stepped in front of me, toward the helpless hosts. I felt the queens pour power into him, until he was a glowing, throbbing, presence. The lost ones felt it, too. In my mind I saw them reach for him, connect to him, and become whole.

A weary voice in my head said, *It is done.*

16

They say the truth will set you free. So far all it had done was to piss everybody off. Carlton's first *orders* to his new hive had been to cooperate completely with the police and the doctors and to "leave Reilly the fuck alone."

The police were not happy. They were not happy at all. Neither was I. Because somehow, in the confusion of healing Rob and binding the vampires, Amanda managed to get away. I had seen the damage to her chest. She should have been dead. She wasn't. The fact was utterly terrifying.

Of course the fact that there weren't any fatalities helped us legally, but there were bodies on the ground. The ER was overflowing with injured vampires, many of whom hadn't seen their seventeenth birthday.

I lay on a bed in a darkened hospital room, suffering from complete exhaustion and a migraine headache. In a few minutes the shot the doctor gave me would take effect and knock me out. I was looking forward to it. Right now the pain was a white-hot ice pick being driven into my left eyeball. Tears were running down my cheeks, and my stomach was roiling. Every time I threw up I was afraid my head would explode.

We were alive. We were all going to be all right. Tom and Rob were sharing the room next to me. I knew Dusty was with them because the migraine had given me super-acute hearing. Eventually the detectives would get around to questioning me. Right now they were busy with Carlton and his attorney.

I closed my eyes and tried to relax, letting my head sink into the pillow. Eventually the drugs kicked in and I slept.

I smelled coffee and felt warm sunshine on my skin. I wasn't completely awake yet, but I was aware enough to realize that I didn't hurt. The complete absence of pain is a wonderful thing. I decided then and there that people really don't appreciate it enough.

"Wake up, Reilly, before your coffee gets cold."

I opened my eyes and found John Brooks sitting in the visitor's chair next to my hospital bed. I hit the button, adjusting my bed to an upright position, and took the coffee from his hands. There was an untouched breakfast tray on one of those metal meal carts. Most of the food didn't look particularly appetizing, but there were some toast and a carton of orange juice that were probably salvageable.

I accepted the Starbucks cup from Brooks's hand and took a little sip of heaven as Brooks scooted the cart over to the bed so I could reach it.

"What are you doing here?"

"I just got back in town and decided to check my messages at the office. Good thing I did. Tom had called and told me what was going on up here. He figured it might be a good idea for me to come up. Things got ugly while you were out." Brooks sat back, stretching his legs. His navy trousers fell perfectly into place. The suit jacket that matched was draped over the back of the chair. His gun holster looked stark and black against the gleaming white of the starched cotton shirt he wore with the sleeves rolled up to reveal muscular black arms.

"Ugly *how?*"

He closed his eyes and let out a slow, controlled breath. "Nobody may have died last night, Reilly, but there are ten teenagers with serious injuries. Some of them are never going to be a hundred percent. All of the wounded are local high school kids. Let's just say that the local citizens are . . . unhappy with you."

"With *me*? How is any of this *my* fault?"

"How isn't it?" He gave an angry snort. "Don't delude yourself, Kate. If you'd called the police instead of charging up here—"

"Amanda would have killed them, Brooks. She was nuts and she had those kids under her sway, ready to do whatever she told them to. Cops would've died."

"Maybe, maybe not. We *are* trained to handle this shit, you know, and we're not idiots."

I finished chewing a bite of toast and forced it down. "You said it yourself. Local kids against the local cops? It would've been a blood bath."

"Hell, Reilly, it *was* a blood bath." Brooks ran his hands over his head in a gesture of frustrated fury. "The only reason you and your friends don't have your asses in jail right now is that every single one of the vamps has said that it was a trap and that you were all just defending yourselves. They're also saying that Lewis Carlton shot Amanda Shea to keep her from murdering you by bashing in your head with a bat."

"He did." I shook my head. "I don't know *why* he did, but he did."

"Right now the local police are guarding your rooms *and* the entrances to the hospital. I've been asked to be here while you make your statement because, as Not Prey, you can't lie to me. Assuming it matches up with all of the others you will be given a police escort all the way to Denver and *encouraged* to stay the hell away from the Western Slope."

"Happy to oblige." I took a deep breath and steadied myself before I spoke. "Are Tom and Rob all right?"

"Doctors say they'll be fine. Now, if you're done eating, I'll let the locals know you're ready to answer their questions."

At my nod, he rose to go to the door. I pulled the sheets up to my waist. The thin blue cotton hospital gown wasn't the most modest garment, and I felt strangely vulnerable. I could see the neck brace standing on the floor between the bed and the windows, its little padlock attached to the hasp. I'd needed it last night, but it couldn't save me from the danger I was facing now.

I turned my head at the sound of the door opening. Brooks was back, along with a local detective. Rage roiled around him in an almost visible cloud. He didn't introduce himself. I suspected it was an intentional slight.

I didn't do it deliberately, but I caught a glimpse into the local cop's mind. He blamed me for everything, and somehow he was going to prove it. I would *pay,* damn it; pay for every single one of those kids who'd been hurt. He knew them, knew their parents. There was no way they'd do something like this. And another thing, all their stories were the same. That just wasn't normal. No way. He didn't know how I'd brainwashed them, but he was sure I had. After all, wasn't I supposed to be some kind of a freaking psychic? Well, whatever I'd done, he'd get to the bottom of it.

I closed my eyes and took a deep breath. "Brooks, I think maybe I should have an attorney with me while we have this discussion."

"A *lawyer.*" The first detective spit the word out like venom.

"Ms. Reilly is entitled to an attorney if she wants one." The words were mild, but there was something in Brooks's eyes I couldn't read.

"It'll take hours for anyone to get here from Denver," he said bitterly.

"Still, she is entitled."

"Fine. Call your lawyer. Although why you couldn't have called before—" he didn't finish the sentence. He was simply too angry.

"I couldn't have called before. I wasn't awake 'til now." I tried to keep the words mild.

"Right." He turned on his heel and stormed from the room without another word.

Brooks settled back into the chair beside the bed, stretching his legs out in front of him and crossing them at the ankles. "I hope you know what you're doing, Kate. Asking for a lawyer makes it look like you have something to hide."

"Brooks, you're a good cop. Hell, most of the cops I've met are great guys with a tough job. But you saw him. He's already made up his mind I'm guilty. He's not going to let me walk away from here if he can help it."

Brooks didn't even try to argue. "No. He's not."

I threw off the covers and swung my legs off of the bed. "Do you have any idea where they put my cell phone?"

"Here." He reached into the pocket of his trousers and pulled out a slender phone made of silver plastic that was incredibly stylish, but looked delicate enough that if it were mine, I'd be terrified of breaking it. He flipped it open, and passed it over to me. "Use mine."

My first call was to directory assistance. They patched me through to the attorney's office. I'd chosen the same man who I'd been referred to about the criminal charges the hospital was pressing. The attorney who'd handled the wrongful death claim didn't work with criminal cases—and I'd heard the one I was calling was one of the best in the business. Unfortunately he was also busy. I explained to his assistant what had happened, and asked that she have him call me back just as soon as possible.

I was released from the hospital at ten and taken directly to the police station for questioning. It was a small brick building painted white that shone in the sunshine. I got to sit in a nasty little room that looked almost exactly like the ones you see on television, only cleaner and less cheerful. The chair was designed for maximum discomfort, and by the time the attorney arrived I'd lost all track of time and my butt was completely numb.

The attorney wasn't the senior partner I'd called. He was scheduled to be in U.S. District Court all day defending an alleged drug kingpin. Instead, I was being represented by a junior associate, one Gary Hamilton. He was short, with a swimmer's build. His round, freckled face and sandy hair made him look like he was all of twelve years old. His suit was expensive, and well cut, but he looked more like a kid dressed up for a wedding or Sunday school than an attorney. Still, I didn't doubt that there was a sharp mind behind those candid green eyes. If there wasn't, he wouldn't have been hired to work at one of the top Denver defense firms.

He asked for, and was given, a few minutes to talk to me privately to find out just exactly what was going on. And from the moment he asked me his first question I knew I was going to have no complaints about his representation. He was obviously shrewd and perfectly capable of using his innocent appearance to his advantage.

"All right. It's a mess, but based on what I learned before I came in here, I think we'll be all right. Just answer the questions, unless I tell you otherwise. Don't volunteer additional information. Just answer each question as asked."

"I understand." I did. It was the same advice I'd been given prior to giving testimony down in Denver.

Gary walked over and opened the door. He leaned out into the hallway and announced, "We're ready when you are."

Brooks came in with the detective. Gary sat next to me. Brooks took a seat on the short side of the table. The detective sat to Brooks's left, directly across from Gary and me.

Gary introduced himself to Brooks and the local detective. I learned that his name was Allcock. I was very good. I didn't laugh. The poor man had probably spent his entire life being harassed about his name. The men all shook hands. No one held out their hand for me to shake, but I already knew Brooks, and Hamilton was representing me. Besides, I was the defendant. I suppose that meant I wasn't entitled to the niceties.

The questioning was relentless, and tedious. Allcock asked questions. Brooks repeated them. When the lawyer didn't object, I answered Brooks.

"Why did you come up to the mountains?"

"I received a message from Amanda Shea saying she'd be up there. I needed to speak with her to find out if she knew anything about the disappearance of some Thrall eggs from a hospital in Denver."

"Did you come up with the express intent of killing Ms. Shea?"

I'd opened my mouth to reply when a touch on my arm shut it. "Don't answer that, Kate," Gary said.

On and on it went. Question after question. I started squirming in my seat. I had to go to the bathroom. My stomach was growling, and I was beginning to worry about Tom and the others.

Eventually even the attorney grew weary of it, and he was getting paid by the hour. "Detective Allcock, my client has been extremely cooperative. You have questioned her extensively, and I *believe* her responses have been borne out by the other witness statements. If you're not going to charge her, it's time to let her go."

The detective obviously didn't want to. But he couldn't legally stop my leaving unless he charged me with something, or made me a "material witness." I could see the temptation to do just that pass over his face. But when he caught a glimpse of the attorney he backed down. He surrendered to the inevitable with ill grace, letting me go with a strong admonishment not to leave the state without letting him know. Then he stormed out, slamming the door hard enough to make the one-way mirrors rattle.

"Charming." I muttered the word under my breath. The attorney smiled. Brooks didn't. "Is there a restroom anywhere around here?"

"Through that door and on the left," Brooks advised.

I left them talking earnestly as we exited the interrogation room. I didn't care what they had to say right now. I needed a bathroom, and sooner rather than later.

I found the restroom and gladly made use of it. When I was done I stood at the sink and washed my hands and face. Amazingly, my purse hadn't gotten lost in all the confusion. It had made it from the Jeep to the hospital, and with me from the hospital to the police station. I was glad. Replacing everything would be a problem, and getting new identification is a damned nuisance. I unbraided my hair and then rummaged in my purse for my hairbrush. By the time I was finished with my toilette I was starting to feel like a human being again.

When I stepped into the hall, neither Brooks nor attorney Hamilton was anywhere in sight. I followed the sound of voices and let myself out through the door at the end of the hallway. I stepped into a tiny lobby area. There were four molded plastic chairs in a shade of dark brown that exactly matched the vending machines. Tom sat in one of them. He wasn't alone. His Acca, Mary Connolly, was with him. She wore a very businesslike black suit with a red blouse, and low-heeled pumps that clicked on the tile as she paced back and forth across the gleaming linoleum. She'd probably come straight from work, where she was a parole officer for violent teenaged offenders. Nobody was talking, and the tension was thick enough to slice.

"Where are Dusty and Rob?"

"They're still questioning them." Tom spoke softly.

"Do they have an attorney?"

"Yes." Mary answered, her voice tight with fury. Her golden brown eyes had narrowed to slits. Her compact body practically vibrated with controlled anger. "Reilly, when this is over, and we can all go back to Denver, you and I are going to have a little *chat* about your dragging my people into danger."

"She didn't *drag* us," Tom protested.

Mary whirled to face him, and he pulled back from her in fear. "Shut *up*, Tom. Don't you even speak to me right now."

I glanced over at the far wall. There was a window of bulletproof glass with a uniformed officer sitting at a desk. At the moment she appeared to be working the radio, but there was a bank of black and white televisions next to her, and I saw the lobby pictured on one of them.

I kept my voice low, making sure my back was to both the window and the camera. "I'm sorry. I was wrong. I shouldn't have brought them along."

I watched her close her eyes and count to at least one hundred. "You admit that."

"They could've been killed. Hell, Rob almost *was*."

"Katie—" Tom started to speak, but a look from Mary silenced him.

"I knew Amanda was laying a trap for me. I suspected she'd stolen the eggs. I *didn't* know she'd made her own nest and was going to try to use the hosts to kill me. I figured she'd want to do that all by herself."

Mary opened her eyes. She gave me a long, searching look, but her body language had relaxed fractionally. I watched her force herself to relax. "God, Reilly, only you can get into such unmitigated disasters. What *is* it with you, anyway?"

"I don't know." It was God's honest truth.

Mary stared at me long and hard. "This isn't over between us. I appreciate the apology, but it's not enough. You put our surrogate in danger along with two of our pack members." She swept her hands outward in a gesture of frustration. "And Rob's got a record. If they press assault charges it could really go badly for him."

We heard the latch of the door I'd come through a few

minutes ago and turned as one. Brooks stepped through. "Kate, you ready to go?"

"What about the Jeep?"

"Impounded for evidence. I'll give you a ride, but we need to leave through the back door. Our escort is waiting outside."

I shot Mary a mute appeal for guidance. I didn't want to abandon Dusty and Rob, but I wasn't sure whether my being here would be a help or hindrance.

"Go home, Kate."

Tom started to rise, but Mary put a restraining hand on his arm, squeezing hard enough that her knuckles whitened. He'd have bruises.

"You stay here. We're going to have a little chat."

Tom swallowed hard, but his jaw thrust stubbornly forward. "Yes, ma'am. Kate, I'll see you in the morning."

Mary gave a low growl. "Reilly, go. Your being here isn't helping anything, and you need to get out of here before the locals get together a lynch mob."

"Do you think they will?" Tom asked.

"Why do you think she's getting a police escort?" She snorted in derision. "It isn't 'cause they like her."

17

I walked out the back door of the police station between Brooks and a uniformed officer who was walking like he had a stick up his butt. I could almost hear his teeth grinding over the crunch of the crusted snow beneath our feet. He was probably about my age, more or less. He looked even younger than Gary Hamilton. It almost made me feel sorry for him. Or it would have, if he hadn't kept his hand hovering near his gun. He was pissed and trying to look intimidating. It wasn't working. I had no doubt he was willing to shoot, but he wouldn't look scary doing it.

At the edge of the sidewalk there were three vehicles with their engines running. The first and last were police cruisers, their lights flashing blue and red in the fading daylight. I'd spent the entire day at the station. It was no wonder I was hungry and tired.

Brooks led me to the middle vehicle, an older model Ford Bronco. Like him, it was big, burly, and well maintained. The navy blue paint gleamed with a fresh coat of wax, and the chrome step-plate reflected the flashing lights.

I climbed into the passenger seat. When Brooks took the wheel, our little caravan was off.

As we passed through the front lot I saw people gathered in small groups talking to each other. There were news vans, of course, and several of the locals were gesturing angrily as they talked to the camera under the glaring lights.

We were moving too slow. I wanted the hell out of here before something bad happened, but the driver in front of us was crawling along. One of the news crews spotted us and pointed. People began shouting and running toward the car. Brooks swore like a sailor and cranked the wheel hard to the right. I saw someone bend down. A moment later one of the landscaping rocks crashed into the passenger window. It was safety glass, so it didn't exactly shatter, but the impact crushed the glass in the spot by where my head had been and sent cracks across the rest of the window as Brooks threw the Bronco in gear and stomped on the gas.

The vehicle leaped forward and right, hard enough to slam my head against the headrest as Brooks ignored the driveway and exited by jumping the curb and going over the grass. I thanked God for the seatbelt and grabbed the panic handle as the shoulder harness jerked across my throat, nearly choking me. As the tires hit the road Brooks shifted again and we left the scene with a squeal of tires, both cop cars trailing behind.

"Idiots! Fucking idiots! Were they *trying* to get us killed?" Brooks slammed a meaty palm against the dashboard, his face livid.

I didn't say a word because anything that came out of my mouth would just make things worse. He was already pissed enough without that. But I couldn't help wondering if maybe, just maybe, the driver in front hadn't been thinking exactly that. At the moment there were just too many people who wanted me dead.

I leaned my head against the seat back and closed my eyes. I was exhausted. But more than that, I was weary. Life had been one crisis after another for months now. I'd been running on adrenaline and determination. Unfortunately, you can only go on that way for so long. Both my mind and body had reached the end of their endurance. I needed rest. If someone attacked right now, I wasn't positive I would be able to lift a hand to defend myself.

I felt Brooks's gaze, but didn't even have enough energy to open my eyes. After a long moment he spoke.

"It's a long drive, Reilly. Get some rest. We'll talk later."

"Reilly." A meaty hand landed on my shoulder and gave me a shake. "Wake up. I need the pass code."

I blinked in confusion. We were at the gate to the garage at my place. Apparently I'd slept through the whole trip. Wow.

"The pass code?" Brooks repeated.

"Yeah, right. Okay." I shook my head, trying to clear it of the cobwebs that seemed to want to take up permanent residence. "82719."

He punched the buttons in sequence. Like magic, the gate began to rise. I yawned, my jaw stretching far enough to make my ears pop. I needed more sleep, but even the little bit of rest on the ride home had helped. I felt better. Not good, but functional.

Brooks pulled the Bronco into the empty spot with Tom's apartment number on it and put the vehicle in park.

I reached to unfasten my seatbelt, but he stopped me with a hand on my arm.

"All right, Reilly, this is as private as it gets. I need you to tell me what in the hell is going on. I got your messages, but they didn't make a lot of sense."

I leaned back, trying to decide where to start. So much had happened. Fortunately I hadn't done anything that wasn't perfectly legal and above-board. One of the great things about honesty is how it really does simplify things.

Taking a deep breath, I started with the meeting with Doug and Carlton. It took a while even though Brooks didn't interrupt. He simply sat there, utterly silent, his eyes getting wider by the minute. When we reached my waking up in the hospital I stopped.

"Jesus. What a mess!" He shook his head, opened his mouth to speak, then closed it without saying a word. We sat in a well of silence so profound that I could hear the traffic outside the garage. I watched as he pulled himself together, putting on his work face piece by piece until, once again, he was the ultimate professional cop.

"All right. I'm still technically on sympathy leave, but I'll make some calls, check on the other Not Prey, see if you're right about our being hunted. They could just be dreams, you know."

I heard *sympathy leave*, but he didn't give away any more information, so I didn't quite feel right about asking. I gave him a long look, but didn't say anything.

"Amanda isn't a host, so technically she is responsible for what she did. Warrants will issue. Sooner or later we'll find her and bring her in."

"I don't doubt you'll find her, but bring her in? Not a chance. At least not if what the queens said is true."

"They can't lie. What did they say?"

I concentrated, trying to remember everything they had said. "She's a monster. What she did to herself has made her powerful enough that the entire collective is absolutely terrified of her. They said she can heal almost any injury, and that her psychic abilities would put Monica's to shame."

Brooks shuddered. Neither one of us was liable to forget how the past Thrall queen of Denver had successfully used mind control on an entire mob.

"Amanda will know they're coming. If we're lucky, she'll just disappear. If not—" I left the sentence unfinished.

"So what, you think *you* should take care of it instead." He was practically quivering with anger, but he managed to keep his voice under complete control.

I shuddered. "Not if I can help it."

He was a smart man. He heard the implication behind the words. "You don't think you'll have a choice?"

"She's not sane and she's fixated on me. What do you think?"

He gave a gusty sigh. "I *think* I'd better call my wife, let her know I'm not going to be home for a while. *Then* I'm going to do some research, see if I can find any records of anyone dealing with something like this in the past: what they did, how they handled it."

"Is your wife going to be pissed?"

Brooks thought about it for a moment, then gave a wry grin. "Probably. But she'll get over it. She knows the drill." He reached into his pocket and withdrew his wallet. He took out a business card and passed it to me. "This has my cell number on it in case you need to reach me."

"Thanks, Brooks. I appreciate it." I unfastened my seat belt and opened the door. As I climbed out of the Bronco I told him, "Someday I'd really like to meet your wife. She's got to be one hell of a woman."

"Yeah." Just thinking about his wife made him grin. "She's something all right. Keeps me in line, that's for damned sure."

"Good that somebody can," I teased.

"You telling me that Tom doesn't do the same thing for you?"

I felt the humor starting to drain away. Tom did that, and so much more. But the way Mary had been acting . . . well, I couldn't be sure what the future would hold. Tom was a werewolf. The pack meant everything to him. If he had to choose—

"You worry too much, Reilly." Brooks spoke gently, his expression softening. "He loves you. He's not going anywhere."

"I hope you're right."

"I'm right. You'll see."

I climbed out of the vehicle and grabbed my purse from

the floorboard. "When do you think I'll be able to pick up the Jeep? The lease company isn't going to be happy. Neither will my credit card company."

"I dunno. I'll make some calls. See what I find out."

"I hate to pay for a car when I can't even use it."

"Yeah, well, all I can say is I hope you got the supplemental insurance."

18

I slept until nearly noon. I might not even have woken then if Blank hadn't jumped onto my chest and started nagging me about giving him a can of soft food. Despite an acute lack of coffee, I felt good physically; better than I had in a while. My head was clear. My body wasn't hurting. I fed the cat, set the coffee brewing, and ran a bath. Sunshine flooded the apartment, and it lifted my spirits. Nobody had died. Yes, things were pretty grim on a lot of levels, but there was hope.

I felt even better when I checked my messages. Tom had called. The district attorney had decided not to press charges against Rob or Dusty. They were on their way back, but it would be a few hours.

The only food in the house for humans was cold pizza, and not much of that. I really did need to go to the store soon. If I managed to get through the next two or three hours without a life-threatening disaster I'd try to get that done. I snorted, amused at my own joke. It's good that I amuse myself, because half the time my sense of humor just annoys the hell out of everybody else.

Speaking of pissy, my brother Joe was due back from his business trip in a couple of hours. I knew I should probably give him a call later, invite him over to watch a movie, find out how the trip went. But if I did he'd ask me about my life. I didn't want to talk about my life right now because it would start a fight. My new goal as of this moment was to get through an entire day without a major argument or physical fight. I was sure I could do it—but it would be a hell of a lot easier if I didn't see Joe. How sad was that?

I heard a horn out front and wandered over to the windows. What I saw made me choke on the last bite of pepperoni. A familiar green Hummer pulled to the curb, and Tom was in the passenger seat.

I dropped the pizza crust and dashed to the door. Vampires and werewolves *hate* each other. What in the *hell* was going on?

I thundered down the narrow staircase, my bare feet slamming against the cold metal as my mind sought Tom's. I panicked when I couldn't feel his presence. *Shit*. My hands slammed against the bar to operate the fire door on the first floor and I dashed through and across the lobby. I was on my way through the front door in time to see Carlton helping Tom up from the seat.

He'd been beaten badly by somebody who knew what they were doing. His hair was matted with blood. One eye had swollen completely shut. His lip had been split. It was obvious that even the slightest movement was causing him pain. He couldn't even stand up straight on his own. The beating wouldn't kill him, but even a werewolf can only heal so much. He'd be miserable for days.

 rushed outside and moved next to them, sliding my arm
 d Tom's waist and his around my shoulder until I was
 ng most of his weight. Carlton took the other side.

He kicked the car door closed and the three of us staggered into the building.

"What happened? Shouldn't we be taking him to the hospital?"

"No," Tom answered. There was force behind the word. It came out clearly, despite the split lip.

"Tom—" I put a pleading note in my voice. This was bad. He could have internal injuries.

"No!" He growled, and it wasn't a human sound. I turned slowly, my eyes inches from that mouth. Up close the damage looked even worse. I was scared, but more than that I was angry. Who in the hell had done this to him and why?

"People are staring. We'd better get him upstairs."

I looked around. Carlton was right. It was Saturday, so there weren't as many people on the street as usual, but there were plenty of spectators just the same. Most were staring at us as if we were putting on quite the show. I glared at one or two, and they quickly averted their eyes.

The three of us made it into the building and across the lobby. We were moving as carefully as we could, but even then there were moments when Tom would give an involuntary gasp of pain. I reached awkwardly with my left hand for the elevator button, with Carlton supporting most of Tom's weight as we waited for it to arrive.

"What happened?"

Tom was being stubbornly silent, so it was Carlton who answered.

"He defied his Acca. She said you were a threat to the pack, told him he had to give you up. He said he wouldn't, that he'd leave the pack first. So she pulled over, beat the shit out of him, and left him on the side of the road in a snowbank."

I stared, openmouthed with shock long enough that the elevator arrived. The doors slid open and Carlton lurched forward.

I hit the button for my floor and the doors whooshed

closed. "Mary did this?" My words were dangerously soft. Anger is hot. Rage, for me at least, is cold. At this moment I felt an icy fury. She could have killed him, wolf or not, he could have died, right there by the side of the road.

"My choice." There was pain in his voice, but determination as well. "Not yours."

Carlton gave me a look over the top of Tom's bent head. I recognized it as a warning. I just wasn't sure whether I was ready to heed it. Because while it might have been Tom's choice, it was *my* fault. Oh, he'd defied her all right. But she'd been pissed at me and had taken it out on him.

"There's always a price for defying the boss, Reilly," Carlton said. "It was his choice, his price to pay. Just like I'm going to pay for this."

"You'll catch hell for bringing him here?" It made sense that he would. But then why had he done it? Even after having seen into some of his thoughts, Lewis Carlton just confused the hell out of me.

"Duh. No shit, Sherlock. They're our enemies." He gave me a look that said as clearly as words that I was being naive to the point of stupidity. "But the trouble I get into for this is *nothing* compared to what'll happen if they find out I told you what I'm about to."

"I thought they knew everything you did?" The tone of my voice made it a question.

He shook his head and smiled, baring his fangs. "Eventually I'll be strong enough to pull out by myself, but not yet. Still, having Fido here with me cut me a break. It's helping me block them out."

The elevator jerked to a stop. Tom gave a small moan of pain and I flinched in sympathy. The three of us shambled forward. Lewis supported most of Tom's weight while I ̶ ̶ ̶ed the heavy steel apartment door, then the two of us ̶ ̶ ̶ him over to the couch. Tom collapsed onto the soft ̶ ̶ ̶ Groaning, he turned and lay down, closing his eyes. ̶ ̶ ̶ the walk-in closet and retrieved one of my mother's old knitted afghans and used it to tuck Tom in. Kneeling by the couch, I stroked his blood-matted hair and fought down alternating waves of rage and sadness as he drifted into sleep. His chest rose and fell in an even rhythm, a soft snore passing his lips.

"You really love him, don't you?"

Carlton's voice startled me. I'd forgotten he was there. It was a stupid mistake to make. Under different circumstances something like that could get me killed.

I kissed Tom's forehead and rose to my feet. "Yes. I do."

"If you try to deal with his Acca on this behind his back you'll be handing him his dick on a platter."

"Poetic."

He grinned. "Maybe, but I know you. You'd ignore subtle."

I couldn't argue. He was right. But it was a little alarming that he understood me that well. He really *shouldn't*.

"So, I'm supposed to just—"

"Let him handle it. He's a big boy. It's his business. Let him deal with it. It's not like you don't have enough problems of your own." Carlton walked over to the recliner and took a seat. I hadn't invited him to, I'd hoped he'd say his piece and leave. It was ungrateful of me. He'd saved Tom after all. But even though I liked him, I couldn't trust him.

I sighed. "I'd offer you something, but I haven't had time to go to the grocery."

"Not a problem." Using the lever on the side of the chair, he pushed it into a reclining position. I fought not to laugh. Big as the chair was, he dwarfed it. The foot rest hit him mid-calf and his head stuck up above the back.

"So what did you want to tell me?"

"We're setting you up." He turned, looking me straight in the eye. His expression was serious enough that I forgot all about the chair.

"Excuse me?"

"Your ex-girlfriend is an abomination. She can't be killed with a bullet. I knew that when I pulled the trigger."

"So what does it take to kill her?"

Carlton settled himself deeper in the chair, his eyes scanned the apartment, taking in everything. "You ever watch the old vampire movies?"

I just stood there staring at him for long moments. I'm sure my jaw had dropped. I could almost feel the breeze on my tongue. "A stake in the heart? You've got to be kidding me."

"Not *just* a stake, Buffy. Once you stake her, you take her head. And, if you can arrange it, you cremate the body." He'd taken off his sunglasses. Looking into his eyes I could see that he was deadly serious.

"Sweet Jesus!"

"I was supposed to let her kill you, *then* take her out." Carlton closed his eyes. He seemed perfectly comfortable, utterly relaxed. He'd been wearing the same clothes for more than twenty-four hours, but they didn't look particularly rumpled. Nor was he half as tired as I would have expected.

"So why didn't you?" I was honestly curious. As he'd said before, disobedience always has consequences, generally severe ones. "She was ready to do the job, and I couldn't have stopped her."

"I *like* you." He turned his head. His eyes met mine, expression intent. "Hell, if I'd met you a year or so ago, I'd be giving Fido here a run for his money."

I blinked. It was the last thing I would've expected to hear. I was flattered, but at the same time thinking about it made me nervous as hell.

"Thank you. I'm flattered. A little startled, but flattered."

A grin lit up his face. "You should be." He hit the lever and stood in a blur of motion too quick for me to follow. "Be careful, Buffy. You're not paranoid if they really are out to get you."

19

Tom slept on the couch. I got up to check on him several times during the night. Each time his face had healed a little bit more. It was fascinating, and a little bit spooky. I was furious with Mary, but Carlton was right. I had to let Tom handle this. I hated it. But that didn't make it any less necessary. If I expected him to respect my ability to deal with the Thrall, then I had to show him the same respect in his dealings with the pack, at least I did if I wanted the relationship to work. But it wasn't easy.

I was wide awake bright and early, despite the interruptions to my sleep to check on Tom. I knew that if I kept moving around the apartment I'd wind up waking him up. It would be far better for him to sleep through as much of the pain as he could than be up and miserable. So I got dressed and ready as quietly as I could, left a note on the refrigerator, and tiptoed out of the apartment to run a couple of errands.

"Bless me, father, for I have sinned—" I spoke the words I had learned by rote back when I was in second grade. Like most Catholics, I hate going to confession. I know I need to. I even feel better afterward. But I still hate it, particularly now that they've instituted their "friendly" policy where you sit face-to-face with the priest and talk. There isn't even the illusion of privacy. I mean, yes, even back in the old days there was a good chance that Father John would recognize my voice and say "Now, Katie—" but if I didn't *want* to be recognized I could go to one of the other churches, walk into one of the old-fashioned booths with a screen, and know I couldn't be recognized.

Today, instead, I was sitting in a nice little room with a statue of the virgin mother and a pair of metal folding chairs. In the seat opposite me was a short, round, middle-aged priest with a mop of coarse dark curls liberally laced with gray. His hooked nose was out of proportion with the rest of his face and would have completely dominated his appearance if it weren't for his bushy dark brows that looked as though they might crawl off his face at any moment.

I needed advice from somebody who didn't have a stake in the situation and would be able to keep his mouth shut. Thus, I'd very deliberately taken a very early and fairly long bus ride to give my confession to the priest at St. Patrick's Parish in Wheat Ridge. St. Pat's is an octagonal building built of white stone. It sits at the crest of a hill and sparkles in the sun, or gleams in the moonlight. The pale stone sets off the colors of the stained glass, so that they glow like jewels. It's not a big church, but it has a healthy, active parish. Masses are well attended every week, not just on the major holidays. I still prefer Our Lady church, but St. Pat's is my second favorite.

I love Michael, but I *so* didn't want to discuss my relationship with Tom with him. No. Just, so no. Oh and my other reasons for going to confession wouldn't make him happy either. So I'd set the alarm painfully early so that I could go to 7:00 A.M. confession at a church in the suburbs.

"What can I do for you, Ms. Reilly?"

So much for anonymity.

"Father—"

"Akins. I'm sorry if I startled you by using your name, but you've appeared prominently in the news a number of times, and I've spoken with Michael about you often enough that I feel as though I know you." He smiled benignly.

Better and better.

"This isn't easy," I admitted.

"It isn't supposed to be. Just talk to me."

I talked. I started with the ordinary sins, things like missing mass. Then I took a deep breath and launched into my relationship with Tom. It was awkward, but not nearly as bad as I thought it would be.

"But that isn't really why you came here, is it?" His small brown eyes were piercing and carried the weight of his intelligence and experience. I got the impression from the look he gave me that there wasn't much he hadn't seen or heard. "You're here because of what happened in the mountains."

"They could have died, Father."

"Your friends?" He leaned forward, putting his elbows on his knees. He had big hands, rough, as though he were accustomed to using them for physical labor rather than the usual priestly duties.

"Yes. They could have been killed. Rob almost was. And in spite of the confessions by all the vampires, the police seriously considered charging him. He could have had to go to trial for assault and he has a record."

"He *did* attack those teenagers."

"It was self-defense. They were Thrall. They were trying to kill us."

"They were trying to kill *you*." He corrected me. He was leaning forward, his dark eyes intent.

"Yes."

"And you feel responsible." The air-conditioning kicked on, making his stole sway slightly.

I met his gaze steadily. "Yes."

"You've been talking about your friends. What about your enemies? I know there were many wounded. Were you directly responsible for any of them?"

"I didn't kill anyone." It sounded defensive, even to my own ears.

"But you would have?" He leaned back, raising an eyebrow. I could feel the weight of judgment in his stare.

There was no getting around the question, and telling the truth wouldn't put me in any worse light. "Yes."

"Did you go up there *intending* to kill?" He was deliberately pushing me. I knew it was his job, but that didn't make me any less angry about it. I had to close my eyes and take several deep breaths to calm down before I answered the question.

"I didn't *plan* on it, but I knew it was a possibility. Amanda is insane. I knew it was a trap."

"And rather than call the police, you went up there yourself."

"Yes."

"I think we can add *pride* to the list of sins." It was a dry observation and probably not far from the mark. I knew I should think about that, and I would. But we had finally come upon the root of my visit here, and I couldn't *not* talk about it.

"The thing is, I learned something up there, something important."

"Yes?"

"Rob was dying. To keep the hosts alive, the queens offered me a deal. They'd show me how to heal him if I helped them connect the hatchlings to Carlton as their queen."

"You accepted?"

"Yes. I helped them, and we healed Rob. In fact, I think . . . I think I might be able to heal other things. Before I started looking for the eggs for the queens they said they could show me how to heal Bryan and some of the other zombies."

I paused and his face took on a whole new light. "That's *wonderful*. Michael will be so happy!"

"It is wonderful . . . and . . . well, *terrifying*. I mean, this is something only *I* can do. No, wait, the queens can do it. They can even heal coma victims. They actually did that once. For a price."

"Ah." He nodded and gestured with his hands for me to continue.

"So how much of it is pride? The Thrall say that Amanda is an abomination. According to the rules they can't lie to me. So I have to believe them when they tell me that she has phenomenal psychic abilities and that the only way to kill her is to cut off her head and stake her in the heart."

The priest was dumbstruck, his eyes wide with shock.

"I could tell the cops, but, if she's as strong as the queens say, Amanda could cloud the minds of the police. They'd be totally vulnerable. Besides, it's me she'll be coming after. She's going to try to kill me. I know it as well as I know my own name. I can't just sit back and let her murder me, and with the powers the Thrall eggs gave her she'd cut through the cops like a hot knife through butter. Am I supposed to 'let them handle it' when I *know* they can't; that good people will *die?*"

"So you intend to kill her." His voice was heavy with disapproval.

"I don't want to." It was the absolute truth. I didn't. I still remembered the good times, when she'd been my friend. I still liked her mother. "But the Amanda the world knew—the human who might have been saved—is already dead and gone."

I'd come looking for advice, for comfort. But I wasn't going to get any. I could tell from the rigid anger in his posture, the stern tone of his voice. "I can't give you absolution for this. You know it is wrong, know it is a mortal sin, and yet you are determined to do it anyway."

"So what do you suggest? Am I supposed to just sit back and *let* her murder me, and kill anyone who might get in her way in the process? Should I walk to my death, knowing full well that all of the zombies who might be saved, will remain trapped in their own minds?"

His fingers clenched together until the knuckles were white and he stared so hard at the candelabra in the corner that it should have been able to float through his will. "There has got to be another alternative."

"Fine. Tell me what it is. I'm *dying* to know." I couldn't keep the sarcasm from my voice. I was starting to get well and truly pissed. I was tired, angry, and afraid. I was sick of this priest implying that somehow the fact that I was being hunted and harassed was all my fault.

"Kate, you are a singular human being. You've been given extraordinary talents. You're supposed to *use* them in the way God intended."

"And how do I know what God intended?"

"*That* is the tricky part. But I'd remind you they're called the ten *commandments,* not the ten *suggestions.*"

"So you don't have any constructive thoughts, right?" I snapped. "It's just good luck and fare thee well, but don't do anything horrible, even though everyone else gets to."

"No." His eyes flashed, but he controlled his temper. "But I'll pray about it."

"So will I."

I got up and left. He hadn't given me absolution or told me my penance. We hadn't said the usual closing prayers. But the conversation was over.

I was preoccupied when I stepped out of the church, which is why I tripped on the first step and fell with bruising force onto my knees.

That stumble probably saved my life.

I heard the explosion a fraction of a second before the stone above my head splintered, sending sharp shards of rock in every direction. I flung myself flat and began belly-crawling backward as fast as I could. A second shot rang out. It hit barely an inch from my face. Jagged bits of stone dug into the skin of my cheek as I scanned the area looking for the shooter.

An old red pickup was parked across the street from the church. There were two men. The passenger was reloading his rifle. The driver had started the engine running.

I heard sirens in the distance. The cops were coming. Out of the corner of my eye, I glimpsed the door to the church opening. Strong hands grabbed me around the ankles, pulling me inside as the rifleman fired again.

As the door swung closed I heard the squeal of tires. I let out a breath I hadn't realized I'd been holding. I tried to stand, but my knees gave out on me half-way up. I would've fallen on my ass if Father Akins hadn't caught me.

"You're bleeding. How badly are you hurt?"

"I'm fine." I gasped out the words.

"You are *not* fine." He half dragged, half carried me into the church proper and dropped me into a pew. "Your face is a mess. There's a splinter of rock sticking out of your skin not a half inch away from your left eye!"

I hadn't felt the pain until he said it. Adrenaline is an amazing thing. It can mask pain and give you the strength to fight or flee. Right now my heart was pounding in my chest so loud I could barely hear the sirens outside or the shouts of the police as they came through the church doors. But by the time the ambulance arrived to take me to the hospital for the second time in less than a week, I was completely wiped out.

I'd told the police everything I knew, but it wasn't much. Two men in a red truck had tried to kill me.

20

Tom, Joe, and Mike burst through the door of the emergency room at Lutheran Hospital looking furious, frightened, and intimidating as hell. I was peeking out of one of those little curtained-off areas that give you the illusion of privacy. A uniformed police officer appeared out of nowhere, stopping them before they could get anywhere near the desk.

"It's all right, officer. They're the good guys." The 's' sound was a little slurred. I'd been given a local anesthetic in my face when they'd started picking out the rocks. It hadn't completely worn off yet, but I already hurt enough to know that it was going to be a miserable evening.

The cop gave me a look over his shoulder that made it clear he wasn't sure he believed me. I couldn't say as I blamed him. Mike might be wearing his clerical uniform, but he's built like the hockey player he once was, and his expression was just as thunderous as the other two. My brother Joe is big, not just tall but *big*—heavily muscled and broad, and he has a redheaded Irish temper that was at full boil. Of the three of them Tom looked the least intimidating, but there was a sense of power around him that would keep anyone the least bit sensitive at bay.

The cop moved out of the way, but reluctantly. The three of them stepped into my "room," pulling the drapes closed behind them.

"Where's Bryan?" I asked.

Tom was the one who answered. "Mary and Dusty came over. They're watching Bryan and the others."

"Oh." I wasn't sure what to say. I was too surprised. It was an amazingly nice thing for them to do, and completely unexpected under the circumstances.

"She didn't do it for you," Joe snarled. "She did it for me. We've been dating for a little over a month now, and when I asked her to help out she said yes."

If I had full control of my mouth, I would have dropped my jaw. As it was, it was already half dropped. But . . . *um*? My brother was dating the Acca of the werewolf pack? Yikes. I guess, thinking about it, they really were well suited to each other. They have the same values, background, even the same sense of humor. Joe can be a bit of a bully. He needed someone with enough strength to stand up to him. Mary was certainly capable of that. But, wow, I just really hadn't seen that coming. And oh shit wasn't that going to complicate matters with regard to me, Tom, and the pack.

"Aren't you going to say anything?" Joe growled. He was glaring down at me, daring me to disapprove.

"Who you date is none of my business. Besides, I like her. I've always liked her. Even when she does stupid shit."

"And until the other day she liked you, too."

Ouch. Well, wasn't he just being a charmer. Then again, that's his way. The more nervous he is, the more aggressive he gets. But I've lived my entire life with my big brother, and I don't get intimidated easily.

Mike looked from one to the other of us and sighed. I

could see him make the decision to interrupt us before things got out of hand. "So what happened?"

I told him the whole story. He shook his head in bemusement. "Do you have any idea who wants to kill you?"

"It'd be easier to make a list of who doesn't," Joe muttered under his breath.

"That is *it*." Tom stepped between Joe and me. His eyes were dark, and his body language more threatening than I'd ever seen it. You could almost see the power vibrating in the air around him. "You will *not* talk to Kate that way in front of me. Ever. And I will sure as *hell* not have you verbally attacking her while she is injured in the emergency room. I don't give a fuck if you're her brother, or who you're dating."

Joe's face got red, and he puffed himself up. The cop appeared at the slit in the curtains just as I slid off of the examining table. Mike was there first. Standing between them with a hand on either of their chests.

"Both of you stop. Right now. The last thing Kate needs is to deal with the two of you." He turned to Joe, giving him a hard look. "You have been baiting him ever since we picked you up at the airport. Hell, *I've* wanted to punch your lights out. And you know I'll do it if you keep it up."

Joe blinked and took a step backward. He opened his mouth, but Mike waved him to silence.

"Kate is an *adult,* Joe. She's not a child. She makes her own decisions."

"If he loved her, he'd protect her—see to it she stayed safe," Joe snarled.

Oh, that pissed me off. It surely did. More so because I saw the words hit Tom like a blow.

"How *dare* you!" I stepped around the examining bed and started toward my brother. Tom reached over to grab my arm as I stalked past him, but I shrugged him off. The cop was through the curtains now, but I didn't care.

Joe turned to me, his face almost purple with rage. Spit

flew from his mouth as he shouted at me. "It's the truth! You have no business getting involved in this sort of shit! You pretend to be so damned tough, like you're some sort of Superwoman. Well, you're not and *somebody* needs to get that through your thick Irish skull before you get yourself killed."

I stared at him for a long, silent moment. I stood in the face of his rage, my mind and emotions gone still and cold. I'd gotten angry. And as frequently happened when my emotions got the better of me my shields had dropped. Without that barrier between us, I'd seen inside Joe's mind. For the very first time I actually understood. Joe might love me, but he didn't like me. He sure as hell didn't respect me. To him, I was just a spoiled little girl who needed to be sent to her room until she learned how to behave around the grownups. Nothing I'd done, nothing I'd ever do, would change his mind. I was a *nuisance*.

"Get out." I said it softly, without rage, or any passion at all.

"Kate—" Mike's expression was almost panicked. He kept his voice very carefully controlled, as though he were afraid that one wrong word would push the situation beyond the point of no return. What he didn't realize was that it was already there.

Joe's eyes had hardened until they were cold green agates. He ignored Mike's warning, ignored everything but me. "You don't mean that. You won't send me away, who'll come riding to the rescue and clean up your mess?"

"Oh, but I do mean it." I smiled, and I knew that the expression was cold, cruel. "I surely do."

Mike flinched. Tom let out a gasp. Even the cop looked nervous.

Joe just stared. In that moment he hated me. I knew it and didn't care. "Fine. You want me to go. I'll go. But don't *ever* expect anything from me again." Joe turned on his heel and stormed past the cop.

I didn't try to stop him. I wanted him gone.

Mike closed his eyes. "I'll talk to him." He started to walk off.

I spoke bitterly to his retreating back. "Don't bother. Nothing you say is going to make any difference. Joe's never been willing to listen to anything that doesn't agree with his own preconceived notions. You'll just be wasting your time."

I heard the hesitation in Mike's retreating footsteps, but he didn't stop, didn't turn around.

The cop followed them out, pulling the curtain closed behind him.

"Kate?" I turned to face Tom. His expression was stricken. "I didn't mean to—"

"This wasn't your fault, Tom. Don't blame yourself." I climbed back onto the examining table. I was tired; so damned tired. Part of it was physical exhaustion. Most of it was emotional. I kept trying so hard to do the right thing, and every time it seemed to end in disaster.

"But—" he struggled to find the right words. "He's your *brother*."

"That doesn't make him any less of an idiot." I spoke calmly, which was odd. I knew I should be upset, should be crying. But the tears just weren't there. I felt . . . empty.

"He loves you and he worries about you."

I sighed "Joe loves me, Tom, but he doesn't like me. He doesn't respect me, or even believe that I'm capable of taking care of myself. I didn't mean to look, but I saw inside his head. He not only doesn't understand, he doesn't *want* to."

Tom stepped forward until he stood barely an inch in front of me. I could feel the warmth of his skin. I could smell the indefinable scent that would identify him to me even if I were deaf and blind. "He does love you. He just doesn't realize how strong you are. And honestly, I don't blame him for worrying. Hell, *I* worry."

"Yes, but it's not because you think I'm a stupid child who's not capable of taking care of herself."

He stopped at that, probably wondering what I really had seen in Joe's mind. He shook his head. "No. You're not stupid, and you are *not* a child. But I have to say, you do have this talent for making the *worst* enemies."

"It is a gift," I admitted ruefully. I was trying to make a joke of it. It was a feeble attempt, but I was trying. Because if we joked, I just might get through this without falling to pieces.

Tom knew me well enough to play along. "Is it too late to exchange it?"

It was a bad joke, but it made me laugh. Yes, the laughter was a little hysterical, but it still helped. That's one of the best things about Tom. He always knows exactly how to bring me back from the edge. Whether I'm angry, depressed, or worried. Whatever the problem is. He's always there, ready to help me if I need it, without trying to make me less than I am.

"I love you, Tom Bishop." I reached over to touch my hand to his chest, just above his heart.

"I love you, too. Let's go home."

"Are you sure? Mary's not going to like it."

Tom's eyes flashed, "If the Acca doesn't like it, she can—" I raised an eyebrow, and he stopped in mid-sentence. "I'm serious, Kate. I love you. I'm not giving you up. If that means I can't be part of the pack anymore, then so be it."

"Tom!" I couldn't keep the shock out of my voice. He's a wolf. Pack meant everything to him. At least I'd thought it had.

"I could've lost you. I know you're Not Prey. I know you're strong. But you can't fight an idiot with a rifle, and I can't protect you from it." His eyes shone with unshed tears, and his voice had taken on a rough edge from the emotions he was fighting to control. "I don't want to lose you. I *refuse* to lose you—whatever the price!"

I put my hand against his cheek as I whispered my answer. "I'm going to do my damnedest to see to it you don't."

He drew a ragged breath and gave a shaky laugh. "I'll hold you to that."

"I expect you to." I kissed him then, a soft brushing of my lips against his. "Now, while I check to see if the doc or the cops need anything else you can call us a cab."

"Sounds like a plan." He leaned forward and kissed me. He was very careful of my injuries, and even then it hurt. The pain reminded me that someone out there wanted me dead. Then again, as my brother had so gracefully pointed out, who didn't?

It took a good half hour before I was able to escape from the hospital. I worked really hard to make sure the cops I'd talked to didn't come in contact with Tom. That would be a bad thing, on a number of levels. Fortunately, the cab was waiting when the release papers were signed, and Tom didn't notice the annoyed, sad shake of the officer's head as I walked out.

I hustled across the sidewalk, my eyes scanning the area for any sign of the pickup. My shoulders were tight with tension. I couldn't help myself. I was afraid and I hated it. I didn't know who had been in the truck, although I was sure it hadn't been Amanda. The fact that we made it back to the apartment without incident only made me feel stupid on top of frightened.

Tom came up with me to my place. Before I'd finished locking the doors he strode over to the windows and hit the switch that controls the window blinds. He closed them fully, so that the apartment was cast into an artificial gloom.

"You want something to eat?" Tom suggested.

I sighed. "I still haven't gone to the grocery store. There's nothing edible in the house." I flung myself onto the couch, shifting the throw pillows around until I had them where it would be comfortable to lie down. Tom had folded Mom's afghan and draped it over the back of the couch. I pulled it over me and snuggled into the soft purple yarn. The adrenaline that had kept me going through the crisis, and the fight with Joe, had drained away completely. I was weary, and in pain both physically and emotionally.

"Actually," Tom said as he came over to the couch. He lifted my legs and sat down under them. Sliding off my shoes and socks, he began rubbing my feet. It felt like heaven. I found my eyes drifting closed as my head sank deeper into the pillows. "After you left this morning I called the grocery store and had them deliver a bunch of stuff."

"They charge a hefty fee for that." I didn't open my eyes. It was just too much bother.

"Don't care." He used his thumb to caress the arch of my left foot, until I sighed with pleasure. "I even," he paused for dramatic effect, "had them bring ice cream. Rum raisin."

I cracked open my eyes and smiled. "You do realize that you are very nearly the perfect man."

"Only *nearly?*"

"You're not filthy, disgustingly rich." I gave an exaggerated sigh, but snuggled deeper into the couch. "But I'll try not to hold it against you."

He laughed and switched to massaging my right foot. "I'll try to work on that." He stopped rubbing my feet. "I think I'll fix us something to eat."

"You don't cook." I managed to mumble the words. It wasn't easy. My eyes had closed and I was nearly asleep.

"Thank God for the microwave."

"Mmmm."

The last thing I felt before I sank into slumber was the pressure of his lips brushing my forehead.

"Kate, dinner's ready." Tom shook my shoulder gently.

I blinked, trying to focus both my eyes and my mind. Neither wanted to work properly. Dinner. What had happened to lunch? How long had I been out?

I glanced over at the clock. I'd slept for nearly four hours. It really was time for dinner. My stomach rumbled in agreement. Food. Right. Good plan.

"Are you all right?" Tom set the dinner plates onto the kitchen island next to the silverware and the folded paper towels we sometime use as napkins. He retrieved clean glasses from the dishwasher, then poured us each a glass of milk to go with dinner. For someone who claims not to be domestic, he's certainly got his moments.

I swung myself upright and tossed off the afghan. I stood up and stretched, arms reaching for the ceiling. Awake. I was awake. Yeah, right. I stumbled to the downstairs bathroom to wash up for dinner. While I was there, I splashed some cold water onto my face, drying off with one of the fluffy, sunshine yellow towels I usually only put out when expecting guests. That reminded me that I needed to do laundry. Which reminded me of Mary's trousers. That, in turn, led me to think of my brother Joe.

Funny how, now that I'd slept my anger wasn't cold at all. I wasn't happy, but was thoroughly awake, when I returned to the kitchen. Tom guessed it from my expression.

"You're thinking about Joe, aren't you?" Tom asked. He had a forkful of green beans halfway to his mouth, but he set it back down onto the plate.

"How'd you guess?" I pulled the stool out and sat down. I automatically said a silent prayer of thanks for the food before I took a knife to the meat, cutting it with a little more vigor than was strictly necessary.

"Other people can make you angry, but only Joe truly gets you *pissed*."

I opened my mouth to explain, but he waved it off.

"It's all right, Kate. Family can drive you nuts." He gave a rueful laugh. "If he were my brother, I probably would've strangled him years ago." He shook his head sadly and picked his fork back up. "But he's not my brother. He's yours. And you're not going to be happy until the two of you fix it."

I shook my head no. I was still too upset to be able to deal with the situation. Hell, every time I even started to think about it my blood boiled. I took a vicious bite of the meat.

"But not tonight." Tom took a long drink of milk. "If we don't get a night away from everything we're both going to go nuts. So after dinner we're watching *Casablanca* on DVD and pigging out on popcorn and ice cream." Brilliant, considerate, gorgeous. No wonder I love him.

We watched *Casablanca, The African Queen,* and a couple of episodes of *Fawlty Towers* for good measure. In between, I ran downstairs and did a few loads of laundry. Connie, my other tenant, had evidently been doing laundry because Mary's trousers had been left, neatly folded, on the shelf I'd put up above the pole for hanging clothes.

It wasn't the most exciting of Saturday nights, but I wouldn't have traded it. A night like this with my honey was better than any night I'd ever spent out in the singles scene.

We went to bed around midnight. No sex, just cuddling. I didn't mind. Sometimes, when you're feeling hurt and angry, cuddling is actually better. I fell asleep, using Tom's chest as a pillow.

I was wide awake at 4:00 A.M., probably because of the nap. I lay in Tom's arms for a little while, but eventually got restless enough that I was afraid I'd wake him. So I climbed from the bed and padded downstairs in my pajamas.

The hive was awake. I could hear them in my mind, a velvet blackness filled with the sibilant whispers of the hive.

What of her? *We should bring her into the hive.*

She will not come. So, she is not our problem.

And the other?

If she *has her way, it will be moot. If it is not, then we continue with the plan.*

I shut my eyes and tried to concentrate on my shields. The voices receded until they were no more than an annoying buzz in the background. I could live with that. Miles MacDougal had told me more than once that I needed to know my enemy, that I should *use* the connection to them. It made sense in a way, but most of the time I preferred to be left alone.

It would be rude to wake Tom, so I was very carefully quiet as I started the coffee brewing and did my meditation. When that was finished I gathered up the soap, a good book, and all my dirty laundry and took the elevator downstairs.

The book was a good one. It kept my mind off of things I really didn't want to think about, including men with rifles, my annoying brother, and Amanda Shea. I was glad to get the laundry done, too. The fresh scent of detergent and the feel of warm clothes in my hands as I folded them fresh from the dryer were very domestic, very soothing. By the time I'd finished and was carrying the basket of folded clothes upstairs I actually felt as though eventually things would be all right. Of course I figured it was probably just the soap fumes.

I continued on the domestic theme when I got upstairs. Tom was still snoring away, so I fed Blank, put away the laundry, and started on the housework. By the time Tom finally rolled out of bed I'd done all the dusting, had AC/DC in my iPod, and was doing a little dance as I ran a mop over the kitchen floor.

He came up behind me to nuzzle my neck and pull me into a hug that was only slightly hampered by the mop. He was wearing one of my favorite tee-shirts over a pair of black sweatpants. It had a pirate on the front pointing his finger outward and read "Dread Pirate Roberts Wants You. Call Me about Franchise Opportunities." The tee was tight across his chest and shoulders, showing off his build to perfection. It also covered all the healing bruises on his chest and abdomen. His face looked better than it had two days ago, but it was still obvious he'd taken a beating. Still, he was up and moving. If he'd been human, he'd be in the hospital.

"What's the plan for the day?"

I slid the headphones off and set the iPod onto the counter. "I figured I'd call Simms's office and see if I could set up a time to try and heal Bryan and the others. Then I thought I'd head over to the church and talk to Mike about things."

"I don't like you wandering around bus stops when someone's been trying to shoot you. I'm amazed the police haven't insisted on offering you protection." He got a very suspicious look on his face and his eyes went dark and deep. "Or did they? What exactly did they say to you while I was calling the cab?"

I turned away. I didn't want to face him, didn't want to lose the last shreds of my good mood by getting into an argument.

Then his hands were on my waist, and he turned me around so I had to face him. Looking into those oh-so-serious eyes from inches away I couldn't lie, couldn't even mislead him.

"Tom . . . ," I started to speak, but my expression told him my answer better than words.

He let go of me and stalked away, going to the farthest part of the living room just to be away from me. "*Damn* it, Katie! *Damn it to hell!* You told them no, didn't you! You refused their protection."

"I—"

"Don't even try to explain. Just . . . don't." He turned toward the window, pulling aside one of the vertical blinds with one hand. I could see the muscles knotted in his shoulders beneath the thin fabric of the tee-shirt he wore. "This isn't the Thrall, Kate. This is some lunatic with a gun. You can't stand and fight. You won't even know it's happening until it's too late. Don't you *get* that? It's a miracle you didn't die yesterday. You *should* be dead. You *would* be if it hadn't been for sheer dumb luck. And he's out there and he's waiting and you're going to make it easy for him because you're too damned *stupid* to get the help you need."

He was shaking with rage, hard enough that the blind rattled. "I love you, Katie, but I can't keep watching you deliberately put yourself in the line of fire. I can't, and I won't." He let the blind drop and turned to face me. "So this is it. Either you call the cops and tell them you'll take their protection, or it's over."

"I don't like ultimatums, Tom." I said it softly. I wasn't angry . . . yet, if the shoe were on the other foot, I'd be doing and saying the same things to him . . . or worse.

He snorted, a bitter sound that carried no humor. "I don't like giving them. But you're not giving me any choice. We can't spend our lives together if you're dead. Take the protection until the shooter's caught. If they get Amanda, too, so much the better. Although I can't imagine the boys in blue putting a stake through her heart."

"You heard that? I thought you were asleep."

"I heard, *Buffy*." He snorted again. I watched him deliberately tamp down his anger, get his emotions in check. Pissed as he was, his control hadn't wavered for an instant. There had been no sign of his beast. And now he was trying to back away from an argument that neither of us wanted and no one would win.

If he was willing to let go of his anger, I was more than happy to play along. "Pretty sneaky of you faking like that, *Fido*."

"I figured Carlton wouldn't talk if he thought I was listening, and I wanted to know what was going on. It just figures he'd have the hots for you." He shrugged. It was an abrupt, angry movement. His words might be neutral, but his body was still tense. I watched him take a slow, controlled breath and let it out slowly.

"You *do* realize I'm not interested." I looked him in the eyes as I said it.

"You'd better not be," he grumbled.

"I'm not." There wasn't a bit of lie in that. I really wasn't interested in Carlton in any sort of romantic sense. He just was an interesting person.

"And what's your decision on the police protection?" Ah yes, back to the subject I'd tried so hard to change. Damn.

"I'll call Brooks. Maybe I'll get lucky and they'll have caught the shooters already."

"It's awfully soon for them to have done that," Tom pointed out.

"Not necessarily. I don't think they were professionals."

"But you don't know. Not for sure. So you need to be careful."

He was pushing, and I hated it. But he was right. I knew he was right. I was in danger from something I couldn't handle myself. And I sure as hell didn't want to lose him. "If the shooters haven't been caught, I'll accept police protection."

He sighed and closed his eyes. I could almost see his lips moving in a prayer of thanks.

I reached over, grabbed the phone, and rummaged around until I found Brooks's business card. I dialed the number for his cell. He picked up on the first ring.

"Hello, Reilly."

"How'd you know it was me?" I didn't bother to hide the surprise in my voice.

"Caller ID," he explained. "Hear you survived another close call. You must have more lives than a damned cat."

I moved the mop out of the way and pulled up a seat on the nearest stool. Tom stayed on the other side of the room, but I could tell he was listening. His ears were good enough that he might even be able to hear Brooks's side of the conversation.

"About that—" I started to explain, but he cut me off in mid-sentence.

"We got 'em. One of the neighbors across from the church got a partial plate number. It was the father and brother of one of the kids from Bear Creek. Dad confessed on condition we drop the charges against his son."

"Think the son will come after me?"

"Nah. He knows we're watching him. You should be okay on this one."

"And Amanda?"

"I'm still looking. I'll call you if I turn anything up. In the meantime, be careful. I've been doing a little research. Apparently Ms. Shea isn't the first one to try this little trick."

"What happened the last time?" I asked.

"Let's just say it ended badly." Brooks sounded tired, but there was a hint of anger as well.

"How badly?"

"The Japanese National Police lost more than a dozen cops in a Tokyo museum before it was all over." His voice was calm and very serious.

"How did they end up taking him down?"

"The riot squad had been shooting him in the chest, and all it did was slow him down. When one of the cops ran out of ammo, he broke through a case and grabbed a set of antique swords off their stand. He used the katana to lop off the guy's head and the wakizashi to stab him in the heart."

I winced, not only from the visual in my head, but from the knowledge that it was something I might have to do, very soon. "Gruesome."

"Very. But it worked." He paused, I heard a muted conversation in the background before he came back on. "Look, I've got to go. I'll talk to you later."

"Brooks—" I paused, trying to come up with better words than just "thanks" and failed miserably. After all, he'd said he was on sympathy leave. That meant somebody close to him was dead or dying. The last thing he needed was to deal with my troubles. But he'd agreed to it, and without complaint. "Thank you. I really appreciate this."

"Yeah, well . . . if you really want to thank me you can use those psychic abilities of yours to get me the lottery numbers for Friday. Camille wants a new SUV."

We were both laughing when he hung up the line. My laughter faded and died when I looked across the room at Tom. He looked fractionally less tense and angry than he had, but his body language was still rigid. He reached behind one of the plants and jabbed at the switch to open the blinds. Bright daylight flooded the room.

"You heard that they caught the shooters?"

One short nod, but he didn't smile. "I heard."

"You still don't sound happy."

I watched him roll his neck, trying to release some of the tension in his muscles. "I'm not happy. You're going to have to deal with Amanda. I hate it, but even if you weren't working with the vamps, you'd still have to. She hates you, and she'll just keep coming after you until one of the two of you is dead." He walked away from the windows, slowly crossing the room until he stood just a few inches from where I sat. "But you weren't happy about the shit with the pack. If you can let that go and let me handle it, then it's only fair that I let you deal with this."

"Yeah. But it sucks."

"Hell yeah," he agreed. "Look, I need to go downstairs, clean up, check my messages, call in to the station. Are we okay?"

"We're fine." I leaned forward, kissing him gently. "I'm just going to call Dr. Simms and Michael to set things up and then maybe start cooking."

"You're not still mad?"

I shook my head no. "You?"

"Only a little." He cupped my face in his hand. "I know you don't mean to, but sometimes you really do scare the shit out of me."

"Sorry."

He kissed me on the forehead and left. I watched him

leave, wondering what I'd done right in this life to have him in it. As the door clicked shut I reached for the pad where I'd written Dr. Simms's number. My heart beat a little faster with nerves. What if it didn't work? What if it did? I tried to remember Bryan as he used to be and honestly couldn't. It had been so long.

I punched in the number and extension. A pleasant female voice answered the line. "Dr. Simms's office, may I help you?"

I took a deep breath to calm my nerves and answered in my best business voice. "This is Kate Reilly. Is Dr. Simms available?"

"One moment please."

I listened to Muzak for a minute or two, my fingers tapping a nervous rhythm against the countertop.

"Good morning, Ms. Reilly. How can I help you?" His voice was pleasant, cultured, and more than a little smug. I'd called. Just like he'd planned. I could actually imagine the obnoxious expression on his face just from hearing those few words. A part of me really wanted to hang up right then and there. But I wanted to help Bryan and I needed to be in a hospital when I did.

"Dr. Simms, I called because I think I know how to cure—*completely cure* my brother and your daughter."

He let out an involuntary gasp of shock. "You *what*?"

"I can't be sure until I actually try, but—"

"What do you want from me?" He interrupted me, his voice still breathless with excitement, his words spilling over each other as a result. Suddenly, the upper hand was mine again. But it didn't really matter to me whether or not I *won* a stupid little pissing match with him.

"I want to try this at the hospital, just in case anything goes . . . wrong."

"How—" I heard him take a deep breath to steady himself. "How does it work? What will you do?"

It seemed silly telling him that I'd sit next to his daughter, take her hand, and *think* at her, but that was pretty much what I was going to try to do. So I used words like "meditate" and "trance" and tried not to sound like a complete idiot. I must have failed because I could hear the skepticism in his voice. "That's it?"

"Look, Dr. Simms, we're in uncharted territory here. I *think* it'll work. It seems logical to me that it should. But if it doesn't, what harm's done? It won't make anything worse."

"I suppose not." I heard an irregular tapping, like the sound of a pen hitting the top of a desk as he considered what I was suggesting. Eventually, he spoke. "Fine. Come by the hospital this afternoon at two. I'll have security escort you to the conference room near my office. But understand this, Ms. Reilly. I am not a man to be toyed with. If this is some elaborate stunt to try to get out from under the charges brought against you—" he let the threat dangle.

It was probably stupid to be annoyed, but I was. "Dr. Simms, *you* are the one who has been pursuing *me. You* offered to drop the charges. Not me. I haven't asked for a damned thing except a place to do this. If things go well, I want my brother kept overnight for observation, but you'd want that anyway so you can gather the press together to make an announcement."

"Yes." His voice was still suspicious, but he couldn't dispute the truth.

"I only ask that you *try* to keep my name out of it." I was being completely honest about that. Because if my name was tied to a true cure, people whose loved ones were trapped as Eden zombies would pursue me to the ends of the earth to get my help. There were thousands, maybe even millions of zombies. There was only one of me.

He paused and then sighed. "If this cure of yours works, that won't be possible—no matter what I do. You know that. Researchers are going to want to know how it was done. They'll want to know how to duplicate the effect. There's too much at stake—"

I cut him off. "Let's just see how this first time goes, shall we? So two o'clock, at the front door."

"I'll see you then."

It took a couple of attempts to hit the button to end the call. I was shaking. I was going to do this. Holy crap. I was going to do this. I used the meditation exercises I'd learned from Henri to steady myself. It took a few minutes, but when I hit the number for Michael on speed dial I was almost calm.

After I'd told him my plan, there were more than a few moments of stunned silence. When he finally replied, his voice was shaking—both with hope and incredible excitement.

"If what you're saying is true, Kate, we could . . . I mean, *you* could . . . how many people would get their lives, their loved ones—" I heard his voice falter again, but not from excitement this time. "But oh dear Lord, there are so *very*—"

He's a bright boy. I knew he'd figure it out for himself, so I completed the thought, repeating what I said to Simms. "So many of them. There's only one of me, Mike. Saving Rob drained me . . . a lot. His injuries were only physical, and he was already a wolf, so he could help. I love Bryan, and I need the hospital's staff, so I'll help Simms, but—"

Concern for me warred with concern for his charges in his voice when he replied softly. "I understand." There was a pause and I let the silence flow, allowing each of us to keep our thoughts for a time.

"You need to tell Joe, you know."

I shook my head, knowing he couldn't see. "I can't, Mike. You saw how—"

"You *have* to, Katie. He has just as much stake in Bryan's future as you do. He's a doctor and a good one. He's read—extensively—on the effects of Eden, and you know it. What if something goes . . . wrong? Could you live with yourself, knowing he might have had a suggestion that could have prevented it?"

He was right, and I knew it. But I couldn't imagine how Joe would respond. Would he be excited at the possibility, or think that, yet again, I was meddling in things beyond my ken?

Score one for pessimism, dammit. Even the logical, reasoned speech I'd rehearsed in front of the mirror, to be certain my facial muscles would convey hope and excitement, wasn't enough.

"You want to *what?!*" Joe's voice held so many emotions that I was glad I'd chosen to call, rather than tell him in person. That much emotional overload would beat at my head like a sledgehammer and make the session with Bryan more difficult. Anger flowed into fear, and tumbled over excitement. But he just couldn't allow that I might actually have enough brains to know what I was doing, so anger won out. "Kate, no! I forbid this. You don't even know this can work. What if—"

"What if *what,* Joe? Just go ahead and say it. What if I kill Bryan? Do you think I haven't considered the possibilities? I'm not *quite* that stupid and irresponsible, regardless of what runs through that excuse of a mind you have. Hasn't it even occurred to you that I wouldn't have suggested it if I wasn't pretty damned sure I could bring him back? I want to do this. I have to . . . at least *try.*"

His voice grew cold. "I didn't think you were going to kill him, Kate. But what if you undo the good already done? You have *no way* to be positive it'll increase his cognitive ability. Damn it, he *recognizes* me, Kate! He smiles when I walk in the room. He laughs at cartoons and—" There was a pause and I heard coughing and a short snuffle that told me Joe was tearing up nearly as much as I was because, yes, that was one of the possibilities I'd considered.

"Fuck it. Do what you're going to do. I know you will anyway."

He slammed down the phone, leaving me to rock on the couch in silent, angry tears, wondering if I was going to lose *both* brothers if anything went wrong this afternoon.

21

A white van emblazoned with the words "Our Lady of Perpetual Hope" pulled up to the curb. Mike was at the wheel. Bryan was bouncing up and down in the passenger seat. Tom opened the sliding door for me, then froze, an expression close to horror on his face.

"What?" I peered around him to see Mary Connolly sitting primly on one of the back seats.

"What in the hell—" I started to protest, but she interrupted me.

"Look, I don't want to be here any more than you want me to, but Joe couldn't get off work on such short notice, so he asked me to be here. It's important enough to *him* that I said yes. So can we all act like grown-ups for the duration?"

The way she said it made it sound like she'd been rehearsing that little speech for the past couple of hours. Maybe she had.

I looked at Tom. He gave me a small nod and helped me get in.

I was wearing the coral suit again, this time with a cream

colored shell and pearls. Somehow jeans and a tee-shirt hadn't seemed right for the occasion. I wasn't the only one who felt that way either. Mary was in a navy business suit. Tom had opted for gray dress slacks and a black dress shirt with the collar left unbuttoned. The only one dressed informally was Bryan. He wore a Notre Dame sweatshirt over faded blue jeans.

"Hi, Ka-tie! Hi, Tom! We're going to the hospital, huh? But this isn't one of the bad trips. It's a good trip—right, Father Mike?"

"Right, Bryan." Mike answered with a smile. But the way his fingers were moving on the steering wheel told me he was trying hard not to get up his hopes.

I was so nervous I was nauseous. Tom had tried to get me to eat, but I couldn't even bear the thought of food. Not right now. Funny, I could face a lunatic wanting to kill me, or a pissed-off vampire just fine, but the thought of trying to cure my brother and possibly failing terrified me. I sat between Mary and Tom, shaking like an aspen leaf in a strong wind. It was bad enough that the seat was actually squeaking.

Don't let me fail. Dear God, please *don't let me fail.*

Tom's hand found mine, and he gave it a gentle squeeze. "It's all right, Kate. It's going to be fine." His voice was a bare whisper in my ear.

I closed my eyes, fighting not to throw up. I needed to get control of myself or this was never going to work. I just wasn't sure how.

"I've never seen you like this before," Mary said, with a confused, quizzical note to her voice. "Even when Monica planted those eggs in your arm you weren't this frightened. Why does this bother you so much?"

Mike spoke before I could. "Because if that had gone wrong, Kate would be the one who suffered the consequences. She's always worried more about everybody else's well-being than her own." His eyes caught mine in the rearview mirror and I squirmed. He was right, but put that way it made me sound all noble, almost saintly. That *so* wasn't me. Just ask Father Akins. Not that he'd say anything, secrecy of the confessional and all.

Mary sat in stony silence, her back rigid. It was almost impossible not to brush against each other in such close quarters, but she managed it. Nor did she say another word during the entire drive. In fact, the silence got so thick that it was even beginning to dampen Bryan's spirits, so Mike turned the radio on to my brother's favorite station—the Disney network—to distract him.

I think all of us were glad when the ride was over and we could climb out and get a little space. Mary took the lead, striding toward the building, her shoes beating an angry tattoo against the concrete sidewalk.

Mike and Bryan went after her, leaving Tom and me standing by the van.

"He's right, you know. You do put everybody else first, even when you shouldn't. You don't value yourself nearly enough."

I started to speak, but he put a finger to my lips. "It's going to be all right. We'll go inside. You'll help your brother and Dr. Simms's daughter, just like you saved Rob. You were able to do that. You can do this. I believe in you." He pulled me close, so that my head was pressed against his warm chest. I took a deep breath, luxuriating in the masculine scent of him. I felt him move until his mouth was next to my left ear. When he whispered, the warm air tickled the delicate nerves. When I shivered against him, it wasn't with fear. "And when all's said and done, and you've saved the day *again,* the two of us are going to go home and have wild passionate monkey sex to celebrate."

It made me laugh, which helped. I was still nervous, but it wasn't the bone-deep terror it had been. I looked up into those sparkling brown eyes and managed to smile. "I'll hold you to that, buddy boy."

"I certainly hope so." He waggled his eyebrows sugges-
tively.

We were laughing and holding hands all the way across
the parking lot. "Are you ready?" He gestured toward the
front door of the hospital where Simms and a security
guard were standing talking to Michael. "They're waiting."

"I'm ready." I didn't believe that—not for a minute, but
ready or not, here we go!

Simms put us in a long, narrow conference room. A pair of
security guards flanked the door, each of them in a starched
white shirt with pale blue uniform trousers and black shoes
that exactly matched the leather of their holsters.

I'd looked around before taking one of the few open
seats. I hadn't liked what I saw. Oh, the room was all right
for an everyday, sundry meeting. The walls were plain
white, without art work or ornamentation. The fluorescent
lighting was bright enough, the carpet tasteful in an indus-
trial sort of way. Even the table was nothing spectacular,
just a long rectangular table of plain blond wood surrounded by twelve chairs of bent chrome.

But there weren't enough seats for everyone who'd chosen to attend, and I couldn't figure out why nobody was
making an effort to get more. Mike and Mary were forced
to lean uncomfortably against one wall, trying to stay out of
the line of sight of the video camera that had been set up to
record the events.

Despite the number of people in the room I was cold.
Part of it was physical. Cold air was blasting through the
vents in the ceiling. But there was a psychological compo-
nent, too. The whole setup reminded me forcibly of the ill-
fated meeting with Samantha Greeley. I vaguely recognized
one or two of the faces from visiting Joe in the emergency
room. Otherwise, the only people I knew were the ones
who'd come with me. The various doctors all talked among
themselves, their voices muted but taut with excitement. All

but two of them kept casting surreptitious glances at me in a way that made my skin crawl.

Bryan was concentrating on the coloring book and crayons Mike had brought for him. Simms's daughter simply stared into space, a beautiful, vacant-eyed doll of about fifteen, with long dark hair and hazel eyes.

Edgar Simms rose, and the murmuring that had filled the room ceased as if cut off with a switch. "Ladies and gentlemen, we're all busy people. Why don't I proceed with the introductions, and then we'll get this meeting moving."

He gestured toward the man to his left, "This is Dr. Leonard Levy," he continued, person by person. I didn't pay much attention. I was trying to focus, find my center.

"Before we get started, I have a few questions," Dr. Levy said firmly. "As Melinda Simms's personal physician, I want to know *exactly* what is about to take place."

Shit. I smiled sweetly and turned my attention to Edgar Simms. "Dr. Simms, may I have a private word with you?" I rose, scooting my chair back from the table.

"Ms. Reilly—" he started to protest, but I cut him off.

"It will only take a moment."

Tom gave my leg a discreet squeeze before I stood and gave me a warning look. I smiled, trying to tell him without words that I wasn't going to do or say anything stupid.

Simms frowned at me, but rose. The nearest security guard opened the door for us and we stepped through it into a nice, empty hallway. The guard followed us through to this side, pulling the door closed behind him. He stood by the door, relaxed but ready, with one hand gripping his other wrist.

"Ms. Reilly," Simms puffed himself up so that he could look down his nose at me. It was supposed to intimidate me. It didn't.

"Dr. Simms," I talked over the top of him. "What in the *hell* did you think you were doing inviting all these people?"

He opened his mouth to respond, but I waved him to silence. "First off, I thought I made it clear that I wanted to do this *discreetly*. But more to the point, what I'm trying to do here involves a psychic trance. Just how am I supposed to manage that with an audience? And a *hostile* audience at that. Do you *want* this to fail? Because I can nearly guarantee I won't be able to achieve the proper trance."

"Ms. Reilly, if this succeeds it will be a hugely important medical breakthrough. From what I understand, you managed to save a wolf's life during *battle* conditions. Surely you understand why—"

"No. *You* understand. I had *help* when I was trying to save Rob—help I'm not willing, or able, to call on this time. I am not even going to try this until the only people with me in that room are Bryan, your daughter, and *one* physician. Whether that person is you or Dr. Levy is up to you. You can leave the camera. You can put the security guards outside the door. But I am not going to just sit there and be cross-examined and treated like some kind of criminal."

"Now see here!" he snarled.

"No, *you* see here." I stepped forward until we were standing toe-to-toe. "I came here to help my brother and your daughter. I haven't asked you for a goddamned thing in exchange. I'm *not* trying to con you. I'm *not* doing anything wrong. But let me be perfectly clear when I tell you that I am also *not* going to be paraded in front of your researchers and subjected to God knows what humiliations. Either that room gets cleared right now or I walk, and *you* lose your only chance at a cure for Melinda. It's your choice."

He glared at me silently for long moments. His breathing was harsh, as though he'd run a long distance. Red anger spots decorated his cheeks. "You'd do it, wouldn't you? Just walk away and leave your own brother to—"

Probably not, but he didn't need to know that. I could find another location and bring in Miles or Joe if I absolutely had to. "In a heartbeat."

He shook his head. He kept clenching and unclenching his fists. A deep flush was creeping up his neck. "Doug said you were a ball-busting bitch."

His mention of the Denver Thrall Queen didn't improve my mood. My voice dripped icicles when I said, "You have no idea how much of a bitch I can be. Now make up your mind, Dr. Simms. I don't have all day."

I could see him consider letting me walk. His pride was such that giving in was almost more than he could bear. But he loved his daughter. In the end, his feelings for her won out. "Fine. Have it your way."

I stayed in the hall with the guard. He went back into the room alone. A moment later angry people began filing out of the room. One or two gave me dirty looks, most chose to ignore me completely.

"Kate," Mary came up to me with Mike and Tom a step behind. "Dr. Simms says you refuse to do the experiment until everyone but Melinda, Bryan, and him leave the room."

"That's right." I decided to head off her temper with an explanation. "I need to concentrate." I gave her a rueful grin. "Besides, there won't be much to see. I'm going to go into a trance and *think* at them. It's liable to be a pretty boring show. About like watching me and Monica negotiate to implant the hatchlings in my arm." I had no doubt she remembered the infinitely tedious stretch of nearly an hour, watching two women staring at each other silently.

"And you think this is going to work?" Her eyebrows rose high enough to disappear beneath her bangs.

I shrugged, because I honestly didn't know. "I saved Rob and the vampires. All I can do is try."

Simms glanced pointedly at his watch. He was holding the door open.

Mary shook her head and looked at me so hard I could feel her power boring into me. "Try hard, Kate. Because if this fails it's going to kill Joe."

No pressure there. "All I can do is my best." I walked through the door. Simms closed it behind me, leaving the three of them standing outside.

Simms took a seat at the head of the table, next to his daughter's still form. I sat between Melinda and Bryan. This was it.

For a few moments, I concentrated on Bryan and Melinda. I put a finger to my lips when Bryan put down his crayons and opened his mouth to speak. "You need to be really, really quiet for just a few seconds, Bryan. Can you do that for me? Maybe you could sing to yourself in your head? How about 'London Bridge'? I know you like that one."

He cocked his head, curious, but then must have seen the intensity on my face, because he nodded and picked up the red crayon, his favorite color, and started to turn the sky in the barnyard scene the color of fire. He tapped his other fingers in time to music only he could hear.

I closed my eyes, taking slow, deep breaths. I willed my power to build, felt it filling me like water fills a cup, until it reached the very brim. With every ounce of will, I blocked myself and those in the room from the Thrall. Not even a whisper of this event would escape to reach the queens. Every hair on my body was standing on end, and an electric tension filled the air in the room like the air before a lightning strike. I opened my eyes and saw Bryan staring at me, his eyes wide. *It's okay, Bry.* I watched his body relax. He'd heard the thought as clearly as if I'd said the words aloud.

Take my hand.

He put down the crayon and took my hand. The touch was the last drop needed to make the cup overflow. I felt my mind slip the confines of my body; as it had when I healed Rob, and before that, when the Thrall egg had hatched in my body.

I knew I should be frightened, but I wasn't. It felt good and somehow *right,* to slide into my brother's mind—as though I'd been here before. Like walking through a familiar building, I knew where things were stored. It was all still there, like the records in the church's basement. The boxes were dusty and water damaged, but the files were readable.

I sent tendrils of power through the scarred passages, felt new pathways form within his brain to connect his old memories to his current awareness. He gave a violent shudder and started to breathe in little gasps, like after being underwater too long. His heart began to beat faster and his palm blossomed with cold sweat. I could hear Dr. Simms push back his chair quickly enough for it to fall over and hit the floor. I managed not to break concentration, but only just.

"It's okay," I whispered with my eyes still closed, and he paused. "Give him a few minutes to adjust."

Simms didn't move forward, but he didn't sit down again, either. He fought against his instinct to rush forward and separate us, but he remained where he was.

I held tight to Bryan's hand as he fought back into his own mind. Finally, he let go of my hand, and I could hear his heartbeat steady. But the power in my head wasn't finished. There was still so much energy. I couldn't hold it all. My mind burned, until I felt as though my skin might explode and my hair would combust. I needed to use it, get rid of it somewhere.

I turned to Melinda Simms and took up her hand.

22

I woke in a hospital bed. All of the lights were off in the room, the curtains had been shut tight so that not a hint of daylight shone through. An IV was attached to my arm, clear fluid dripped slowly into the tube.

Tom sat on the opposite side of the bed, his hand holding mine.

"You're awake!" His whispered words sounded as loud as a shout. Pain stabbed into my left eyeball like a heated ice pick. I rolled over in the bed, grabbing frantically for something to throw up into, barely managing to grab the little plastic pan in time. The monitors had started beeping vigorously. The pitch was penetrating and loud enough to bring tears to my eyes.

I hate migraines. I've only had four in my life. This was the second one in about a week. Both times it came after trying to manage a psychic healing. If Bryan was okay it would be absolutely worth it. If not, I was going to be seriously pissed. I knew I should care about Melinda Simms, but I just didn't. I remembered bits and pieces of touching her mind—finding it horribly disfigured and burned. There was so much damage and it took so much energy, not only to *find* the memories, find what had been Melinda, but to connect them. I'd used all the power filling my mind, and then some.

I'd come to know Melinda Simms through her memories, but she wasn't such a wonderful person—much like Amanda had been. Pretty, popular, and . . . intentionally cruel . . . petty because she *could* be. There was a certain poetic justice to the damage inflicted on her and I'd wondered at the time if someone had given her a bad dose intentionally. Her last memory was of the satisfied look in the girl's eyes when she'd handed over the syringe.

I'd also wondered if she was worth saving.

But in the end, I did—because I also saw those around her who didn't deserve to live in misery because of her fate. Her father, and mother, friends and a handsome boy who had love in his eyes in her faded memories.

But either she was better, or she wasn't. I couldn't remember how it had come out before I'd fallen off my chair to the floor, weary beyond belief.

"How is he?" The words came out in a hoarse croak.

"Bryan is fine. So is Melinda." Tom's voice was thick with more emotions than I could sort in my current condition. "*You're* not. You . . . died, Kate. Your heart stopped. You weren't breathing. It was all they could do to bring you back."

I lay very still beneath the stiff cotton sheets and thought about what he said. I didn't remember dying. Shouldn't I? The knowledge of that felt . . . odd.

The door opened and a doctor came in carrying a manila folder with my name on it. Bright light shone in from the hallway, and I shut my eyes. The afterimage of the light burned against my lids.

"Good morning, Ms. Reilly. I'm Dr. Watkins. I'm a neurologist. I was called in after the . . . incident yesterday afternoon."

I opened my eyes to see that he had used the dimmer switch to up the light so that he could see more clearly, but had kept it dim enough that it wouldn't be painful to my hypersensitive vision. There was a button on the side of the bed to change positions. He held it down until I was propped in a sitting position.

Dr. Watkins was a tall, gangly man with crisply cut graying hair and a hang-dog face. His eyes held a keen intelligence and more than a hint of kindness. I would've guessed his age in the fifty to sixty range, but it was hard to tell. Other than the gray, he'd probably looked exactly the way he had now for the past twenty years, and would for another twenty should he live that long. He held out his hand and I shook it. He had a good, firm handshake. The skin of his hand was rough, and I wondered briefly what hobbies he had that would give him calluses. Not that it mattered, but I was curious.

Without my really willing it, my mind slid into to his. Gardening: he was an avid gardener. Digging in the earth relaxed him, helped him get rid of the inevitable stress of dealing with patients who were generally frightened and in pain.

With a blink, I was back in my own head. He was talking, but I'd only missed a word or two.

". . . I want to congratulate you. We're going to do extensive testing, but at first glance both your brother and Melinda Simms appear to be back to normal. A truly miraculous feat."

His expression held equal parts awe and astonishment. "I've never seen anything like it, and I've been working with Eden zombies for most of my career. It's absolutely amazing." He turned to look at the printouts spewing from the nearest machine. "But my concern now is for you. Whatever you did appears to have caused you some slight brain trauma and swelling. It triggered the onset of a major migraine headache with light and aural sensitivity and nausea."

I nodded and immediately regretted it. He noticed it, and a small frown crossed his face.

"Have you had migraines prior to this?"

"Once or twice."

"When was the last one?"

"Last week. It was right after I used my psychic gifts to heal someone for the first time."

He took a pen from his pocket and folded open the file. His hand sped across the page with a soft scratching sound as he took notes. His large hands shouldn't have been able to move with such delicate finesse.

"And after that healing, did you collapse?"

"No, but I was working with . . . someone else that time."

He made a little harrumphing noise and scribbled some more. "When was your last migraine prior to the one last week?" His gray eyes locked with mine over the folder.

"Not for years."

"Approximately how many years?"

I thought about it and couldn't remember for sure. It had been when I was in high school. "Probably a decade anyway."

"Two incidents isn't exactly conclusive, but it's probable that the use of the psychic talent is triggering the migraines."

I gave a minuscule nod. The less I moved, the less it hurt.

The doctor sighed. He looked from me to Tom, and back. "All right. We'll need to do more tests to determine if there's any permanent damage. But until we know more about what's going on . . . no more healings. And you need to *rest* for the next couple days. I'm going to schedule an MRI for you for early next week and compare it to the one we took yesterday after your collapse. I'll check to see if there are any from when you had the concussion a few years ago. Your brother mentioned you'd had X-rays, but couldn't remember if they'd done an MRI. I'll let you check out of the hospital tomorrow if the migraine is under control, but I want you to take it easy."

He took a deep breath and I could tell he was annoyed. He lowered his voice until it was actually at a really comfortable level for my hypersensitive ears. "The media are going to want interviews. So far, the hospital management is allowing me to call the shots because of your condition. But if possible, you need to avoid them even after they overrule me. I never said that, though. Is your phone number unlisted?"

I managed to stop myself from shaking my head. "No. I run my own business out of the house."

His face took on a sour look, as though he'd bit into something bitter. "You'll need to unplug the phone or change the number. Distraught families are going to want you to heal their sons and daughters. I heard on the news that a prince from the Middle East announced an offer of ten million dollars to heal his son."

At that, my jaw dropped and it caused a brief spasm in my temple. "You're kidding me!"

Tom shook his head no. Apparently he'd heard about it, too. Wow. That was a lot of money. Not worth dying over, of course—but . . . *damn.*

"Katie—" Tom's voice held a warning. Apparently I'd looked interested. I wasn't . . . much. But *damn!* Ten *million* dollars. "Don't even think about it!"

"I'm with your fiancé on this one." The doctor said. "No more healings for now. Agreed?"

I tried to hide my shock at his use of the word *fiancé*, but my voice was a little higher and breathier than normal when I replied. "Agreed."

Dr. Watkins slid his pen back into the pocket of his lab coat. He closed the folder and tucked it under his arm. "I need to go talk to your brothers. They've been pestering the hell out of me, but I've insisted on only one visitor at a time."

"Thank you, doctor." Tom and I said it in unison. It made

me smile—for a brief second before the pain spiked behind my eye again.

"You're welcome." He smiled at the two of us. "The nurse will be by in a few minutes with the medicine for your headache. I'll check back to see how you're doing in a couple of hours." He left the room, closing the door quietly behind him.

"Fiancé?" The lilt in my voice made it a question.

The light was dim, but I saw a flush rise to Tom's cheeks. "Joe and I got into it in the hallway. He was going to have them throw me out after they rushed you to the ER. I told him they *couldn't* throw me out, because I was your fiancé and had more right to stay than he did." He hung his head but thrust out his jaw. "I'm sorry, Kate, but I couldn't stand to let them send me away. I had to be here. I *had* to."

"I don't mind." I took his hand in mine and squeezed it until he would meet my eyes. "What was the fight about?"

Tom shook his head no, letting me know he wouldn't tell me. "It doesn't matter. He was scared. He was frightened and lashed out. I was just the closest target."

"Asshole."

Tom squeezed my hand, hard. "Don't," he admonished me. "I don't blame him, and neither should you. Loving you is just terrifying. Because it's always something."

"I don't do it deliberately."

"I know." He gave me a tired echo of his usual smile. "But that doesn't make it any easier on the rest of us. I swear, I've considered taking you up to a cabin in the middle of the wilderness, but I'm pretty sure you'd somehow manage to piss off the local bears."

I was spared coming up with an appropriate answer to that by the arrival of the nurse with my medicine.

I met with Bryan for the first time post-healing after they'd taken away my lunch tray. My headache was finally gone.

Whatever it was that Dr. Watkins had prescribed, along with a stomach full of amazingly exceptional hospital food, had done the trick nicely. I had a whole new appreciation for the absence of pain. Tom was more than willing to relinquish his place at my bedside once he knew for sure I was going to be okay.

Meeting with my baby brother was amazing. More than amazing. Bryan was just *back*. It showed in every move he made, in every word out of his mouth. And boy was he being mouthy.

"What in the *hell* did you think you were doing? Are you *insane?*"

I shrugged and looked him square in his handsome, animated face. "I wanted you back."

"You *idiot!* I would *never* risk you for me. Never." He was stalking back and forth across the hospital room, his face flushed. Even his hand gestures were exaggerated. It was exactly the way he'd acted when we'd argued as teenagers. It made me grin in delirious joy.

"It was worth it."

"Worth it—" He stopped at the end of my bed to glare at me. "Damn it, Katie, it's not like I'm not grateful, but you *have* to stop risking yourself. Yeah, you're tough. But one of these days you're gonna go too far—" He stopped talking in mid-sentence and glared at me through lowered lids. "You're *smiling* again."

"I'm sorry, Bryan. Really I am. It's not that I'm not taking you seriously. But . . . it's *you*. It's really, really *you*. You're yelling at me and I can't tell you how happy that makes me." I could barely get the last sentence out, my throat had tightened so much. God I'd missed him. I looked up and said a silent prayer of thanks as I held open my arms for him.

Bryan stepped forward into the hug, carefully avoiding the various tubes still sticking out of my arms. He gave me a tight squeeze and said. "You realize you're making it really hard for me to be pissed at you right now."

"Good. I don't want you to be."

He touched my arm while still warm against my chest. The scars were still an angry crinkled pink against my pale, pale skin. He traced the knife wound Brooks had made, nearly the full length of my forearm, to remove the Thrall eggs as though I'd break. "I can't even *imagine* the things you've been through since I've been out of it, Katie. No wonder Joe is such a basket case." He let go of the hug and took a small step back. I shifted my legs to give him room to sit on the edge of the bed. "You know he's out there, driving the doctors crazy, wearing out the floor tiles in the hall."

He rose up to get a better look at me, and the mattress shifted slightly under his weight.

"But he won't come and talk to me."

"No." Bryan's face fell. "He won't. He's just unbelievably angry with you. Keeps saying that if you insist on getting yourself killed, he can't stop you, but he doesn't have to watch. Katie, what the hell has happened between the two of you? I don't get it. I mean, you've always fought, but this . . . this is different."

The hurt in Bryan's eyes was hard to bear. I wanted to explain it away, but I wasn't sure I could. Bryan had turned into a zombie before I got engaged to Dylan. He'd missed so damned much history between Joe and me.

"You know I'm Not Prey, right?"

"Yeah, I heard. What's up with that?"

"Make yourself comfy, bro. This is going to be a long story."

I tried to give him the Reader's Digest Condensed version of my life while he was out. Even that took time. He tried not to interrupt too much, but sometimes he couldn't help himself. By the time we'd finished, my throat was parched and it was nearly time for dinner.

"My God, Katie, no wonder Joe's half-crazy. What the fuck."

"Yeah, but what was I supposed to do? Can you tell me one thing I could've done differently?"

"You could've left Dylan to the Thrall. If you'd done that one thing, let him live with the consequences of his own stupid choices, *none* of the rest of it would've happened."

I shook my head no, but took his hand. "I couldn't do that. I loved him. I couldn't just leave him to die or be infested, any more than I could leave you to your own private hell—despite the fact that taking Eden had been *your* choice. Besides, once Larry knew I had psychic talent he'd decided he wanted me as a possible queen. If I hadn't gone in, he'd have just come after me." Larry had been Monica's predecessor. He'd wanted me and Monica to duke it out to become queen. I still remembered the burning excitement in his eyes as he'd tried to bite me.

Bryan couldn't meet my eyes. "You don't know that's true."

"Actually I do. Larry as much as said so before I fought him."

Bryan sat quietly for a moment, mulling that over. "But you still won't leave things well enough alone. Not if there's *any* chance." He patted my leg with one hand. "Don't get me wrong, I'm grateful as hell to be back but I can see why Joe can't handle it."

"Do you see any solution? I mean, I am what I am."

"Yeah, and he is what he is," Brian grumbled. "I'll work on it." He rose from the bed and started for the door. He turned to look at me with his hand on the doorknob, his expression grave. "Because I'm telling you now—I *will* have my family back." His expression softened. "But right now I need to get out of here. I've technically been released from the hospital. Joe and Mike are making all the arrangements to sneak me out without the press seeing me. The other girl and her folks did a press conference, but I *so* don't want to go there."

"Where are you going to stay?"

"I've got some options. Joe offered to let me move in with him, but he's living with Mary, I'd just be in the way. Mike said I could come back there, but I don't really want to."

"So—" My tone made it a question.

"Tom suggested that I take his place. If that's okay with you?"

I smiled. "It's fine. It's *great*."

"I love you, Katie. And I'm sorry . . . for everything." A shadow passed through his eyes. I knew what caused it. It was the guilt for having done the drugs in the first place, for needing to be rescued.

"I'm sorry, too."

He crossed the room, giving me a quick impulsive hug, then left. The room seemed awfully empty without him.

A tray was wheeled in for my dinner shortly after he left. None of it was particularly appetizing this time, from the thin tomato soup to the hamburger that bore more resemblance to shoe leather than actual meat. There must be a different cook on the dinner shift. I'd honestly never had trouble chewing green beans before in my life. Still, it was food. Not particularly *good* food, but it was healthy, good for me, and I was hungry enough that I was willing to eat pretty much anything.

I tried to kill time watching television, but couldn't find anything I wanted to see. I kept channel surfing, hoping there would be something I could enjoy. It reminded me of the Springsteen song, you know the one, "57 Channels (and Nothin' On)." If I had a gun I might've even followed his example. Fortunately, I didn't. And before too long Mike came in with the plan for how to get me out of there.

The dial on my watch read 10:15 P.M. Moonlight reflected off of the snow piled outside the windowsill. Distant stars sparkled, barely visible because of the orange glow of the street lamps outside. The lights in the room were turned off, as though the occupant were sleeping. The bed, however, was freshly made, the room completely clean except for the flowers. Those had been promised to the nurses as a gift for all the bother they'd been through.

I felt like I was in the middle of a prison break. Representatives of the local, national, even international news agencies had surrounded the hospital, and every one of them was trying to find a way to get *the* interview. They had been driving hospital security absolutely nuts and had camped out on the lawns near the main entrances and exits of the hospital.

I checked my reflection in the mirror one last time. There wasn't much light in the room, but there was more than enough for me to see by. Dr. Watkins had thought the light sensitivity was part of the migraine. But the headache was long gone, my EEGs were normal, and still bright light was intensely painful for me. I shook my head, making the black nylon wig I wore over my hair sway. I looked utterly ridiculous, like Sydney Bristow, superspy—on a particularly bad hair day. Still, passing for an employee was my best chance of getting out of the room and off the floor unnoticed.

I patted the pocket of the pants. The small plastic identification badge belonging to Miles MacDougal was still in the pocket. He'd given it to me, along with the pass code for the door to the research wing of the hospital. If anyone ever found out, he'd be in deep trouble; could even lose his job. But I wasn't telling and *he* sure as hell wasn't, so we should be safe.

I checked my watch again. Time to go. I grabbed the lightweight black tote that held my personal items, took a deep breath, and stepped through the door and into the hall.

Squinting against the bright fluorescent lights, I turned left and took a couple steps down the hallway toward the elevators, but came to a skidding stop at the sound of voices arguing at the nurse's station.

"What are you doing here?"

"We understand Kate Reilly has a room on this floor."

I recognized that voice. It was the reporter for Channel 4 News. I'd first run into her at the Shamrock Motel when Monica showed up. She'd seen me before; knew what I looked like. Up close, my disguise wasn't going to fool her for a minute. *Shit!*

"There is no patient by that name on this floor. Ms. Reilly checked out earlier this evening." The nurse was curt, but it wasn't enough to discourage the reporter.

"What are you doing? I'm calling security!" I heard the sound of hurrying feet, and the nurse's voice on the telephone calling for assistance.

There was no time to run, so I did the only thing that I could think of. I ducked into the nearest room and hid behind the door.

I heard footsteps right outside the door of the room where I was hiding. Someone opened the door across the hall. I heard them step inside, then call out to the people waiting in the hall. "She's not here. Are you sure you've got the right room number?" A male voice asked.

The female reporter's heels clicked angrily against the floor tiles. "Damn it!" she swore. "Look at the cards on the flowers. It was her room all right, but she's gone now."

I heard the man swear softly under his breath. "We may as well go. Security is on their way. I don't know how she managed to get out of the hospital without being spotted, but apparently she did."

"Maybe she switched rooms," the woman suggested.

"Well, we don't have time to check."

He was right. In the distance I heard the ding of the elevator bell and the crackle of radio static. The cavalry had arrived in the form of hospital security.

I glanced at my watch. Fifteen minutes had passed. Brooks was probably sitting in the van wondering what in the hell was taking me so long. I didn't dare risk digging out my cell to call him. If I could hear the folks from Channel 4 News through the door, the reverse would be true as well. So I stood in the deep shadows of an empty hospital room and listened impatiently to the newswoman's Academy Award–worthy performance and the guard's unimpressed response. All in all it was almost thirty minutes before they were gone and I could emerge from hiding.

I stepped out of the room, and ran straight into Mike.

"What in the *hell*—" he spluttered.

"The team from Channel 4 arrived just as I was leaving."

He made a disgusted sound. "Figures. Come on. When you didn't make it out to the van in thirty minutes I decided to come looking for you."

"Thanks."

He didn't answer, just strode down the hall at a brisk enough clip that I had to hustle to keep up with him. The squeak of my tennis shoes on the polished linoleum seemed amazingly loud to my ears, but Mike didn't seem to notice. It was probably just nerves.

Mike hit the lever to open the door to the emergency stairwell. "You do realize that you're eventually going to have to face the press. What you did—" I watched his Adam's apple bob as he swallowed nervously. "It was just amazing. Nothing like that has ever happened before. I don't know if Tom's told you yet, but you had a message from Barbara Walters on your machine this morning." I had started to pass him, but when he said that I just froze in place, my jaw hanging down somewhere around my navel.

"Barbara—"

"Walters wants to do a special interview with you and Bryan." Mike made a shooing gesture with his hands and I started down the steps. I didn't know what to say. I mean . . . holy crap. A Barbara Walters special? My nerves *so* weren't up to this.

"Have you talked to Joe yet?" Mike's words interrupted my thoughts.

I flinched. No, I had not talked to Joe. If Bryan hadn't told me he'd been hanging around I wouldn't even have known it. He hadn't come in to see me. There'd been no card, no flowers. My throat tightened, and I felt the sting of tears. Damn it! A part of me knew I should probably make the first move, but he was the one in the wrong! Would it kill *him* to apologize first for once?

"I take it that's a no." Mike was angry. I knew it even before I looked at him over my shoulder. His face was flushed, his jaw set in an aggressive line. "Damn it, Kate. Joe loves you and he worries about you."

"And I love him. But you and I both know that he can be an interfering, overbearing, bully sometimes. He was out of line. Would it kill him to apologize?"

Mike ran his free hand through his thinning hair. "I think it actually might." He blew out an exasperated breath. "Between the two of you, I swear—"

We had reached the third floor. It was time to go out into the hallway and down to Mac's lab. I really hoped I hadn't gotten turned around. The directions he'd given me were from the elevator.

I needn't have worried. Mike knew where he was going. He had one of those internal compasses that never let him get lost. I followed his broad back down a long bright hallway that smelled of antiseptic and other chemicals, the nylon bag bumping against my legs in an irregular rhythm.

We turned left and I found myself in a familiar corridor. He'd led me right to the hall with Mac's lab. I took the lead again, going over to the security door they'd installed since my last visit and punching in the numbers I'd been given. Like magic the light on the mechanism turned from red to green, and there was a metallic click that let me know the door was ready to be opened.

Mike took the lead again, and I followed him through the empty corridor to the marked fire door. A few flights of stairs later, I had my hand on the doorknob, ready to go outside and make the short trip across open lawn to the employee parking garage.

Mike went first. I waited a couple of minutes, the door cracked open so that I could listen in case he called out. Instead, all I heard was the crunch of feet on frozen snow.

The wind sneaking through the crack of the open door was frigid. My breath misted in the air. I started swearing under my breath, wishing heartily for my heavy coat. I didn't have it; wasn't exactly sure what had happened to it. So I was left to shiver in my borrowed scrubs and hope to hell that Brooks had the heater on in the car. Otherwise I was in for a long, miserable ride.

Steeling myself, I opened the door. The wind hit me like a full-body slap, cutting through the thin cotton as if I weren't even wearing it. I took off at a run across the frost-limned grass. The breath coming into my lungs was clean, but sharp as broken glass.

Mike was waiting by the back door to the garage. I slowed to a stop and pulled Miles's identification card from my pocket. I swiped it through the locking mechanism. Once again a green light flared and I heard the mechanism click.

Mike opened the door, holding it open for me.

"*Damn* it's cold." I blew on fingers that had gone red.

"I should have thought to bring you a coat. I'm sorry. At least the van will be warm."

"Thank God for that!" I stepped through the door. I'd expected to see a rental mini-van. Instead, an old white work van was parked right where it was supposed to be. A thin wisp of gray smoke trailed from its tailpipe, adding to the prevailing smell of gasoline and exhaust that permeated the concrete structure.

The van door slid open as I ran toward it. Bryan was inside. The minute he saw me his face lit up. His grin was just as open as it had been before, but there was a spark of knowledge in his eyes, in his body language, that showed just how much the healing had changed him. Individually the differences were so minute that I couldn't pinpoint them. Collectively it made all the difference.

"Hey, Katie, 'bout time you got here!"

He took the bag from my hands and scooted out of the way so that I could climb in. He slid out of his brown leather bomber jacket and threw it over my shoulders. "Here. Wear this. You look like you're freezing."

"I am." I managed to say it through chattering teeth. The metal floor was cold through the thin fabric of my trousers, but the jacket helped. Since Bryan was wearing a heavy fisherman's sweater he could afford to lose the coat, even if people saw him through the window. I watched as he pulled the side door closed as Mike climbed in to the passenger seat and strapped on his seatbelt.

"Hey, Reilly." Brooks turned to look over the driver's side seat. "Good to see you up and about." He turned to the front of the vehicle and made minute adjustments to the rearview mirror. "We've had a change of plan. Rob called. I'm supposed to let you know that he and Dusty will take care of Blank for you. I'm also supposed to tell you that the Channel 4 News crew just showed up at the church. They're looking for you and Bryan, or at least to talk to Mike. They figure he knows where the two of you are."

Brooks put the van in reverse. It jerked into gear. I wasn't prepared and wound up sliding a couple of inches across the floor.

"Why would they think that?"

Brooks laughed. "All they had to do is talk to someone you know. Anybody who's ever met you knows the first person you go to when you're in trouble is Mike."

I thought about that for a minute. He was almost right. I'd been relying on Michael O'Rourke since we were kids. He'd been the one who helped me through my parents' deaths, through my breakup with Dylan. But he wasn't the first person I ran to any more. Tom had taken that place in my mind, in my heart. I wasn't sure exactly when things had changed, but they had. The knowledge made me both happy and oddly sad.

Mike turned to meet my gaze. His look made me wonder if he knew what I'd been thinking. He often did. He gave me a wistful smile before turning to face the front.

"So, what's the plan?" Bryan asked. It was the tone that startled me. His voice had a confidence and aggression that had been missing for years. I wondered if I would ever be able to take the changes in him for granted. Would it always surprise me? Or would I eventually become so used to him being back that I forgot the hollow shell he'd been for so long: the empty eyes that stared back at me with no recognition whatsoever.

Brooks answered Bryan's question, but his eyes met mine in the mirror, checking for my approval. "You could use my mother's . . . old place." There was an odd tone to his voice, and it occurred to me that his mother must be the reason for his sympathy leave. He'd just lost one of his family, and I'd never said a word. But he kept going, his voice getting stronger with each word. "No one would think to look for you there. We haven't even started boxing up her stuff, so you should be comfortable, and I didn't like leaving it empty anyway."

"You're sure it's okay?" I had to ask. Having someone else in her place, so soon . . . well, I would've had a hard time with it. "I'm sorry about your mom, Brooks. I should have said so earlier." Mike and Bryan murmured their agreement with my condolences.

"It's fine," Brooks answered. I heard the click of the turn signal and felt the van shift left as he took a corner. "She was sick for a long time, and in a lot of pain. It was time."

An awkward silence descended on the car. I'm Catholic. I truly believe in heaven. I'd never met Brooks's mother, but I'd be willing to bet good money she'd gone there. Her son seemed more a man who embraced his past than over-came it.

The van slowed and lurched, sending me sprawling side-ways as we turned into a rutted driveway. I winced as the spot where the IV had been slammed against the seat's floor support.

"We're here."

I slid open the side door and climbed out to see a small, neat house with green shingles, the trim and front porch painted a pure white that gleamed in the moonlight. The porch light was on, casting a warm golden glow over the pair of old-fashioned metal chairs painted a green only slightly darker than the house. There was a braided rug on the floor in front of the door in place of a welcome mat. The floorboards of the porch creaked as we walked across them and the hinges of the wooden screen door squealed in protest as Brooks opened it. I recognized the neighborhood as one at the very edge of Denver, in a little triangle of confusion where three cities met. On the plus side, since nobody was certain of the boundaries, a 911 call usually brought instant response from all three cities.

Pulling keys from his pocket, he unlocked the main door and held it open with one hand as he reached in to turn on the light switch with the other.

The minute I stepped through the doorway I felt an abid-ing sense of home. It felt *right* somehow. Old hand-painted lamps cast a warm glow over well worn, but lovingly tended furniture. One corner of the room was dominated by a huge upright piano that had to be an antique. Its dark wood gleamed from years of polish. A lace cloth had been spread on its top with a collection of family photographs arranged in an attractive display. I saw pictures of Brooks as a child, playing catch with a young man in front of this same house; pictures of his graduation from high school and the police academy. It was obvious he'd been an only child and that his parents had been very proud of him.

I moved away from the photographs, turning to look at the rest of the room. A brick fireplace took up most of the north wall. Built-in bookcases flanked both sides up to chest height, the leaded glass wavy with age. The finish was old-fashioned varnish, not polyurethane, and while it was less practical, it gave the cabinets a glowing warmth that the newer finishes never quite seem to match. Mrs. Brooks had been a mystery buff, the cabinets were mostly filled with paper- and hard backs by the masters of mystery fiction. The entire bottom two shelves of one cabinet were filled with a set of familiar yellow covers. I walked over to check. Sure enough, the entire collection of Nancy Drew mysteries had been set out in numeric order.

He cleared his throat as I took in the room, smiling. "The fireplace works. I had it cleaned just a couple months ago, and there are some of those chemical logs in a bin on the back porch. You should probably crack open one of those if you decide to use it." Brooks gestured to the small windows on either side of the chimney.

"The bedrooms are back this way." Bryan and I followed him down a narrow hallway. There were two bedrooms. The largest was probably twelve by twelve. It was wallpapered in a pattern I'd never seen before, but liked very much—a cream background overlain with tiny bunches of flowers in white, gold, and vivid crimson. The dark wood bed and dresser were a matched set of antiques, with delicately carved leaf designs on the head- and footboards matching the design above the dresser mirror. A matching end table had a lace doily under a large reading lamp. Heavy crimson drapes covered the large windows on two of the walls, exactly matching the fabric and pattern of the spread on the bed.

"I figured you could sleep here. Mom would have insisted. There are fresh sheets in the linen cabinet in the bathroom." Brooks stepped back into the hallway and gestured at a closed door.

"Bryan, this is the other bedroom." Brooks pushed open the door to reveal a smaller room that had been painted a shade of sky blue. This was the first room to have carpeting rather than hardwood floors, and it was a thick plush the intense dark blue of a midnight sky. The walls were trimmed with wide baseboards painted bright white. There was one window. The curtains on it were white with navy and powder blue stripes crossing to form a loose plaid. The twin bed was black and had a metal tube construction on its head and footboards. The bedspread was a white chenille. In the corner a four-drawer chest of drawers stood. It had been painted a glossy black that looked good with the bed. A pair of shelves had been mounted on the wall. They held an assortment of ribbons and sports trophies—the only remnants of the childhood Brooks must have spent in this room.

The three of us trooped back to join Michael in the living room. Brooks was still talking. "You're welcome to whatever is in the pantry, but you'll need to go to the store for perishables."

"I can't tell you how much we appreciate this, John." Bryan said. It seemed strange that Bryan felt free to call him by his first name, but I never had.

"It's no problem." His eyes flickered as he had an idea. "If you really want to thank me you can start cleaning out the garage. It's filled with old junk. The real estate agent says the house will show fine with the furniture, but the garage is a disaster."

"I'll take care of it," Bryan promised with a confident nod. He flexed muscles that Mike had made certain were toned through hard work and frequent exercise.

"Thanks. You can just take it all out to the dumpster in the back alley. The city comes around to empty it every Friday morning. I'd stay inside as much as possible for a few days. Maybe take things outside after dark. People here know me, but they don't know you, and I don't want to walk around knocking on doors tonight. I'll explain things in the

morning. The neighbors are the *Neighborhood Watch* sort."
He reached into his pocket and withdrew a set of keys. He
tossed them to me. "Here. The one with the pink plastic
ring on it is the front door key. The little one is the padlock
to the garage. The car keys are to the Oldsmobile parked
out front. You can use it all you want."

"Brooks—" I was at a loss for words. He was being incredibly generous.

"Don't thank me until you see the garage." He joked.
"Padre, you ready to hit the road?"

"Any time you are." Mike stepped forward and gave me a
hug. It felt . . . odd. We've been hugging each other comfortably for years. But this time he gripped me fiercely,
tight enough to take my breath away. He buried his face in
the silly black wig and whispered in my ear. "Good-bye,
Katie."

"Mike?"

He pulled back abruptly and nearly dived out the front
door. Brooks and Bryan both gave me an odd look. I
shrugged. I had no more clue as to what was wrong than
they did.

"I'll talk to him." Brooks started toward the door, but
stopped with his hand on the handle. "I almost forgot to tell
you. Henri Tané *is* dead, but Antonia and Emily are both
fine. We can't be sure about Digby Wallace. Nobody's seen
him for a few days, but that's not unusual. One of the cops
in the nearest town volunteered to go out and check on him.
So it looks like it was just good, old-fashioned nightmares."

"You're sure?" I couldn't keep the relief from my voice.

"Sure as we can be. Still, I warned everybody about
what you saw, so they know to be careful. I'll call you
when I hear from Australia." He left then, without saying
good-bye. The screen door slammed shut behind him.

"So," Bryan said. "I'm starved. What do you say we
check out that pantry?"

I rolled my eyes, but followed him into the kitchen.

It was a small, neat room. The white painted cabinets had old-fashioned silver handles. The kitchen table was one of the old-fashioned ones with chrome legs and a wide chrome band around a smooth gray-flecked top. The chairs had chrome legs and metal seats and chair backs that had been painted fire engine red. Imitations of this exact set were being sold for ridiculous amounts of money at high-end furniture stores and galleries, but this was the real thing. The stove and refrigerator were both older models that had been top of the line back in their day. They were sparkling clean, without so much as a fingerprint or scorch mark marring the surface.

The floor was covered in scarred red linoleum that was probably loaded with asbestos. It had been waxed until it practically glowed. And on the wall, hanging above the stove was a white metal sign with bright red letters that read "The kitchen is the heart of any home."

There was pancake mix in the pantry, unspoiled eggs and milk in the refrigerator. In no time we were eating scrambled eggs and pancakes, while I answered Bryan's questions and caught him up on what had been happening in the big, wide world.

No surprise that he was most interested in the advancements in . . . video games.

23

*B*ryan and I spent a quiet few days in the house. I got to reread the old Nancy Drew novels I'd loved as a girl, lose at backgammon to Bryan in front of the fireplace, and generally rest up until I felt like myself again. I missed Tom dreadfully. I hadn't realized how much a part of my life he'd become. But it was wonderful spending time with Bryan. It felt like a part of my life had clicked back on, like a speaker you hadn't realized was shorting out.

We spent some time walking around the neighborhood, just to stretch our legs. It was a quiet, middle-class neighborhood with a fair ethnic mix. People mostly kept to themselves, although they were friendly enough when you ran into them at the grocery store or saw them walking their dogs. I guess Brooks had stopped in to tell people some quiet lie.

There was a little, neighborhood pizza place, a liquor store, and a privately owned grocery that had a meat shop where they'd cut your meat to order. At one point during the week Bryan called Joe. The two of them went out to a movie, then to Bernardo's afterward to shoot pool and drink beer. Bryan hadn't given up on getting Joe and me to make up. He'd back away for a little while, before trying again. He worked on each of us in turn, hoping that one of us would have the good grace to be the first to apologize.

After a week the worst of the media frenzy had died down. *The* hot superstar couple had given birth to their twins. The president had made a major announcement. There were other things to report. Oh, there was still interest, but we weren't being treated like hunted animals any more. Brian, Melinda, and I had agreed to do a Barbara Walters special on condition that the network make a major donation to the church's zombie care program. There would be mention of the program and Michael, broadcast at the beginning and end of the show. That should win him some points at the Vatican.

Since there was no more need to hide, Bryan and I would be going home tomorrow. Before we could leave, though, we had a promise to keep. Brooks hadn't been kidding. The garage was a disaster, packed floor to ceiling so that you couldn't even take two steps inside.

Thursday morning Bryan decided to try Joe yet again. He used the work cleaning out the garage as an opportunity to bridge the gap in our family. He asked him to come help. Joe refused, saying he "wasn't ready" to forgive me. I wasn't sure what he was supposed to be forgiving me for. Since I didn't think I'd done anything wrong, I refused to apologize. It hurt Bryan. He hated being caught in the middle. He loved us both so very much. A big part of me thought I should just say whatever it took to get Joe to back off, that the whole situation was childish and stupid. After all, Bryan was back, when we'd thought him lost to us forever. But another, stronger part sincerely believed that if I didn't make a stand Joe would be bullying me and harassing Tom for the rest of our natural lives. I didn't want to live like that. So I kept my mouth shut and enjoyed my time with Bryan away from Joe.

Brooks drove Tom to the house when he got off shift on Thursday afternoon at one. As agreed, we waited for John and Tom to arrive before getting started. First, because we were enjoying the quiet rhythm that we'd fallen into while staying here. But also, because neither Bryan nor I wanted to throw anything in the garage in the trash without checking with Brooks first. He might say "it's all junk," but we didn't want to accidentally dispose of some priceless family heirloom.

At one-thirty we opened the door and started digging in.

It was hard, physical labor, but it was a little like a treasure hunt as well. There were boxes of clothes, kid's toys, and board games piled next to boxes of old newspapers, some of them from before I'd been born. She'd only saved the special ones, and I was amazed to find yellowed copies of the *Denver Post* and *Rocky Mountain News,* one proclaiming the assassination of JFK and the other of Martin Luther King. Those *had* to be worth some money. I set them aside in a special pile.

There was a box of beautiful crystal, pale blue etched with a pattern of flowers. It was exquisite. I'd never seen anything like it. Brooks added it to the *save* pile. He'd let Camille decide whether she wanted it, or if they should donate it to the Salvation Army.

Three Bronco loads of books, children's games, and old clothes did get donated. There were probably more such things further back behind the mower and gardening tools, but we hadn't reached them yet.

I checked my watch as Brooks and Bryan each took an end of a battered old box spring and started shuffling their way around the house to the alley. We were making progress, but it was getting late and there was still an awful lot to do. I stared at the remaining mess, feeling tired and more than a little discouraged. A few minutes later, when Tom stepped through the garage door carrying cold beers from the fridge I was more than happy to take one in exchange for a quick kiss. He handed one each to Bryan and Brooks when they got back and said, "This is the last of the beer."

Bryan wiped the sweat from his forehead with one hand, smearing dirt in a long line. "There's a liquor store a couple blocks from here. I'll go buy some more and maybe pick us all up some sandwiches. Gotta tell you, I really missed beer."

I raised my brows in mock disapproval and crossed my arms—being the good big sister. He hadn't been of legal drinking age when he'd become a zombie. Brooks and Tom each reached into their pocket to retrieve a wallet while Bryan winked at me and grinned.

"I've got it," Brooks announced. "It's the least I can do considering how much work the three of you are putting in."

Tom started to argue, but Brooks cut him off with a wave of his hand. "I *said* I've got it."

Bryan took the money from Brooks's hand and went inside to grab the keys to the Oldsmobile. I watched him go with something akin to amazement. He remembered how to drive. I mean, yeah, his license was still technically valid from when he'd gotten it at sixteen. But he actually *remembered* how to drive. I hadn't believed it was possible, but he'd proven it to me in an empty church parking lot the previous afternoon. It was so cool, and so . . . weird.

I flipped open the can and took a long drink. I'm not much of a fan of beer, but it felt good going down. I was hot, sweaty, sticky, and no doubt stunk to high heaven. Of course, so did they. Every one of us had set aside our jackets hours ago to work in our shirt sleeves. The temperature outside was cold, but we were doing heavy physical labor that had us sweating like pigs.

I set my beer on the floor just outside the door, then gathered up the last bundles of old magazines that had been tied together with string. I crossed the lawn, carrying my burden into the alley and toward the third dumpster down from the house. We'd filled the first two to overflowing, but the neighbors had been more than happy to donate their space to the house cleaning and save their trash for the next week. Brooks's mother had been a lifer in the neighborhood. It was their way of showing respect. The first two were already full to overflowing with odds and ends of lumber and other miscellaneous crap.

The street lights were spaced far enough apart that sections of alley were in deep shadow. One of the neighborhood dogs barked, leaping against the chain-link fence as I passed. His lips curled back, exposing a set of fangs Tom or Rob would be proud of. I hoped the fence would hold and moved away quickly.

I had to set down the magazines so that I could flip open the dumpster's hinged lid. Grunting with effort, I lifted the first bundle and flung it over the lip of the container. I was tired. My shoulder was starting to hurt. I'd been careful, tried not to do too much, but the old injury was letting me know that it wasn't going to put up with much more. I hated it, but pushing harder would just reinjure it, and put me through more months of expensive, painful physical therapy.

I was bending down to get the next bundle when I heard the roar of an engine and the crunch of gravel. A pair of headlights pierced the shadows as an SUV barreled toward me.

There was no time to think. Instinct took over. I dived to the side, rolling as I did. I took most of the impact on my shoulder with bruising force, driving dirt and broken glass through the fabric of my shirt and into my skin.

There was a squeal of tires as the driver slammed on the brakes, but the SUV's momentum was too much to overcome. The vehicle slammed into the Dumpster right where I'd been standing, the impact sending the heavy metal canister back six feet, through a tall wire and picket fence with a deafening scream of metal on metal and the crunch of splintering wood.

It took a few seconds for me to pick myself up off the ground, staring at the crushed front end of the vehicle. Distantly I heard Tom and the others approaching, but my attention was all on the SUV. I limped forward, planning to check on the driver. The airbag had deployed, and I couldn't see inside in the uncertain light.

"Kate, are you all right?" Tom called.

"I'm fine. But you'd better call the cops and an ambulance."

"Right."

I heard his running footsteps retreating toward the house. I had rounded the rear corner of the vehicle, intending to check on the driver when I saw the door was open. In that same instant, out of the corner of my eye I saw movement reflected in the paint.

I spun, and the scrap of two-by-four sped by me in a blur of speed before slamming into the fender. The metal bent and tore with a heavy sound. Almost before I could react the board was pulled back again.

"Amanda!" I gasped out the name.

She looked like the villain from a slasher movie. Her face was contorted with rage. The entire front of her body was soaked with blood so that her clothes clung wetly to her. She smelled of blood, and meat.

I screamed, loud and long. She cursed, swinging the two-by-four with the same deadly ferocity she'd used to swing the bat at me up in the mountains. I opened my senses, using my psychic talent. It was the only way I could stay ahead of her deadly swings.

"Drop the board." Brooks's voice rang out through the night. He stood beneath the street light, gun aimed steadily at the center of her chest.

She hissed, spinning in his direction. I tried to shout a warning, but it was too late. The board flew at him like a missile. Brooks dived out of the way, firing as he did. The board clipped him, and I heard the gun clatter to the ground. I didn't dare look to see if he was hurt. Even as I watched blood blossom from the exit wounds, her body jerking like a badly handled puppet, she tried to lunge at me.

I could see her heart beat through one of the holes in her chest, but as I watched in horrified fascination the hole was shrinking. Her body was actually healing the damage *while I watched.* That was even faster than Tom's wounds had healed.

Time seemed to slow, everything seemed preternaturally clear. I backed away, trying to get ready for what she was about to do. Tom was coming. I could see the large furred shape of him running toward her unprotected back.

Amanda reached down, grabbing another scrap of lumber to use against me. Her voice when she spoke was . . . eerie, high-pitched and breathy, yet weirdly calm.

"I went to the church looking for you." She swung, the board hitting the SUV. The tail light shattered with a crash, causing a rain of shards of yellow, white, and red plastic. "I knew Mike would know where you were hiding." The board missed me, by the merest fraction. She'd put enough force behind the blow that it threw off her balance for a second, giving me time to move further out of the way. "I had to kill the wolf to get to him." She looked annoyed. "He almost got away. I caught him in the church basement. I used to like him, you know. I would have been easier on him, but he fought me. He wouldn't tell me, no matter what I did to him."

Caught *who*? Rob? Or Mike? I didn't dare reach out with my mind. I needed every spare brain cell for the here and now. But shouldn't I have known? Why hadn't my senses warned me while she was at the church?

She faked to the right with lightning speed, but the move threw her off balance. She stumbled, and Tom leaped, the momentum of his body against her back taking her to the pavement with a wet thud as his teeth sank into the back of her neck. Growling, he jerked his head sharply back and forth. I heard her spine snap; saw her head tearing away from her body. I remembered then, what Carlton had told me, what Tom had overheard.

To kill Amanda we had to stake her, and take off her head. Tom could take her head, but he couldn't stake her, not in his present form.

Brooks was bent over, picking up his gun. The sirens were getting close. There wasn't much time.

I reached behind me, grabbing a broken picket in my right hand. With one final jerk of Tom's jaws, Amanda's head rolled free of her body. Her blue eyes blinked, her lips pulling back from her teeth in a snarl, even as the head rolled across the pavement, leaving a bloody trail behind it.

I grabbed her shoulder with my left hand, rolling her headless body onto its back. Blood was spurting from her neck, but the gunshot wounds were almost completely healed. As if distantly, I heard Brooks gasp in shock. Her chest was still rising and falling with labored breaths that made whistling noises from her open windpipe. I raised my "stake" above her chest. Using all my strength I drove it home. Amanda's body gave one last shudder and stilled.

24

The rest of the night passed in a blur. I have no real memories of what happened, just scattered images. I recalled being curled up in the worn metal chair on the front porch of the house, my body wrapped in a heavy quilt Brooks had pulled off his mother's bed. The police had separated Tom, Brooks, and me to take our statements. I was waiting for my attorney to arrive before I said anything.

The next image was of being questioned at the nearest branch of the Denver P.D., with Gary Hamilton arguing back and forth with the assistant DA.

Finally, there was a late morning cab ride to Denver General.

Jake was dead. Amanda had killed him. I hadn't liked him much, but I mourned his passing none the less. Mike was in ICU. They'd had to do massive surgery. He might not make it, but even if he lived, he'd probably be paralyzed from the chest down.

Joe blamed me for everything. He said it was my fault Mike was here and Jake was dead. He stood an inch in front of my face shouting at the top of his lungs, his spit spraying my face. He said my "lifestyle choices" were deadly for the people around me. I didn't fight back. I couldn't. If Amanda hadn't wanted me dead, none of it would've happened. She hadn't had any grudge against Jake, the zombies, or Michael. She'd wanted me dead and was ready to destroy anything and anyone who got in her way. We'd killed her. But the damage was done.

Monica, Amanda . . . my enemies. But when they'd wanted to hurt me, they'd struck out at my family and friends. Because they knew that would hurt me the most, and that was where I was the most vulnerable.

I turned to walk away from the fight, but Security had arrived. I left the building under escort . . . again, wandering out of the hospital into the cold, clear winter day.

I didn't bother to call a cab to take me home even though I was miles from the warehouse. I walked, tears streaming unchecked down my cheeks, my breath misting the air in front of me. I walked with my hands in the pockets of Bryan's leather bomber jacket, neither seeing nor caring about the world around me.

I prayed hard for Michael and for Jake's soul. Then I prayed for guidance and thought about my life. Had I brought all this onto myself and the people who loved me? I tried to be brutally honest. If I had acted differently, would things have been better? Had I done something wrong that was the root of my problems? I couldn't come up with a damned thing. Amanda had been jealous of me in high school and blamed me for what happened to Monica and the others. Before that, Monica had hated me for taking out Larry's nest to save Dylan.

Bryan said I shouldn't have saved Dylan. But I couldn't not. He hadn't believed that Larry would hunt me down. I knew better. He had chosen me to be next in line based on the things he'd heard about my psychic talent. If I hadn't gone into the basement after Dylan Larry *would* have come after me. One way or another, I would've had to fight. I knew it without a doubt in my mind. The time and place might have been different, but the result would have been the same.

A strange peace settled over me as I waited for the light at the crosswalk at Speer and Colfax. I was almost halfway home. I was cold. I was tired. But I was as clear headed as I'd ever been in my life. Joe was wrong. He was terrified and angry and I was the easiest target for him to direct that at. But he was wrong. I wasn't responsible for Michael's injuries or any of the other things he was laying at my door. Monica and Amanda's actions had been horrible, violent and *evil*, but they were *their* actions—*not mine*.

A horn honked, and I turned to see a familiar Oldsmobile pulling to the curb with Bryan at the wheel. He stopped a short distance in front of me and threw open the passenger side door. I trotted over and climbed in.

"It wasn't my fault, Bryan. Part of me really wishes it was so I could just go throw myself off a bridge and save all my enemies the trouble. But none of it was my fault."

He turned to me, rolling his eyes. "You're just now figuring that out? Jeez, Kate, I thought *I* was the stupid one in the family."

I pulled the car door closed and strapped on my seatbelt, reveling in the warmth pouring from the heat vents. "You are not stupid. As I recall, you got straight A's and were top of your class." I held my hands in front of the heat vents, trying to get them warm.

He gave me a pitying look, as if he couldn't believe I was so naive. "Only because I played varsity football. If I'd had to earn those grades I'd have flunked Algebra, and had a solid D in English Lit."

I turned and stared at him. "You're kidding!"

He raised his right hand from the steering wheel. "Nope. Hand to God. And Emily Carter did my homework for me in U.S. Government in exchange for . . . *carnal favors*." He paused for effect. "Services which, by the way, I was more than happy to render. I wasn't a saint, Kate. No matter what you and Joe thought." His grin was positively wicked.

"Bryan!" I was shocked, although come to think on it, I probably shouldn't have been. My baby brother had many shining qualities, but his work ethic had never really been one of them. Coach Cooper had wielded a lot of influence in the school, and men's varsity football had been huge with the alumni association.

Bryan hit the turn signal and pulled back onto the road at the first opening. "This bullshit is so like you, taking the blame for everything." He kept his eyes on the road, but his expression was intense. "Joe was always the smart one—when he wasn't acting like an idiot. You were the stubborn one . . . the athlete. You never quit. You don't know how. You give everything you've got, everything you *are,* on the field."

He slowed the car for a stoplight, and glanced at me across the seat. "The other night, when I said Joe and I went to a movie? I lied."

I didn't say anything, but I gave him a questioning look.

"Mary was pissed at Joe. She said he didn't have a clue who you really are, that maybe if he took the time to really understand you, the two of you would get along better."

I blinked rapidly as I tried to accept what he was telling me. Mary Connolly couldn't possibly have stuck up for me. It would be a miracle if she didn't blame me for Jake's death as well. I couldn't imagine why she would be trying to help me with my family problems. Of course, she could be trying to help Joe get his head back on straight. It was something she'd do . . . if she loved him.

"Anyway," Bryan's voice pulled me back to the present. "She pulled out this old videocassette, slams it in the VCR, and hits play. It was your last volleyball match. The one where you got injured so badly, and still wouldn't quit: wouldn't give up. Your damned arm was almost totally useless. It hurt me just to *watch* you trying to use it. But you would *not* give up."

The light changed, and he pulled the car forward in traffic. "The video crew had a camera focused on your huddle with your partner, and they'd turned up the sound as high as they could to try to catch what you could possibly be saying to each other."

He switched lanes, hitting the signal to turn right onto the road that would lead to the lofts. "And I heard you say to your partner, 'This is the last game of this tournament, my career, and my *life*. I am *not* going to fucking lose. So you had *damned well* be ready to fight.'"

I winced. I'd said it, and at the time I'd meant every word. Now it seemed a little . . . I dunno, *melodramatic*. "I wouldn't have thought they'd let the profanity through on television."

"They didn't. They bleeped it, but Mary had the *director's cut*."

We rode in silence for almost a block. I wasn't sure what to say. Looking back on it, what I'd done was probably . . . no, it just *was* idiotic, no probably about it. But I couldn't have done any differently. It wasn't in my nature.

"After we watched that Joe just sat on the couch, not saying a word. I left. I went down to Bernardo's, shot pool against some guy named Leo. He said he was a friend of yours. Nice guy, and pours a mean rum and Coke. When I came back to the house, you were already in bed."

He pulled the car up to the gate of the parking garage and typed in the code.

"Why are you telling me this, Bryan?" I shifted in my seat and looked away from him, staring out the window.

He didn't answer until he pulled the car into Tom's open spot and put it in park. He turned in the seat until he was facing me, but I still wouldn't look at him. "Couple of reasons. I was pissed at both of you. I'm back and I wanted things to be back to normal for the three of us. But the two of you are just being complete assholes. It wasn't like this before. So I talked to Mike. I figured if anybody could help with this mess he could."

I swung my head around to meet his gaze. "What did he say?"

"He said that Joe doesn't respect you, and that's the one thing you can't forgive."

I flinched. It was a perfect one-sentence summation. "Did he have any suggestions?"

"He told me to pray."

I unbuckled my seatbelt and opened the door enough to turn on the dome light. He turned to face me, his face half hidden by shadow. "What was the second thing?"

"You've spent so much time thinking of me as a kid that I needed to remind both of you I'm an adult. Hell, I was an adult *before* the Eden. I was nearly seventeen—ready to graduate and get my own place. I'm back to that person." He reached out and touched my hand, took it in his and squeezed it. "You don't have to be my keeper anymore, Kate. You get to live your own life." He paused for effect. "It's time to let go—of a lot of things."

25

Tom's alarm sounded and he groaned his way to wakefulness. His pulled his arm from around me and half rolled, half reached for the clock. "It's morning." He didn't sound happy to be making the announcement. I wasn't thrilled about it either. We'd stayed up very late the night before, talking. Mike was out of ICU, but still in critical condition. The werewolves were in shock over Jake's loss. It was a small pack, and a very close-knit one. Losing a member was hitting them very hard. I couldn't imagine how Tom was managing Jake's loss, or why he hadn't noticed anything wrong when Amanda had attacked. I'd never asked him how, or whether, the wolves were connected mentally. Maybe Mary was a better person to ask.

Tom scooted away, until he wasn't spooning me any more, and climbed out from beneath the covers. I watched him cross the room and disappear into the bathroom. A moment later the shower was running. Closing my eyes, I dozed off. I didn't wake again until he was bending over to kiss me good-bye.

The kiss was tender at first, almost tentative, but it grew in passion until it was a wild, hungry thing, devouring us both. We both needed a touchstone right now to start to heal the hurt.

Fierce, hot need poured through me, leaving me breathless. I was glad I was already laying in bed, because if I'd been standing my knees would've given out on me. He laughed. It was a confident, masculine sound that should have been annoying, but somehow wasn't. "I love that I can do that to you, love the way your body reacts to mine."

I smiled over at him. "If we had just a *little* more time I'd show you what *my* body can do to you. But *you* have to go to work."

"Damn it anyway. Maybe if we hurry?"

"I am *so* not going to hurry." I laughed. Tom needed to go to work and I needed some time alone. I loved him, but there were things I needed to do that just never seemed to get accomplished when he was around. "You're just going to have to wait until you get off shift, *knowing* that I'm going to have three whole days to come up with all sorts of creative things to do to you."

He gave me a long look. "You're *sure* you're all right?"

I sighed. Last night we'd talked about a lot of things, among them my problems with Joe and my worries about Mike. Only family was being allowed into ICU, so it wouldn't even do any good to go to the hospital until he was in more stable condition. The nurses were being polite, but vague.

"I'm fine!" I assured him, mostly to hear myself say it. "Now *git*. Shoo! You don't want to be late."

He gave me one more quick kiss good-bye and left. I watched him go and felt a bit of relief when he was gone. I needed time alone to think about the things we'd talked about and to digest everything that had happened. Now that Amanda was gone, I was hoping I could live a little more normally, not be looking over my shoulder *quite* as much.

I cleaned up, then spent the morning working on my finances. Between one thing and another, I had enough to pay the worst of the bills, but that was it. The good news was that I would no longer have to pay for nursing care for Bryan, but if I didn't get some serious income through the door soon I was going to lose everything. I couldn't in good conscience accept disability any longer. My body was fine, or at least good enough to get back to business.

Working would also get me out of the house so I didn't spend my days sitting around moping.

I paced the apartment, trying to come up with a plan of attack. First, I needed to contact all of my old clients and see if I could win them back from whoever had been taking care of them during my absence. Next, I'd need to do something to get my name out there to potential new clients. A flyer would be cheapest and easiest. After all, Tom's computer was right there on the desk, and he had an art program that I could probably figure out how to use. If I *had* to do actual advertising, I would. But the cost of ads is staggering, particularly in the kind of high-end publications that would appeal to a clientele that would use a bonded courier. At least my bond was safe. The not guilty verdict assured that, and I'd just mailed in the check for the annual fee.

I popped one of Tom's packaged meals into the microwave and sat down with the telephone and my address book.

The first number I called was to Ramon and Celeste's art gallery. She answered on the first ring.

"Tres Chic, how can I help you?"

"Hi, Celeste."

"Kate!" She let out a squeal of delight. "Ramon, it's Katie!" She didn't cover the phone through any of this, and I had to hold the receiver back from my ear so as not to lose an ear drum. "Darling, it's so good to hear from you! I'm so happy about your brother! Absolutely *amazing*. You must be ecstatic!"

I had to smile. Every sentence was uttered with breathless excitement. It was very, very Celeste.

"But oh dear, this latest thing . . . and the other, up in the mountains . . . Kate, you need to be careful. *They* are terrible enemies to have. I really do worry for you." She would know all about that. She'd been enthralled by one of Monica's old hosts. While I was pretty sure it was partially voluntary, I was happy to play stupid since Monica's death had gotten her back together with Ramon. He'd been heartbroken to think she'd cheat on him, but forgave everything when he realized she'd been bitten. Sometimes love really is blind—and not terribly bright. Still, who was I to judge?

"Thanks Celeste, I appreciate that."

I heard Ramon pick up the other extension. "Kate, sweetheart! It's so good to hear from you. No doubt Celeste has told you how happy we are about Bryan."

"Yes, she has, thank you."

"To what do we owe this honor?"

I took a deep breath and steeled myself. I've always hated cold calls, and I wasn't *positive* that Ramon wasn't going to be pissed at me for what I'd charged him for serving papers on Celeste. I'd been ticked off at him, and charged him ten grand for a ten minute job. I felt like a heel spending the money, and couldn't afford to repay him the difference. But whether or not I was back in his good graces was another thing entirely.

"Well, I'm fit to go back to work, so I thought I'd give you a call and see if you had anything for me." The words came out a little rushed, but at least I didn't sound as nervous as I felt.

"I hope you don't intend to charge me as much as you did last time." Ramon's tone made it a joke—sort of. I could tell he was definitely not over being angry with me.

"Ramon!" Celeste scolded her husband.

"Kate knows I'm teasing, darling." He tried to placate her. I knew no such thing.

"It's Kate that saved me from those . . . things, Ramon."

"And for that I am forever in her debt." Ramon said suavely, and I had no doubt he bowed to her over the railing. They kept offices on different floors of their shop, even after they reunited, for reasons unknown to me. "And while we have been using someone else lately, I haven't really been that happy with their level of service."

I let out a breath I hadn't realized I'd been holding.

"Darling, what about the Anderson statue?" Celeste was pushing him.

There was a long pause as Ramon considered his options. I had no idea what the Anderson statue was, but I wanted the job.

"Fine." He agreed, but he didn't sound entirely happy about it. "We have acquired a statue through the Anderson estate. Quite beautiful, really. We're having it auctioned at Christie's in London. Will Friday work for you? I assume you'll want to make your own flight arrangements."

I let out a breath that sounded just a bit like a squeak of delight. "Friday will be fine."

"We'll give you your usual fee. The man we've been using is a bit cheaper—" he let the phrase dangle for a few seconds, no doubt hoping that I would offer to reduce my rate. When I didn't bite he sighed and continued. "But, as I say, we haven't been entirely happy with him."

We chatted for a few more minutes before ending the conversation. I took a break to eat, then came back to the phone and the next number on my call list.

I wanted to call Gerry Friedman, but it was too late because of the time difference. So I skipped his name and moved further down the list.

It took longer than I expected, but the results were gratifying. People had actually missed me. There was work to be had. Hallelujah!

At four thirty I stopped calling. I stood, stretching to relieve my stiff muscles. After a quick dinner of frozen pizza I sat down at Tom's computer and went to work designing a business flyer.

I was completely immersed in the project, to the point

where I was startled to look up at the clock and find it was already 10:00 P.M. I decided to finish the project in the morning and went upstairs for a hot bath before bed.

The sheets still smelled of Tom's cologne and I snuggled against his pillow as I drifted off to sleep, warm and cozy.

The small wood-frame house was painted pale yellow. It had green shutters and bright white trim. A white picket fence enclosed the backyard. There was a flower bed along the fence. The bare stalks of rose bushes climbed upward, stark and black against the white of the pickets, made darker by the long shadows cast in the moonlight.

The moon rode high in a sky scattered with wispy clouds. There were stars, but only the brightest of them shone down. Every window in the neighborhood was dark. Only the occasional front porch light had been left on.

Behind the picket fence a dog started barking. I could tell it was a big dog. It had one of those deep, resonant, no-nonsense barks that makes you pause and worry about the amount of damage a dog that size can do. It was angry, frightened at the scent of something I could sense but couldn't see. The barks grew more frantic.

A light came on in one corner of the house. I could hear a man grumbling about "checking on the damned dog." He stumbled toward the back door. The back porch light came on. Through the screen door I heard him call "What is it, Brutus? What's the matter boy?"

I knew that voice! Knew the face behind the screen door. It was Brooks standing there in a white tee-shirt and boxers. I scanned the area, looking for the source of the dog's barking. She was here, somewhere. I knew it, and I knew who it was.

"What's wrong, John?" A woman's voice called from the house.

"Doesn't look like anything's wrong."

"Well he doesn't just bark over nothing. You'd better let him in before he wakes the neighbors."

Brooks grumbled, but opened the screen door. As he bent down to unhook the dog's chain there was a blur of movement, too fast for the eye to follow. A dark shape slammed into Brooks, driving him to the sidewalk with an impact that drove the breath from his lungs and smashed his head against the concrete.

Brutus the Rottweiler attacked, his full bulk lunging at the person riding his master's body, fangs bared to tear out the intruder's throat. The swing of a gloved fist sent the dog flying. His impact against the garage was loud enough that lights began coming on all over the neighborhood.

The dog rose painfully to its feet. Growling, it struggled to drag itself forward, using only its front legs.

A woman came to the doorway. She wore a flimsy red silk robe with nothing under it. She was beautiful, fierce, and proud. She held her husband's gun in a teacup grip the way he had taught her and took aim . . .

I woke with a jerk, sending Blank leaping from the bed with a startled meow. Rolling onto my side, I checked the clock on the nightstand. It was only 1:00 A.M. I groaned and tried to focus. What had I just dreamed about that had my heart racing so fast? Was it another nightmare? It seemed desperately important . . . like there was something I needed to do right away, but the details were just . . . gone. Damn it, I needed to *sleep*. These nightmares had to stop before I was too exhausted to handle another day.

I climbed from beneath the covers and padded over to the bathroom. If Tom found out what I was about to do he'd raise holy hell with me. But I was desperate and not stupid enough to tell him.

I opened the medicine chest and pulled out the bottle of muscle relaxants that had been prescribed for my shoulder. I didn't need them for the pain any more, but I recalled that I'd slept like a dead thing every time I'd taken one.

I poured a single pill into my palm and popped it into my mouth. I washed it down with water from the sink held in my cupped palm. I dried my hands on the hand towel, crossed back to the bed, and curled up beneath the covers next to where the cat had snuggled into the warm spot I'd vacated. Within minutes I fell into a deep, sound, sleep.

I woke at 9:00 A.M. feeling utterly refreshed. I bounded downstairs to feed the cat and call Gerry Friedman. I knew their offices in Tel Aviv were closed, so I left a message, telling him I was back in business and asking him to call. That done, I sat down to finish work on the flyer and mailing list. When I finally had them printing I climbed back upstairs and pulled out a set of sweats and sports bra. I wanted coffee. Not coffeemaker coffee, either: the good stuff. I brushed my teeth, pulled my hair into a tight ponytail, wrapped my knee, and pulled on the exercise gear. In just less than ten minutes I was jogging up Seventeenth Street, my breath fogging in the chill morning air, my shoes beating a steady rhythm on the concrete sidewalk.

There's a Starbucks on the first floor of one of the office towers on Seventeenth. It does a booming business pretty much all day long. I waited in line behind a bunch of executive types and one or two bicycle couriers. When I finally got to the front of the line I ordered the biggest cup of heaven I could get my hands on, along with a double-fudge brownie with walnuts baked in.

I took a seat on a stool next to the long counter that ran along the far wall. I stared out the window, entertaining myself by people-watching as I sipped my coffee and ate breakfast. A familiar green Hummer pulled to the curb across the street and Lewis Carlton unfolded from the driver's side.

He was wearing glossy black warm-up pants with a pair of red stripes down the side and a dark red fishnet tank that showed off an upper body that was finely chiseled and covered with expensive body art. A gold ring glittered in his left nipple, clearly visible through the sheer fabric of his shirt. Gold-rimmed sunglasses with dark lenses hid his eyes. If he was cold, I couldn't tell it. He jaywalked across Seventeenth, ignoring the honking horns and accompanying hand gestures from drivers who'd been trying to run the yellow light.

He strolled into the store, taking his place in line. Everyone stared. It was almost impossible not to. Whatever else you might say about him, the man had style. He chatted amiably with the people in line, accepting the adoration of the sports fans, signing his autograph on cups, napkins, even on one woman's abdomen. He nodded a greeting at me. I nodded back, not really even tempted to leave.

Eventually he managed to get his coffee and break away from his fans to join me. "Mornin', Buffy. How's tricks?"

He lowered himself onto the stool next to me, facing in so that he could stretch his ridiculously long legs out into the aisle.

I smiled in spite of myself. "Fine, Carlton. You?"

"Not bad. Gotta give you props for offing Amanda Shea. I didn't think you'd be able to do it." He lifted his coffee cup in salute before taking a sip.

"Tom did most of it." I didn't say more because, while it appeared that there wouldn't be charges pressed against either of us, I didn't want to risk it. Besides, people were listening. They were trying to pretend they weren't, but the guy with the newspaper was holding the silly thing upside-down, and the woman with the book hadn't turned a page since Carlton walked in.

Carlton nodded as he sipped his coffee. "Fido's all right. He's good for you." He grinned, flashing fangs. "Mind you, I'd be better. But he's all right."

"I'll tell him you said so."

He laughed. "You'd do it, too." He took off his sunglasses and hooked them into the neck of his shirt. When he set the cup on the counter, his face was utterly serious. "You can't do any more healings, Buffy. I don't care how guilty they make you feel or how much money they offer."

"Funny, my doctor says the same thing." With everything that had been going on, I'd forgotten all about the MRI scheduled this week. Oh, and then there was the interview. My stomach tied itself in a knot just thinking about that.

"It'll kill you." Carlton's words brought me back to the present with a start. "Hell, it was *supposed* to kill you to heal your brother. That, or leave you a mindless shell. That was sort of the plan—hook you in with the promise of it and then let you do yourself in. Without a symbiont, the human brain isn't wired to handle that much psychic energy." He shook his head in amazement. "You are one stubborn bitch. You just won't *die*. Do you have any idea how much that pisses them off?"

"Them? Not you? They're not listening in right now?"

He put his cup to his lips. Taking a long pull he looked at me over the rim of his cup before he spoke. "You hear any buzzing in here? Nah. You're all right. From what I can see, when we leave you alone, you leave us alone. Only time you ever went out lookin' for trouble was when they took that boyfriend of yours . . . what's-his-name."

"Dylan Shea," I prompted him. I watched him react to the name, just a flicker of . . . something that passed through his eyes and was gone before I could guess what it was. It puzzled me. But what puzzled me more was why he'd be helping me. "Why are you telling me this?" I really wanted to know. If the rules still applied, he couldn't lie to me. But if he was telling the truth, it was bound to piss off the queens and the hive. I'd seen the queens fell members who defied them with the psychic powers they could command. Why would Carlton risk that? It didn't make sense.

Then again, almost nothing about the big black man made sense to me. He was a very big, very tough enigma.

"You helped me save those kids. You could've said no. They were working with Amanda Shea to kill you. But you helped us save them. They're my hive now. My peeps. So I figure I owe you one."

"Bet the rest of the queens don't see it the same way."

He flashed his fangs again. "No bet. I'm not letting you take my money on a sure thing."

Setting his cup on the counter he rose and extended his hand for me to shake. "Take care of yourself, Reilly. They want you out of the way. Truth. They'd do pretty much anything to manage it. I've been sent off to Pueblo with the kiddies. Can't have two queens in the same city. Besides, for some reason they don't like me running into you." He winked and then covered his eyes with the so-dark shades. "They seem to think I talk too much. Go figure."

I laughed. I couldn't help it.

"Anyway, I saw you sitting here and figured I'd stop by and tell you good-bye and good luck." I took the hand he held out for me and shook it, feeling the strength of those fingers as his hand gripped mine, his playoff rings digging ever-so-slightly into my flesh.

"You too."

He left the way he came, loping across the street to the accompaniment of car horns and hand gestures. I doubted I'd ever see him again, and I wasn't positive that I wasn't sorry. Carlton might be a Thrall, but he was an amazing individual. God help me, I actually liked him. That wasn't a good trend.

I finished my coffee, dumped the trash into the container, and left for my run home.

It was clouding up. It might blow over. Then again, it could snow sometime this afternoon. If it did, I didn't think it would amount to much. It was probably just one of those

here-today-gone-in-the-morning snows that happen so often in Denver.

I made good time getting back to the apartment. When I got home there was a message on the machine from Gerry telling me how happy he was to hear from me. It was good to hear his thickly accented English. He promised to make a couple of calls. That was a relief. Business might not be booming yet, but it was a start. Gerry had a lot of connections in the jewelry industry. The people he worked with had been some of my best customers in the past. Morris Goldstein might be dead, but I didn't doubt that someone had taken his place. Commerce, like nature, abhors a vacuum.

There was another message from the television network, confirming the time for the interview. I'd hoped that when the word got out about Amanda's death they'd cancel. Not a chance. I was not only famous, I was *infamous*. The ratings would be *huge*. They'd do it here, in Denver, in my apartment. Could I please call and confirm that next Tuesday would be good for me? My mouth went dry with absolute terror. Why in the *hell* had I agreed to this? But Tuesday would probably work. I could be back from London by then. Oh, crap. I took deep, steadying breaths and reminded myself that a good charity would be getting a lot of money in exchange for my doing this.

So, afraid or not, I picked up the phone and called them back. I don't run from my fears—most of them, anyway.

I also called the hospital to check on the date for the MRI. I was wrong. It was next week, not this one. At least I hadn't missed it. Whew. I asked to be transferred to ICU, but there was no change in Mike's condition. Still no visitors. Still no information other than he was in serious condition.

After spending a few minutes worrying about him, and praying a lot, I hung up. I started a stew cooking in the crock pot and spent the next several hours cleaning house and trying to find places to put all Tom's stuff. I hung the picture of his family and the group shots of him with his firehouse buddies on the same wall with all of my photos, including the one of Tom as Mr. August from the firehouse calendar. It's amazingly hot and stays just this side of decency because of the careful placement of a coiled fire hose.

Blank convinced me that he was starving to death and hard food just wouldn't do. He also lured me away from my work for a while with a wild game of "attack the feather duster." Eventually he tired of the game and curled up in a sunbeam between a pair of potted plants.

By dinner time the place looked pretty good. Oh, it would need more work before the crew showed up, but the place definitely looked better than it had in a while. I was feeling pretty self-satisfied when the phone rang.

"Hello?"

"Hey baby, it's me." Tom was in a good mood, which probably meant that thus far this shift he hadn't had to deal with anything bad. We'd been together long enough now that I could recognize the strain in his voice when he called after a bad fire, one with injuries or fatalities. He tried to hide how he felt every time, but it always affected him.

"Hi gorgeous. Hope you don't mind. I've been unpacking your things. You get the right half of the bedroom closet and the bottom two drawers. Oh, and I hung your photos."

There was a long silence on the other end of the phone. "Tom? Is that all right? Did I do something wrong?"

He laughed. "Wrong? Hell no! I just never expected you'd let me move in without pitching a fit, and here you are hanging my pictures for me."

"Yeah." I grinned. "Kind of surprises me, too. I guess you'll just have to repay me in *creative* ways."

"Oh, I can *do* that."

I mentioned the interview, and my job prospects. He told me it had been a good shift thus far, and that Rob had found another job. Then we said we loved each other, joked about what we'd do when he got off shift the next day, and hung up the phone.

I was in love. And it felt really good.

I ate the stew while watching *Danger Mouse* on DVD. It's a British cartoon, with a one-eyed white mouse as a secret agent. Tom's not a big fan but I am, so I watch it when he's not around. I had a wild case of giggles watching "The Bad Luck Eye of the Little Yellow God" when there was a knock on the front door.

I felt outward but for some reason, couldn't tell who it was. I furrowed my brow and asked, "Who is it?"

"It's me, Bryan."

That seemed odd, but I was glad he was here. I hit the pause button and walked over to unlock the door and let him in.

He gave me a hug as he came through the door. I noticed there was a dusting of snow on the bomber jacket he wore. Apparently while I had been watching the television it had started snowing. His hands were red and cold, which meant the temperature was dropping, too.

"I heard you laughing all the way up the stairs."

"I'm watching cartoons."

Bryan stripped off his jacket and draped it over the back of one of the stools by the kitchen counter. "Cool! *Danger Mouse*. I love that one! Any chance I could talk you out of some of that stew? I'm famished. I spent all day at the hospital and didn't get a chance to eat."

"Sure. Help yourself. Any news on Mike since this afternoon? I called, but they wouldn't tell me anything."

Brian reached into the kitchen cabinet and pulled out a large bowl. He was filling it with stew as he spoke. "They've upgraded his condition to stable." I raised my eyes and offered a sincere thank you while Bryan kept talking. "He's conscious and aware. He was worried as hell that Amanda might have gotten you. I told him you were fine, that you'd be there if you could. When Joe came by, Mike raised hell with him for getting you kicked out. Told me that as soon as they get him in a room with a phone he'll call you, and that you are *not* supposed to blame yourself."

I snorted and the cat sneezed in unison. "Yeah, right."

"We've already talked this to death, Kate. You can't help it that you're a magnet for nut cases." An impish grin lit up his face. "It's like that curse Willow put on Xander accidentally, making him a demon magnet."

I laughed at his joke. My little brother had shown a grim determination to get reacquainted with pop culture while we were at Brooks's house. He blew through the movie and DVD rental section at the local grocery with a vengeance. *Buffy the Vampire Slayer* was becoming one of his absolute favorites. He was trying to catch up with the rest of the series. He'd watched a couple of seasons already, all in a row.

Bryan opened the fridge and pulled out a can of soda. "Okay if I have one?"

"Go ahead."

"Thanks." He hooked the refrigerator door with one foot and pulled it closed before moving over to take a seat at the counter with the food in front of him. It was such a familiar gesture that it made me smile again. He took an experimental spoonful, blowing on it to cool it a little before putting it in his mouth. He got a look of rapture on his face. "Damn this is *good*. I don't remember you being able to cook like this before. This is as good as Mom's was."

"I've been practicing," I admitted with a small blush. "But I'll never be as good as her."

He dug in, alternating bites with sips of soda. I wandered back over to the couch and settled down to make myself comfortable.

"Katie." Bryan's voice was more tentative than I'd heard it since he'd come back to himself. None of us Reillys are exactly known for timidity, so I had to wonder what was up.

"What?"

"I did something, and I don't want you to be pissed at me."

That didn't sound promising. "What did you do?" It sounded suspicious, even to me.

"I went to look up some of my old friends from . . . before."

My stomach tightened into a hard knot. I closed my eyes and fought down a wave of rage. I wanted to scream at him, ask him why in the hell he'd do something so stupid. They'd gotten him into drugs, and when it had gone badly they hadn't even had the decency to take him home or to a hospital. They'd dumped him at the side of the road in a strange town like so much trash. Why would he care about what had happened to them? But he did. Just like I'd cared enough to save Dylan, even though I knew he'd cheated on me with Amanda.

I grabbed a throw pillow and clutched it to my stomach with both arms, clenching the soft fabric in both fists so that I wouldn't scream or throw something at the wall. I've gotten much better about controlling myself. I've only gone through two alarm clocks in the whole time I've been with Tom. A new record. But this was definitely pushing my limits. "And? What did you find out?" My voice actually sounded neutral. I was proud of myself for that.

Bryan started listing the names of the people he'd hung out with. I remembered a few of them. Others I hadn't really known. A lot of them hadn't liked me, or I them. Even the ones who didn't dislike me had thought I was either a hard-ass or a stick-in-the-mud. Watching his face as he spoke, I saw the depth of pain he tried to hide behind a mask of calm. "Max died of an overdose. John was killed in a car wreck. Mindy and April got scared after what happened to me and stopped using. April got married to Josh last June. They're expecting their first baby." He smiled, grateful there'd been at least some good news.

"What about Toby?" Toby had been his best buddy. The fact that he hadn't mentioned him first was probably a bad sign, but I couldn't not ask.

He paused and I could almost feel the heartbreak flowing off him in waves. "Toby's a zombie."

Shit.

"I'm sorry, Bryan." I was sorry. I hadn't liked Toby much, mainly because I'd blamed him for getting Bryan into the Eden scene in the first place. But on my worst day I wouldn't have wished he'd become a zombie. It was just too horrible.

"I know you hated him."

No sense denying it. "Only because I blamed him."

"You shouldn't. It wasn't his fault I took drugs, Kate. It was stupid, but it was my choice. You can't blame anyone else for that."

Yes I could. And I most certainly *did*. But I wasn't going to say that out loud. Nope. Nope. Nope. "We should probably change the subject."

"Why? It's over. I'm not going back. Why can't you talk about it?"

I couldn't stand any more. "They dumped you at the curb like trash, Bryan! I had to go find you in a strange city, without any clue where you were. Nobody would tell me. If I had any idea for certain who'd been with you that night I would have hunted each and every one of them down and beaten the living *shit* out of them for that. Yes, I blame them. You're damned right I do."

It occurred to me that I sounded *exactly* like Joe had when I'd agreed to help Dylan. It was a flash of insight like a blinding light that illuminated some of the darkest corners of my mind. I owed my older brother an apology. Maybe not the one he wanted. But I definitely owed him.

Bryan was still talking. I'd missed part of the conversation. He'd moved on to some other tangent and I hadn't followed it. I shook my head to clear it and turned to look at my younger brother.

". . . you just don't get it! You never have. Joe's the smart one. He's a doctor. You were a professional athlete. More than that, you're utterly fearless. How could I possibly live up to you two? I wasn't a good enough athlete to pursue professional sports. I wasn't smart enough to get a scholarship. I didn't *want* to do anything else. What was I supposed to do? What was I supposed to *be?*" He was ranting now, not really expecting an answer. His face was flushed, his hands waving in broad gestures.

"Whatever you wanted." The words were just a shade above a whisper. He was on the verge of really losing it. I wanted to talk him back from that ledge. I just wasn't sure how.

"I didn't know—" he paused, taking a deep breath. "I *don't* know what I want. That's the problem. I'm alive, but I only have my *old* life, and no hope of any future. I don't have a fucking clue."

I let out a sudden burst of bitter laughter. "Welcome to my life, Bryan. Do you think *I* have a clue? I wish I could help you, but you'll have to figure it out for yourself. Maybe when you're at college—"

"I'm not going to college." He glared at me as he blurted out the words, defying me to argue. When I didn't, he had the grace to look puzzled. "You're not upset?"

I sighed. "Bryan, it's *your* life. I'm just glad to have you back. Go to college. Don't. Get a job. Go on welfare. It doesn't *matter.* Don't you understand? You're alive . . . you've got the whole world to play with. Whatever you do, I'm still going to love you."

He snorted and thrust out his jaw. "Joe was pissed."

I shrugged because I wasn't surprised. "Joe spends most of his life being pissed. He'll get over it."

Bryan gave a rueful laugh. "Yeah. I expect he will . . . *eventually.* But it really bothered him hearing that I took a job at a grocery store over by Brooks's mom's house."

"You got a job?" I tossed the pillow aside and stood up. "That's *terrific.* When did you do that?"

"The other night. You know how I told you I didn't make it back in time to help you deal with Amanda because I was applying for a job? Well they called me back. I went for an interview and they gave me the job. I start Monday."

"Congratulations!" I hurried across the room to give him a huge hug. "I'm so proud of you."

He returned the hug with interest, "You really are, aren't you? For a minimum wage job moving lettuce around."

"Of course I am. It's got to be hard, coming back like this. A lot has changed. But you're diving in. I mean, you're not asking for a thing. You're just dealing with the reality. But you do realize that's clear on the other side of town. You're going to have quite a bus ride every day—especially in the winter."

"That's partly why I'm here. I was hoping you could give me Brooks's telephone number. I was going to see if he'd sell me the Oldsmobile."

"Ooo! Good idea." I let go of him and started rummaging through the stack of papers that had accumulated at one end of the counter. I'd done most of the cleaning, but I'd run out of steam before I got to the paperwork. Of course, I'd left it for last because I hate it so much. But the card with Brooks's cell phone number was here somewhere.

I finally unearthed the card and read off the number so that he could make the call.

He dialed and waited. But apparently there was no answer because he left a message explaining what he wanted and asking that Brooks call him back at my number to let him know one way or another.

Brian put the phone back in the cradle. Rising to his feet, he walked over to the kitchen sink and began rinsing out his stew bowl before putting it into the dishwasher. Keeping his back to me so that I wouldn't see his face he asked, "Are you going to apologize to Joe?"

I lowered myself onto the nearest stool. The thought had been simmering in the back of my mind for a while, but was particularly strong since my insight a few moments before. But damn it, if I apologized he wouldn't. He needed to. Not so much to me, as to Tom. My sweetie might hide his feelings well, but he'd been badly hurt by the things my older brother had said. Joe had been wrong. He'd been deliberately cruel, and I wanted him to be sorry about it and say so. The thing was, I was pretty sure he didn't think he'd done anything worth apologizing for.

"If you'd apologize first, he'd follow. He really does realize that he was wrong about you." Bryan grabbed his empty pop can from the counter and threw it into the trash with excessive force. "But you're both so damned stubborn. Neither one of you wants to be the first to give in and admit you were wrong."

I closed my eyes and counted to ten before I answered. I didn't want to snarl at Bryan. I didn't. But he was pushing me into a corner. "If Joe apologizes to Tom for the things he said, I'll apologize to him for—" I tried to think of the right words for what I was sorry about.

"Um . . . maybe not being more careful? For making us worry?" Bryan prompted.

A part of me wanted to shout, *I know what I'm doing. I can handle it.* But I didn't. Not really. Most of the really dangerous things that came up didn't give me a lot of warning. Or if they did, I wasn't bright enough to put together the pieces. I would've thought the psychic abilities would help, but they didn't. Which nightmares were dreams, which ones premonitions? If there was a way to tell, I sure didn't know what it was.

Bryan stepped forward. He put a hand on my shoulder, giving a gentle squeeze. "I know it's not fair to ask. You were *always* the first one to give in. But I know Joe won't, and damn it, I want my family back. Is that so much to ask?" He was pleading with me; the look in his eyes so raw that it clawed at my heart. My throat tightened with emotion.

Put that way it shouldn't be. It really shouldn't.

"Please, Katie," he whispered. "Do it for me?"

I took a deep shuddering breath. Slowly, painfully, I reached for the phone and hit the speed dial for Joe's number.

26

The phone rang at 3:00 A.M., waking me from a sound sleep. I fumbled around for the portable extension next to the bed, grateful that I had taken the trouble to hunt it down and put it back on the charger.

I was in bed alone. Tomorrow afternoon Tom was due back from his shift at the firehouse.

" 'Lo?"

"Kate, what are you doing asleep?" Mary's voice on the other end of the line sounded annoyed.

I blinked dumbly at the clock on the bedside table. "It's 3:00 A.M." My mind was thick with fog and definitely not firing on all cylinders.

"Which is why you need to wrap up the conversation you're having with your brother and send him back here. He's got to be at work at seven."

"Huh? Bryan's not here." I was waking up now. The reality of what she was saying was breaking through the sleep-induced fog. "He left hours ago."

"Not Bryan, you idiot. *Joe.*"

"Joe's not speaking to me, Mary. This is the last place he'd be. I haven't seen him since he kicked me out of the hospital."

"What do you mean . . . he's not there? I gave him your message when he got home at ten and he took off for your place. He said he wanted to talk to you in person."

The words hit me like a blow. I jumped out of bed. Propping the telephone between my ear and shoulder I started grabbing whatever clothes were handy and pulling them on. I wound up in one of Tom's dirty tee-shirts, gray sweatpants, and an ancient pair of Pumas with no socks. "He's not here. Hasn't *been* here. I haven't heard a word from him. I swear, Mary."

Closing my eyes, I sent my mind outward looking for him. All I found was an impenetrable barrier of will. My body was shaking from the effort I was putting my mind through. "Shit! I can't find him, Mary. I should be able to find him, but I can't."

"Oh God, Kate! I have to hang up. I'm going to call the emergency rooms. I'll call you back."

The line went dead in my ear. I sank down on the edge of the bed, my knees weak from fear. I had to call Bryan. Had to let him know what was going on. I hit the number for Tom's apartment on speed dial and listened as the phone rang and rang. On the fourth ring voice-mail picked up. I left a fairly hysterical message for my brother and hung up.

My stomach tightened into a knot of pure fear. My psychic senses were screaming that something had happened to Joe, but I didn't know what, and didn't have a clue what to do. I rummaged through the bedroom, gathering up my knives and strapping them on. Once I'd done that, though, I could only wait in terror for some word.

I sat praying as I waited for Mary's call. The phone was in my lap. When it rang, I jumped a good foot, nearly spilling the phone onto the floor. I fumbled with it for a minute, then hit the button with a trembling finger. "Mary?"

"No. I'm not Mary." It was a woman's voice, cold and pitiless, with just the tiniest hint of amusement. There was silence in the background, followed by a man's shriek of agony.

"Who is this?" I practically screamed the words into the receiver. "What do you want?"

"Really, Ms. Reilly, don't you recognize my voice?" Her voice was a seductive purr, and I heard Joe's hoarse shout "Don't do it, Kate. Whatever she wants, don't—"

I did recognize her voice. Samantha Greeley let out a roar of rage. I heard the thud of a blunt object impacting against skin, then silence. I swallowed the bile that had risen. I wouldn't throw up. I *wouldn't*.

"What do you want?" My voice was strangled with fear and rage.

"I asked you a question. Do you recognize my voice?"

My mouth didn't want to work, but I managed to choke out, "Samantha Greeley."

"*Very* good," she purred.

"What do you want?" I swallowed hard, trying to keep my voice normal in spite of the panic that was threatening to overwhelm me.

"I want to kill you, just like I did the others." Her voice was all the more terrifying because it was completely bland, even pleasant. "Did you watch the news today?"

"No." I concentrated on keeping her talking. If she was paying attention to me she wasn't hurting Joe. But while I talked I was using my psychic abilities in a desperate attempt to find where she was.

"You remember Antonia, don't you? She was such a pretty girl. They found her head yesterday. Digby is still missing, as is Emily. They may find their corpses eventually. Then again, perhaps not. I went to quite a bit of effort to make it difficult."

Fuck! I thought Brooks said he'd checked on them!

"I'm really very annoyed about Mr. Brooks. If it hadn't been for that damned dog—"

Oh God! I remembered the nightmare as she said the words. *That* was what was so important, and I'd taken a fucking sleeping pill! Bile rose into my throat until I could barely swallow it down again. She sighed. "Oh well, he's in intensive care. There's no way they'll get him evacuated in time. The bomb will take him. But I digress. I have your brother. You slaughtered my siblings. Can you give me one reason *not* to kill yours?

A *bomb?* In the hospital? How many people was she willing to kill? "Because I'm the one you want. Not him. Killing Joe would be like shooting fish in a barrel."

"Or spraying alcohol in an incubator?"

Her rage beat at me across the distance, hot enough that I expected the phone to melt in my hand or the skin to burn from my bones. But in her anger, she let her shield slip. I knew where she was calling from now: in the lab, at the hospital. Where it all began.

I ran blindly down the stairs, hoping the signal would hold. I needed to keep her busy, but I needed a car, and the cops, and—what the hell—the cavalry, if I could get it. I tore across the living room. I flipped back the locks on the front door with trembling hands and threw it open. I was already halfway down the hall when I heard it slam closed.

"What do you want me to say?"

"There's nothing you can say. I'd make you beg, but while it would be fun to humiliate you, we both know it wouldn't do any good."

"Then why did you call?"

I opened the door to the staircase. Bryan wasn't home but one of the downstairs tenants had to be, had to have a car. Dusty and Rob would be preferable, but Connie would do in a pinch. My mind was racing, trying to come up with a plan for rescue while at the same time I struggled to keep up my end of the conversation. I had to keep her occupied. There hadn't been any fresh screams since we'd started talking. There were low moans, but that meant Joe was alive. So long as he was moaning, and there were no more screams, there was hope. I sent a wordless prayer upward that God would help me save my brother as I skidded to a stop at Rob and Dusty's door.

"A good question. Maybe I just want you here to see him die."

The connection went dead.

"*FUCK!*" I screamed it at the top of my lungs, throwing the telephone handset with all my strength against the wall of the hallway. It shattered, batteries and sharp pieces of colored plastic raining down on the floor.

I raised my fist to pound on the door, but it opened. Rob was there, wearing nothing but a pair of pajama bottoms.

"Kate, what's wrong?"

Time, there was no time. I wanted to voice my rage and fear in a long, endless scream. Instead, I fought for control; fought to sound sane and reasonable as I told Rob what I needed. "I need car keys. She has Joe, she's going to torture him to death. Call Tom, tell him there's a bomb in the hospital. They need to evacuate it now. Then call Mary and have her meet me at St. E's. I'll fight her, but I need Mary to get Joe out and to the doctors. Damn it, Rob—*GIVE ME THE GODDAMN KEYS!*"

"*Who* is her, Kate? Who has Joe? Amanda's dead, isn't she? Tell me—for God's sake! Tell me she's dead!" He was babbling and deserved an answer, but I didn't have time to give him one.

Dusty didn't ask any questions. She just looked at me and, in that instant, she *knew*. "It's Samantha Greeley, Rob. Go! I'll call the police." She grabbed the keys from a hook on the wall and threw them to a swearing Rob, who caught them in the air with his left hand. I saw her pick up the phone in the instant before Rob shoved me out of the way and slammed the door closed.

We were running down the hall, shards of plastic crunching beneath my shoes. Rob got to the door first, I caught it on the rebound and was through before it could close. Then we were in the parking garage. Rob tossed me the keys an instant before I felt the surge of power and heat that signaled he was ready to change. By the time I'd unlocked the door to Dusty's Mustang he was in wolf form. When I flung the door open he leapt inside and between the seats.

I jumped inside, slamming the door. I had the car started and seatbelt on in an instant. With a squeal of tires that left patches of rubber on the concrete we were off.

I drove Dusty's car as though the hounds of hell were after me. They may as well have been. Joe was being tortured. She was going to kill him. If the police came after me, so much the better. But they didn't come after, they came before. The entire hospital was crawling with police, fire rescue, ambulances.

It was mass confusion, insanity. Blue and red flashing lights strobed the night. People in open-backed hospital gowns were being shuffled toward private vans and city buses, while gurneys were being wheeled into the back of ambulances parked in rows six deep. Dusty must have made more than one call. Attagirl.

News vans were parked across the street, but the crews were on the lawn, their lights shining bright on the perfectly made-up faces of excited reporters.

I pulled the car to the curb behind a fire truck. Rob and I climbed out. My goal was the back of the building. I still remembered Mac's pass codes. If I could get to a back door I could get us inside.

I forced myself not to run, not to panic. I needed not to be noticed. It wasn't to be. One of the doctors I knew from the ER shouted my name. One or two others turned to look.

I ran, around the corner of the building. Tom and a pair of cops were arguing by the back door. He saw Rob and me coming, and his eyes went wide. The cops turned. The first one paled and grabbed for his gun. Before he could draw, Tom slugged him, sending him sprawling to the ground. The second cop turned, his hand just starting to raise the weapon when Rob leaped, and he was down as well. I didn't stop to watch what happened next. I was through the door and inside the hospital.

It wasn't until I was around the bend and halfway up the next flight of stairs that I stopped. Joe had been screaming, *really* screaming. He couldn't be in the lab. Too many people would have heard him. But if not there . . . where? I needed to think, but panic was making it hard. I heard someone come through the door below me. "Do you know where she was headed?" Mary's voice echoed through the stairwell. She sounded preternaturally calm, not hysterical at all.

"Mary? I'm up here. I just thought of something."

I heard her footsteps on the concrete stairs, along with the click of claws.

"What?"

"She doesn't have Joe in the lab. She couldn't. He was screaming too loud. She has to have him somewhere sound-proof. But I don't know where it would be. Can the three of you search the hospital, track him by scent?"

She appeared just below me. She looked grim in black jeans and a blood-red scooped neck tee. Her eyes blazed an inhuman gold, and I could feel the power she held barely in check.

"Easily."

"Do it."

"And may I ask what you'll be doing?" I was pretty sure she didn't trust me not to make it worse. I couldn't really argue, but I had an idea that just *might* work.

"Springing a trap."

She gave me a long look, and raised her hand in salute. "Happy hunting."

"Just save my brother." She gave a sharp nod and was off, with Rob at her heels. I didn't stay to watch them go. I had an appointment to keep. I did glance over at the pony-sized wolf beside me. Tom was with me. I wasn't surprised. I wasn't sorry. In fact, I couldn't think of anyone I'd have wanted with me more.

We were just coming out of the stairwell into the hall near the lab when the building was rocked by an explosion that rattled the glass in the walls and sent papers flying from the desk at the nurse's station. The overhead lights flickered and died. A moment later I heard the generator kick in and there was emergency power. That lasted as long as it took us to get to the far end of the hall.

The second explosion was either closer or bigger. It knocked me off my feet as the building seemed to shift beneath me. The sound of it hit my ears like a blow, and for a few moments it wasn't possible for me to hear properly.

The lights in the hall were out except for the occasional brilliant flash of the battery-operated alarm lights. It gave everything an odd, strobe effect. I didn't dare look at it too closely, either, because the searing light would ruin my night vision.

The acrid stench of smoke was faint, but growing stronger. I tasted concrete dust on my tongue. Tom moved in front of me. In wolf form he could see in the near pitch dark, and his training in fire rescue could only help keep us from getting lost.

I worried for Joe, Mary, Rob, and for all the poor souls who hadn't been evacuated yet and the emergency crews who'd been sent in to save them. I prayed, as much as I was able, but my thoughts were as fractured as the windows of the building. The cold air blew fiercely through the open panes, rattling the Venetian blinds. When I heard it I realized my ears were working again, and I tried to concentrate, listening for the sound of anything unexpected.

My eyes stung and burned from the dust, and the smell of smoke was growing stronger. Tom stopped, turning his body to block my progress. I felt his hackles raise, heard a low growl rumble from deep within his chest.

I would've given anything to have him tell me what was wrong, but he couldn't talk to me in wolf form.

"Come out, come out wherever you are." Samantha Greeley's voice sang through the devastated hallway. "I know you're here, Katie, and that you brought your puppy dog with you."

I used the light from the flash to choose a place to hide in ambush. There was an open doorway on the left, next to the wall-mounted fire extinguisher. When the light flashed off I squeezed Tom's shoulder, then moved as quickly as I could to take my place. I would've wished for silence, but it wasn't possible. There was too much trash on the floor. But there was a lot of ambient noise coming in through the broken windows. Maybe it was enough.

The light flared again, and I saw a brief shadow of movement. It was too tall for a wolf, and shaped like a human, but moving faster, and with more confidence in the dark than any mere human could.

I looked for Tom, but he wasn't where I'd left him.

There was the sound of a scuffle, and a fierce growl that changed to a yelp of pain. I focused on the sound, pulled my knife. Waiting for the flash was the hardest thing I'd ever had to do. But I waited, and when the light came I saw Samantha Greeley locked in combat with Tom, a bloody knife in her hand. Before she had time to see me, or do anything, I threw.

She shrieked with pain and rage. I heard the heavy thud of Tom's body hitting the wall where she'd flung him. He slid limply to the floor, stunned or dead.

I felt more than saw her charging toward me. At the last second I stepped sideways. Grabbing the back of her shirt and the waist of her pants I used her own momentum to slam her face first into the shattered wall.

I'd hoped to break off her fangs, send the Thrall within her into shock. But she'd sensed it, or was lucky, and turned her head at the last instant, taking the blow on the side of her face. There'd been enough force behind it to dislocate her jaw and break her cheekbone. Her eye didn't spill from its socket, though it looked as if it might. It had been a good blow, but not enough. Her teeth, and her mind, were intact.

She spun, knife drawn, forcing me to leap backward. I reached to draw my second knife, but it wasn't there. I'd lost it at some point. I was unarmed.

She kept advancing, forcing me back across the cluttered floor. I was finally getting used to the uncertain light; using it when it was there to plan, moving when it was not. I tried to search for something to use as a weapon. A flash of the light reflected off the red paint of the fire extinguisher a few feet away. The door to its cabinet hung forlornly open, its glass cracked, but the extinguisher itself was still inside and intact.

It was tantalizingly close, but terrifyingly far away. I opened my senses, hoping to use my psychic ability to dodge the knife strikes as I had dodged the blows from Amanda's bat.

I felt the hive watching, and knew that if I tried I'd be able to pick out individual members. The connection was stronger now than it had ever been. Whether it was because of my panic, or the strengthening of the bond when I'd helped them in the mountains I didn't know. But it gave me an idea; something I could do to distract Greeley, maybe even long enough to get to the fire extinguisher.

I opened my psychic senses to their fullest, grabbing on to that connection with everything I had before the queens could slam it closed, bar their mental doors against me. It was an amazing amount of power. The pain was excruciating. My mind felt as though it were on fire, as if it might explode from the pressure of all the power I fought to contain.

But even then, I knew it wouldn't be enough. I reached out further, to do something nobody had ever done. I found Tom. He was alive, but hurt badly. I reached into that cool blankness of power, drew on it—and, in turn, the pack as another lifeline. He let me, held me in his mind with fierce determination. The Thrall recoiled from the touch, as did the wolves. But I didn't care. I needed the love of my life now as I'd never needed anyone ever before.

I dropped my guard just a little, enough to draw her forward. I had to touch her for it to work. She lashed out with the knife, a vicious slash that tore through the fabric of my tee-shirt and cut a long line of skin beneath it. It stung immediately and burned. I didn't know if the cut was deep enough to be dangerous, to bleed me to death. But in that instant it didn't matter. I had her.

I grabbed her knife arm with both of my hands, squeezing hard on her wrist. She shrieked in rage and frustration, using all her strength to fight against my grip. In that moment she had no shields. Her anger had left her completely vulnerable. I forced a connection between my mind and hers and poured every ounce of psychic energy I had, everything the *collective* had, and the pack had, into her unprotected mind.

It drove her to her knees, her eyes wide and vacant. Her mouth opened in a silent scream of agony. The knife fell from her nerveless fingers into the piles of debris and blowing papers on the floor.

I didn't reach for it. If I bent down now I would fall over and might not ever be able to get back up. I let go of the collective and the pack. There was nothing more they could do to help. The last was up to me.

Tom was stirring against the far wall. He let out a small whine of pain as he pulled himself onto his feet. I knew I was glad, but I was too drained to actually be excited about it. Besides, this wasn't finished. She was still alive. She was swaying on her knees. But she was alive.

I stumbled over to the fire extinguisher cabinet. I pulled the canister free with a vicious yank that set my torn skin on fire. I ignored the pain, and the light wash of blood that followed it. In three steps I was in front of her. Holding the canister in both hands, I swung it backward, then slammed it with all my might into her open mouth.

She swayed on her knees for a moment before she collapsed. She didn't move. She wasn't breathing. Even so, I had to be sure. I let go the canister and dropped to my knees so that I could put my finger to her throat and search for a pulse.

There wasn't one. She was dead.

Tom limped over to me. He whined, nudging his nose against my chest. I didn't want to move; wasn't even sure I could. Tired. I was so very tired. At that moment, I didn't mind if I died, if only I could just *rest*. But the smoke was burning my eyes and throat, making it hard to breathe. It was getting thicker, so that it was hard to see, even in the flashes of light. It was hot, too. There was sweat mingled with the blood on my belly.

Tom whined again, butting me with his head. He was trying to get me to move. I forced myself to crawl forward, ignoring the pain each movement cost me. He circled me. One moment he was behind me, nudging me forward. The next he was ahead, barking encouragement, leading me forward through the smoke to the stairs.

I used the railing to haul myself upright, my body raging in protest at the abuse. But I wasn't taking the stairs on my knees. Too slow. Too *hard*. So I forced myself to do what needed to be done and, one step at a time, made it down the first flight and part of the next with Tom barking his encouragement.

It was after one of his barks that I heard . . . something. I stopped, and so did Tom. He bolted up the few steps to the doorway. Backing up a pace, he shifted all his weight onto his back legs, using his front paws to depress the bar of the fire door. He dived through the opening, moving quickly despite his injuries.

He returned a moment later, pulling an injured woman by the shirt collar while a small boy crawled behind. A few minutes later the four of us shambled out of the building and into the arms of the waiting EMTs.

27

They took me to Denver General. It has one of the best-rated trauma units in the country, maybe the world. It's sort of sad that it's gotten that way from repetitive use. I was in and out of consciousness for most of the ambulance ride. They put me under completely for the surgery. The knife wound wasn't as bad as it could've been, but all the fighting and crawling around hadn't done it any good.

I woke up in the morning in a semi-private room. There were two hospital beds, with a cotton curtain on a track that could be pulled closed to separate them. I was in the bed by the window. I couldn't see out because the blinds were closed. The lights were off, too. The dim light made it difficult to be sure whether the walls were a pale blue or gray. Tom was in the chair beside my bed, his head leaning against the wall, eyes closed. He was wearing a plain white tee-shirt and jeans.

My head didn't hurt. After what I'd done to Samantha, I had expected to get another one of those truly spectacular migraines. In fact, the only thing that hurt was my abdomen. I lifted my hospital gown and saw a long row of stitches that ran in a diagonal across most of my torso. They'd covered it with a kind of rubbery goo that I recognized from hearing Joe talk about it. It was supposed to help keep the wound sealed shut. It looked and felt very weird, but I wasn't going to argue.

"Tom?"

He was instantly awake and alert, his dark eyes focused on me.

"Joe?" It hurt to talk. My voice was a harsh rasp from all the smoke and fumes I'd inhaled.

Tom grimaced. "He's in surgery. Mary and the others found him in time and got him out. Some of his injuries are fairly hideous, but the doctors know what they're doing. Bryan and the others are with him now."

I closed my eyes, my body going limp with relief. He was alive. They'd found him. They got him out.

"They got everybody out of intensive care. The bomb she planted there didn't go off."

I shuddered. It had been bad, but it could have been worse. The people in ICU were utterly helpless. Samantha Greeley had been willing to kill them all to get at Brooks. Insanity. Total insanity.

"The cops didn't press charges against Rob and me for assaulting a police officer, but I'm suspended, and may lose my job for dereliction of duty." His voice was matter-of-fact when he said it, but I knew how much his job meant to him.

"Tom—" I tried to come up with the right words.

He shook his head with force. "No. Katie, it's okay. It's not even important. Your brother's alive. Brooks is alive. I knew what the consequences would be when I left my post. I made my choice. Besides, there's going to be a hearing. My counsel is going to try to prove extenuating circumstances, since I saved lives in the hospital. We'll just have to wait and see."

I blinked back tears. I wouldn't cry. I wouldn't. When I

had myself back under control I asked one of the questions that was bothering me. "How many bombs were there?"

"Seven. She put them in strategic points throughout the building. Apparently she used to date a guy in demolitions. She knew a hell of a lot about explosives and bringing down a building. We were damned lucky the casualty count was as low as it was." Tom pinched the bridge of his nose with the thumb and index finger of his right hand. It was an unconscious gesture that he only used when he was completely exhausted.

"Have you gotten any sleep at all yet?"

"No." He admitted. "I needed to be sure you were all right, and let you know the people you cared about were going to be okay."

I looked at him. He was practically swaying in the chair, his skin gray from exhaustion and stress. It was a semi-private room, but nobody was in the other bed. He needed rest.

"Lay down next to me."

"Kate—"

"Seriously, what is the worst that will happen? A nurse will come in and tell you to move? Whoooo. You're exhausted. You need rest. Come lay next to me." Now that he wasn't slouched over I could see the bulge of bandages beneath his tee-shirt.

"Oh God! You're still hurt?"

"I'll be fine. They didn't even need to keep me overnight." He bent over the bed and gave me a gentle kiss. "Unlike *some* people, who seem to spend half of their nights in a hospital bed." He grinned at me and moved the blankets aside. I scooted across the bed, trying to make room for him. The bed was narrow, but I knew we could both fit if we snuggled, and I wanted to snuggle. "Your insurance company must *hate* you."

Tom kicked off his shoes and slid into the bed beside me. He spooned against my back, his arm wrapped around my waist. I pulled the blanket back up over us both. It wasn't long before I felt his breathing change. He was asleep.

The doctor checked in on his rounds at ten and woke us up. He didn't make any comment about Tom being in the bed, but he did give us an eloquent *look* before telling me that I was welcome to check out of the hospital.

My clothes from the other night were completely ruined. They were filthy, blood-stained, and smelled of smoke. I couldn't leave in a hospital gown. So Tom went down to the gift shop to see if he could find anything for me to wear. A few minutes later he brought up a truly tacky souvenir tee-shirt and a pair of men's extra-large white pajamas with red vertical stripes. I had no doubt I looked silly. Even with the drawstring pulled tight the pants were huge. But I was decently covered and didn't stink of smoke, so I didn't complain.

Hospital regulations required that a nurse wheel me to the hospital door in a wheelchair. I tried to argue. It didn't matter. So I rode down with the nurse pushing and Tom beside me. And when we wheeled to a stop at the curb I immediately stood up, walked back into the hospital and to the elevators. Surprisingly, there were no camera crews. Maybe I hadn't made the news after all.

Joe was in surgery for hours. I sat in the waiting room with Tom, Mary, and Bryan. We didn't talk much. In the background a television was playing the news. The sound was off, so I didn't have to listen to what was being said, but the bombing of St. Elizabeth's was being featured on all the networks. There were images of flames shooting upward and the evacuation of the patients. But no pictures of me graced the screen. Thank God for small favors.

A sound made me turn my head away from the television. A doctor was walking in. His shoes were still covered with little surgical slippers, and he still wore a cotton elasticized cap over his head.

He looked from one to the other of us, but he stopped in front of Mary. She sat on the uncomfortable waiting room chair, pale as a ghost, her back rigid. I watched her throat bob as she fought to swallow her fear.

"Ms. Connolly," the doctor spoke quietly. "I wanted to let you know, the surgery went very well. He's stable. Barring unexpected complications, he should be fine."

28

The phone was ringing as Tom and I headed out the front door. I heard P. Douglas leaving an "urgent" message on the machine, but I didn't go back to take the call. Whatever the Thrall queen had to say could wait until later. I didn't want any bad news tonight. Tom and I were celebrating.

My interview with Barbara Walters was over. It hadn't been quite as horrible as I'd feared. She was actually a very nice woman and the ultimate professional. At my request she asked one specific question. "I understand you haven't used your talent to heal any more zombies since that first time. Why?"

I wanted to make sure the world knew I hadn't just chosen to quit on a whim, or was holding out for the best offer, but because the Thrall collective warned me, and Dr. Watkins agreed, that I would be risking my life if I tried to repeat what I'd done for Brian and Melinda.

I don't really believe it will stop people from approaching me, but it's worth a try. I had to do *something*. Everywhere I go people come up to me. They cry, they beg, they offer to pay anything. It kills a little part of me to say no. If I thought I could help them without it killing *all* of me, I would. But I don't think Carlton was lying. I've changed my telephone number. I've even tried to change my appearance. It hasn't helped much. I don't blame people for grasping at the only hope out there. I remember the pain, the desperation. I wish I could help. I can't. It sucks.

I forced my mind away from that problem. Tonight was a celebration, damn it. Joe was getting better. We'd talked. He thanked me. We both apologized. It's still a little awkward, but we're working at it. Good thing too. Mary asked me to be her maid of honor at their wedding and I'd said yes.

Tom and I walked hand-in-hand up the sidewalk to the Old Spaghetti Factory. This was *our* restaurant. It was the first place we'd gone together, and still my favorite. I love the food. I love the funky atmosphere. Where else can you sit and eat *inside* a trolley car, or at a table converted from an old brass bed?

A server escorted us to a table for two in the trolley car. It was the same table we'd been at that first night. I didn't know if Tom would remember, but I did.

"Can I get you something to drink?" The waitress smiled and gave each of us a menu.

"Sure. And if you don't mind, we can go ahead and order. I think we both know what we want."

"Certainly." She pulled a pen and pad from the pocket of her apron.

We placed our orders, and she left.

We'd been among the first to get here, the restaurant had just opened for the evening. But it was a popular place. People were trickling in. There were couples, families, even a few large groups.

Tom had suddenly grown quiet, and I turned my attention back to the table. He was on one knee with a blue velvet jewelry box in his hand. I stared at him, openmouthed. "I've been working really hard for you not to read my mind tonight. I wanted to surprise you. Mary Kathleen Reilly, will you marry me?"

For some reason my tongue wouldn't work. It seemed glued to the roof of my mouth. I managed to nod yes. His smile lit up the whole car. He pulled open the hinged lid to show me the most beautiful ring I'd ever seen; a delicate gold band set with a large marquis-cut diamond flanked by four emeralds. It caught the light and splintered it, shooting sparks of color.

"This was my mother's ring," he explained, both proud and shy. "Otherwise I would've had to go for something simpler. I hope you like it."

"I *love* it. And I love you." I held out my left hand, and he slid the ring onto my finger. It fit perfectly, as though it had been made for me.

Tom smiled and kissed my fingertips before rising and getting back into his seat. "How soon do you think we can get hitched? Do you think next week might be rushing it?"

I laughed. "It's not that simple. There are pre-Cana classes, and—"

Tom groaned. "It figures. Here I'm trying to get you to make an honest man of me before the pack or anyone else has a chance to come up with any objections and *you* start dragging your feet."

"I am *so* not dragging my feet!" I didn't ask why the pack would object. I knew the answer. Rob had gotten Dusty pregnant; and Ruby was expecting Jake's baby. But, while Rob was employed and could do his duty as a dad, Jake was dead. There was a good chance the pack would want someone to take his place with Ruby, be a father to the baby. Oh, the whole pack would take part in raising and caring for the child. But the wolves are an old-fashioned lot. They like their children to be brought up in a two-parent household. I don't disagree.

"I don't want to risk losing you again, Katie." Tom smiled when he said it, reaching across the table to take my hand. I looked into those oh-so-sincere brown eyes and my heart skipped a beat. "I swear, if you weren't Catholic I'd suggest a quick trip to Vegas. But I'm not brave enough to face Mike and tell him we got married outside the church."

"We could do both," I suggested.

That raised his brows. "*Both?*"

"Why not? We'll get the legal stuff and the honeymoon taken care of right now, and do the big Catholic wedding after we get back."

"You'd do that?" He asked incredulously. "Mike will *kill* us!"

I smiled at him. "You're not the only one who doesn't want to take any chances. The sooner we're married, the safer I'll feel. I'm willing to risk Mike's wrath. He'll get over it."

He laughed and it lit up my heart when he said, "Las Vegas, here we come!"